Praise for
The Summer Place

"A meditation on mothers and daughters, Weiner's latest novel also explores class conflicts, identity issues, and real estate dramas."

—*The New York Times*

"The natural beauty of the Outer Cape is the backdrop for plenty of family drama and romantic intrigue in Weiner's latest novel, which incorporates the challenges of the COVID-19 pandemic but still manages to feel breezy and delicious to read."

—*Vogue*

"*The Summer Place* is so good, it will be on every beach this summer. [It] gets at the core of just how life's twists and turns, choices and moments can consume us—and how beautiful that entanglement can be, despite the hardships. . . . With its Cape Cod setting that evokes seashells, cool water, melting ice cream, and summer bliss, it's sure to be the must-have beach bag item this year."

—*USA Today*

"From steamy affairs to juicy family secrets, bestselling author Jennifer Weiner's scintillating beach read has it all."

—Apple Books

"In Jennifer Weiner's latest . . . expect all of the hijinks, heartbreak, and happiness of a messy reunion."

—*The Boston Globe*

"[A] funny, tender read. A new novel from Weiner heralds the start of beach reading season, so prepare your collections accordingly."

—*Booklist* (starred review)

"A family's secrets and entanglements flare up during a Cape Cod wedding in this first-rate page-turner from Weiner. [She] is a master of emotionally complicated narratives, and her smart and witty writing is on full display here. This engrossing novel will please her legions of fans."

—*Publishers Weekly*

"Weiner creates a story with all the misunderstandings and miscommunications of a screwball comedy or a Shakespeare play (think *A Midsummer Night's Dream*). But the surprising, over-the-top actions of the characters are grounded by a realistic and moving look at grief and ambition. . . . Even when the characters are lying, cheating, and hiding from each other, they still seem like a real and loving family. . . . [A] poignant look at family bonds."

—*Kirkus Reviews*

The
Summer
Place

BOOKS BY JENNIFER WEINER

FICTION

Good in Bed

In Her Shoes

Little Earthquakes

Goodnight Nobody

The Guy Not Taken

Certain Girls

Best Friends Forever

Fly Away Home

Then Came You

The Next Best Thing

All Fall Down

Who Do You Love

Mrs. Everything

Big Summer

That Summer

The Breakaway

NONFICTION

Hungry Heart

FOR YOUNG READERS

The Littlest Bigfoot

Little Bigfoot, Big City

Jennifer Weiner

The Summer Place

A Novel

POCKET BOOKS

New York   London   Toronto   Sydney   New Delhi

Pocket Books
An Imprint of Simon & Schuster, LLC
1230 Avenue of the Americas
New York, NY 10020

This book is a work of fiction. Any references to historical events, real people, or real places are used fictitiously. Other names, characters, places, and events are products of the author's imagination, and any resemblance to actual events or places or persons, living or dead, is entirely coincidental.

This Pocket Books paperback edition July 2024

POCKET and colophon are registered trademarks of Simon & Schuster, LLC

Simon & Schuster: Celebrating 100 Years of Publishing in 2024

For information about special discounts for bulk purchases, please contact Simon & Schuster Special Sales at 1-866-506-1949 or business@simonandschuster.com.

The Simon & Schuster Speakers Bureau can bring authors to your live event. For more information or to book an event, contact the Simon & Schuster Speakers Bureau at 1-866-248-3049 or visit our website at www.simonspeakers.com.

Manufactured in the United States of America

10 9 8 7 6 5 4 3 2 1

ISBN 978-1-6680-3366-1
ISBN 978-1-5011-3359-6 (ebook)

For Bill Syken
In memory of Frances Frumin Weiner

"Are you sure
That we are awake?
It seems to me
That yet we sleep, we dream"

—William Shakespeare,
A Midsummer Night's Dream

PROLOGUE

～～～

For forty years, the house had stood on the edge of the dune, overlooking the waters of Cape Cod Bay. Over time, the dune had eroded, shearing away in gentle showers of sand. Beach plums and bayberry shrubs clung to its sides like the splayed fingers of a clutching hand. Down below, the water in the bay had crept higher each season, paring off slivers of the beach. The dirt path that once led to the house's front door had been widened and covered in crushed oyster shells. Her grounds had been landscaped, lavender and hydrangeas and bright-blooming roses added to the pin oaks and crabapple trees. A pool had been dug out of the gentle slope of the meadow, a guesthouse and garage added on; then more decks, a hot tub, and an outdoor shower with a crescent moon cut into the arch of its door so bathers could look out at the sea.

Through all the changes—the coats of paint, the loose boards nailed down for the second and third times, the hinges oiled, and the windows replaced—the house had waited, patient and steadfast. The molecules of her walls vibrated with the echoes of every conversation ever held in her rooms; the ceilings and the floors and the dirt below held the resonances of all she had seen. She knew things: good and bad. She'd seen sorrow and happiness, tragedy and joy, and plenty of the mundane, the cheerful low hum generated by families at the beach in the summertime.

Thousands of meals had been cooked and eaten in her kitchen; hundreds of hamburgers and hot dogs grilled and served at the picnic table on the top deck. She had witnessed the preparation of fresh clams and lobster, local corn on the cob and sun-warmed tomatoes sweet as sugar and right off the vine. Couples, young and old, had danced on her floors and embraced in her bedrooms. She'd seen tender kisses and heard blissful sighs and whispered declarations of love. Babies had been conceived beneath her roof, and those same babies had grown up and come back to her, with babies of their own. She'd watched a mother bathe her newborn daughter and, many years later, had seen that daughter set her own baby in a crib, then walk toward her mother and embrace her, whispering, *Thank you. I had no idea how hard this was going to be.* The house had welcomed them all; she'd borne witness to their histories and had held them close in her embrace.

In all those years, through all that time, she had only ever been able to watch. All the pain, all the mistakes— *no, not that party; no, no more to drink tonight; no, not him; no, not her; no, don't open that door, don't answer the phone, do not let that man back in your bed*—she had never been able to assert her own will or even make herself known. For years, she'd tried, but she'd never managed to do more than cause a few odd ripples in the hot tub or make the same screen door fall off onto the deck ("that damn door," the families muttered, as they lifted it back on its tracks).

The house never gave up. She kept working at it, patiently, assiduously, trying to find ways to let her people know that she heard them, that she saw them, that she wanted to help. They might take her for granted; they might leave her empty all through the winter, letting mice chew through her insulation to make nests inside her walls, but she cared for them, and always would.

And now, another summer was approaching, the days getting longer, the air getting warmer, and her mission had never felt more urgent. Changes were coming. She had so many things to tell her people, and she was running out of time to figure out how.

PART
ONE

~~~~~~

RUBY GETTING MARRIED

SARAH

On a Friday night just after sunset, Sarah Weinberg Danhauser lit a match, bent her head, and said the blessing over the Shabbat candles in the dining room of her brownstone in Park Slope. Dinner was on the table: roast chicken, glazed with honey; homemade stuffing with mushrooms and walnuts, fresh-baked challah, and a salad with fennel and blood oranges, sprinkled with pomegranate seeds so expensive that Sarah had guiltily shoved the container, with its damning price tag, deep down into the recycling bin, lest her husband see.

Eli, said husband, sat at the head of the table, his eyes on his plate. Their sons, Dexter, who was eight, and Miles, almost seven, were on the left side of the table with Eli's brother Ari between them. Ari, twice-divorced and currently single, his jeans and ratty T-shirt contrasting with the khakis and collared shirts Sarah insisted her sons wear on Shabbat, had become a Friday-night regular at the Danhausers' table. Ari was not Sarah's favorite person, with his glinting good looks and sly smile and the way he'd "borrow" significant sums of money from his brother once or twice a year, but Eli had asked, and Sarah's mother-in-law had gotten involved ("I know he's a grown man and he should be able to feed himself, but he acts like Flamin' Hot Cheetos are a food group, and I'm worried he's going to get rickets"), and so, reluctantly, Sarah had extended the invitation.

On the other side of the table sat Ruby, Sarah's stepdaughter, and Ruby's pandemic boyfriend, Gabe. Sarah supposed she should just call Gabe a boyfriend, minus the qualifier, but the way his romance with Ruby had been fast-forwarded thanks to COVID meant that, in her mind, Gabe would always have an asterisk next to his name. Gabe and Ruby had been together for just six weeks in March of 2020 when NYU shut down and sent everyone home. Ruby had come back to her bedroom in Brooklyn and, after lengthy discussions, Sarah and Eli had agreed to allow Gabe, who was from California, to cohabitate with her. The two had been inseparable that pandemic year, all the way through their virtual graduation, snuggling on the couch bingeing Netflix or taking long, rambling walks through the city, holding hands and wearing matching face masks, or starting a container victory garden on the brownstone's roof deck that eventually yielded a bumper crop of lettuce and kale, a handful of wan carrots, and a single seedy watermelon ("Next year will be better," Ruby promised, after posting a series of photos of the melon on her Instagram).

Ruby and Gabe had stayed together through the summer, into the winter, and, after the New Year, when the pandemic had finally loosened its grip, they'd gotten vaccinated, gotten jobs—Ruby as assistant stage manager in an independent theater company in Jackson Heights; Gabe as a proofreader—taken several of their favorite plants, and moved out of Brooklyn and into a tiny studio in Queens, where they'd been living for just over a month.

Sarah finished the blessing over the wine and the bread. The platters of food had made their first trip around the table (Ari, Sarah noticed, helped himself to the largest chunk of white meat). She'd just finished reminding Dexter to put his napkin on his lap when Ruby, beaming blissfully, took her boyfriend by the hand. "Gabe and I have some news," she said.

Sarah felt a freezing sensation spread from her heart to her belly. She shot a quick, desperate look down the table, in Eli's direction, hoping for a nod, a shared glance, any kind of gesture or expression that would say *I understand how you feel and I agree* or—even better—*I will shut down this foolishness, don't you worry.* But Eli was looking at his plate, completely oblivious as he chewed. Big surprise.

Sarah made herself smile. "What's that, honey?" she asked, even though the icy feeling in her chest told her that she already knew.

"Gabe and I are getting married!" Ruby said. Her expression was exultant; her pale cheeks were flushed. Beside her, Gabe wore his usual good-natured, affable look. His dark hair was a little unruly; his deep-set eyes seemed sleepy; and his posture was relaxed, almost lazy, as Ruby put her arm around his shoulder, drawing him close. Sarah liked Gabe, but she'd always felt like he was a boy and not a young man, a mature adult, ready to take a wife and, presumably, start a family. Not that Gabe wasn't a good guy. He was. He was well-mannered and considerate, supremely easygoing. He never got angry. He almost always looked pleased. Or maybe he just looked stoned. Sarah had never been able to tell, and these days, with pot being legal, she couldn't complain about the smell that had sometimes seeped down the stairs from the attic when Ruby and Gabe had been in residence. *It's no different from having a beer,* Eli had told her, and Sarah agreed intellectually, but somehow it still felt different, illicit and wrong.

"Way to go!" said Ari, extending his hand across the table so Gabe could high-five him. "Up top!" he said to Ruby, who grinned and slapped his palm.

"Can we be in the wedding?" asked Dexter. Dexter

looked like his father, tall and lanky, with curly dark-blond hair, pale, freckly skin that flushed easily, and elbows that always seemed to find the nearest pitcher or water glass.

"We can be best men!" said Miles. Miles was more compactly built than his brother, with Sarah's heart-shaped face and fine brown hair. If Dexter was an exuberant golden retriever, Miles was a small, neat cat, his movements careful and precise as he maneuvered his silverware and dabbed at his lips with his napkin.

"We've got an even better job for you guys," said Ruby. "We're going to get married in July, on the Cape. I already asked Safta, and she says it's fine. She knows it's my favorite time of year there."

"So soon!" Sarah blurted, then gulped at her wine. Ruby had always been a determined girl. She hated to be thwarted; despised hearing *No*, or *Let's think it over*, or worst of all, *Slow down*. Even a whiff of a hint that her stepmother opposed this match, or thought that Ruby, at twenty-two, was too young to marry anyone, would have Gabe and Ruby at City Hall by the end of the week with a marriage license in hand. And what was worse, Sarah thought, was that Ruby had told Sarah's mother before she'd told Sarah herself. She felt a clenching toward the back of her throat, a feeling that had become all too familiar during the pandemic, as she choked back what she wanted to say.

Sarah had met Ruby fourteen years ago, when Ruby was just eight years old, a skinny, pigtailed girl walking down the hall of the Manhattan Music School, where Sarah was the executive director. She'd noticed Ruby right away. Or, rather, she'd noticed Ruby's father, tall, bespectacled, and a little awkward, one of a handful of men in the sea of women; towering over most of the moms and nannies who sat, waiting on the benches outside the kids' classrooms as their children shook maracas or thumped at drums. "Miss Sarah, do you have a boyfriend or a girlfriend or a husband or a wife?" Ruby had asked one day after class, staring up at Sarah very seriously.

Sarah had been charmed. "Not at the moment," she'd said, and Eli had put his hand on Ruby's shoulder, gently steering her toward the other kids, saying, "I've got it from here."

Eli had taken Sarah to dinner that Saturday night, and to a Philip Glass concert at the Brooklyn Academy of Music the following week. Eli was more than ten years her senior, divorced, with full custody of a child, employed as a periodontist. Back when Sarah had made lists of what she wanted in a husband, any one of those facts would have been an automatic disqualifier. She'd thought she had wanted a man her age, unencumbered by either children or ex-wives; a painter or a writer or a musician, not a man who did root canals and gum grafts for a living; definitely not a man who'd failed at marriage and already had the responsibility of a child.

But Eli won her over. He wasn't a musician himself ("Six months of recorder," he'd said cheerfully, when she'd asked), but when they started dating he began reading reviews and following classical music blogs. He took her to hear chamber music concerts and piano recitals, where he listened attentively and was unstinting in his admiration for the musicians. "Someone has to be the audience, right?" he'd said. "We can't all be soloists." She'd smiled, a little sadly, because once, being a soloist had been her plan. There was a version of her life where the closest a man like Eli could have come to her would be as a member of the audience, where he'd paid for a ticket to hear her play. But Sarah had abandoned that dream long ago.

Sarah loved the way Eli had pursued her with a

single-minded intensity; the way he noticed what she liked, the way he always thought about her comfort. If they went out and the weather turned cold, he'd wrap her up in his jacket and insist that she wear it home. If he noticed her enjoying a certain wine at dinner, he'd have a bottle sent to her house the next night. He bought her clothes without asking for, or guessing at, her sizes (later she learned that he'd discreetly asked her best friend); he gave her a pair of beautiful gold and amethyst earrings to mark their first month of what he unironically called "going steady." The first time he took her to bed, she'd been delighted, and a little surprised, at how much she liked it. In the real world, Eli was respectful, almost deferential, a feminist who had no problem working with women or treating them as equal. With his clothes off, he was different—self-assured, a little bossy, in a way that Sarah was surprised to find thrilled her.

Best of all was his devotion to Ruby. A man who loved his daughter, Sarah had thought, a man who was a good father, would be a good husband, too. She'd been right, for the most part. Eli had been a wonderful husband, even if Ruby had been a handful early on. Ruby had liked Sarah just fine when she was Miss Sarah at music school, had resented Sarah terribly when things went from being theoretical to actual, and when Sarah went from being a fun companion who showed up on the weekends and took Ruby to get mani-pedis or tea to a full-time, live-in partner to Ruby's father, who made sure that Ruby did her homework, cleared her dishes, and finished her chores.

It hadn't been easy, but Sarah had persevered, ignoring the resentment and nastiness, enduring the tantrums and the tears. She'd made allowances after Eli told her that Ruby's mother, Annette, had walked out before Ruby's first birthday, and she had done her best to not take it personally when Ruby made rude remarks or hid her house keys or left unflattering drawings of Sarah (her chin extra-pointy, her mouth gaping open, presumably mid-yell) lying around where Sarah was sure to find them. She learned not to flinch when Ruby made a point of correcting anyone who got it wrong: *Sarah's not my real mother.* It had taken Sarah years of patience, years of ignoring slights large and small, years of extending her hand and having it slapped away, to finally arrive at the moment, right around her thirteenth birthday, when Ruby had started to soften and began to let her in.

It hadn't hurt, Sarah thought, that Annette had no discernible interest in parenting. Annette was an artist with no actual career and no permanent address. She had always focused on herself and her current passions, whatever they were at the moment: learning to throw pottery or to apply henna designs, performing slam poetry in Seattle, or building costumes for an avant-garde theater company in Brazil. (Annette loved to tell the less theater-literate that the proper terminology was not sewing or creating costumes but building them.) Annette's creative pursuits came first; her romantic partners came second. Her only child might not have even made the list.

And now Ruby was getting married! Maybe if Sarah had been Ruby's birth mother, she'd have been comfortable telling Ruby no, she was too young to be promising her entire life to someone; that her brain was not done baking; that she still had the whole world to see and explore. Her father and her biological mother could have said those things, and Ruby might even have listened; but Sarah, as a stepmother, had to keep quiet, knowing that if she spoke up she'd only send Ruby running faster in the wrong direction.

"We don't want a big wedding," Ruby was saying, with Gabe's hand still clasped in hers. "Just family and our closest friends. There's not a lot of planning that we need to do. So there's really no reason to wait." Daintily, Ruby speared a drumstick from the platter and set it on her plate.

"What about your dress?" Sarah managed. "And flowers? You'll need a caterer . . . and invitations can take weeks. Months!" Maybe she could convince Ruby that there were actual, practical reasons why this plan would never work. When Sarah herself had gotten married, she and her mother had spent six months planning the big day. There'd been a rehearsal dinner at her parents' house in Truro, then the ceremony on a bluff overlooking the ocean, and, finally, the reception at a vineyard, underneath a tent, on a gorgeous night in early September, when the air was still soft and full of the smell of summer rose hips, the bay still warm enough for skinny-dipping. Late at night, after their rehearsal dinner, she and Eli had gone down to the beach, taken off their clothes, and run into the water. *I thought it was bad luck to see the bride the night before the wedding*, he'd said. *So close your eyes*, she'd whispered back, wrapping her legs around his waist and her arms around his shoulders.

"We're going to do email invitations," said Ruby, waving one hand in an airy dismissal of Sarah's concerns.

"What?" Sarah squawked, wrenched out of her memory of skinny-dipping and rudely returned to the tragedy currently in progress.

"Better for the environment," said Gabe, making his first contribution to the conversation.

"Siobhan said she'd make me a dress as a wedding

gift." Siobhan, Sarah knew, was an NYU classmate who'd majored in costume design. "And Safta said she'd help me with the rest of it."

Again, Sarah mentally cursed her mother. Again, she wondered why Ruby hadn't told her first, or at least at the same time. She looked down the table, at her husband, wordlessly begging him for help. Eli's face was expressionless. He still had his eyes on his plate and his fork in his hand. As Sarah watched, he shoved another wad of stuffing into his mouth and started chewing.

"Can we be ring bearers?" asked Miles.

"Are dogs invited?" asked Dexter. "I bet we could tie the ring around Lord Farquaad's neck!"

At the sound of his name, Lord Farquaad, the family's corgi, who'd been sleeping on his bed in the corner of the dining room, lifted his head and peered around. Once he'd determined that no food was on offer, he gave a chuffing sigh, settled his snout back on his paws, and closed his eyes, looking vaguely disgusted at having been woken up for nothing.

"You guys can be ushers. How about that?" Ruby offered. The boys had cheered and Sarah relaxed the tiniest bit. When Sarah had gotten pregnant, she'd worried that the new arrival would further alienate Ruby, but Dexter's arrival had been the event that finally turned them all into a family. Prickly, angry Ruby had loved the baby unreservedly. The first day in the hospital, she'd begged to hold him. As her dad watched, murmuring instructions, Ruby had seated herself carefully in the armchair and tucked the blanket-wrapped bundle against her chest. "Hello, Dexter," she'd said. "I'm your big sister. And when you're old enough, you can come stay with me, and I'll let you do anything . . . you . . . want." Eli had looked a little alarmed at that assertion, but Sarah's eyes had filled with tears. *Maybe this will be all right*, she'd thought. She'd greeted Miles with just as much enthusiasm, and all through college no matter what else she had going on, she'd spent a week or two each summer with her half-brothers at Sarah's mom's place on the Cape, shepherding them through meals and nap times, driving them to swim lessons and Audubon camp, hunting for clams or hermit crabs on the beach, or going for a bike ride and an ice-cream cone.

"What's an usher do?" asked Miles.

"You get to be in charge of where everyone sits. You help people find their seats, and you ask if they're with the bride or the groom. It's a very important job," Gabe said, with one of his easy smiles. Ruby beamed at him, and Gabe reached over to give her ponytail an affectionate tweak. Ruby's cheeks were pink; her usually sharp expression was almost dreamy. Her eyes sparkled behind her glasses as she leaned her head on Gabe's shoulder.

"Have you told your mother?" Sarah asked quietly.

Ruby's expression darkened. "We've talked," she said.

Which meant what, exactly? Sarah shot her husband a frantic look, which Eli, still chewing, either didn't see or chose to ignore. What had Annette said when Ruby called her with the news? Why hadn't Sarah's own mom called to warn her? And what was she supposed to do now? Congratulate those two children? Propose a toast?

Before she could decide, Dexter asked Gabe, "Did you give her a ring?"

Ruby flipped her hand over, curling her fingers into her palm. "We're going to pick one out together." Ruby leaned over and kissed Gabe's cheek. Sarah swallowed hard. She knew Ruby so well. She knew how Ruby dreamed of being a Broadway director, how Ruby would tell everyone her favorite show was *Angels in America*, but how she secretly loved *Phantom of the Opera*, how she hated celery and loved capers, and was so ticklish that she had to cut the tags off any item of clothing that touched her skin. She knew that Ruby hated being short and was secretly vain about her curls and that she'd been delighted when an eye exam revealed that she was near-sighted, because she thought heavy, Clark Kent–style glasses would make people take her seriously.

Unlike Ruby, with her singular focus—Ruby, who'd known, since she'd seen her first Broadway show, that she wanted to grow up and work in theater—Gabe hadn't settled on a career. While Ruby had earned a BFA in production and design at NYU's Tisch School of the Arts, Gabe had drifted through the general studies program, graduating with a degree in liberal arts and, as far as Sarah could discern, no idea of what he might use it for. He'd fallen into proofreading, and seemed to like it well enough, but when Eli had asked about his future, Gabe had just shrugged.

This concerned Sarah enormously. "Are we worried about this?" she'd asked Eli, right after the pandemic had started, before Gabe and Ruby had arrived. They hadn't met Gabe yet, and had managed to gather only a sparse handful of facts about him—that he'd grown up in California, that he'd graduate with Ruby, with a degree in liberal arts, and that he was still trying to figure out what to do with his life.

"Why would we worry?" Eli said.

Sarah pointed at her husband. "You knew what you wanted to be when you grew up by the time you'd finished college."

"Probably by the time I finished high school," Eli agreed.

Sarah thought the idea of an eighteen-year-old dreaming of dental implants and root canals was a little weird. She let it go. "I knew what I wanted to be pretty early on." *And then decided not to be it*, she thought. But even though she hadn't become a concert pianist, she'd found a way to make music her life. She hadn't floundered around for years, trying this, sampling that. Her own mother, as far as Sarah knew, had always loved books and writing, and had always known her career would involve those things, somehow, and her stepdaughter was the same way. "Ruby's always known that she wanted to be in theater."

"Since she saw *Phantom*," Eli said, smiling fondly. Sarah had heard the story, early on, of Ruby's first Broadway show, how enraptured she'd been, how she'd stood at the stage door and waited until every single actor had come out. "We were lucky with Ruby. Just like your parents were lucky with you."

Sarah pressed her lips together, not wanting to dwell on how often she found herself doubting her choices and thinking about the life she hadn't pursued.

"I don't understand what Ruby sees in him. Doesn't it worry you at all?"

"Not really." Eli was in the bathroom with the door open. Sarah could see him studying his hairline in the mirror. "It's probably the sex."

Sarah chucked a decorative pillow toward the bathroom door. "Thank you for that. Now I'll just sit here imagining . . ." She waved her hands. ". . . that."

"Ruby's twenty-one. Of course she's having sex," said Eli. He tilted left, then right, frowning, and handed Sarah his phone. "Will you take a picture of the top of my head?"

"No. Down that road lies madness." Eli's hair was starting to thin, but whenever he asked about it, Sarah assured him that everything was fine. His bald spot, she'd decided, would be her secret. *Men are vain about their hair*, her mom had told her. *Even though it's not as big a deal for them, they don't like getting older any more than we do.*

Eli reclaimed his phone and gave his wife a look that was equal parts fond and exasperated. "I think Gabe sounds like a nice guy." He plugged his phone into the charger on his bedside table, then retrieved the throw pillow, setting it on the love seat. "Not everyone has it all figured out before they graduate."

"But Ruby does," Sarah countered, swinging her legs off the bed, heading to the bathroom to brush her teeth and floss (life with a periodontist meant you never got to slack on your flossing). "Ruby is going full speed ahead."

"It's called balance," Eli said, a touch smugly. "He complements her. You can't have two type-As getting married. You need one person who's all drive and determination . . ." With a flourish, he'd pointed at himself, in his white undershirt and his plaid pajama bottoms. ". . . and someone who's laid back and happy to let their partner lead the way." He'd pointed at her. "That," he'd concluded, "is the key to a happy marriage."

Sarah had shaken her head, smiling, and Eli had come to bed, wrapping his arms and legs around her like a vine around a tree. "Wife," he'd murmured into her ear, and she'd fallen asleep, warm and content, knowing that she was loved.

How glad she would be now for Eli to tease her like that again, to whisper "wife" in her ear! How grateful she would be for a moment of connection, however brief, during a disagreement. How she wished that she and Eli could keep talking when dinner was over, so that then, gently, she could turn the conversation toward him, and what was going on, and why he'd shut down on her just as the pandemic had started and her job and the kids' schools had gone virtual and Ruby had come home and Gabe had moved in—the moment, in other words, when she'd needed him more than ever. But before she could start, she knew Eli would make some excuse about work, a Zoom call, a deadline, something he needed to double-check that sounded both vague and urgent, and he'd go padding down the hall, the flip-flops he swore were helping with his plantar fasciitis slapping noisily against the floor.

It was ironic. She and her husband had spent the pandemic year working less than fifty feet apart. Eli handled emergencies when they came up, but usually he was home doing telehealth visits and virtually teaching a class at Columbia's dental school. He had an office. Sarah did her Zooms from the vanity in their walk-in closet, where a fancier lady might have sat to do her makeup. She helped the school's two dozen teachers, including the Luddites who'd never so much as sent a text on an iPhone, figure out how to teach lessons online. She brainstormed with the development office about ways to raise money without the draw of in-person performances that doubled as fundraisers; she coordinated an online holiday choir concert. When she wasn't on camera, she worked in bed, with her back against the headboard and her laptop on a pile of pillows in front of her. The boys' school had been on a split schedule—two days a week in person, masked and distanced, the rest of the time at home, in virtual school. When they were home, each boy was in his own bedroom on the third floor, unless they were taking gym down in the living room, grunting or giggling their way through sit-ups and jumping jacks while a teacher called encouragement through the screen. Ruby and Gabe had been on the fourth floor for their classes. All that proximity, the way they lived and worked right on top of each other, meant that Sarah had never felt closer to her sons and her stepdaughter. But she'd felt increasingly distant from Eli, and every day it seemed like he was moving a little farther away.

You think you know someone, Sarah thought. She looked at her husband now, at the head of the table, cramming dinner into his mouth, clearly not tasting the food she'd spent hours cooking, not looking at her or at his daughter. *You think you know someone, then you're locked in a house together for over a year, and it turns out, you never knew him at all.*

"Well, if no one else is going to do it, I'm going to address the elephant in the room," Ari announced with a smug smile. It was so unfair, Sarah thought, that Ari was the taller, more classically good-looking brother. He didn't use reading glasses, he'd never had back trouble, and his hair wasn't thinning at all.

"What elephant?" asked Miles, looking around.

"Is there going to be an elephant at the wedding?" asked Dexter. "Arjun at my school went to a wedding with an elephant."

Ari ignored them, waggling his eyebrows at Ruby and Gabe. "Anything else you two want to tell us? Is Uncle Ari going to need to get his shotgun?"

Gabe's brow furrowed. Then he ducked his head with a shame-faced grin, as Ruby flushed more deeply.

"No! God, no!"

Ari held up his hands, palms out. "Okay, okay! All good! Just checking!"

"Uncle Ari," said Dexter, looking deeply disapproving, "you don't really have a gun, do you?"

"It's just an expression," Ruby said.

"Well, mazel tov!" said Sarah, lifting her wineglass. "To the happy couple!" Her celebratory declaration, even to her own ears, was far too giddy, too hearty, patently fake. She watched as Eli, with his mouth full, raised his own glass, then started to cough.

Miles and Dexter raised their plastic cups. Miles did it carefully. Dexter sloshed grape juice on the tablecloth, even though his glass was only half full. Eli managed a strangled "Mazel tov," before starting to cough again.

"Dad?" Ruby asked, as Eli hacked, bent over his plate with his face turning red. "Dad?"

"He's choking!" yelled Dexter, jumping up and knocking his chair to the ground. Miles got up, too. So did Lord Farquaad, who'd sensed either danger or a chance to snag some roast chicken.

"I'm fine," Eli wheezed, waving them off.

Sarah stood and bumped the edge of the table with her hip, knocking over the wine, sending dark red liquid cascading down over the tablecloth, soaking her legs, and dripping onto the carpet, which she'd had steam-cleaned the week before. Lord Farquaad *grrr*ed when the decanter bounced past his head. Sarah pictured the dog snapping at her ankle; pictured herself falling, pulling down the tablecloth as she went. She imagined the lit candles rolling onto the carpet; she pictured the curtains, then her beautiful home, then the whole of her beautiful life, going up in flames, burning down to nothing.

Eli kept coughing, then hiccuped, then reached for his napkin and finally managed to hack up whatever had gotten stuck in his throat. "I'm okay," he said, waving away the glass of water that Gabe had poured. "I'm okay. Don't worry. Everything's fine."

I'm not, thought Sarah, staring at her family, thinking that Ruby and Gabe's engagement was not off to a particularly auspicious start.

RUBY

~~~~~

When dinner was over, Ruby and Gabe cleared the table. The boys helped them, carefully carrying glasses and dirty forks and knives into the kitchen (Miles stacked the plates neatly; Dexter grabbed whatever he could reach). "Bride's side or groom's?" Ruby overheard Miles asking Dexter, and she smiled, imagining the two of them in button-up shirts and bow ties.

Gabe put the food away, portioning it into Tupperware. Ruby washed the dishes that couldn't go into the dishwasher. She felt a strange sensation, an unfamiliar tension in her chest. It eased a little when Gabe settled his hand at the base of her neck, rubbing gently.

"You okay?"

"I'm fine," said Ruby. "That was just a little weird."

"Mmm," said Gabe, pulling her close. "They're happy for us, right?"

She understood his confusion. Gabe hadn't grown up with a father, or in close proximity to a marriage. During their time in Brooklyn, Ruby had seen him watching her dad and stepmother carefully, a little enviously, sometimes struggling to interpret a look or a joke or a gesture.

"Yes," said Ruby. "They're happy."

"Are you sure you're okay?" Gabe asked.

"What?"

"You shivered," said her boyfriend. Ruby promised she was fine, that her dad and her stepmom were fine, that everyone was happy for them. She hugged Gabe, feeling that delicious sensation in her belly, a softening, melting feeling when he whispered "You're my sweetheart" in her ear. Then he went to get a broom, and Ruby bent back to the dishes, feeling a dozen different things at once, her head a tangle of emotions that she couldn't unpick or even name.

Gabriel Andrews was the first boy Ruby had ever loved. He'd also been the last boy she ever thought she'd have a chance with. Ruby knew she wasn't beautiful. She could look cute, at best, and that was only on the days she put a lot of effort into her outfit selection and used at least three different products in her hair. Gabe was effortlessly gorgeous, with his slow, relaxed smile and his deep-set dark-brown eyes. She'd noticed him the day she began classes at NYU. She'd exited her dorm room on the twenty-fourth floor, stepped into the elevator, and been hammering at the button to close the door even though she understood, rationally, that those buttons didn't do anything but make you feel like you had some control. The doors had finally started to slide shut when an arm shot through the gap between them, and a male voice called out, "Hold up!" The doors slid obligingly open. Someone toward the back of the elevator had groaned. And there was Gabe, who'd smiled a genial apology at the other passengers before plugging in his earbuds and spending the rest of the trip swaying to his own private soundtrack. He'd stood right next to Ruby, close enough for her to smell the soap on his skin and to hear, faintly, the sounds of circa-2000s Britney Spears. Ruby had been entranced.

"He's from LA," Ruby's roommate's friend Amara

had told her, three months later at a party, when Amara had caught Ruby staring at Gabe while he danced.

"Is he seeing anyone?" Ruby asked.

"I don't know," said Amara, and blinked eyelashes so long that they brushed her cheeks. Oh, how Ruby had coveted those lashes, and Amara's long, long legs! "He's a cutie, right?"

Ruby had nodded woodenly, blushing as she watched Gabe make a fluid turn from the girl he'd been dancing with toward the guy who'd been grinding on him from behind.

"Is he bi?" she asked.

"Bi. Or maybe pan. Anything and everything," Amara said with a wink.

Ruby nodded, feeling like she'd swallowed stones, like her competition for Gabe's attention had just effectively doubled, that her chances had just gone from slim to nonexistent, even though she knew it wasn't true. Liking men and women, one of her friends had once explained, didn't mean that a bisexual person would like all men and all women. The question was, could Gabe ever like her?

Ruby couldn't stop staring at Gabe as he closed his eyes, lost in the music, rocking his hips against those of the guy who'd embraced him. He looked like a fallen angel, which was a weird thing for a Jewish girl to think, but it was true. With his beautiful face tilted toward the roof and his hands gripping the other guy's hips he was a picture of corrupted innocence, like he'd been pure and now couldn't wait to be filthy. Ruby felt herself shiver. At that instant, Gabe opened his eyes, looked right at her, and gave her a teasing smile before beckoning for her to join him. Ruby shook her head and managed a wave— a stupid little half-hearted waggle of her hand—before turning away. He was, she'd decided, like a statue in a museum. Fun to look at, impossible to take home.

She and Gabe had moved in and out of one another's orbits through their first three and a half years of college. She'd dated one of his freshman-year roommates for a few months sophomore year; he'd been in her History of Cinema seminar two years after that, loping into the lecture hall seconds before the professor started talking, flipping open his laptop with one languid hand, and lounging in his chair like it was a velvet-covered chaise and not nubbly preformed plastic. Finally, in the fall of senior year, they'd worked on a production of *The Bacchae* together. Ruby had been the stage manager, and Gabe, who'd enrolled in an Introduction to Stagecraft class, had somehow been assigned the role of assistant lighting designer.

"Danhauser!" the director, Professor Caldwell, had shouted, waving her over. Professor Caldwell was short and round, with a notable wart on his nose. In the course of his acting career, he'd played hobbits, gnomes, and, in a long-running children's TV show, a troll who lived under a bridge. Each year, the seniors invited all of Professor Caldwell's new advisees to a party where, at midnight, they screened a highlight reel of the professor making children answer riddles, offering pithy wisdom to questing heroes, and eating second breakfast. "Danhauser! This is . . ." He spent a moment groping for Gabe's name, then gave up and just waved toward him. "This young gentleman is going to help run the lights."

"Hey," said Gabe, with a friendly smile. "I'm Gabe." He offered Ruby his hand.

"Hi. Have you ever worked a lighting rig before?"

"I don't even know what a lighting rig is," said Gabe.

"It's up there, right?" He'd gestured vaguely toward the ceiling.

Oh, boy, thought Ruby.

"I just changed my minor to Theater Arts, so this is kind of a last-minute thing." Gabe shuffled his feet, looking so crestfallen that Ruby felt her crusty, on-task stage-manager heart thaw and crack.

"Don't worry," she told him. "I'll show you what to do."

They'd worked together for eight weeks, through rehearsals and tech week and Caldwell's inevitable dress-rehearsal-day meltdown, where he'd raged and screamed, announcing that this was going to be the worst show, the absolute *worst* show that he'd ever had the dishonor of being associated with in all his years in the theater. Ruby, who'd seen this performance three times previously, had watched with a jaundiced eye, with Gabe cringing beside her. "He looks like Rumpelstiltskin when the miller's daughter gets his name right," Gabe had whispered, after Caldwell tossed his script to the floor and stomped on the ground. Ruby bit her lip to keep from laughing, and whispered back that Caldwell had actually played Rumpelstiltskin in a direct-to-DVD movie.

Through all that time, Gabe had been friendly, maybe a little flirty. He, like Professor Caldwell, referred to her as Danhauser. Sometimes he'd clap her on the back or touch her on the arm, and he always insisted on escorting her home when rehearsals ended after midnight. She learned that he was the only child of a single mother, that he'd never known his dad and had always wanted to attend college in New York City, where his mother had lived and where, he suspected, he'd been conceived. But he'd offered those courtesies and told her his story while

Ruby knew he was hooking up with other people, first with two different members of the all-girl Greek chorus and then with the guy understudying Tiresias. She hadn't let herself hope. At the cast party, she'd contented herself with standing in a dark corner, sipping white wine from a plastic cup, watching Gabe dance, wondering why he hadn't made that his major as he waved his arms in time to the beat. She'd been chagrined when he'd caught her staring again, then surprised when he took her by the hand.

"Danhauser. Dance with me." It hadn't been a question, and Gabe hadn't waited for an answer. He'd pulled her through the throng of people and began to dance. Ruby did her best to keep up.

"Close your eyes," Gabe shouted. She did . . . and then she felt him pulling her closer, felt his fingers in her hair, tucking one of her curls behind her ear. "You're so pretty," he'd said, his mouth close to her cheek, and Ruby had been so startled that she'd blurted, "What?" loudly enough for all the dancers near them to hear.

"You," Gabe said, his mouth very close to her ear. "I can't stop thinking about you. With your beautiful hair and your cute little stomping boots." Ruby stared down at the Doc Martens she'd started wearing after someone had dropped a prop marble bust on her left foot during a junior-year production of *The Play That Goes Wrong* and broken two of her toes.

Gabe had backed Ruby into the corner where she'd been hiding. He'd cupped her cheek in his hand, bent down gently, looking into her eyes, waiting for her nod. Then he'd kissed her, first softly, then more boldly, licking at her lips until she tipped her head back and then slipping his tongue into her mouth. *He's done this a lot,*

Ruby told herself. *It doesn't mean anything.* She told herself she was an observer, that she wasn't feeling anything but a clinical, almost scientific interest in how Gabe went about seducing someone. She'd never liked kissing all that much, but as Gabe nibbled at her lips and slid his tongue against hers, she had to admit that she was finally getting the point of it.

They'd kissed for what felt like hours, first in the corner, then on a couch. Ruby felt hazy, lust-dazed, her body more liquid than solid when, finally, Gabe had whispered, "Can we go somewhere a little less public?"

"Okay," she'd whispered back. "But you have to stop calling me Danhauser. You have to call me Ruby."

"Ruby," Gabe said. Then he'd nibbled at her earlobe, making her moan out loud. She'd taken him back to her apartment, and they'd spent their first night together.

They hadn't had actual, all-the-way sex that time. But the following weekend there was another party, at a rooftop bar in SoHo, and they'd both had a few drinks. Back in Ruby's bedroom, the kissing had, once again, been sexy and luxuriously slow (later she'd learned that Gabe had eaten an entire edible before the night began, which meant that everything unfolded at a deliciously languorous pace). By the time they were both naked, Ruby had never been more aroused, but the actual intercourse had been disappointing, clumsy, quick, and unremarkable. "You good?" Gabe had whispered at the end. Ruby had nodded, not wanting to confess that she hadn't come anywhere close to an orgasm or wanting to show him what it would take to get her there. Gabe had fallen asleep with his head against her chest, and Ruby had spent a delightful hour running her fingertips over the silky, almost hairless expanse of his chest and his shoulders. Gabe's skin was the brown of hulled walnuts where the sun touched it, warm golden where his clothes covered him up, and what body hair he had was inky black and silky straight, finer than the hair on his head. Ruby, pale and freckled as she was, prone to sunburns and betraying blushes, loved Gabe's skin. She loved that Gabe got her sense of humor, that he admired her ambition, that he thought that she was beautiful, with her curls and what he always called her stomping boots. Even though they'd grown up very differently, she knew they were the same. Ruby had been abandoned by her birth mother; Gabe had never even known his dad. And even though that first loss had made Ruby a planner, a maker of lists who'd pictured her future in elaborate detail, while Gabe's life with a single mother had left him relaxed and easygoing, willing to roll with whatever life dealt him, Ruby knew that they were more alike than they were different. They were broken in the same places; they were both survivors, who knew how the world could bruise you, and that shared knowledge meant that they would never hurt each other.

Her senior year, Ruby was sharing a one-bedroom apartment with two other girls, in a high-rise that overlooked Washington Square Park. Ruby and her roommates had decided to keep the kitchen and the living room as common spaces, to share a communal wardrobe (they were all more or less the same size), and to partition the bedroom into three private cubicles. Ruby had the cubicle on the left, a space she and Gabe had dubbed the sleep box, a narrow, windowless rectangle with barely enough room for a twin-sized bed and a three-drawer Ikea dresser.

For the first few months, living there had been an adventure, like crossing the Atlantic in steerage, or traversing the country in the sleeper car of a train. Having sex in the sleep box meant that your roommates and their partners all heard your business, and would occasionally cheer you on, or call out suggestions. Eating ramen, or black beans and rice, using her roommate's parents' account to watch premium cable, getting her hair cut by cosmetology students, and going to bars that offered cheap drinks and free food during happy hour—all of it felt fun, even romantic. Ruby understood that, unlike Molly, one of her roommates, unlike Gabe, she was cosplaying poverty, experiencing it with a safety net underneath her, which meant she wasn't really experiencing it at all. She was lucky; she was privileged. She didn't have to worry about student loans, or, once she'd graduated, about surviving on what she'd be earning as an entry-level stage manager without a union card. Nor did she have to worry when COVID happened and NYU had gone virtual.

Come home, her stepmom had said, her voice tight with fear, right after Two Weeks to Slow the Spread became Four Weeks to Stop the Spread, and it was clear to anyone who was paying attention that the spread was neither slowing nor stopping.

"I'm fine," Ruby had insisted. Sarah was a hoverer, a worrier, always reminding Ruby to wear sunscreen and her retainers. Ruby was pretty sure Sarah also tracked her on her iPhone. It was annoying, but also obscurely comforting, to have someone who cared.

"I don't think it's safe, being on the subway or out on the streets," Sarah had said.

"You can't catch it from touching things," said Ruby.

"They don't know that," Sarah said. "They don't know how it spreads. And what if they stop letting people go in and out of the city? What if you get sick, and we can't help you? Or if we get sick, and you can't help us?"

Ruby had to admit that Sarah had a point. She also knew that the Brooklyn brownstone where she'd lived since she was eight years old had much to recommend it: an expansive kitchen, a fully stocked refrigerator and pantry, a washer and a dryer and a home theater, with a flat-screen TV that got all the premium channels, not to mention the fourth floor that was hers alone. No more schlepping her laundry to the wash-and-fold two blocks away; no more roommates who could hear her and Gabe through paper-thin walls.

Brooklyn was tempting. But Ruby wasn't eager to relinquish her independence. Nor was she willing to give up her boyfriend. "What about Gabe?" she'd asked, assuming that would be a deal-breaker, but Sarah hadn't even hesitated. "Gabe can come, too," she said. "Except he can't keep delivering food."

"Mama," Ruby said. After Sarah and her dad got married, Ruby and her father had decided that Sarah would be Mama and Annette would be Mom, although, for the first few years, Ruby never called Sarah anything at all. She'd also never guessed that when she was twelve, Annette would say, "How about you just call me Annette?" and that by then Sarah would feel like more of a mother than Annette had ever been. "Gabe has to work. He's got loans."

"I understand that," said Sarah, whose usually low, melodious voice was getting high and slightly shrill. "But your dad and I don't feel safe with him in and out of people's apartment buildings, being around all those strangers, and then coming back home. How do we know that the people he's delivering to aren't sick? Or that the people working in the restaurants aren't?"

Ruby opened her mouth to argue, then reconsidered. Put that way, Sarah had a point.

"Gabe has to work," she repeated.

"I understand that," Sarah said. "But he doesn't have to deliver food. Let me make some calls."

Ruby had agreed, and Sarah had gotten the music school where she worked to hire him to digitize their student performance archives. Ruby was almost certain that at least some of Gabe's salary was coming out of Sarah's own paycheck, which made her feel like crying; that Sarah would quietly make that kind of sacrifice and never say a word, so that Gabe could have his pride, and so that Ruby could have Gabe. She had been so excited to make the offer, to give Gabe the town house and, by extension, her family, like a peasant laying a gift at a king's feet. He and Ruby had only been exclusive for about six weeks by then, and Ruby couldn't wait to spend more time with him, to get to know everything there was to know about him. If COVID fast-forwarded them through months of dating, then God bless COVID, Ruby thought.

"Come live with me and be my love," she said, quoting "The Passionate Shepherd to His Love," hoping that Gabe would get the reference from the literature class that they'd both taken, even though she suspected she'd paid more attention than he had.

Frowning, he'd asked, "Are there sheep involved?"

"Definitely," said Ruby. "Also little kids. But we'd have our own bathroom."

She'd expected delight, immediate excitement. Instead, Gabe had frowned, his dark eyebrows drawing down. "It sounds amazing. But are you sure it's okay?"

"I'm sure," Ruby had said, looking around, letting her face crinkle in distaste. "And you can't stay here."

Gabe's apartment was even worse than hers: a five-bedroom home in Bed-Stuy, shared with seven roommates who always smelled like weed and feet.

"You're positive your dad and your stepmom don't mind?" he'd asked.

She'd assured him that they were fine with it . . . but, it seemed, Gabe was struggling to believe her. "Are you sure?" he'd asked her, over and over, while he packed. "Are you sure it's okay?" She'd promised him; she'd helped him carry his bags downstairs, where they waited for the Uber that Sarah had insisted they take. When the car turned the corner onto the block where she'd grown up, Gabe had gone very still.

"Jeez, it's a mansion," he'd said when they were both out of the car. Ruby felt her face get hot with one of her betraying blushes. "It's not that big," she'd mumbled. "And this neighborhood wasn't so expensive when they bought it." Both of those statements were lies, and Gabe probably knew it.

Ruby had told Gabe that her stepmother was a music-school administrator, and her dad was a periodontist. As they walked up the sidewalk, she could see him trying to figure it out, trying to do the math that would add up to this house in this neighborhood.

Ruby decided to explain. "It's my step-grandmother," she said. "Sarah's mom. She was an author, and one of her books was turned into a movie a long time ago. She helped my stepmother buy this place." Sarah's mother, Ronnie Levy, Ruby's *safta*, had also paid for Ruby's college education, the same way she would take care of tuition for Miles and Dexter, and her cousin Connor, Ruby's uncle's stepson, when Connor was old enough; but Ruby felt shy about mentioning it. Gabe's mother was a nurse now, but she'd worked as a waitress when Gabe had been little. Savings and scholarships had paid for most of Gabe's tuition, but he'd had to take out loans his senior year. No wealthy grandmother had covered his bills or would buy him a brownstone once he had his degree.

Ruby unlocked the door and led Gabe inside, through the foyer and the parlor and the living room and the dining room, up the stairs, past her dad and stepmom's bedroom and her dad's office on the second floor, past her brothers' rooms on the third floor, all the way to the fourth floor, the playroom and the suite that had been Ruby's when she'd lived at home.

Gabe set his duffel bag down. Ruby followed his gaze, trying to see the room the way that it would look to him: the stained oak floors, the bookcases that stretched from floor to ceiling along the north wall, the cushioned, curtained window seat, where a kid could curl up with a book, or perform a play or a puppet show. She saw Gabe take in her old, kid-sized drum kit, the bins of blocks and Legos, the baskets full of stuffed animals, the painted wooden rocking horse, and the three-story dollhouse that had once been her very favorite thing. He looked at the cubbies full of art supplies; the full-length mirror, the chest full of princess gowns and fairy wings, wooden swords and magic wands, and the little refrigerator stocked with bottles of water and apple juice.

"Is this where you sleep?" Gabe's voice was a little faint.

"No, that's in here." She showed him the bedroom, the queen-sized bed with its white-painted wrought-iron frame and the padded bench, upholstered in apple-green linen, at its foot. "And there's a bathroom over there."

Gabe sat on the bed, his expression uncharacteristically serious, his brows drawn together, his lips in a straight line, a little white at the edges. "I don't get it," he finally said. "If you could have just been living here, why were you in that crap apartment?"

"Um, because I don't want to live with my family? Because I'm an independent woman?"

Gabe just shook his head. He didn't say anything, but Ruby could imagine what he was thinking: *You actually pay rent to* not *live here?*

Ruby twisted a lock of her hair around her finger. She and Gabe had talked a little about the differences between them. But their conversations had been general, not specific. She didn't know about the neighborhood in Los Angeles where Gabe had grown up, or much about his life before he'd come east for college. She knew that his mother had lived in New York, before he was born, and that she and Gabe had lived with her parents, in her childhood bedroom, for a while when Gabe was little. She knew that Gabe hated cilantro, that he'd been raised nominally Catholic but never went to church, that he was bisexual and could understand but not speak Spanish. Beyond that, Ruby could make guesses, based on what she saw: the way Gabe had worn the same pair of black-and-white checkered Vans for the entire time she'd known him, or how he always bought used textbooks and sold them back to the university bookstore at the end of the semester, or the way that, when he'd packed, his entire wardrobe had fit into the duffel he'd set at the foot of the bed. At college, rich kids and poor kids and all the kids in between wore versions of the same clothes, ate the same meals, attended the same classes, studied from the same textbooks, and typed their papers on the same laptops. There were differences, of course: some kids' jeans cost twenty dollars and some kids' cost two hundred; some kids owned the newest laptops and some just leased them from the school—but you had to look for them. College didn't erase the differences between how everyone grew up, but it disguised those differences—except, of course, for the kids who went out of their way to drop the names of the places they'd vacationed or brag about getting bottle service at some club, and those kids were easy enough to avoid. Only now that Ruby was home, she had been unflattened, her circumstances brought sharply into focus, so that Gabe could see her life in all its dimension. And what must that look like, what must she look like, now?

I know how to fix this, Ruby thought. She took Gabe's hand and tugged him toward the bed. A few minutes later, she was on her back, with Gabe's mouth hot against hers, his hands warm at her waist, and her bra and sweatshirt both shoved up around her neck. Ruby hummed happily as she felt his lips against her cheek, then her neck. After the first few times they'd gone to bed together, she and Gabe had learned each other's bodies, figured out each other's rhythms, where, and how, they liked to be touched. When they made love, it was always satisfying, even if Ruby worried sometimes that it wasn't the kind of explosive, world-shaking sex that would strip their souls bare and forge the kind of eternal, intimate communion that the movies and books—including her *safta*'s—had taught her to hope for. Maybe the books and the movies had it wrong, she thought, as Gabe cupped his hands under her bottom and Ruby wrapped her legs around his waist. Maybe even the best sex was more akin to a good meal than a revelation. Maybe she'd bought into a bunch of stupid, paternalistic myths and was being dumb to worry about how, when she came, it was hardly ever during actual intercourse, and usually with the help of Gabe's hand, or her own. Maybe . . .

"Stop thinking," Gabe had murmured in her ear. The feel of his breath on her skin made her shiver. Ruby closed her eyes. The scent of her sheets, her stepmother's fabric softener, was all around her, the feel of her down comforter beneath its crisp duvet cover. The slant of the light through the window, the hardwood floor creaking underneath them, all of it was wonderfully familiar, and as she felt Gabe slide inside her, Ruby felt content, her monkey brain ceasing its chatter, until everything was quiet and she felt herself, finally, at peace, at home. Only Gabe could ever make her feel that way. She never wanted to let him go.

That was the night that Ruby decided she wanted to marry her sweetheart . . . and what Ruby wanted, Ruby got. When she'd decided to learn to play the drums she'd worked on her dad until he'd agreed, and when she'd wanted to do theater she'd convinced the head of her high school's drama club to let her join when she was just in eighth grade. She'd gotten into her first-choice college; she'd gotten both of the internships she wanted once she was there. She knew how to apply herself and work toward the goal of a future together, and it helped, of course, that Gabe wanted it, too. He loved living with her, although sometimes Ruby worried that what he loved even more was being with a family, in a big, capacious house with two adults who were accomplished cooks and two little boys who idolized him. In the end, it hadn't been hard at all. "We should get married," she'd said, after they'd made love on a night six months later. It had been a Friday—Shabbat dinner, a movie in the basement screening room (which was just an extra-large flat-screen TV and an extra-wide couch). Bowls of buttered popcorn and Sarah's seven-layer bars, which were better than any candy. Slipping away when the movie was over, shedding their clothes in the playroom so they were naked by the time they reached the bed. A perfect night, and when Ruby had whispered her plan—*we should get married*—Gabe had said, "I'm in." For months it had been their secret. As soon as they'd found their own place, and started their jobs, Ruby had called her *safta*, and Gabe had called his mom, and they'd gone back to Brooklyn, to give Sarah and Eli and Dexter and Miles the news.

When the kitchen was clean and the boys were in bed, Ruby and Gabe said goodbye to Sarah (Eli had already gone up to bed) and took the subway back to Queens. In their new apartment, they'd made love, and then they'd lain awake, legs entwined. Ruby pillowed her cheek on Gabe's chest.

"Tell me about your mom." She said it sweetly, as if she hadn't spent months of their relationship asking and cajoling and finally demanding that Gabe tell her something—anything—about his life in California. He knew all about her—how her mom had left when she was a baby; how, when she was little, she used to wish that her mother would come back and take Ruby away with her. How she'd been so awful when Sarah had tried so hard.

Gabe knew Ruby's whole story, but she knew very little of his. Now that they were engaged, Ruby felt that he'd forfeited the option of silence. "I need to know about your mother. She's going to be my mother-in-law," Ruby said. The thought gave her an odd twinge.

She felt Gabe's body tense. "She's . . ." He paused, and sighed, and didn't continue. Ruby held her breath, prepared to wait, for as long as she had to, until she got some answers.

"She's what?"

"She's proud," Gabe finally said.

"Proud of you?" asked Ruby.

"Proud in general," said Gabe. "And a little prickly about things. And . . ." Another long pause. "I'm not sure my mom and your stepmom are going to have much in common," he finally said, his voice low.

"That's okay," said Ruby. "They don't have to be besties."

"No," said Gabe, "but . . ." He rolled onto his side, so he was facing the wall, turning his back to Ruby as he spoke. "Your parents have that beautiful place. My mom and I lived in my grandparents' house until I was in fourth grade, because my mom couldn't afford a place of her own. She'd sleep on the pullout couch so I could have the bed."

Ruby nodded. This was one of the handful of facts Gabe had shared. "So you think that Sarah . . ." Ruby groped, sensing what he meant, not quite sure how to say it. "You think she's going to be, like, snotty to your mother? You think that she'll look down on her?"

"I know she won't," Gabe said bleakly. "She'll be nice. She'll be kind. And that," he said, "is going to be worse. Worse than if she acted like my mom wasn't good enough for her; like I'm not good enough for you. Because my mom will think she's faking. Even if she isn't."

"But Sarah doesn't think that!" Ruby said to Gabe's back. "And she's not just going to pretend to be nice. She loves you! Both of my parents do! And they're both excited to meet your mother. That's not fake!"

"I know." Gabe's voice was mournful. "I know it's not, because I know your parents. But my mom doesn't."

"So what can we do?" Ruby asked.

He finally rolled back toward her, and pulled her against him, holding her tight. "We'll just have to give it time. You can be patient, right? I know you're great at waiting."

At that, Ruby smiled, because, as Gabe knew, Ruby was famously impatient, or infamously impulsive, depending on who was doing the telling. According to her dad, her very first sentence had been *Want that one*, uttered as she'd pointed, imperiously, to a teddy bear in a toy store window. Ruby had always known what she'd desired, whether it was a pattern for a new duvet cover (blue polka dots, not pink flowers) or what she wanted for her seventh birthday dinner (sushi and dumplings and a chocolate cake with chocolate frosting) or where she wanted to go to college and what she wanted to study while she was there. She made up her mind and never second-guessed herself, or deviated from her decisions. *Ruby For Sure*, her dad used to call her. Once, when she was thirteen, and absolutely settled on the theme and the location of her bat mitzvah party, she'd overheard him talking to Sarah. "Losing your mom the way she did has to be the worst kind of uncertainty," her dad had said. "I think that's why she's got to be so certain about everything else." Sarah had murmured something Ruby couldn't hear, and Eli had laughed, and had said, "Right now, all she can see is black and white. When she grows up, she'll start to see shades of gray." If it was true, Ruby thought, it hadn't happened yet. Right was right; wrong was wrong. Her father and Sarah were good, or at least they tried to be, which amounted to the same thing, and her mother was bad, or at least selfish, which, again, was the same. Thinking of Annette made Ruby remember that she hadn't called her yet. For a moment she imagined telling her mother the news. *I'm in love. I'm getting married. And, unlike you, I will never leave.* Except that thought gave her an odd pang, too: *But what if I wanted to leave?* she thought, and then, immediately, made herself stop thinking.

Ruby wrapped herself tight around her beloved and kissed his cheek, then his forehead. Her boyfriend. Her sweetheart. Her husband-to-be! "Don't worry, all right?" Gabe said, pushing a lock of hair off her forehead, twining it around his finger, and letting it boing back into place. "My mom will get along fine with your family. And if she doesn't . . ." He bent close, nuzzling her neck in a way that never failed to make her shiver. "If she doesn't, she'll be all the way in California."

"I won't worry," said Ruby. "I promise." She tilted her head up, and he bent down to brush his lips against hers.

They both used the bathroom. Gabe dotted prescription acne medication on his cheeks and his chin. Ruby popped in her retainer. Gabe kissed her forehead, then each eyelid, then rolled onto his back and was almost instantly asleep. Ruby lay awake in the dark. In Brooklyn, the attic was always quiet. Now, in their walkup in Queens with windows that faced the street, her nights were punctuated by laughter, shouting, sometimes the sound of breaking glass. Cars and buses drove by, along with police cars with their sirens wailing. In Brooklyn, it was easy to imagine that she and Gabe lived in a castle, that they were a prince and a princess, high in a tower. Their time in Park Slope had felt enchanted, with delicious meals magically appearing, where they had people around when they wanted company and solitude when they wanted to be alone, or together, just the two of them. Now that they'd moved out, Ruby wondered if what she was feeling was that enchantment fading, the luster of new love disappearing, evaporating like a dream, revealing the reality of the world. *Maybe I'm homesick*, she thought, and told herself that she just needed to get used to the new place, that she and Gabe would make it cozy and soon it would feel like home. She tried to ignore the tiny voice inside of her that was whispering, *This is a bad idea, you're rushing into it, you're too young, this won't work*; tried to ignore the growing certainty that what she was feeling was surprise and disappointment. When she'd called Ronnie, she'd expected her to say, *Ruby, please tell me you're kidding?*; when she'd told her stepmom and her dad, she'd been waiting for them to laugh, to shake their heads and tell her, *Absolutely not!* She'd been counting on one of the grown-ups to put an end to it. *No, Ruby. This isn't going to happen.* But they hadn't said that. They had congratulated her. They'd smiled their approval; they'd raised their glasses for toasts, they'd treated her like an adult who could be trusted to make decisions about her own life. Except, Ruby wondered, what if she was making a bad decision? What if she couldn't be trusted? And, if that was true, what was she supposed to do now?

ELI

~~~

Elijah Danhauser was a good man.

Growing up in Massapequa with his parents and his brother, he had been a good son and a good brother, hardworking and decent and kind. He'd worked hard at school and treated his elders with deference, his peers with kindness, and his parents with respect. While his brother, Ari, was crashing cars, flunking out of colleges, and getting arrested, Eli drove carefully, studied hard, and graduated with honors. In adulthood, Eli had tried to be as good a husband as he could to his first wife, Annette. He and Annette met in college, at Syracuse University, at a fraternity party. Annette was petite, with big hazel eyes underneath a wide forehead, wavy brown hair, and a quick, bright smile. They'd fallen in love when they were both juniors and were inseparable for two years. After graduation, they'd set out together to see the world. For eight years they traveled, working menial jobs for six months to save enough money to fund six months of adventures. Eli had a strong back and was good with his hands and could always find work doing carpentry or construction. Annette had an ear for languages and, with her cheerful personality, usually ended up bartending or waitressing. Together, they had biked from Canada to Mexico and worked on a ranch in Montana, with Annette helping in the kitchen and Eli repairing miles of fence on the range. They'd spent a summer at a hotel in

Iceland and three months crewing a billionaire's yacht. They'd followed the Dave Matthews Band on its world tour in the late 1990s (Annette's choice, not Eli's), and spent half a year living in Madrid, where they could visit the Prado every day (Eli's choice, not Annette's). They'd led cycling trips through the Lake District in England and through the wine country of France and up and down the hills of Tuscany. They swam in volcanic lakes in Guatemala and spent six weeks in a yurt in Saskatoon. When their thirtieth birthdays were approaching, Eli wanted to get married, buy a house, start a family. He'd assumed Annette would want the same things by the time she turned thirty. He'd been wrong. Annette, it turned out, wanted none of those things. She had no interest in marrying Eli, or anyone else, and had even less desire to buy a house and stay in one place. "I can't do it," she'd said tearfully, in the midst of one of their discussions that always seemed to turn into fights. "I'm not exaggerating. At all. If you make me live in a suburb, I'll die." She'd swung her long hair over her shoulder and started to braid it, a thing she did when she was trying to soothe herself, and Eli had promised no suburbs, but couldn't they find a city they both liked?

They'd still been talking it over when Annette had gotten pregnant. Eli realized what had happened before she did. In their years together, he'd gotten used to caring for her every month when her period started. No matter where they were, he'd dig her heating pad out from her backpack or under their bed, find an adapter that would let him plug it in, and spend that first night rubbing her back, bringing her Advil and hot tea. When a month came and went without any requests for back rubs or heating pads or painkillers, he'd figured it out, and when he'd found the positive test in the trash his suspicions, and his fears, had been confirmed. She was pregnant, and she hadn't planned on telling him.

Eli had put aside his anger and tried to convince her that it was a sign. He'd told her that a baby didn't have to change anything. They could keep traveling, only they'd be a trio, not a pair. Maybe, he told her, they could rent an RV and tour the country's national parks! Or they could visit Sweden, like she'd always wanted to do, and try to find her relatives there. They could live on a houseboat, or in a yurt, or sail around the world. He'd begged and he'd pleaded and he'd threatened and he'd even cried, and finally, Annette had agreed.

"Fine," she had said with a shrug—the same shrug with which she'd eventually assented to Eli's proposal. Pregnancy made some women glow, but it turned Annette exhausted and slow-moving, her skin pallid and pimply, her beautiful long hair hanging greasy and limp.

After the briefest of ceremonies at City Hall, so that the baby would be legitimate and, more important, so that Annette could get on Eli's insurance policy, Eli had brought his wife to New York City and the apartment his parents were paying for. He'd enrolled in dental school in New York City. "Dental school?" Annette had asked, her eyebrows all but disappearing into her bangs. As she started worrying the end of her braid, Eli told her not to worry, that dentistry was akin to learning a trade, that dentists could work anywhere in the world— "because everyone's got teeth, right?"—Annette had nodded, looking disheartened and unconvinced. That night, she'd woken him up just after three o'clock in the morning, gripping his shoulder and shaking him out of a sound sleep.

"You're going to move me to Long Island," she'd said, and started to cry.

Eli swore that he wouldn't. He promised his wife that nothing would change, that her fears would never come true (while of course he was thinking, secretly, guiltily, that once the baby came Annette would welcome the idea of a fenced yard, safe streets, and that, once the baby came, she'd start to see things his way). Eli worked hard at school. At home, he struggled to convince Annette that the future, while not exactly what she had envisioned, would be fine, even better than fine. He would provide, and they would find a way to be happy.

Annette planned on looking for work, but first she'd suffered from nonstop nausea, and then she'd started spotting, and her doctor put her on bed rest. Eli's parents were happy to pay his tuition and to help the young couple with rent and utilities and money for groceries. Eli went to classes and study groups while Annette shut the door to their bedroom and lay there, day after day, growing quieter and quieter as her belly got bigger and bigger. Eli would rub her feet and brush her hair and bring her the foods she could eat: plain toasted white bread, cups of clear broth and herbal tea. Annette would sip or nibble, sadly, answering his questions with one-word answers, braiding and unbraiding her hair, barely meeting his eyes. By that time, people were starting to talk about postpartum depression, but Eli had never heard of during-partum depression. He also suspected that Annette wasn't really sad but, rather, angry. She felt like he'd tricked her, like he'd trapped her. Deep down, Eli was not sure that she was wrong.

"A beautiful girl!" the doctor said, handing Eli the wrapped bundle, after the endless hours of Annette's labor and the eventual C-section that had gotten Ruby out of Annette and into the world. Eli had looked into Ruby's calm blue eyes, had taken in her finely etched brows and her fuzzy halo of brown hair and had been enraptured, instantly in love.

"Look, honey," he'd said, but Annette had barely glanced at the baby. "You hold her," she said to Eli, in a voice that was barely audible. "I need to sleep." Eli had ascribed her indifference to exhaustion. "I've got her," Eli said, cradling the baby close as Annette's eyes slipped shut. "Don't worry, baby," he whispered into Ruby's ear, aware that his life's priorities had been reordered, instantly and eternally. From now on, this tiny, precious scrap of a girl would come first.

Eli was besotted with his daughter. He could have spent hours staring into her fathomless dark-blue eyes, tracing, with one fingertip, the lines of her tiny nose, her plump cheeks, her silky soft eyebrows, her pink gums, with her baby teeth waiting to erupt beneath them. Everything about her, each fingernail, each curl of her hair, enchanted him, everything she did—her little mewling yawn, the first time she rolled over, or successfully grasped her own foot, and shouted in triumph—delighted him.

Annette did not have the same interest in their baby. She kept Ruby clean and changed and fed, but she had a hard time recovering from the delivery. Even after she'd healed, it was abundantly clear that she wasn't finding any joy in marriage and motherhood.

She complained to Eli that she was bored, home alone all day with the baby. When he encouraged her to make friends, she told him that the other mothers, the ones she met in the park, or at Little People's Music,

were also boring. "All they want to talk about is their babies," she said. Which made sense, because Ruby was all
Eli wanted to talk about, too, but Annette couldn't tol-
erate even a few minutes of conversation about whether
rice cereal was really the best first food or exactly how
early you needed to get on the wait list for the YMCA
preschool.

"So get a job," Eli suggested. "Go back to school!"

"And what happens to her?" Annette asked, gesturing
at the baby.

Eli promised he'd find a way to make it work. His
mom could take the train in from Long Island, or he'd
hire a nanny. He'd do whatever it took to keep his wife
happy, and his little family together.

One Friday afternoon when Ruby was six months
old, Eli came home from school to find Annette packing her bags. He assumed she was going to her sister's,
where she'd retreated once before, when she was pregnant and they'd had a terrible fight. Eli was all for it.
"You'll take a break, you'll get some sleep, and you'll feel
better when you come home."

"I'm not coming back," Annette said. She told him
that she wasn't doing him or Ruby any good; that she
had never wanted to be a mother or a wife.

Eli was astonished. Yes, Annette had talked about
leaving, and yes, he'd told her, while she was pregnant,
that if she truly hated motherhood she could walk away,
but he'd never, ever expected that she'd actually be capable of doing it. "Ruby," Eli said. "How can you do this
to Ruby?"

Annette told him she had tried. She told him she
felt exhausted and lost, each day a plodding repetition
through gray, despairing hours. She reminded him that

she'd said that this might happen. And, even though he'd cried, and promised to do whatever she needed, even though he'd begged her to stay, Annette had been resolute. When he'd said that Ruby needed a mother, she'd replied that she was sure he would find her a great one. He'd cried, and she'd kissed him, and walked out the door, down the hallway to the elevator, without once looking back.

Eli had watched her go, numb with disbelief. *She'll be back,* he told himself. No mother could walk away from her child. When Ruby had woken up from her nap, he'd collected her from her crib, changed her, and held her against his shoulder. Ruby had just cut her first tooth. Eli caught flashes of it as Ruby shoved first one wet fist, then the other, into her mouth, chomping down vigorously.

"That," he said, "is your incisor. You're going to get eight of those bad boys, four on top and four on the bottom. Then you'll get your canines. Those are the sharpest teeth in your mouth. Oh, yes, they are!" he said, as Ruby swatted at him and burbled laughter. "Oh, yes, they are!"

That night, he'd given Ruby a bottle, then a bath, taking care to wash behind her ears, gently sponging the folds of her thighs, the backs of her knees, and between her toes. He'd toweled her off, dressed her in clean pajamas, and brushed her single tooth, telling her that it was never too early to start a good oral hygiene routine. He read *Hippos Go Berserk* three times and soothed her until she'd finally fallen asleep, a warm, boneless weight in his lap. Sitting there, imagining his wife buying a ticket and boarding a plane to somewhere, he could admit that he'd lied to her. Or, rather, he'd told her what she'd wanted to hear, about travel and adventure and seeing the world.

He'd assumed that she wouldn't want it forever. He hadn't listened when she'd told him that, indeed, she had. "I never wanted to be a mother!" she'd shout, and he'd yell back, "Well, I never wanted to be a periodontist!" But it wasn't true. He had played at being a free spirit, a modern-day hippie, rootless and untethered, and he'd enjoyed that life, knowing it wasn't permanent, knowing that, deep down, he'd always wanted conventionality; a life like his own parents had, only, of course, not miserable. He'd wanted a suburb, a family, a house with a swimming pool. Just as Annette had foretold.

Eventually Annette had surfaced in New Orleans, where she'd moved in with a tattoo artist named Phred. When Eli proposed joint custody, he heard his soon-to-be-ex-wife sigh from over a thousand miles away. "Ruby can spend time in the summers with me," Annette finally said. "But, Eli, let's be honest. You were the one who wanted kids. Not me."

Eli opened his mouth, ready to ask Annette what was wrong with her, how it was possible for her not to love the baby they'd made together, how anyone could not want Ruby. Then he closed it. Annette wouldn't have any answers. At least, not answers that would satisfy him.

"I'll never understand you," he let himself say, and, again, he heard Annette sighing.

"I know," she said, and ended the call.

For the next seven years, except for one month a summer, it was just Eli and Ruby, in a one-bedroom apartment financed, at first, by his parents, on the Upper West Side. When Eli started working he could handle the expense, plus private school for Ruby. Eli might have failed at marriage, but he was determined not to fail at fatherhood. He arranged his schedule so that he could be home for as many of Ruby's waking hours as possible. His mom came to the city twice a week, and he'd found a wonderful nanny to stay with Ruby when neither of them could do it. He mastered a variety of hairstyles and kid-friendly meals; he hosted playdates and sleepovers; he never missed a single choir concert or parent-teacher conference. At every school play or class picnic or non-denominational holiday assembly, Eli was there, camera in hand, cheering for his girl.

Ruby had been seven years old when she'd decided that she wanted to learn to play the drums. Eli had enrolled her in music school, and that was where they'd met Sarah. He'd seen her while he waited for Ruby, a woman of medium height and build with shoulder-length dark-blonde hair; a woman who walked fast and had a determined jut to her chin. She wore crisp blouses and creased pants, or colorful print dresses and high-heeled boots. The kids called her Miss Sarah, and all of them adored her. She seemed calm and good-humored, utterly unflappable whether she was dealing with a parent unhappy about how quickly her kid was progressing or a preschooler who'd thrown up in the middle of drum circle. He'd planned to do nothing more than admire Sarah Weinberg from afar, especially because he sensed that bringing a new woman into Ruby's life would be disruptive. By the end of her first month in second grade, he'd been called to the school twice because Ruby's teachers had overheard her making up wild stories to explain her mother's absence. "I have to give her points for creativity, but the trouble with telling the other kids that her mother was a lion tamer who was eaten by one of her lions is that now they think it'll happen to their moms, too," said Mrs. Levinson. Eli promised he'd have a talk with Ruby, which had been just as excruciating as he'd known it would be. "Honey, you know your mom isn't in the circus," he'd said gently, and Ruby, her face twisted, her eyes full of tears, had said, "Why won't she come back?" And what answer could Eli give her?

Eli did what he could to make up for Annette's absence, and Ruby was a generally good-humored girl, but sometimes she got quiet, her mood turning mournful. At her birthday parties and around Chanukah, he'd catch his daughter looking at the door, like she was hoping Annette would come through it, arms full of presents, heart full of regret. "That woman really did a number on poor Ruby," said his mother, who'd refused to so much as speak Annette's name once Annette had gone and referred to Eli's ex-wife only as "that woman."

Eli was loath to start a new relationship, because introducing a new person would be difficult, and having another woman leave would be even worse. His daughter had already been abandoned by the most important woman in her life. He wasn't going to risk letting it happen again. He wouldn't complicate things for Ruby for the sake of his own happiness. As far as he was concerned, parents forfeited their rights to make their own pleasure a priority as soon as a baby arrived (Annette, of course, would still probably be putting herself first when she was seventy years old, even if she'd had a dozen kids by then). But Ruby had taken matters into her own hands.

"Miss Sarah, do you like grilled cheese?" she'd asked, in her most winsome voice, after determining that Miss Sarah was single.

"I do!" Sarah had answered with a smile. "It's one of my very favorite sandwiches."

"My dad makes the very best grilled cheese in the world," Ruby said. "I think you should come to our house so he can make us grilled cheese."

Sarah and Eli had looked at each other. Then Eli had smiled, and Sarah had shrugged, and somehow, she'd ended up walking six blocks to their apartment, where Eli had, indeed, made her a grilled cheese ("With sweet pickle slices on the side!" Ruby insisted). Sarah offered to take him out for coffee during Ruby's next lessons, and those coffees became a regular fixture of his Tuesday afternoons. After the fourth one, Sarah asked if he wanted to get dinner. Regretfully, Eli had explained the situation, stumbling through what sounded even to his ears like an excuse, concluding with, "If I was going to date anyone, it would absolutely be you."

Sarah had listened to this recitation with her face expressionless before sitting back, her eyes narrowed and her arms crossed over her chest. "So you're not going to date until Ruby's, what, in college? In ten years?"

Eli didn't answer because he couldn't imagine Ruby being in college, or Ruby growing up and leaving him. Then again, he'd never been able to picture Annette walking out on a baby, and she had, which showed the limits of his imagination. Ruby would leave, someday, and then where would he be? Almost fifty. Still alone.

"I like you," Sarah said. "I like that you're so concerned about Ruby's happiness. And I definitely don't want to do anything to hurt her. But I know there are single parents who date, and the kids manage to get through it. And it's just dinner," she said with a smile. "We're not pledging our lives to each other or anything." She looked at him, her heart-shaped face open and expectant. "We could try. If you want to."

He decided that he did.

Right away, Eli had seen a future with Sarah. Even though she was twelve years younger than he was, Sarah was an old soul, grounded and practical and unusually mature, ready to start a family and buy a home. She was also, it emerged, financially equipped to do so in a way few of her contemporaries (or his) were, although Eli didn't find that out until after he'd proposed and Sarah had consented, and then, a little shyly, asked if he would be okay with a prenup.

"Sure," he'd said. Then, belatedly, "Why?" That was when he found out that Sarah's mother wasn't just an English professor. She'd been a bestselling novelist who'd had a book turned into a movie, and then a miniseries, back in the 1980s. "She made some money, and she did well with her investments. She put me and my brother through college and gave us each some money when we turned twenty-five." Eli was glad he hadn't known about that until after he'd proposed, because he had to admit, in his most private thoughts, that the money made the woman he loved even more appealing. The idea of having Sarah in his life, and in Ruby's, and being able to buy a beautiful home in a good neighborhood, and also not having to worry about college tuition . . . it seemed like the universe was making up for his disastrous first marriage by handing him a near-perfect second chance.

Still, he'd promised himself that if Ruby disliked Sarah, that if the three of them couldn't get along, he would end it. Ruby hadn't asked to be the child of divorced parents, bouncing between New York City during the school year and a few weeks in New Orleans, or Antigua, or wherever Annette had landed in the summer. Eli was determined to keep the promise he'd made to himself that he'd never do anything to make his daughter's life harder.

At first, Ruby had been delighted when Miss Sarah the music lady showed up at her house or picked her up after school or spent time with her in the park. When Sarah's presence went from being a novelty to a constant, when Sarah went from being a friend to someone who took away some of Eli's attention and reminded Ruby to clear her plate and clean her room, Ruby was far less enamored. Sarah, to her credit, hadn't been offended when Ruby had acted out. She never got angry when Ruby would ask, "When are you going back home?" or when, at breakfast on the weekends, Ruby asked her father to take her to the diner, just the two of them, because Sarah's scrambled eggs tasted funny. "She's gotten used to having you all to herself," Sarah said when Eli apologized for Ruby's behavior. "If I were her, I wouldn't want to share you either."

Sarah seemed to know, intuitively, just when to go meet friends for a movie or return to her own apartment to give them a few hours or a few days. She gave Ruby space, and let Eli handle the discipline. She tried hard not to try too hard, giving Ruby enough room to come to her. And, eventually, Ruby had.

It helped that Annette was so inconstant. Her flakiness compared poorly to Sarah's dependability; the way Sarah was always there, quietly standing by, ready to help, when Ruby would let her. It also probably hadn't hurt that Sarah's parents, Lee and Veronica, adored Ruby. They would buy her toys and piles of books, and Ronnie would let her take whatever she wanted from Ronnie's extensive collection of costume jewelry when they visited them. Ronnie and Lee would host them in Boston or on the Cape and plan special outings for Ruby—Broadway shows, museum visits, a trip to a fancy hotel for tea. When Sarah brought Eli and Ruby to their summer place on the Cape, Ronnie had taken Ruby on hikes through the dunes to the cranberry bogs and taught her how to use a clam rake to retrieve shellfish from the bay. Ronnie had been the one to teach Ruby how to ride a bike and sail a Sunfish; how to do a racing dive and a flip turn in the pool. Ruby and Ronnie would swim across ponds together, both of them in navy-blue tank-style suits, Ronnie with a bright-orange personal flotation device looped around her waist. They would ride their bikes into Provincetown for ice-cream cones and sit on the Provincetown Library lawn to watch the Portuguese Festival and the Carnival parade. "All the stuff she used to do with me and my brother, when we were kids," Sarah said.

Ronnie and Lee had helped. The Cape itself had helped. The house they'd eventually purchased had, too. Eli and Sarah and Ruby spent three months of weekends house-hunting, looking for a place that they could all share. Eventually they'd found a slightly dilapidated brownstone that had been owned by just one family for the last eighty years. "It's like a castle!" Ruby said when she'd first glimpsed the place from the sidewalk. Eli supposed that, after life in an apartment, a four-story house might, indeed, look that way to a little girl. While Sarah stood in the kitchen, quizzing the contractor about the HVAC and the pipes (a conversation she'd spent the previous night prepping for with a book called *Home Heating and Cooling for Dummies*), Ruby had walked slowly up the staircase, stopping on each floor and counting the number of rooms out loud. When she got to the attic,

Eli had been right behind her. He'd watched as she'd stopped, mouth agape. Her favorite book at the moment was *A Little Princess* (Eli didn't doubt that, in her head, Ruby had assigned poor Sarah the role of cruel Miss Minchin, who banishes the orphaned Sara Crewe to the attic). Ruby had looked, then gone racing down the stairs to find Sarah and tow her up to the attic, pulling her by the hand. "Please, please, can we buy this house and can this please be my bedroom?" she'd asked.

Sarah pretended to think about it. "Really? You want to be all the way up here? By yourself? Are you sure?"

"Yes! Please! I'm sure! It's so so perfect!"

"Okay, but only if you promise you'll help me pick out the wallpaper."

"I promise! I promise!" Ruby had yelped, and she'd thrown her arms around Sarah's midriff, almost tackling her to the ground.

Eli and Sarah had gotten married six months later. By then, they were coasting on the fumes of the last of Ruby's initial goodwill and her excitement about the new house. The hard years were coming, but back then, Ruby had been thrilled about the wedding, insisting on writing vows welcoming Sarah into the family, and giving Sarah a special necklace that she and Eli picked out, a gift just from her. When Sarah had promised, before the rabbi and God and all their guests, to love them both, for as long as she lived, most of the guests and both Eli's mother and Sarah's were crying.

For years, Ruby had reigned as queen of the attic. Eli and Sarah got used to the sound of Ruby's little feet stomping up those stairs, the door closing at a volume just short of a slam. Then Dexter arrived, and then Miles. Ruby had loved her brothers, and had, finally, let Sarah love her. And Eli was happy, happier than he'd ever hoped he'd be after Annette had left him. He had a circle of friends, hobbies he enjoyed. He cycled with a local club, played squash once a week, brewed his own beer in the basement. He was grateful for his good fortune, for his marriage, his beautiful family, his second chance, and he'd taken care to behave in a way that showed that gratitude. He'd been kind to his patients and generous with his colleagues, to the students he taught and to the people he employed. He gave money to charity; he supported diversity initiatives and Black Lives Matter and the women who spoke out when #MeToo became a thing. He added his pronouns to his online biography and refused to speak at seminars or on panels to which only straight white men had been invited. He called his parents every week and visited them every month. When his brother, Ari (at fifty-four, still the family fuck-up), forgot their parents' birthdays or anniversaries, Eli added his name to the card or the gift that he, Eli, had purchased, and lied when their mother asked. *Oh, yeah, Ari helped me pick it out. He knows orchids are your favorite!* When Ruby came home with friends Eli would ask what pronouns they used. He did his best to be respectful and apologized when he got it wrong. He tried to move through the world gently, to follow the Hippocratic oath: *Do no harm.*

For his entire life, Eli Danhauser had been good. Except for four days, more than twenty years ago, when Eli had not been good, when he'd been the exact opposite of good. And now, he feared, the result of that single, brief lapse had come back to haunt him, the way he always knew it would, and the truth, instead of setting anyone free, was going to destroy everything he'd worked for and hurt everyone he'd loved.

RONNIE

~~~~~~

Veronica Levy hung her towel and her cover-up, one of Lee's old button-down shirts, on the knobby branch of a scrub pine. She kicked off her Crocs and stood, looking out at the pond, its water the gray of a tarnished nickel in the early morning light. Wisps of steam rose from the surface and dissolved into the air. The water would be cold, but there was no better feeling than the handful of seconds after that first wincing shock, when she'd force her arms to paddle and her feet to kick, and she would feel her heart start beating again, her skin tingling, her body absolutely, irrefutably alive.

Ronnie clipped an inflatable float on a belt around her waist and made her way down to the water. Once, the belt hadn't had quite so far to travel, and her legs hadn't been quite so jiggly, or her skin so fine and slack. Once, she'd been deliciously curvy, even though she'd wasted years despairing of her body, trying to wish and diet and Jazzercise the weight away; starving off the same ten or fifteen pounds that always came back, usually with friends. She'd been pretty back then, her skin smooth, hair shiny, eyes bright. These days, everything was dulled and faded, and every part of her body from her breasts on down had developed an unseemly droop. In clothes, or even in a swimsuit, she could still look not-terrible. Out of clothes ... well, out of clothes she just tried not to look. She tried to be grateful for everything that her body could still do, that she could still drive and carry her own groceries; that she could walk. That she could swim. That she was still here at all.

Veronica waded out until the water lapped her thighs, then took a deep breath, braced herself, and submerged, ducking down, shuddering as the water rose over her shoulders, her neck, her face, sending her hair drifting in a cloud around head.

She rose to the surface, gasping, wiped water from her eyes, and set off across the pond, her arms lifting and falling smoothly, legs flutter-kicking, the flotation device trailing on its rope behind her. She was not as fast as she'd once been, but she could still make it across the pond and back again in under an hour.

This early in the morning, this early in the season, there were no other swimmers. Just Veronica, and the schools of darting, silvery minnows, the croaking frogs and the tadpoles, the sunfish and the snapping turtles who hadn't yet emerged to take their place on the sun-warmed rocks. Veronica stroked smoothly through the water, feeling it lapping at her shoulders, cupping her body and bearing her up, like a strong hand in a silken glove.

When she'd made it across the pond she slowed her pace, dog-paddling into the reeds, peering around to see if the Pond People, the families who owned the cabins and camps in the woods, had put up new signs yet. Yes, there they were: three ankle-high admonishments painted on planks of scrap wood, hammered into crosses, with the words NO TRESPASSING in blaze orange, jutting out of the soft sand.

Ronnie swam closer, treading water, trying to be quiet. She could see an older woman—in other words, a woman about her age—standing on the shore, observing her. The other woman wore a linen caftan in faded pink, with an oversized sun hat on her head. Her feet were bare; her legs were deeply tanned, with varicose veins twisting over her calves and up her thighs. She was probably naked underneath that caftan. The Pond People were avid skinny-dippers. Veronica used to tell her husband that it was weaponized nudity; another way for them to claim the pond as their own. Which it wasn't. People on the Cape could own land right up to the shoreline. They could not own the water, either salt or brackish or fresh. Not the ocean, not the bay, not the marshes, and not the ponds. This fact did not prevent the Pond People from scowling, or shouting, at any swimmer who dared come too close to shore. "Get off of our PRAH-per-ty!" she remembered a little boy yelling at her, and at Sam and Sarah, when they'd made the swim one summer. Stalwart Sarah had glared right back at him. "Make me," she'd muttered under her breath. While Sarah was giving the boy her most scorching stink-eye, Sam, her sensitive soul, had turned and started swimming back. He'd spent the rest of the morning brooding on the shore.

"Why are they so mean?" he'd asked on the bayside beach later that day. "We weren't even on their property!"

"Because they're assholes," Lee had said succinctly, and winked at his son as Veronica frowned and said, "Language!"

"They are, though," her husband said, opening a new section of the *New York Times*.

"They're jerks," she'd said primly, and told Sam that he hadn't done anything wrong.

Ronnie had her own ideas about why the Pond People were so possessive of the shoreline, and why they reflexively despised people like the Levy-Weinbergs. *Once upon a time*, she imagined telling her son, the entire Cape was theirs (*the entire world*, she could hear her husband thinking, his good-natured face wearing an unusually cynical expression). Back then, Jews weren't allowed to buy houses in their neighborhoods. They started beach clubs and neighborhood associations, just to keep people like us out. But we worked hard, we became successful, and some of us did well enough to buy our own homes in the handful of towns that would have us. Maybe some of the people who lived near the pond are unhappy about that. Maybe they wish the whole world still belonged to them alone.

Veronica had never set foot in a Pond Person's home, but one of her friends had. "It was unbelievable," Dolores had reported to the other members of the book club that met at the Truro library. "There's one building with a kitchen, a living room, four teeny-tiny cabins that hardly look big enough for a bed, and one toilet for everyone." Her eyes had gleamed as she'd shared all the details. "Everything was held together with duct tape. Literal duct tape. And they had barrels of booze and no food. Nothing to eat except a sleeve of Ritz crackers and supermarket cheddar." She'd sniffed. "Not my idea of entertaining."

Veronica had murmured something about the expense of keeping a place on the Outer Cape in good repair, how, between the damage the salt air could do and the paucity of trustworthy, available contractors, everything was more expensive and time-consuming than it would be on the mainland. "And it sounds like it's very eco-friendly," she'd added.

"Oh, it sounds just like my husband's family's place in Maine," said Trudy, one of the other members. "Towels so thin you can see through them, sheets that are seventy years old, one bathroom in a six-bedroom house. It's their idea of fun," she'd said. "I think it takes them back to summer camp, or something." She'd had them all laughing with stories of her stay in Maine as a young bride, how she'd driven twenty minutes to the nearest town each morning to use a gas station restroom after she'd caused her in-laws' single toilet to flood her first night there.

Of course, back then there'd been a way to tell who was playing at poverty and who was genuinely broke. The local paper had published a biannual list of property owners who'd fallen behind on their taxes. Everyone in town had condemned the practice. Everyone had also read the lists the second they were published. But the paper had been purchased by new owners. These days, Ronnie wasn't sure which of the Pond People were like Trudy's in-laws and which of them actually, genuinely didn't have enough money for the upkeep of a summer home. All she knew for sure was that the Pond People all seemed to be fanatics about keeping everyone from the public beach away from their shores . . . and that once, years ago, one of their children—Son of the Pond People—had hurt her daughter.

In the water, Veronica kicked and stroked until she could make out the purse-lipped expression on the woman's face. "Good morning!" she called, and gave a cheery wave. "Beautiful day, isn't it?" The woman's lips tightened. Without a word, she turned and walked back to the cabin, mostly hidden by the reeds. Ronnie saw faded, peeling paint; the ripped screen of the door, the old chintz cushions of the daybed on the porch. She could hear the screech of unoiled hinges as the door creaked shut.

Ronnie sighed, submerged, and started the return trip. Back to the shore, back to her car, back to her house, which had central air and bathrooms in multiples. *Flashy. Showy. Nouveau riche*, they'd say, these people with

Mayflower pedigrees and first names that were indistinguishable from last names. Forty years after she and Lee had bought their house, they were still newcomers. Forty years meant nothing to people whose ancestors had arrived in America when Ronnie's had still been in the shtetls, picking potatoes and running from the Cossacks.

Forty years might not mean much, but Ronnie still felt, would always feel, that the Outer Cape was her place. She hated to think of leaving the house that she had loved so much and for so long; the house where she'd lived for the last ten years, after she and Lee had sold their place in Cambridge and become year-rounders. When the kids were little, they'd added on a guest house, dreaming of summers surrounded by their children and eventually their grandchildren. She wanted her grandkids to have the kinds of summers she'd been able to give to her twins: days spent on the beach or the bike paths, eating lobster rolls and ice-cream cones and going to the Wellfleet Drive-in. But, after years of dreaming and invitations and increasingly pointed hints, she had to acknowledge the reality. Sam lived all the way on the other side of the country, so he and his stepson couldn't visit often, even if they'd wanted to. Sarah was close enough, but she had decidedly different opinions about summer than her mother. At eight, Dexter was already studying Mandarin and judo and the violin; Miles, at nearly seven, played on two soccer teams and had just started to learn ASL ("It was his idea," Sarah said, sounding defensive, when Ronnie had asked). Their school days were scheduled from morning until night; their summers were even worse. The boys came to the Cape for a week in June, right after school ended, before their camps began, and much of that week was occupied by mandatory practice of their respective instruments and sports. Ronnie had felt like a teenager trying to avoid Mom's censorious eyes when she'd sneak the boys out of the house for a walk on the beach to look for shells, or for a quick bike ride.

It was ridiculous, but Ronnie knew better than to say so. Sarah was sensitive to criticism; quick to unfold her tales of woe, about how abandoned she'd felt as a little girl when Veronica was working. "You were always fobbing us off on the mother's helpers," Sarah would say. "You were always busy." That did not comport with Veronica's memories of the kind of parent she'd been. Yes, there had been mother's helpers, but she'd stopped publishing when the kids were young. She'd been a full-time academic, which meant she had plenty of work in the summer months, but at least it was work that was portable, work that let her stay with them on the Cape. She remembered spending every summer day with the twins, the mornings of swimming lessons at Gull Pond, the afternoons on the beaches, Corn Hill or Longnook or Head of the Meadow.

True, Veronica had needed a few hours a day to grade papers or talk to the graduate students she advised, to plan her lessons and read for pleasure. True, there'd always been a mother's helper, an extra set of hands to help with the showers and the meals and the bedtime routines, but she remembered being an attentive, hands-on, present mother who'd taught her kids to swim and ride their bikes and then gave them the gift of empty hours to fill, with books or swims or walks or Frisbee games with friends. And was telling a kid to amuse herself in a beautiful house right on the ocean really so awful? *Poor you*, Veronica would think, but never say, when Sarah got going on her lonely childhood and her neglectful mom.

Of all the kids, it was Ruby, her bonus grandchild,

with whom Ronnie had gotten to spend the kind of summers she'd dreamed about. Eli had recognized the Cape, and Ronnie and Lee, as a refuge for his prickly little girl. "Between you and me, she's giving Sarah a hard time," he'd confided to Ronnie late one night. This was before he and Sarah had gotten married, when the three of them had come to the Cape for a long weekend. Ronnie saw her opportunity. She'd begged and pleaded and finally convinced Eli to let Ruby stay.

"Are you sure you've got time for this?" he'd asked. "We'll enroll her in camp, so you don't have to entertain her all day . . ."

"I would be happy to entertain her all day," Ronnie had said. The next morning, she and Ruby had waved goodbye to Eli and Sarah from the half-moon-shaped deck off the kitchen, where Ronnie grew sage and mint and basil and rosemary. Ruby plucked a leaf of mint. She'd sniffed it, and then she'd peered up at Veronica, her face solemn, the breeze ruffling her curls. "What are we going to do?"

"We could go for a walk and look for box turtles and horseshoe crabs," Ronnie proposed. "Or we could kayak through the marsh."

Ruby chose the walk. They kayaked the next day. The day after that, they rode the bike path to get an ice-cream cone in Eastham, and on the rainy day that followed, they went to Wellfleet for a matinee and completed a five-hundred-piece puzzle at the kitchen table. Ronnie taught Ruby how to play gin. Ruby taught Ronnie how to play Bananagrams. When it was dinnertime, they'd grill hot dogs and hamburgers. Some nights they'd just eat freshly buttered corn and sliced tomatoes from the farm stand up the road, and when Lee arrived on Friday nights they'd make challah for a special Shabbat/ welcome-home dinner. Ruby was good company. A little solemn, and almost frighteningly competitive ("You aren't letting me win, are you?" she'd asked, eyes narrowed, after Ronnie had praised her lavishly for playing a z on a triple-word-score space, and Lee had to assure Ruby that his wife never let anyone win at Scrabble). Ruby was focused, and determined, but also funny, and usually cheerful, and willing to try new things. Best of all, she loved the water the way Ronnie did. The first time she and Ruby had swum across the pond together, Lee told her that he'd never seen Ruby looking as delighted as she had when they'd emerged from the water and gone running to him, saying, "I made it the whole way across without stopping!" That night, in bed, he'd brought up the idea of getting a place in New York City. "A pied-à-terre!" he'd said, rolling the words with a flourish. "Why not? You'll be able to see Ruby all year round, and Sarah's going to want you close if she has babies." Regretfully, Ronnie had told him no. She'd reminded Lee that he had no plans to retire in the near future, and that his firm was in Boston, that a place in Manhattan wasn't practical. She didn't mention her own reasons for avoiding New York.

Two weeks had sped by. When they were over, Ruby hadn't wanted to go. "Why can't I stay longer? Can I come back next summer? Can I stay longer next time?"

Ronnie smiled, remembering as she swam, until her thoughts drifted from her grandchildren to her children. She'd always believed the major crisis of Sarah's life had happened years ago, when Sarah had been eighteen and had to decide whether to pursue a career as a pianist. Sarah had been in agony, struggling to make up her mind. One morning she'd say, "That's it, I'm done," and that afternoon she'd be back at the grand piano they'd bought when she was twelve, playing the same bars of a Chopin nocturne or a moody Beethoven concerto over and over and over again. "I've worked so hard. I don't want to just quit on myself!" she'd told Ronnie, and Ronnie hugged her, telling Sarah she'd support her no matter what she chose, never voicing her own secret wish, that Sarah would stick with it, that she'd be recognized as one of the best young pianists in the world, rewarded with all the fame and glory, the accolades and the newspaper profiles, the applause of crowds and the admiration of strangers. A version of the world that Ronnie herself had walked away from, before Sarah had even been born.

Sarah had chosen the safer path. She'd gone off to Wellesley glowing the way only a teenage girl who has, for the first time, been told *I love you* by someone who wasn't a relative could glow. Less than a week later, that boy had broken Sarah's heart. Ronnie, remembering, kicked at the water a little harder than was necessary, telling herself what she'd told herself then: that maybe that heartbreak had been a good thing, a distraction from Sarah's previous sorrow.

Sarah had gotten over it, eventually. She'd dated other boys; she'd moved to New York City, and eventually she'd met Eli. Ronnie had liked Eli, but she'd worried about Sarah trying to make a life with an older man, a man who'd already been married and had a daughter. She worried, too, that Sarah was throwing herself into marriage and motherhood and a ready-made family mostly because it was a prescribed path with clear landmarks and borders, and that's what she wanted after abandoning music, where her journey would have been just as regimented, the steps just as clear: the competitions and the recitals, the lessons and the master classes and the practice, practice, practice.

Lee had been Eli's booster from the start. "He's old," Ronnie would say. "He's seasoned," Lee would reply. "And I think Sarah could be good for Ruby. They'll be good for each other." *She'll be happy*, Lee had said, and he'd been right. At least, that's what Ronnie had always believed, although lately she'd been worried. When the stay-at-home orders came, Sarah said she loved having Ruby home again; she was glad that the boys were safe ("and thank God they're old enough to not need me every second of the day," she'd added, and Ronnie had shuddered, thinking of the women trying to work remotely in a house or apartment with infants or toddlers or preschool-aged children who did need attention every waking moment, and with husbands who might not see helping out as part of their job). When Ronnie asked, Sarah would talk about how Eli seemed distant and distracted, which didn't sound like the son-in-law Ronnie knew. And when Ronnie didn't ask, Sarah didn't bring up her husband at all . . . which, more than anything Sarah did say, suggested trouble.

And Sam! Her baby, her darling, who'd finally fallen in love and gotten married, only to lose his wife so quickly. His wife *and* his home, Ronnie thought as she kicked, kicked, kicked through the water, wondering if she'd need a second trip across the pond to calm down. How could God or fate or the world be so awful to Sam?

Ronnie paused, treading water to catch her breath. When she set off again, she swam at a more sedate pace, reminding herself that the world was not a rancid bag of garbage. At least, it wasn't *just* that. There was happiness, too. Like Ruby's wedding! A *simcha*, a happy occasion.

A bittersweet one, too; the sign she'd been waiting for that it was time to let go of her dream house, and all the hopes she'd had for it. *The Summer Palace*, Lee had called it when he'd teased her, but they'd been happy there, the four of them. Then Ronnie and Lee had been happy there, together, and they'd been happy with Ruby when she'd come to visit. Now it was just Ronnie, alone, all the time, even though she imagined she could still hear her husband's voice, could still almost see him, out of the corner of her eye, doing the crossword puzzle at the picnic table, or standing at the deck with his hands on the railing, admiring the sunset. She had to be realistic. The house might be her heart's true home, but it was far too big for just one person. The children and grandchildren she'd hoped would come and fill it weren't going to materialize. And the time would come when she wouldn't be able to manage the stairs, when she'd need her bedroom, bathroom, and kitchen all on the same level.

At least, Ronnie thought, she would get her family together one last time, for one big party. A wedding! What could be happier than that? She'd take lots of pictures; she'd send her children and grandchildren home with happy and hopefully lasting memories. And then she'd tell Paul Norman, who'd sold her the place years ago, that she was ready to let some new family enjoy this beautiful place.

Ronnie stroked through the water until it was shallow enough to stand. The sun was coming up, the water shading amber and gold, and she could catch flashes of the sandy bottom. Water weeds swayed in her wake; minnows flickered around her feet as she climbed slowly back onto the shore and stood, wringing out her hair, letting the water drip from the skirt of her swimsuit to soak the sand at her feet.

She dried off, got dressed, and drove slowly along the rutted dirt road until she could turn onto Route 6. At home, she spent her day puttering, planting new herbs in the kitchen garden, sorting through her books and collecting a bag of them to donate to the library. It had been close to forty years since she'd published her last book, but her editor and, eventually, her editor's assistant continued to send her galleys of new novels. First they'd hoped she'd offer an endorsement. Eventually, when so much time had passed that her name no longer meant anything, they'd just send her books they thought she'd like. Ronnie carried the bags out to the car. She'd moved on to the kitchen and was trying to unpick a mesh bag that had somehow gotten tangled in her garbage disposal (*the glamorous life of a former bestselling author*, she thought) when her phone buzzed on the counter.

Veronica breathed in deeply, sent up a brief prayer for strength, and hit the "answer" button. "Hello, Suzanne."

"Is this really happening?" her sister demanded. "Is Ruby actually getting married?"

"It's actually happening," Ronnie confirmed.

"But she's a baby!" said Suzanne.

"She's twenty-two," said Ronnie. "How old was Mom when she got married, nineteen?"

"That was a different time," said Suzanne. "Is anyone going to try to talk some sense into her?"

"She's in love," Ronnie said, keeping her voice mild. "And Ruby's always been stubborn. If someone tried to talk her out of it, do you think she'd listen?"

"So Sarah and Eli are just letting this happen? *You're* just letting this happen? At your house? On your deck?"

"Suzanne," Ronnie said patiently. "They're both of age. If we told them no, they'd elope. And then where would we be? They'd still be married, and we wouldn't even have the pleasure of a wedding." And oh, how Ronnie was longing for the pleasure of that wedding! Dexter and Miles and Sam's stepson, Connor, splashing in the pool, collecting hermit crabs on the beach. Sam and Sarah and Ruby in the kitchen with her, using Lee's recipe for linguine with clam sauce; all of the adults playing Pictionary or Trivial Pursuit at night.

"Some pleasure," Suzanne grumbled. "Watching a twenty-two-year-old child throw her life away."

"Think of it this way: at least we'll get some nice family pictures," Ronnie said, as she triumphantly pulled the last bit of netting out of the drain.

"Hmph," said her sister, and changed the subject to a mole on her forearm with irregular edges and how her dermatologist was working through a post-quarantine backlog of patients and couldn't see her for months. Ronnie half paid attention, offering "mmms" and "ohs" and "that's too bad" as she emptied the dishwasher, still lost in a fantasy of the whole family, together, eating steaks and fresh corn out on the deck, piling into the minivan for a trip to Longnook Beach, where the kids would bodysurf and boogie board. Swimming across the pond with her daughter and stepgranddaughter alongside her. And Suzanne, she thought, frowning. Of course she'd have to invite Suzanne.

Ronnie and Suzanne had never been close. These days, her sister called her once a week, mostly to complain about her children, her various health ailments, and all the problems she and her husband were having with the house that their parents had left to Suzanne and Veronica, a recitation that included lots of hinting that Veronica had gotten the better part of the bargain by allowing Suzanne to buy her out. Suzanne was just three years older than Ronnie, but in Ronnie's opinion, Suzanne and her husband, Matt, had gotten old a long time ago. They were always fretting about osteoporosis or a suspicious colonoscopy, forever sending her forwarded emails about how Barack Obama was actually a Muslim or how COVID was a government-engineered virus, or telling her about the last seniors-only bus trip they'd taken in endless, excruciating detail.

Lee used to call Suzanne and Matt Doom and Gloom. Ronnie smiled at that memory as Suzanne launched into a story about a friend who'd been rear-ended in the parking lot of the Stop & Shop. ("Was she hurt?" asked Ronnie. "No. But she could have been!" Suzanne replied.) She could almost see her husband rolling his eyes at her from across the room as Suzanne droned on.

"What do you think they'll want for a wedding gift?" Suzanne asked. At some point, she must have brought the conversation back around to Ruby and Gabe.

"Cash," said Ronnie.

"Oh, but that's so impersonal. Ruby's still into drama, right?"

"That was her major in college, and she's working in a theater, so I'm assuming the answer is yes."

"Good, because I'm giving her a pair of Ma's earrings, and I bought her a coffee table book about Broadway musicals of the 1970s."

If you already know what you're giving them, why did you ask? Ronnie thought. And then, *You're buying a coffee table book for a couple whose apartment probably isn't big enough for a coffee table?* Although, of course, Suzanne and Matt wouldn't be buying, she imagined Lee saying. They'd be regifting.

Ronnie kept her mouth shut, wiping down the kitchen counters and sweeping the floor, half-listening while Suzanne blathered about the impossibility of shopping for her own grandchildren, two of whom, evidently, had asked for a birthday gift of a specific kind of sneaker that was both insanely expensive and impossible to find.

"I sent Sam and Sarah those DNA kits for their birthday last week, so at least they're taken care of," Suzanne said. Ronnie felt her heart stop. She jerked her head up and lurched toward the phone.

"What?" she asked.

"Those 23andMe kits," Suzanne repeated. "Amazon had a sale, on Prime Day. And I've been watching that show on PBS, with that African American professor, where they get some famous person to come on, and they analyze their DNA and tell them where they're from, and if they're, like, related to any presidents, or serial killers." The relish in her voice suggested that she much preferred it when the celebrities turned out to be related to criminals and not politicians.

Ronnie's tongue felt like it had gotten very heavy, and her lungs felt like they couldn't expand to take in air. "Did you send the kits already?" she made herself ask.

"Yes," said her sister, oblivious to Ronnie's distress. "Or I guess Jeff Bezos did. I emailed them and told them to send them back right away, so we'll be able to discuss it when we're all together. That'll give us something interesting to talk about, right?"

Something interesting, Ronnie thought. Her blood was pounding in her ears, and she could taste old pennies under her tongue.

Ronnie made some excuses and ended the call. She stood in her kitchen, the hand that held the phone pressed against her chest. For the first time since his death, she was glad that her husband wasn't there, glad that Lee hadn't lived long enough to see what might happen next.

ROSA

osa had been leaving her car after a shift at the hospital when the phone call came. "Mom? Mami? It's me. Gabe."

"Hello!" she said, feeling her heart lift, as it always did, when she heard her son's voice, the way he'd always announce himself as if she didn't know who was calling.

"I have news! Can you put me on FaceTime?"

Heart pounding, already guessing at the news, Rosa fumbled with her phone until she'd hit the right button and her son's handsome, beloved face filled the screen. His girlfriend was there with him, and both of them were smiling. Rosa couldn't help but smile back as Gabe and Ruby told her that, indeed, they were going to be married, in three months, on Cape Cod over the Fourth of July weekend.

"I'm so happy for you," Rosa said, over and over. *I'm thrilled,* she said, and *Cape Cod! I've never been there,* and *Ruby, I can't wait to meet you in person!*

"Ruby, can you send me your parents' names and phone numbers? I'll need to get in touch with them." Both Gabe and Ruby assured her that they'd handle all the wedding planning, that it was going to be an intimate, casual affair; that Rosa didn't need to do a thing except make the trip and be their guest, but Rosa had insisted. "Please. I want to congratulate them," she'd said. Finally, finally, the call was over. Thirty seconds later, her phone dinged with a text. Sarah and Eli Danhauser, and an address in Brooklyn.

Eli Danhauser.

For a minute, Rosa sat frozen and motionless, her hands on the steering wheel, feeling shame pulse through her with each beat of her heart. Here was the retribution that she always knew was coming; here were the consequences you could postpone but not avoid. Soon she'd be exposed as the worst kind of liar. And Gabe, her angel, the one person she'd managed to love successfully, the only relationship in her life she hadn't ruined, the one person she'd never betrayed, the one thing she'd done right in her life, Gabe would hate her, too.

Rosa Alvarez Andrews had grown up in Los Angeles. Her mother, Maria, had emigrated from Mexico, slipping over the border with two of her brothers and one of her sisters. The Alvarez siblings had picked strawberries and lettuce on the big farms in Ventura County. Eventually her mother had fallen in love with and married Glenn Andrews, whose family owned one of those farms. Maria and Glenn had moved to a suburb of Los Angeles, where Glenn, who'd never much liked farming, had run a garage and Maria had been an administrative assistant in the city's school district. Glenn and Maria had three kids— Emmanuel, Rosa, and Amanda, the baby—and there was a path those children were meant to follow, a path that began with a high school diploma and continued on to college and white-collar, respectable employment, followed by marriage and families of their own. Manny, Rosa's big brother, got a chemical engineering degree, and made his parents proud. Mandy, Rosa's little sister, was a professional party girl until she turned twenty-one, settled down, and went to cosmetology school—not ideal, but still okay, still a profession, especially since Mandy eventually ended up owning her own salon. Rosa, who'd never liked any of her classes besides art and music, who'd been the prettiest girl in her high school, the lead in every musical, had completed a single semester of community college at her parents' insistence. When she turned nineteen, she'd packed her belongings—mostly clothes and makeup—taken the money she'd saved, and gotten on a bus to New York City. Her parents wanted her to be a nurse or a dental technician or a paralegal. Rosa, with her long, dark hair and big, dark eyes, had other plans. She wanted to be a singer, a dancer, a star.

Rosa found an apartment in Crown Heights that she shared with three roommates, and a job as a cocktail waitress at a nightclub in Manhattan. She could have made more money stripping, or letting the customers at the nightclub take her home. Some girls did. Rosa didn't judge them, but she wasn't ready for that—at least not yet. She signed up for dance and acting classes. She got a subscription to *Backstage* and started going out to every open audition and casting call for every show that she could find.

It took Rosa maybe a month to realize that being the most talented girl in her high school did not make her even close to one of the best singers or dancers in New York; that having been prom queen wasn't enough to allow her to compete for the spots in the chorus line with girls who'd been models, or looked as if they could have been.

She hung on for two years, slinging drinks, singing with a cover band that played Pat Benatar and Heart and Fleetwood Mac songs at the local bars (but only on Wednesday and Thursday nights—they never got quite good enough to headline on the weekends). She got called back twice but, ultimately, wasn't cast as Mimi in the off-Broadway revival of *Rent*, and she'd played Fantine for six weeks doing *Les Misérables* at the Bucks County Playhouse. That was the extent of her theatrical success.

Rosa kept trying. And while she was trying, she had sex. Lots and lots of sex. Being admired, being desired, being pursued, all fed her self-esteem, which was being regularly decimated by the audition process. Her sense of herself as beautiful and talented and worthy was diminished every time she didn't get a role, every time a casting director hollered "Next!" without even looking at her face. Sex let her feel good about herself, even if only for a few hours—or, in the case of her trysts with the cover band's bass player, Benji, a few minutes. Handsome men were, in her experience, the worst lovers, assuming that women were so thrilled to be in bed with them that they didn't have to make any effort to ensure their partner's pleasure, and gorgeous Benji with his glossy black hair and pillowy lips and the hollows under his cheekbones that made him look like a tubercular poet instead of a guy who hadn't picked up a book since high school was no exception. When Rosa went to bed with a man, she could feel, again, like she was the most beautiful girl in her class, the most sought-after and desired, and even though the feeling never lasted for long, it could give her enough of a boost to get her through another week of waitressing and auditions. She counted on the Pill to keep her from getting pregnant, and the Planned Parenthood clinic to take care of any other unpleasant consequences of her adventures.

By the time she was twenty-one, Rosa had realized that she was never going to be JLo, or even a plain old working singer or actress with a spot in the chorus or the ensemble. She'd been to too many auditions with too many women who were prettier, or more talented, than she was, and now, even worse, she was beginning to see women younger than she was. Her options, as she saw them, were limited. She could keep trying and find a man to marry who'd support her while she did. She could keep trying on her own, and resign herself to always having low-paying, exhausting day jobs. Or she could give up, go home, go back to school, and become the nurse or the paralegal her parents had always wanted.

Then the world handed her Option Number Four: just after her twenty-first birthday, Rosa had gotten pregnant.

She was almost positive that Benji the bass player was responsible. One of his friends had a place in the country, and Benji had invited Rosa to come with him for a weekend. They had stayed in a rambling, drafty old farmhouse, where almost all the bedrooms had fireplaces. It had been March, with gray skies and a raw, biting wind that made it unpleasant to be outside. Benji had built a fire in their bedroom, and they'd spent most of the next three days huddled under the covers, doing everything they could to keep warm.

Two weeks later, she'd missed her period. Maybe, Rosa thought grimly, the amount of sex they'd had during that freezing weekend had overwhelmed the hormones in her bloodstream. When the pregnancy test she'd bought at the Dollar Tree came up positive, and then the name-brand test for which she'd paid fifteen bucks at CVS gave her the same bad news, Rosa called in sick to work. She took a long shower, wrapped herself in her favorite robe, and sat on her bed. It was early in the afternoon on a Tuesday. The apartment was empty for once, all her roommates at work or at class or at auditions of their own. That rare solitude gave her an opportunity to think, but there was really no thinking to be done. Rosa was in no position to be a mother, with less than two hundred dollars to her name and an apartment she shared with three roommates, and Benji, even broker than she was, was in no position to help.

Instead of calling Benji with the news, she called her sister. Amanda had always been a schemer, the cleverest of the siblings, the one who could usually talk her way out of trouble. Rosa knew Amanda would know what to do, and Amanda did not let her down.

Find some guy with a wedding ring who looks like he has money, Amanda said. *Screw his brains out. Don't give him your real name. Make sure you know where to find him and that he doesn't know where to find you. Wait two weeks and show up at his door. Tell him you're in trouble, and that you don't want to keep it, and that you need money to take care of it. He'll be so terrified that you'll tell his wife he'll pay you, no problem.* Rosa had considered asking how many times Amanda had used that particular scam herself, then decided that she didn't want to know.

She'd followed her sister's instructions, and they had worked just like Amanda told her they would. With the money in hand, she'd scheduled the procedure back home in Los Angeles, and bought the cheapest one-way ticket she could find. New York hadn't worked, but there was still LA. She could get new headshots taken, find new acting classes, sign up with the agencies that cast extras, and start getting herself out there. But then, as the plane crossed over the Rockies, Rosa had a realization. *I am never going to be a singer*, she thought. *I'm never going to be famous. I will never be a star.* And a baby . . . a baby would be a companion, someone who adored her and needed her and would never reject her and never leave. Rosa pictured a little girl, with big dark eyes and soft dark curls, with Benji's beauty and Rosa's talent, a girl who would love her forever.

By the time the pilot announced the start of their descent, Rosa's mind was made up. She'd had her big adventure, and now she would be a mother . . . and a good one.

She put her hand on her still-flat belly, her little question mark. "It's you and me, kiddo," she whispered. She was scared. But there was also, in the swirl of her fear and confusion, a thin, bright ribbon of hope. Rosa bounced a little bit as she made her way through the concourse, feeling the way she'd felt as a kid, picking up a wrapped gift from under the Christmas tree, wondering what was inside.

Glenn and Maria did not welcome their prodigal daughter home with fatted calves and open arms. Instead, it was sour looks and *I told you so*s in two languages. Rosa's mother made it clear that she was not interested in being an *abuela*, that she'd done her time changing diapers and getting up in the middle of the night for midnight feedings. With her troublesome daughters finally out of the nest, Maria had retired, swapping the school district for the local casinos. She was happy spending her days at the San Manuel Indian Casino, in front of the nickel slot machines. Glenn still worked full-time at the garage; Amanda was still in beauty school; and Manny had moved to Phoenix, where he'd found a job in a lab.

Her parents allowed Rosa to move back to her old bedroom, with the stipulations that she do her own cooking and cleaning and laundry, and pay them two hundred dollars a month in rent. For the duration of her pregnancy, Rosa worked the kinds of jobs you could get with a high school diploma. She waitressed, she cleaned homes and office buildings; she worked as a cashier at a drugstore. At home, she took her high school posters off the wall and put up pictures of the alphabet, and Mickey and Minnie Mouse. She replaced her vanity with a changing table and her desk with a secondhand crib. She bought a mobile that sent pink butterflies swirling to the tune of the "Blue Danube" waltz when you wound it up. She filled her dresser with miniature pink and white onesies and socks no bigger than her thumb. She found a Bugaboo stroller on Craigslist, and rented a fancy breast pump from the hospital. She was ready for her princess to come home.

Then Gabe had arrived . . . and Rosa, who'd been so convinced she was having a daughter that she hadn't asked for an ultrasound, had, for the first time in her life, fallen in love. From the minute she'd held her son, tracing his full cheeks, the snub of his nose, his bowed lips, touching the dark curls covering his head, she'd felt something inside of her shift. It was what you felt, she thought later, when you gave your heart away, the click you experienced when your focus changed completely. The moment she held her son in her arms was the moment she became an adult.

Gabe was her angel, her darling, a sweet-natured, easygoing baby who was happy to be held, eager to nurse, and content when he dropped off to sleep, lying in his crib, staring at the glittery butterflies, or being pushed along the sidewalks in his pink stroller, which Rosa couldn't afford to replace. By the end of the first month of his life, he'd thawed his grandma's heart sufficiently that she was willing to give up two of her casino days to stay home and care for him. Rosa's dad was similarly enchanted. At night, he'd sit on the couch in front of the TV with the baby beside him, tucked under his arm, explaining the finer points of the professional wrestling match on the screen to his grandson, who'd sit, content, gnawing at his fist and seeming to pay attention. Even Mandy was willing to give up a few hours of her busy social life to stay home with Gabe on a Saturday night.

With that patchwork of family assistance in place, Rosa navigated Gabe's infancy and toddlerhood. She got a job at a steakhouse frequented by wealthy industry types, who'd tip lavishly when you remembered their names and their drink orders. She told herself that she hadn't given up, that she'd start auditioning again someday, but someday never came, and Rosa was only occasionally regretful. How could she be sorry when she got to spend her days with her gorgeous, sweet, bighearted boy?

When he was three, Rosa enrolled Gabe in preschool at a local synagogue, where Gabe learned his ABCs, his shapes, and his colors, along with, to Rosa's amusement, the Hebrew blessings for bread and wine and the prayers for Shabbat.

Gabe had started talking late, but when he spoke, it was in complete and thoughtful sentences. By four, he'd learned to read, and he read voraciously—street signs, cereal boxes, movie posters, and any book Rosa would hand him. He had a lovely, clear singing voice, and, with his huge brown eyes and glossy dark curls, he was so handsome that strangers would stop them on the street to ask if he'd ever modeled, or if he'd be interested in acting. Rosa would accept their praise and their business cards politely, then toss them as soon as she could. Having been through the scrutiny and rejection herself, the last thing she wanted to do was subject her son, her darling, to that kind of pain.

As he got older, Gabe's essential nature never changed. If anything, with each year that passed he became more kind and empathetic, more amiable and good-natured, as lovely on the inside as he was on the outside. *Mami, how was your day?* he'd ask when he came home from school. He'd sit at the kitchen counter, and, wondrously, he'd actually listen when she told him, which made him unlike the majority of the boys and men she'd ever known.

By the time Gabe was in fourth grade, Rosa had enrolled in nursing school, and had saved enough money to move them into a one-bedroom apartment, an easy walk from her parents' house. Gabe had the bedroom, where there was a little bookshelf and space for his toys, and a desk where he could do his homework. Rosa slept on a pullout couch in the living room. She didn't mind. She hadn't dated since her return from Los Angeles. She didn't mind that, either. Even though she could feel men's eyes on her, even though she'd been asked out by coworkers and bosses and Gabe's math teacher on Parents' Night at the school, by customers and fellow commuters and strangers on the street—she wasn't interested; nor did she feel lonely or deprived. Gabe was all she needed. Everything was for him.

When Gabe had decided to go to college in New York City, Rosa had been quietly devastated. History was repeating itself. Now, instead of being the child who couldn't wait to fly away from the nest, she was the mother left behind.

She told herself not to feel sad; that this was the way of the world. She would let her beloved only child go, and maybe, someday, he would find his way back to her. Only, instead of Gabe's return, the pandemic had come, and he'd moved in with his girlfriend, Ruby Danhauser, whose last name should have sent alarms whooping in her brain, instead of causing just a prickle of suspicion that Rosa had brushed aside.

She should have paid more attention, but she hadn't. Not even when she saw pictures of Ruby, with her light eyes and her dark-blonde curls, not even when she learned that Ruby's father was a dentist. None of it had registered until the day Gabe had called to tell her that they were getting married, and she'd finally, belatedly thought to ask for Ruby's father's first and last name. By the time the alarms were shrieking, the sirens were strobing, it was too late.

Rosa had managed to drive herself home, back to the apartment in Silverlake that she'd shared with her son. She went to Gabe's bedroom, where she sat on the edge of his bed. He'd left things neat when he'd gone off to college. An orderly row of books (*Animal Farm*, *To Kill a Mockingbird*, *The Old Man and the Sea*) was arranged on his desk; pictures of friends, and ticket stubs from concerts had been neatly thumbtacked to a corkboard on the wall. In a silver frame on top of his dresser was a photograph of his high school graduation. Gabe was smiling at the camera, and Rosa was smiling up at him.

Potted plants lined his windowsill: an aloe vera, sending spikes in every direction; a small, prickly cactus; a houseplant he'd told her was called a mother-in-law's tongue. He'd made her promise to take care of them and had left a schedule telling her when each one needed to be watered, showing her how to test the soil. When he was little, she remembered, that was what he'd ask for. Not candy, not toys, but the cheap half-dead plants from the clearance aisles in Home Depot. *Please, Mami, it's only a dollar and I know I can fix it!* he'd say. *It just needs some love!* Most of the time, he'd been able to bring those withered brown things back to life.

I don't deserve him, Rosa thought. For a long moment she just sat, her hand on Gabe's pillow, her eyes on his picture, imagining she could still catch a ghost of his scent lingering in the room. She could feel the name that he'd texted her, the name of Ruby's father, pulsing in her brain. *What are the chances?* she asked herself, shaking her head. Whatever those odds were, she'd beaten them. She'd gambled and she'd lost, and now, after all these years, the bill had finally come due.

SAM

~~~~~~~~~

When his step-niece, Ruby, called to tell him she was engaged, Sam told her he was thrilled, and meant it. He hadn't seen his mom or his sister and her family since before COVID. Now he had an occasion to visit. And, of course, he had his own personal reasons for wanting to make a trip to Cape Cod.

"It'll be a small wedding, out on the deck," Ruby said. Sam told her that it sounded fantastic. He asked about the dates and dress code and promised to get Connor a suit and a tie, all the while thinking that the world, or fate, or God Himself had sent him this opportunity, had placed it right in his lap. Now all he had to do was gather the scraps of his courage. He'd been standing on the very edge of the diving board for months. Ruby's wedding was the push he'd needed. Now, maybe he could jump.

Samuel Levy-Weinberg had been born into a loving, upper-middle-class family, with happily married parents and a twin sister who served as his guardian, clearing the way for him, speaking up for him, happily fighting his battles, because Sarah loved a good fight. Sam had talked late, because Sarah had talked early, and in complete, declarative sentences, and Sarah had spoken for both of them: *No bath. Want cookie.* On the playground, she'd walk fearlessly up to a new group of kids and announce herself and Sam to them: *Hi, I'm Sarah Levy-Weinberg and this is my brother, Sam. We're twins.* That was usually enough to start a conversation. Everyone had questions: *Are you identical?* Obviously not—identical twins had to be the same gender. Besides, they didn't even look alike. Sam had his father's brown hair and changeable hazel eyes, while Sarah's hair was lighter and her eyes were a mixture of gray and blue. *Did you have a secret language?* Not exactly, but they'd always had a sense of what the other was feeling, a kind of twin telepathy informed by their shared history. If Sarah had gotten in a fight with her best friend, Sam would have sensed trouble, and he'd have known to get her a scoop of Purple Cow in a sugar cone and bring it to Gull Pond, where he'd find Sarah swimming. When Sam got cut from the baseball team, Sarah collected him in the car they shared, and they spent an hour or two driving on the highway, listening to the radio.

When they were eighteen and Sarah had given up on her piano soloist dreams and had gone to study music and English at Wellesley, Sam decided, in the way of thousands of young men before him, to head west. He'd enrolled at UC Berkeley, where he'd found, without his sister, that he'd felt unsurprisingly adrift.

It didn't help that he kept getting dumped. Most of Sam's friends had gone through breakups where they'd been the ones to call it off, or where the end had been mutual. Sam, in spite of his best efforts, in spite of the romantic gestures that he made, in spite of being considerate and thoughtful, and always remembering birthdays and anniversaries, was never the dump-er, always the dump-ee. Somewhere between the three- and six-month mark, when the first glow of infatuation was waning, first Tory, then Rebecca, then Celia had decided that she needed to be free. Tory, his senior-year-of-high-school girlfriend, had gotten interested in another guy (a college guy, and what could Sam do about that?). But Rebecca had just shrugged when Sam asked her why she didn't want to be with him, looking as sad and as puzzled as Sam had felt. "I don't know," she'd said. "There's just something missing. Something that isn't there. I can't say it better than that."

Celia had been more explicit. "I ask you what we should do on the weekend and you say 'Whatever you want.' I ask where you want to go to dinner, and you tell me I can pick. And then, when we get there, you don't even order for yourself! You just make me pick two things I want, and you order the one I don't get!"

Sam was bewildered. "Isn't that a good thing? That way, you get two things you like."

Celia had given an exasperated sigh. "I want a guy who respects my opinions, sure, but I want him to have a few opinions of his own."

After a twenty-minute debriefing with his twin ("I never liked her anyhow," Sarah told him. "She had weird teeth"), Sam sought the solace of his fraternity brother Marcus—more specifically, the solace of Marcus's bong. Marcus lived on the fraternity's third floor, in a room so cluttered with clothing and notebooks and classwork and pizza boxes and care packages from his well-meaning mom that it was impossible to see the floor. Sam had to carefully plot a course by identifying stable surfaces on which he could step. Gingerly, he made his way from a geology textbook to a pair of gym shorts to an open graphing notebook before finally reaching safe harbor on the bed. In spite of his slovenly habits and a room that looked like an ongoing audition for *Hoarders*, Marcus managed to attract an astonishing variety of women with what looked, to Sam, like an almost magical ease.

"You want to know the truth about women?" Marcus asked as he applied his lighter to the bottom of the bong. "They call themselves feminists. They think they want to be in charge. But do you know what they really want?"

"No," Sam said. "Clearly, I do not."

With his free hand, Marcus thumped his chest and gave a Tarzan-like yodel. "They want a caveman."

Sam frowned. His father was not a caveman, and his dad had been married to his mom—happily, as far as Sam knew—for almost twenty-three years. Sarah, his sister, did not seem drawn to chest-thumpers.

"They might not say that's what they want," Marcus clarified. He hit the bong, held his breath, and let it out in a series of coughs that made the air even thicker with resinous smoke. "They might not even really know that's what they want. But women like decisiveness. Strength."

"So, they want to be bossed around?" This was sounding disturbingly like some of what Sam had read in the men's-rights subreddits, where every man was owed sex and where women were targets, or Bettys, or bitches, or worse.

"Some women like that, I guess," Marcus said. He scratched at the scruff on his cheeks. "But most of them just want someone who knows what he likes, and knows what he wants, and knows that he wants her. And a woman wants to feel like you went out there and fought to get her."

Sam must have looked confused, because Marcus got up, dislodging several textbooks, an iPod, and half a basket of laundry, and crossed the room to pat Sam's shoulder. "Just watch me tonight."

A few hours later, Sam and Marcus stood in the fraternity's living room, each holding a beer. Sam had shaved and changed his shirt. Marcus had done neither of those things. The scent of pot still clung to his clothing; his eyes were red-rimmed, but still sharp as he scanned the crowd.

"Pick a girl," Marcus said.

Sam considered his choices, finally nodding at a girl with a dark-brown ponytail and glasses in a denim dress and sneakers.

"Target acquired," Marcus murmured, and headed out to the dance floor with Sam a few steps behind him. "Hey there," he said with a smile when he reached the girl. "Those are great glasses."

The girl touched the frames, looking puzzled and— Sam could see it already—charmed. "Thank you."

"I think I might need glasses," Marcus said.

"You should get your eyes checked," the girl replied.

"If I do that, will you help me pick out a pair? Like, where'd you get those?"

The girl told him the name of the store. Then she told Marcus the name of her ophthalmologist, and how long she'd been wearing glasses, and how it felt when she got her first pair and discovered that the green blur above every tree trunk was comprised of individual leaves. Marcus listened attentively, touching the girl's arm, then her shoulder, finally playfully tweaking her ponytail. A few minutes later, they were on the dance floor, the girl's arms draped over Marcus's shoulders and her glasses perched on his face.

Sam attempted to put Marcus's lessons into action

when he spotted Gracie Chen Cohen around the campus. Gracie had a notched eyebrow and a pierced belly button and a tattoo of a koi fish, brilliantly orange and green and gold, spiraling down the length of her left hip and thigh. Sam had noticed the tattoo when he'd seen Gracie striding through the quad in a pair of cut-off denim shorts. Remembering Marcus, Sam had approached her the next time he saw her. "Hey," he'd said, "that's a great tattoo."

"Isn't it?" Gracie had said with a grin.

"I'm thinking about getting a tattoo," Sam lied. "I don't have any yet."

"Oh, yeah?" She didn't seem too interested, but Sam was undeterred.

"Where's the best place for a tattoo virgin?" When Gracie told him, Sam asked, "If I decide to do it, can you come help me pick one out?"

She'd agreed. ("Toldja so," said Marcus when Sam gave him the news.) That weekend, Sam had gotten a tiny infinity symbol inked on the inside of the second toe of his right foot, and a date for Friday night. He and Gracie had been a couple for six ecstatically happy months. Gracie had been the most sexually confident woman he'd ever been with. She had a vibrator, insisted on equal-opportunity orgasms, and was happy to show Sam how to help her have them. Sam and Gracie had sex in a bar's bathroom. In her off-campus apartment, he'd gone down on her until she'd almost writhed off the bed in delight, and then she'd hopped back onto it to return the favor. Sam was blissfully content, and imagined that Gracie was, too. But then, precisely at the six-month mark, Gracie had dumped him. She'd done it kindly, she'd sworn it wasn't him, it was her; she'd told him that his person was out there, but that she wasn't it. Two weeks later, she'd started dating a woman named Elise.

"So you're gay?" Sam asked when he'd gotten Gracie to agree to meet him for coffee. "You like women now?" It was, he thought glumly, the logical next step in the progression. First women would stop liking him, then they'd stop liking men completely.

"I don't know about women," she said, and smiled a dreamy smile. "But I definitely like Elise."

Sam glared at her. Gracie's smile disappeared. "Sorry," she murmured.

"So you're bi?"

"I'm Gracie," she replied with a shrug. "Just Gracie. And I know who I am." She put one of her small, capable hands on top of Sam's. "Do you?"

"Of course."

She kept looking at him, her gaze unyielding. "Yeah, but do you really?"

"Yes!" he'd said, his voice rising. "Yes, I do!"

Gracie had followed him home to pick up the last of her things. Not five minutes after she'd collected her toiletries from Sam's bathroom and retrieved her vibrator from under his bed, the phone rang. Sam knew immediately who was calling.

"Hey."

"What happened?" Sarah couldn't always tell when something had gone wrong for him. Sam didn't always know when something was upsetting Sarah. But, more than half the time, he would feel something—a pain behind his eyes, a twinge in his side. Usually, Sarah could feel his tug at the other end of the rope that would always connect them.

"Gracie and I broke up."

"Oh, Sam." Sarah sounded sympathetic but, he noted, not especially surprised.

"She says I don't know who I am."

Instead of saying *That's bullshit* or *Of course you know who you are!*, his sister said nothing.

"What?" Sam asked. When she didn't answer, he asked again, more loudly. "What?"

"Well." He could tell Sarah was being careful, taking time to choose her words. "It's just that you can be a bit of a chameleon."

Sam frowned. "What do you mean?"

"Okay. Remember in middle school, when you started playing hockey? And you were, like, Mister Hockey? All hockey, all the time?"

"I liked hockey!" Sam protested.

"And then, senior year of high school, you started dating Tory, who thought that contact sports reenacted the toxic gender dynamics of the patriarchy?"

Sam was impressed that Sarah remembered, verbatim, exactly what his girlfriend had said when she'd held forth at Thanksgiving dinner at the Levy-Weinberg house.

"So you stopped playing hockey, and you joined that a cappella group."

"I like singing!"

Sarah's voice was infinitely patient. "I'm not saying you don't. You have a very nice voice." She hummed a few bars of "My Coney Island Baby." Sam ignored her.

"What else?" he asked.

"Then, when you and Tory broke up . . ." Sam mentally thanked his sister for not saying *Then Tory dumped you*. "And, by the way, remind me why you decided to go to Berkeley?"

Sam pressed his lips together, remembering Tory lecturing him. "You need to figure out who you are as a person. Not as a twin." It was Tory who'd urged him to look at schools in California, luring him with pictures of sand and sun and surfing (and, of course, with the fact that she was going to Stanford). Then Tory had dumped him, and Sam had been stranded, single and three thousand miles away from home.

"Then you get to college, and you start dating Celia, and you join a fraternity."

"I wanted to make friends!" Sam realized he was almost shouting. He lowered his voice. "Berkeley is a very big school. A fraternity helped to make it feel more manageable."

"Of course."

"I felt like I had a community."

"Makes sense."

"And Phi Kappa Psi wasn't, you know, one of the toxic fraternities."

"Yeah," Sarah said dryly. "I'm sure women are treated with consideration and respect, and the brothers are all very big on consent."

Sam closed his eyes.

"So then you're Mister Greek Life. Until you and Celia break up, and you drop out of the fraternity—"

"It was costing a fortune. And I got busy with my thesis. I was never there, and it didn't make sense to—"

". . . and you start dating Gracie."

Sam squeezed his eyes more tightly shut.

"And Gracie's an artist. So you move in with her, into that . . ." Sarah paused. ". . . place. That commune or whatever it is."

"It's a co-op," Sam said wearily. "A vegan co-op." It

was actually, per its charter, a long-running experiment in meat-free, mutually respectful communal living, one of Berkeley's longest-running off-campus houses, with generations of pot smoke and patchouli fumes contained within its plastered walls.

"And you start doing morning pages, and you grow out your hair and you get a tattoo . . ."

Sarah was the only one in the world, aside from Gracie, who knew about his tattoo. Sam hoped she hadn't told their parents, who would undoubtedly freak out. "I know you better than anyone in the world," Sarah said. "And I feel like there's this piece of you that maybe you're not entirely sure about yet."

"So I'm missing pieces." Sam could hear the bitterness in his voice. But why shouldn't he be bitter? No one else he knew was missing anything. They'd all found their place; they all had their thing. His father had known, since reading *To Kill a Mockingbird* in sixth grade, that he'd wanted to be a lawyer; his mom had known, even sooner than that, that her life would involve reading and writing. Sarah, of course, had been a pianist, a serious musician who'd never wavered from her path until she'd segued—painlessly, as far as Sam could tell—to music education. Gracie would surely end up being some kind of artist, but even if she didn't, she'd always have her style, her tattoos, her piercings, her sense of who she was.

Sam had never felt that kind of pull toward an activity or a hobby or a profession. He'd liked hockey well enough, but it hadn't hurt him to drop it. Same with a cappella, and the fraternity, and he could already tell that he wasn't going to miss morning pages, even though he'd enjoyed sitting with Gracie every day, watching her bent over her notebook, scribbling intently in purple ink. He certainly wasn't going to miss his mom sniffing as she announced that "journal" was not a verb.

"Maybe I'm wrong," Sarah said, hearing condemnation in Sam's silence. "But Mom did always say you were a late bloomer."

"She said that?" Sam felt angry. More than that, he felt tired.

Sarah's voice was small. "Oops." Then she said, "Look, you'll figure it out. There's no rush. If you are missing something—and I'm not saying you are—you've got plenty of time to find it."

Sam would have many occasions to revisit Gracie's assessment, and Sarah's, and his mom's, as the years went on, as he graduated from college and followed Marcus to LA ("Where the grass is green and the girls are pretty!" Marcus had crowed). Marcus wanted to be an agent, and got a job as an assistant in one of the big talent agencies while Sam, who'd studied coding, found a niche in the legal world, in internet security, search engine optimization, and reputation management. He helped law firms establish their online profiles, ensuring their names came up first in the searches that people conducted, that the articles and links the firms wanted highlighted appeared near the top of the queue, and that anything less positive or flattering got pushed toward the bottom. He could have done his work anywhere, but he figured that Hollywood was the land of reinvention, a place where people changed their faces, their names, their bodies, their entire identities. If Sam was going to figure out who he was, there were worse places to do it.

He and Marcus were roommates for the first few years. Then Marcus had gotten engaged and moved out, and Sam had kept the two-bedroom apartment in Los Feliz, turning the second bedroom into a home office. He thought that he'd miss the seasons—the fall foliage, the first snow in the winter—but he quickly got used to the temperate weather, the sunny days and cool nights, and found that he didn't miss the blizzards that turned the roads into impassible, ice-rutted obstacle courses, or the bleak, gray days of late winter, or the August humidity.

He worked. He took up hiking and joined a tennis club, where he played tennis two mornings a week. He saw friends, from college and the few new ones he'd made at the office. He kept in touch with Gracie, who was living in Seattle as part of a throuple, managing a clothing boutique. Every few months, she'd find a cheap flight to LA. She'd sleep in the second bedroom and cajole Sam into taking her on the star tours, or to Universal Studios, or to Malibu, where they'd drive along the twisting roads and Gracie would insist that every middle-aged man they saw was Kelsey Grammer.

Sam had no trouble meeting women—at work, at the tennis club, in line for the movies. He had a number of relationships, even though none of the women he'd dated had ever set him aflame the way Gracie had. He told himself it was because he couldn't get out of his own head. When he'd been with Jamie, a sommelier, she'd taken him to wine tastings, and together they'd spent a week in Napa ("I like wine!" he'd told Sarah, who'd just shrugged). When he'd been with Miranda, who worked in Business Affairs for one of the networks and loved to ride her bike, he'd started taking bike trips ("It's an excellent workout. Very low-impact," he said, when Sarah merely raised her eyebrows at the five-thousand-dollar carbon-frame road bike he'd bought). And, instead of getting dumped, whenever a relationship hit the six-month mark, when it was time to either break up or commit to going forward, with everything that would entail, Sam would always opt to leave. He'd never been sure, with the bone-deep certainty that marriage required, that the woman he was with was the right woman for him; the one he could be with for the rest of his life. *When you know, you know*, everyone from Sarah to Marcus to his own father had said, and, so far, Sam hadn't. He didn't want to waste anyone's time, especially as he, and the women he dated, both got older. He also, he realized, didn't want to get his heart broken again, or told that there was something missing about him, so he made sure that he was the one who did the dumping.

Then he'd met Julie. He'd been in line at Whole Foods, paying for his hot-food-bar dinner of salmon and greens, when he heard the woman in front of him apologizing as she rooted frantically through a leather purse stained black at one corner, where a pen had exploded.

"I'm so sorry . . . I think I left my wallet in my other purse." She was wearing a long, loose-fitting sundress and dangly gold earrings, with her brown hair slipping out of a bun that appeared to have been secured with one of the elastic bands that postmen used to wrap the mail. Sam watched her pull things out of the seemingly bottomless bag: a pair of leggings, a single kid's-sized sneaker, a water bottle, a lip gloss, a sample-sized box of dental floss, a plastic bag full of goldfish crackers. Her face flushed when she pulled out a tampon. She was biting her lower lip, sweat beading faintly at her hairline, as the boy beside her tugged at the skirt of her dress and said, "Mama, I have to go potty!"

"Oh, God," the woman breathed.

"Can you use Apple Pay?" asked the cashier, nodding at her iPhone. There were five people in line, counting Sam, and a few of them were starting to grumble.

"What? Oh, no. I'm sorry. I've been meaning to figure it out. God, I'm such a ditz, I'm so sorry . . ." She started rummaging in her bag again, and Sam saw her eyes shining with tears. She didn't appear to be broke—Sam thought her bag and her dress both looked expensive—but she was obviously ashamed. Beyond the immediate chagrin, Sam saw resignation in the slump of her shoulders, the twist of her lips. *This is what always happens*, her face and her posture projected. *This is the way it will always be.*

"If you can just maybe put my things aside, and I'll run right home, and . . ."

"Here." Sam reached past her, extending his credit card. "I've got it."

"Oh, no, really, that's so nice, but I can't let you—" The woman and the boy were both looking at him. They had the same pale skin, the same round faces and fine brown hair and eyes that tilted down at the corners.

"It's no problem," he said, handing the cashier his card.

"Oh, God, thank you, thank you so much! That's so kind of you." Her face was alight, and Sam felt something in his heart shift as the cashier handed him back his card.

The woman's name was Julie Barringer. Her son's name was Connor. Julie told Sam that she managed at a music store on the Sunset Strip, that she was divorced, and that she and Connor lived with Julie's father in a mansion on Coldwater Canyon. Officially, Julie and her ex-husband shared custody, but, for all practical purposes, Julie was raising Connor alone. "His dad means well," she said on her first date with Sam, at a sushi restaurant near her shop. Connor's father's name was Jason. He played the guitar—Julie had met him when he'd brought it in to have his truss rod adjusted—and he'd been a member of four different bands. Each one of them had, Julie said, been on the cusp of success at one point, but none of them had ever quite made it. "Jason does studio work, mostly, and he travels. And he doesn't make a lot of money, so he's not too consistent with his child support."

"Well, I guess it's good that you've got your father," Sam said.

Instead of answering, Julie nibbled a bit of seaweed salad and asked Sam about his own family. Sam was happy to discuss his twin sister (married, stepmother of one and mother of two, all of which, he thought, recommended him as a suitor), as well as his parents, who'd just celebrated thirty-five years together.

"My father's a lawyer. He did mostly corporate litigation, but lately he's gotten involved in more pro bono work. Tenants' rights, immigration, things like that."

Julie nodded her approval as Sam talked about his dad: how Lee Weinberg hadn't been especially athletic, but had volunteered to coach all of Sam's youth league teams; how he wasn't a fan of classical music but had faithfully attended every one of Sarah's recitals; and how, on the weekends, he'd been the one to drive them both to their various camps and games and lessons, so that their mother could have some quiet time. "My mom's retired now, but she used to be an English professor. She wrote two novels, back in the 1980s, before my sister and I were born."

Julie set her chopsticks down. Her round eyes were open wide; her face was curious. "Why'd she stop?"

Sam shook his head. His mom had never talked much about her writing days. "I'm not sure. I think she didn't like going on book tours, or being away from us."

Frowning, Julie asked, "But wouldn't that only have been for a few days a year?"

"If that," Sam said. "I don't know if she didn't like writing anymore, or if she just liked teaching and being a mom better."

"I can barely remember my mom." Julie's voice was wistful as she smoothed her chopstick wrapper, before starting to fold it into pleats.

"What happened?"

"Leukemia. It was very fast. I was five." She gave an unhappy, cynical smile. "My father was so mad."

"Mad at who?" asked Sam.

"Oh, her doctors, for not figuring it out fast enough. God. My mother, too. I think he felt like she'd failed him." Julie shrugged. "He got married again less than a year later, so at least he wasn't afraid to get back on the horse that threw him." She smoothed out her wrapper, then started to fold it again. "Then—when Jason left—I remember thinking that I knew I could get through it, because I'd gotten through my mom dying. I remember thinking, *Well, at least it won't be as bad as that was.*"

She bent her head, and Sam wanted to touch her, to hold her hand and tell her everything would be all right. He walked around the table, sat down on the booth beside her, and pulled her close, letting her lean against him, thinking that he wanted to keep her safe and make sure that nothing would ever hurt her again.

After a few minutes, Julie lifted her head and managed a tremulous smile. "I'm going to the ladies' room. And if you want to leave right now—if you want to just walk out the door and get in your car and pretend we never met—I'm not going to judge you. I promise that I won't."

Sam stared at her, incredulous. "I'm not going to run out on you," he said.

Julie sighed. "I might as well give you the whole story," she'd said, "before you waste any more time on me."

The waitress set down a platter of sushi. Sam picked up his chopsticks, and listened as Julie told him that her father, Saul Barringer, had once been in-house counsel for one of the biggest film studios (hence, Sam supposed, the mansion in the hills). Saul had been married three times, and had outlived all three of his wives, along with a son, Julie's half-brother, who died of an overdose in 1993, and another daughter, an older half-sister, who drowned in a scuba accident in Belize in 2007. Saul was now, Julie said, in the late stages of kidney disease. "He's ninety-one, and he's had a quintuple bypass, plus skin cancer, so he's not really a candidate for dialysis or a transplant." Just a week ago, following his last hospitalization, his doctors at Cedars-Sinai had sent him home to die. "I guess that's why I've been losing things," Julie said sadly, explaining that, in addition to her wallet, she'd managed to lose her car keys, her garage-door opener, and her phone, all in five days' time. Shaking her head, she said, "At least I haven't left Connor anywhere."

Julie had arranged for her father to have round-the-clock nursing care, plus visits from the hospice nurses. Then she'd moved back home to oversee her father's death. "He didn't ask, but I wanted to be there for him." She'd sighed, her face resolving into what Sam would come to recognize as the expression she wore when discussing one of the men who'd let her down. Her eyes were downcast, her lower teeth dug into her upper lip. "I thought maybe he'd have, like, a moment of clarity, and he'd tell me he loved me, or tell Connor that he loved him, but I think all my dad ever really loved was his job. And earning money. And screwing other people out of it." She'd shaken her head, looking disgusted, either at her father, for being so heartless, or at herself, for speaking that unpleasant truth out loud. "But he's still my dad, and I don't want him to be alone." She'd sniffled, wiped her eyes, and tried to smile, even though Sam could see tears trembling on her eyelashes. "I bet all of this is sounding delightful. Deadbeat ex-husband, dying father, five-year-old every night of the week." Her voice was shaky. Sam reached for her hands again. He didn't desire Julie the way he'd once desired Gracie, all those years ago. It wasn't a return of that desperate passion, but there was something about Julie that called to him, that made him feel capable and strong. Julie and Connor needed him, and that need would give him an identity, a role he could assume without wondering if he'd just glommed on to someone else's interests or hobbies or way of being in the world (and wouldn't entail his sister lifting her eyebrow and quietly observing that it was a good thing he'd never dated a woman who'd been in a cult).

Julie needed him, and Sam discovered that he liked feeling needed. Julie believed the world to be a terrible place full of unkind people, and Sam wanted to show her that it wasn't. There was also Connor, who was curious and smart and affectionate and who would slip his hand into Sam's when it was time to cross the street, or ask for help zipping his jacket.

"You're sure you're cool with the whole stepdad thing?" Marcus asked. Marcus and Aubrey had three kids of their own by then. Marcus had swapped his stoner ponytail for a gelled pompadour, and had traded his collection of ratty T-shirts and cargo shorts for thousand-dollar suits and raw silk ties. These days, he used his confidence—what he referred to, unironically, as his "raw animal magnetism"—to attract clients instead of bed partners. He was a devoted father to his daughters, a loving husband to his wife, and still Sam's sensei when it came to all things female-related.

"Why wouldn't I be?"

"Raising another man's kid . . ." Marcus's voice trailed off.

"Connor's father's barely around," Sam said. "And his grandfather's terrifying."

Marcus shook his head. "Dementia's a bitch," he said, and Sam, who thought that Saul Barringer was probably a terror even before he'd started losing his faculties, had nodded in agreement.

"And you love Julie? This isn't about, you know, riding to the rescue? Slaying the dragon and rescuing the damsel in distress?"

"I love her," Sam said, without hesitation. "And I love Connor."

Marcus clapped him on the back. "Well, good for you, buddy. If you're happy, I'm happy."

Sam had moved in with Julie and Connor six weeks later. Julie had warned him that her father's house was a horror show, but even her descriptions had left Sam unprepared for the place, an enormous, vaguely Italianate pile of white marble and pilasters and columns, all odd angles, ill-considered additions, and massive plate-glass windows that seemed to scowl down from the top of a serpentine driveway. "How many people lived here?" he asked after he'd gotten the tour. The house felt endless, full of rooms with pointlessly high ceilings and windows that caught the light at the wrong part of the day, which meant you were always either blinking through the glare or squinting in the gloom. Julie's mother had liked Spanish architecture, so there were arched doorways and a tiled roof and a fountain inlaid with Moorish mosaics just off the kitchen. Her successor had preferred mid-century modern, so there was a boxy, flat-roofed addition that served as a guest house. Saul had insisted on a grand library, with a hulking antique rolltop desk and floor-to-ceiling shelves stocked with leather-bound, gold-embossed books whose spines had never once been cracked, and a ladder, should anyone want to reach them. Just off the Art Deco kitchen, there was a solarium that could have been cheerful if it held anything besides a StairMaster that looked like it had been abandoned around the time Sam's mother had published her last book. Finally, running the length of the house, there was a living room where giant canvases covered the walls, paintings done exclusively in smears of ocher and maroon and brown.

Saul Barringer ruled this kingdom from the throne of his hospital bed. Old age and poor health had taken his ability to walk; cataracts had stolen most of his vision. He'd started going deaf years ago, and refused to wear hearing aids ("because, according to him, nobody says anything he wants to hear," Julie said). None of those ravages had touched his voice, a raspy, phlegmy, Brooklyn-inflected bellow, which he employed from early in the morning until very late at night, with the occasional break for naps.

Saul yelled at the nurses when they turned him, to

prevent him from developing bedsores. He screamed at the home health aides when they helped him with toileting or tried to bathe him. He berated his daughter. "Stop treating me like an invalid!" he'd howl, and Julie would murmur apologies, while Sam thought, *How else is she supposed to treat you? You are an invalid!*

"Who are you? What are you doing in my house?" he'd holler every single time he caught sight of Sam (whether he genuinely failed to recognize his daughter's partner or was making an existential point, Sam was never sure). Sometimes, Saul would think Sam was the housepainter employed by his first wife. ("I don't care what Laurie wants, you paint that bathroom pink and I'm not paying you one single cent.") Sometimes he thought Sam was a partner, or a client. One terrible night he'd thought Sam was his dead son, Jerry. "I don't understand why it's got to be heroin," Sam said, in a bellow that somehow managed to be almost plaintive. "Can't you just be a drunk?"

It was brutal. But it wouldn't be for long. "The doctors told me he's got weeks. Maybe a month at the longest," Julie said. Sam had no reason to doubt her. Not until he watched Saul hang on for weeks, then a month, then months, plural, shouting at the nurses, screaming at the physical therapists who'd been brought on board, at one of the more optimistic doctors' urging, to help improve Saul's strength and mobility. "Why should I walk?" he thundered. "You think I've got anywhere to go?"

The nurses quit and were replaced by new ones, who quit and were replaced in turn. The therapists left, and so did the aides, sometimes just walking out at lunchtime without giving anything resembling notice. Julie even had an entire agency quit on her, refusing to send any more of its staffers for Saul to abuse. After six months of this, Sam was convinced that Saul had been pickled in his own nastiness, that he was too awful to ever die.

In spite of this—maybe because of it—Sam was spending most of his nights at the mansion. The agencies tried to send male aides, because they were the ones who could lift Saul and maneuver him without risk of injury, but there were only so many men doing that work, which meant that, at least once a day, Sam would end up wrestling his girlfriend's father in and out of bed, or rolling him from one side to another. "You're so good to me," Julie would say. "I don't deserve you." Sam would kiss her and tell her the truth: that it was no big deal; that he was happy to help. Julie and Connor needed a defender, a champion, someone who spoke to them kindly and treated them well and could stand up to Saul's curses and bellows, and Sam was happy to play that role.

Sam did his best to ignore Saul's abuse. He settled into what had been Julie's childhood bedroom and found his own routines within a household that moved to the rhythms of Saul's sleep, Saul's therapies, Saul's needs. He'd get up early to start a pot of coffee, exchange good mornings and updates with the nurse who'd had the overnight shift, and make Connor his lunch. He'd bring Julie a cup of coffee in bed, and she'd sit up, propping her back against the headboard, wrapping her hands around the mug, gazing up at him, saying, "I don't know what I'd do without you."

After six months, he knew he wanted the three of them to be a family. He discussed it with his own parents—"if you're happy, we're happy"—and with Sarah, who'd come through her own wars with Ruby, who was, by then, a senior in high school. "Being a stepparent is a lot to take on, but if you love her, it's worth it." Finally, he'd talked it over with Connor. "How would you feel if I married your mom?"

Connor considered it carefully. "You'd be my dad, then?" he asked, his voice hopeful.

"Stepdad," Sam said.

"But you'd be here? Every day and every night? You wouldn't leave?"

"No," Sam promised. "I wouldn't leave."

"That's good," Connor said. That was all he'd said, but that night, when Sam went to bed, he saw that Connor had taken his most prized possession, his Lego *Millennium Falcon*, and left it on Sam's pillow, as a gift.

He'd taken Julie out to dinner, then for a drive in Malibu. They were at an overlook, with the ocean crashing underneath them, when he gave her the ring. She'd said yes, then she'd cried, then hugged him, then asked if he was sure, then cried some more. "I'm so happy," she'd said, and wiped her eyes. "Boy, did I get lucky that day I forgot my wallet. Best mistake I ever made."

"Do you think—should I ask your father for your hand?"

Julie looked stricken. "Oh, God. Please don't. What if he says no?"

"Do you think he would?"

Julie gave him a long look. Then she sighed. "He's ninety-one years old. He can't eat solid food, he can't smoke cigars, he can't golf, he can't drive, and he can't chase women. Tormenting people is the only joy he's got left."

"I'm still going to talk to him," Sam decided, and Julie gave him a thin smile and said, "On your head be it." The next morning, after he'd brought Julie her coffee and seen Connor safely into the morning's carpool car, Sam made his way across the vast living room. Mornings were usually Saul's most lucid period. By late afternoon, he'd be raving, yelling at Julie, or at a long-dead assistant or travel agent or wife.

Once, the room had held a sectional couch and a table that sat eight, with eight heavy chairs made of dark, carved wood. There'd been floor lamps and tables, all of them, to Sam's eye, almost exquisitely ugly. When he'd gotten sick, Julie's father had demanded that every piece of furniture be pushed against the walls so that his bed could be set up in the very center of the enormous room. It gave the space the appearance of a theater, with Saul center stage and all those empty chairs and couches waiting for an audience to fill them. To the left of his bed was a rolling tray table covered in bottles of medication, rolls of gauze, tubes of various ointments, a box of baby wipes, a bottle of talcum powder, a bedpan, and a urinal. Sam dragged a chair over the right side.

"Saul?" he called.

For a moment, Saul Barringer's body remained motionless. Then Saul craned his tanned, wrinkled neck upward and peered around, his bald head turning slowly. He looked like a turtle, Sam thought. Not a kindly one, but an ancient, crafty tortoise with a brutal bite.

"Who's that?"

"It's me. Sam. Sam Levy-Weinberg."

"What kind of name," asked Saul Barringer, his lips curling in a sneer, "is Levy-Weinberg? Why don't you just call yourself Jew?"

Sam didn't respond. *The thing about Daddy is, you can't let him bait you*, Julie had told him. Plus, Sam knew that Saul Barringer had been born Sol Bernstein. "Mr. Barringer," Sam said, "your daughter and I would like to be married."

Saul pursed his lips. "Which daughter is this?"

The only one you have left, Sam thought. "Julie."

Saul closed his eyes. "Julie. Her mother was Laurie." His lips thinned in an approximation of a smile. "Laurie was my favorite." *Well, that's nice*, Sam thought, as Saul tried to push himself up straight. There was an uncharacteristically fond expression on his face; a softening around his mouth and his eyes. Saul smiled, gently, lost in memory. Then he said, "She could suck the chrome off a trailer hitch."

That isn't nice at all, thought Sam, and considered how awful it would be if Saul Barringer had ended up being the man in Connor's life. "Julie and I love each other," he said.

"Sweet," Saul said dismissively.

"I think we can make each other happy."

"Not your job."

"Pardon?"

"I said," said Saul, shouting each word, "that it is not your job to make someone else happy." He glared at Sam suspiciously. "A person's happiness is his own business. Or hers."

Sam didn't know what to say. "I love her, and I love Connor."

"Connor?" Sam supposed he could have ascribed Saul's confusion to his age or his failing health, but Julie had told him that he'd never bothered to acquaint himself with any of his grandchildren. "That's her boy, right? The musician's son."

"Yes, that's Connor. Your grandson."

Saul thought it over, and eventually grunted, "Fine.

Only don't think I'm paying for anything!" he'd added before Sam could thank him. He lifted one arthritic finger, with its horny nail, in the air, and jabbed it at Sam. "I already paid for one wedding. It's one per customer!"

"We'll pay," Sam promised, and Saul had waved him away with one age-spotted paw and started looking around for a nurse to berate. That afternoon, Sarah called Julie to start planning the wedding—a ceremony at a restaurant, with dinner and dancing after, and Connor serving as the ring bearer, Marcus as Sam's best man, and Sarah as his best woman.

Julie's father wasn't well enough to leave the house, which Sam regarded as more of a blessing than a disappointment. Lee and Ronnie flew in from Boston. Sarah and Eli and their kids had come from New York, and Gracie had come from Seattle, and Marcus had arranged a bachelor party (Sam had bargained him down from a strip club and a steakhouse to Cirque du Soleil and In-N-Out Burger).

The wedding had been exactly what Sam and Julie had hoped for. Julie told Sam that she'd already survived a two-hundred-person blowout that her parents had insisted upon when she'd married Connor's father and had hated the entire experience. "I just want a great party, where there's a fifteen-minute interlude for the ceremony," she'd said, and Sam, with his mother's and sister's help, had done his best to oblige her. Julie had chosen the restaurant; his sister had helped her plan the menu. His parents had come out a week early to help. "Tell me about the kind of work you did," Lee Weinberg had said to Julie's father, pulling a chair up to Saul's hospital bed, and Saul, recognizing a fellow attorney, had expounded at length on the advantageous deals he'd made over the years, and was happier than Sam had ever seen him.

Sarah stood up with him at the ceremony, holding one of the poles of the chuppah, beaming her approval as he slipped the ring on Julie's finger. "Mazel tov!" Marcus yelled, after Connor carefully placed a napkin-wrapped lightbulb under his heel, and Sam had stomped down, hard.

Julie's typically tremulous, worried face was wreathed in smiles for the entire night, except for the few minutes when she'd cried, during their vows. Sam and Julie had danced until two in the morning, and spent the night in a bungalow at the Beverly Hills Hotel. "Promise you'll never leave me," Julie had whispered, holding his shoulders with a panicky force, pressing her body against his, so tightly it felt to Sam like she was trying to push herself through his skin.

"I'll never leave," Sam had whispered back. The next morning, Sarah brought Connor to the hotel. His sister and stepson and parents had joined them for brunch, then Sam and Julie and Connor had left for a family honeymoon in Maui, at a resort that offered a kids' camp, so the newlyweds had plenty of time to be alone.

Sam found that he liked cooking. He'd FaceTime with his sister every morning while he made Connor's lunch, filling bento boxes with radish rosebuds and edamame and neatly portioned servings of grilled chicken and rice. He would make Connor's bed, after a few bad run-ins with Legos taught him to wear shoes before entering the boy's bedroom, and when Connor came home from school, Sam would prepare a snack, and together they'd watch a half hour of anime on TV. On weekends, Sam would take Connor to visit dogs at the pound, in hopes of getting their own pet, at some un-specified date, when Grandpa Saul, who hated animals as much as he hated most people, had gone on to his reward. They started reading *James and the Giant Peach* together at night. Connor was enchanted with the idea of a giant, inhabitable fruit. "Do you think something like that could really happen?" he'd asked, and Sam said, "I don't think so," but he still caught Connor looking wistfully into the backyard, where apricots and avoca-dos and oranges grew. Julie was reluctant to leave her father for any length of time, but Sam coaxed her to spend a weekend camping at Big Sur, and a week of ski-ing in Jackson Hole during spring break, where they'd shared a house with Sarah and Eli and Dexter and Miles. In June, Sam's parents hosted them and Sarah and Eli and Ruby and the boys for a week on the Cape, and Sam and Julie and Connor visited Sarah and Eli in New York City right before Christmas, where they saw two Broadway shows, and took Connor to see the store's holiday displays, and went skating in Rockefeller Center one cold, starry night.

For the duration of the marriage, Sam and Julie and Connor were a merry little band of three. They did their best to ignore the malevolent, shouting presence in the living room, a thing that sometimes seemed more dead than alive. Each night in bed, instead of *I love you*, Julie would say, *It won't be much longer*, and Sam would say it back: *It won't be much longer*.

One afternoon in May of 2019, just over a year after he and Julie were married, Sam had been home, prep-ping salmon fillets for dinner, when the doorbell had rung.

"Tell them we don't want any!" Saul had yelled from

his bed in the living room. "Tell them we gave at the office!"

Sam wiped his hands on a dish towel and went to answer the door. Two police officers were standing there.

"Mr. Barringer?" the first one, a woman with a close-cropped Afro, said.

Sam's heart gave a great thumping kick in his chest. "No, that's my father-in-law. I'm Sam Levy-Weinberg." Terrible thoughts were running through his mind, all involving Connor, who'd gone to a birthday party at the La Brea Tar Pits that afternoon. "Did something happen? What's wrong?"

The second officer, a tall man with tanned white skin and curly reddish-brown hair, said, "Maybe we should talk inside."

Sam led them to the kitchen. "Who's there?" his father-in-law was yelling. "What's going on?" Ignoring him, Sam said, "Would you like coffee? Water? Something to drink?"

"Does Julie Barringer live here?" the female officer asked.

Sam was still holding the dish towel, twisting it in his hands. "I'm her husband. She—she kept her last name."

The male officer bent his head. "I'm sorry, sir. We have bad news."

They told him that there'd been a bad accident on the 405. Julie's Prius had been rear-ended, shoved into the guardrail at the median by kids joyriding in one of their daddies' Range Rovers. The driver of the Rover had a concussion. Julie had been killed.

While the officers were talking, the two nurses on duty had come to the kitchen, where they stood to hear the news. The three of them were standing there, motionless, speechless, when Sam heard the front door swing open, and heard Connor's happy shout. "Sa-am! I'm ho-ome!" followed by the unmistakable tootle of a kazoo. Connor came skipping into the kitchen, carrying a paper gift bag full of party favors, with the instrument in question in his other hand.

"Maya's mom says that Rexton's parents were sadists for giving us kazoos, but she wouldn't tell us what a sadist is," he announced breathlessly. Then he turned and saw the police officers and went immediately still.

Sam felt the horror of what had happened settle into his bones. *I have to tell him*, he thought. *Oh, God. How do I tell him?* Connor's dark eyes swept the room—the two police officers, the nurses, Sam with a dish towel twisted in his hands, his grandfather braying "What's happening?" from the living room and being, for once, ignored.

"What's wrong?" Connor asked, in his husky voice.

Sam hunkered down, so he could look Connor in the eyes. *My God*, he thought. *How do I do this? What do I say?*

"Connor," he said, and cleared his throat. "I have bad news."

"Is it Mom?" Connor asked, his voice rising. "What happened? Just tell me!"

"There was a bad car accident," Sam said. "I'm so sorry, honey. Your mom is dead." He watched as Connor's eyes got big and saw the moment the news landed. He held the boy while he cried and, after a murmured conversation with the nurses, dispatched one of them to give Saul the news. "What?" he heard Saul shouting, as Connor sobbed, "No! No! No!" and pummeled Sam's shoulders with his fists. "Who?" Then "I'm going to sue those sonsofbitches! Get me Abrams on the phone!" Meanwhile, Connor clutched at Sam with panicky arms.

"Are you going to stay here? Please don't leave, Sam."

Sam swallowed hard. He felt dizzy, his brain overloaded. He could smell salmon, and garlic, and could hear his father-in-law shouting, and could see the table he'd just finished setting for three. Julie's yoga mat stood, curled up by the front door, her rolled-up grippy socks beside it. Her favorite coffee mug rested in the drainer; the olive-oil cake she'd baked two days ago was still in its pan, covered in tinfoil. Everything was here, except Julie. It didn't feel real.

"I'm not going anywhere," Sam promised Connor. "No matter what."

That night, after Connor had been coaxed to eat a few bites of macaroni and cheese, after Sam had struggled to answer question after question about where his mommy was now, and what would happen to her, and had it hurt when the car had hit her, and was she going in the ground and what would happen to her there and was she going to watch over him from heaven, because that's what Logan P. at nursery school told Connor people did after they died, Sam had tucked the boy into bed, made his way downstairs, and poured himself two fingers of whiskey. He'd decided to sleep in Connor's room, on the floor beside Connor's bed. He couldn't even look at the room he and Julie had shared; couldn't imagine sleeping in their bed without Julie beside him.

He was hunting through the closet for his sleeping bag when the phone rang.

"Sam? Hey, hi. Is everything all right? Are you okay? I got the strangest feeling this afternoon."

That old twin ESP, he thought, and cleared his throat. "Julie's dead."

"What? *What?*" his sister cried, then, "Oh, God, you're kidding me. What happened? Oh, my God, that poor little boy." Sarah had started to cry. "I mean, poor you, poor Julie, but my God, my God. Poor Connor."

Sam was crying. He'd held it together for Connor, but now he couldn't have stopped the tears if he'd tried.

"Come home," said his sister.

"Sarah, I don't know if I can. I can't leave Connor, and his father is here—"

"Oh, like he'd give a shit," Sarah said, her voice uncharacteristically sharp. "Like he'd even notice. And didn't you tell me he'd be out of town for three months?"

"He's playing in Branson," said Sam. "But California's the only place Connor's ever lived. And," Sam continued, "I don't know if I'm even allowed to take him anywhere." Sam called himself Connor's stepfather, but he'd never officially adopted Connor. He had no idea what his legal standing might be.

"Find out," said his sister with her voice cracking. "I just can't stand thinking about you and Connor, being there, in that house, without Julie."

Sam promised that he'd consider it, but, in the end, it was Saul Barringer who decided for him, summoning him to the living room in his familiar obnoxious bellow early the next morning.

"What's the plan, son?" Saul demanded, when Sam was standing in front of his hospital bed.

"For Julie?" Sam swallowed. "Her body is still at the morgue. They have to do an autopsy because . . ." He gulped again. "Because of how she died. Once they release the body, I thought we'd bury her—"

Saul interrupted. "Her mom's at Hillside Memorial. So is her sister. She should go there."

"That's fine," Sam said. "I'll make the arrangements."

"Good. Now." He craned his neck up, baring his teeth. "I'll give you two weeks to pack up and clear out."

"I—" Sam stared at his stepfather. "Excuse me. What?"

"You don't have to go home, but you can't stay here," the old man said. His lips curled back, revealing his dentures.

Sam stared at him. "Excuse me?"

"It's my house. I want you out. You and the kid."

Sam's hands were forming fists of their own accord. "Julie was your daughter. That kid is your grandson."

"Is your name on the deed of this domicile?" The old man paused, head cannily tilted. "No? Didn't think so. I'll evict you if I have to, but it doesn't have to get ugly. Just pack your things and go."

"You'd do that," Sam said. His voice was faint with disbelief. He felt like he'd been hit over the head, hard. He wanted to hit Saul someplace, even harder. "You'd put your own grandson out on the street?"

Saul waved one large, spotted hand dismissively. "He'll have plenty of money once I'm gone. But hopefully that won't be for a while." The old man drew himself up straight. "I want the place to myself."

This cannot be happening, Sam thought. This can't be real. He made his way out of the living room, through the foyer, out the front door, where he stood, breathing the cool desert air. Then he thought, *Why should we stay?* True, this house had been Connor's home for years. But just because it was familiar didn't mean it wasn't toxic, full of dread and bad smells and the echoes of Saul's querulous shouts. Sam had enough money to provide one little boy with a stable existence outside of these walls. *He can stay with me and I can take care of him*, Sam had thought. *Maybe we can actually go home.* And, six weeks later, when the school year ended, that's what he and Connor had done.

"Tell Connor hi from me," said Ruby, as she said goodbye to her uncle, after giving him the date and time for the ceremony. "Tell him we're so excited to see him." Sam promised that he would, and congratulated her again. Then he'd hung up the phone, pleased and unsettled, a fizzing sensation in his bloodstream. *I'll have to tell Sarah*, he thought, of this thing that he'd only just figured out about himself. *I'll have to tell Mom.* But he wouldn't need to tell them immediately.

After the wedding, Sam thought. He'd leave Connor with his mom and his sister for a few nights, and finally get some answers.

SARAH

~~~~~~~

He's . . . having . . . an . . . affair," Sarah said, gasping the words between breaths as she and her best friend speed-walked through Prospect Park. It was just after seven o'clock on a cool late-March morning, and the park bustled with walkers, joggers, cyclists in Lycra leaning hard into the turns.

"Oh, he is not," said Marni Silver, who'd gotten divorced, after her own affair, when her third daughter was just nine months old ("and lived to tell the tale," as she liked to say). Marni and Sarah were both dressed in leggings with sheer cutouts and sneakers with excellent arch support. Marni had on a light jacket with stripes of silvery reflective tape; Sarah wore a long-sleeved magenta T-shirt made of some magical sweat-wicking fabric. Both women pumped their arms as they walked and dreamed (or at least Sarah did) of the days when they'd been runners, before hip pain or back problems had slowed them down.

"None of us left our houses for most of last year," Marni said to Sarah as they rounded the curve by the pond. "When would he have met someone? When would he have seen her?"

"Maybe online?" Sarah said. "Maybe it's an emotional affair."

Marni turned her head to look at Sarah without breaking her stride. "I'm just checking. Are we talking about the same person here? Eli Danhauser, the most devoted husband in history?"

Sarah allowed herself a brief flush of pleasure at her friend's words before letting anxiety replace satisfaction. "Something's off. Something's wrong. I know it is."

Marni pursed her lips. "You don't think maybe you're being paranoid because everything is so . . ." She waved both her hands, a gesture encompassing, Sarah presumed, the pandemic, the election, the shelter-in-place orders, the vaccine rollout, virtual school, and maybe even Sarah's father's death, a few months before the first case of COVID was reported, an absence that still felt raw and new.

"He's changed," Sarah said. "He looks right through me. It's like I'm barely even there." That was especially painful because for years, as Marni well knew, Eli had been the very best of husbands. He'd always been attentive, solicitous, respectful, and kind. Not to mention, surprisingly sexy. For the duration of their marriage, every few months, on a Friday afternoon or Saturday morning, Sarah would get a text: *Meet me at the bar at Towne.* She'd go through her closet, selecting her clothes and, especially, her underwear with special care, feeling her pulse quickening. She'd arrive at the bar and Eli would be there, wearing something that she'd never seen—a new tie or shirt—and, always, different cologne. *Buy you a drink?* he'd offer. I'm Dave. Or Mike, or Mark, or Gary, from Bar Harbor, or Cleveland, or Des Moines. He'd give her a name and a job. Sarah would invent a character of her own. She'd been a journalist, on an out-of-town assignment; a painter, in town for a bridal shower; a sorority girl having her first legal drink. She and Eli would sit at the bar, exchanging details of their made-up lives. Eventually, their hands would brush, or she'd feel Eli's hand on her leg, one sure finger crooked against the soft flesh underneath her knee. *Want to get out of here and go someplace we can be alone?* he'd ask, or *Can I show you my hotel room?*

They'd go to the room that Eli had reserved and make love, for the first time, as these invented people. Sometimes it would be tender—she'd pretend to be a virgin who'd never even touched herself, and Eli had eased her onto the bed, kissing her for long, languorous minutes, slowly pulling off each piece of clothing, asking *Can I touch you here? Can I kiss you?* as he led her, gently, toward her very first orgasm. Sometimes it would be rough. Eli would open the hotel-room door, and almost before it was shut, he'd have her by the shoulders, pressing her up against the wall, grabbing one wrist and tugging it down to his erection while he bit her neck, and kissed her lips, and whispered, *You're driving me crazy, you know that, right?* He'd yank off her panties, pull up her skirt, drop to his knees with his face between her legs, and then he'd stand up, grabbing her hips, spinning her, making her put her hands flat against the wall, panting, *I can't wait anymore, I need to be inside you.*

As good as their at-home Eli-and-Sarah sex was, that hotel-room sex was spectacular. It showed that Eli never took her for granted, how he worked to keep things interesting. How, on each one of those dates, he'd woo her and win her all over again. And now, Sarah couldn't remember the last time they'd had any sex, of any variety at all.

She missed it. She missed him. She missed having a partner, someone intimately familiar with the details of the life they'd built together. Right now more than anything, she missed someone who would join his voice to hers and tell her stubborn stepdaughter that getting married at twenty-two was insane, and that she couldn't, shouldn't, do it. And Eli was completely oblivious, physically present, emotionally gone.

It would have been bad if Eli had just ignored her, but that wasn't all. For the years they'd been married, Sarah had done her best to ignore Eli's annoying habits: the volume at which he chewed; the way he'd leave his sweaty workout clothes in a sodden pile on the bathroom floor, and how he never remembered to clean his beard stubble out of the sink after he shaved. In the early days of their marriage, Sarah would fret about his shortcomings. She would discuss these failings with him calmly; she'd remind him politely, she'd even screamed at him a few times before realizing that she was, as the self-help books said, sweating the small stuff. Eli was never going to change. She had two choices: she could expend her time and energy on getting him to act differently, or she could make peace with his minor acts of slovenliness. Sarah went for the second option.

She knew that it could have been worse. The evidence was all around her—a friend's husband who'd been hiding a meth addiction; another friend whose husband had drained their bank accounts during a year's worth of secret late-night online poker sessions; a third marriage that had ended after the wife had an affair with her spin instructor, which, in addition to being shameful, was a total cliché.

Sarah remembered how when Dexter was in kindergarten, a wave of divorces had swept through his class, almost as if marital discord were a cold that was catching. Sarah would hear about one couple after another after another being in counseling, or "taking some time apart," or separating or divorcing. One little boy or girl after another would become the owner of two separate backpacks, one for Mommy's house and one for Daddy's, and go trudging stoically between two domiciles, usually, at that point, with a therapist of their own. It broke Sarah's heart, even though Dexter thought those kids had won the lottery. Two bedrooms! Two doting parents, or sets of parents! Two holiday and birthday celebrations, with twice as many gifts! In a plaintive voice, Dexter would ask why he couldn't have two birthday parties like Madison or celebrate Christmas *and* Chanukah, like Taylor S., or go to Florida like Taylor Z. and her dad and her dad's new girlfriend. Sarah had felt proud, even the tiniest bit smug, about her own marriage.

It was a version of the same pride she'd felt, starting seven or eight years after her own wedding, when all the friends and colleagues and classmates who'd asked if she was sure, *really* sure, about Eli, if she was positive about becoming a stepmother, if she'd thought about what she was getting into; all the women who'd told jokes that weren't really jokes about how Sarah was a child bride and how she'd be the Wicked Stepmother, no matter how kindly she behaved. By the time they were in their mid-thirties, all of those women had ended up scrambling around, as Marni put it, like the very last shoppers at the Filene's Basement semiannual sale, only instead of grabbing at discounted wedding gowns they were snatching up any presentable, employed, marriage-minded man who hadn't already been claimed. *Who's laughing now?* Sarah had thought as friend after friend had walked down the aisle with her own Mister Not Quite Right, a man who looked or sounded or behaved like clearance merchandise, the dinged or damaged goods you'd find on the shelves at Marshalls or TJ Maxx; the imperfects. Sarah watched, sympathetic but unsurprised, as some of the marriages wobbled unsteadily forward and some imploded after a year or two. Meanwhile, she had been a decade into her own marriage. She and Eli had two gorgeous babies, her beautiful boys, and Ruby had stopped hating her and had become one of Sarah's favorite people.

Staying married, she'd decided, was a choice; one that had less to do with love and more with forbearance. You recommitted yourself to your spouse every time you overlooked a pair of sweat-soaked boxer shorts in the corner of the bathroom; every time you swept, without comment, toenail clippings from the bedroom floor; every time you'd pick a different coffee shop after finding yourself buoyant and flushed and a little too eager to see that one barista with tattoo sleeves and the large, capable-looking hands. Every day, at least once, Sarah would find herself looking around her beautiful kitchen, with the skylight she'd added, or at Ruby as she came bounding through the door, and she would think, *I made the right choice. I did the right thing.*

But all those years of tamping down her annoyance must have had some effect, nibbling away at her patience. When the pandemic hit, and Eli went from spending his days out of the house to being inside with her, all the time, staring into his patients' mouths on his computer screen, lecturing on oral anatomy for the course he taught at Columbia's school of dentistry via Zoom, Sarah found that whatever tolerance she'd cultivated over the years had frayed to the point of nonexistence, and whatever reserves of goodwill she'd stored up had been drained. Just the sight of a bowl crusted with the residue of cereal around its rim, or one of those sweaty T-shirts she'd spent years ignoring, could make her murderous; just the sound of his orthopedic flip-flops slap-slapping up the stairs made her incandescent with rage.

"Maybe it's perimenopause," she said to Marni as

they finished their last lap and slowed their pace. "But it used to be I'd only want to kill him maybe once a year." She considered. "Maybe twice a year. Only now, it's like weekly. Sometimes daily." She felt herself scowling and did her best to relax her face, not wanting to end up prematurely wrinkled. It was a warm spring morning, the trees all glowing gold and green, the air sweet and clear, and Sarah couldn't enjoy it at all. Between her stepdaughter's ill-conceived plans and the husband whose life she wanted to end, she'd lost the ability to notice the weather, or to appreciate a beautiful day.

"Just so I understand: you're terrified that he's cheating, and you also want him dead?"

Sarah considered the contradiction. Then she said, "Yes."

"Got it," Marni said, nodding as if that made perfect sense. "Maybe it's proximity," she said. "Look, all of our routines have been disrupted. Everything's upside-down. And you're planning a wedding on top of it all, so he's probably freaking out about his little girl getting married and the inevitability of his own death." She paused to inhale. "Give it time. Next September, God willing, the boys will be back in school full-time, the wedding will be in the rearview mirror, and Eli will be back at the office. Things will be better."

It made sense. Except Sarah didn't know how much longer she could hold on. The pandemic had left her spacious house feeling punishingly small. Ruby and Gabe had claimed the fourth floor, Dexter and Miles had taken over the third; Eli's office was on the second story, but he'd roam up and down, from the first floor to his office and back down again, flip-flopping all the way. From her desk or her bed, Sarah could hear everything that happened in the house, the creak of the floorboards as Eli paced, Miles's voice during his classes, the crashes and exclamations as Dexter dropped things, and even, God help her, the thump of the headboard against the wall and the occasional moan from Ruby and Gabe's aerie.

Sarah loved her family. She loved her boys, especially because their existence had never been a given. Her life could have gone in a different direction. If she'd devoted herself to her music, the way her teachers had wanted; if she'd gone to a conservatory for college instead of getting a liberal-arts degree, if she'd pushed herself to the very limits of her talent, forsaken all her other interests and hobbies and practiced five or six hours a day, she could have made it; could have been performing with symphonies or doing residencies in Vienna or making records for Deutsche Grammophon.

Maybe she'd chosen the safer path; the easier, more familiar road, where she played for herself and occasionally dazzled one of the kids who came into her office at the music school. Sarah would play one of her old recital pieces, Grieg's Concerto in A Minor or Chopin's "Fantaisie-Impromptu" and watch their eyes get wide and their mouths drop open. "Miss Sarah, you're good!" they'd say, or they'd put their hands at the sides of their heads, then draw them outward, making exploding noises to suggest that their minds had been blown.

I was good, Sarah would think. *And I might have been great, if I'd worked for it.*

But she'd made her choice, and she'd tried not to look back or think about the road not taken. For the most part, she'd been happy. When the babies came, au pairs and babysitters and, eventually, Ruby's help meant she could go back to work and know that her babies were safe and well cared for. She'd had her solitude: the hour in the morning after Eli had left for work and the kids had left for school, when she could sit with her second cup of coffee and do the crossword puzzle, or fold a load of laundry, or straighten up the kitchen, or read a chapter of a book, or just enjoy the quiet. She'd loved the weekend afternoons when the kids would be at sports practices or playdates and Eli would be out with his buddies, riding his bike or playing pickup basketball with the other dads. She would sit in the living room by herself and listen to music or half-watch some show about tiny houses on TLC while she made her weekly shopping list. At night, she'd savor a quiet hour alone in the kitchen, after everyone had gone to sleep, prepping the next night's dinner or paging through cookbooks while she sipped a cup of tea.

Eli knew how much her alone time meant to her, and all through their marriage, he'd done what he could to preserve it. When Ruby was little, Sarah and Eli had allowed her to spend time in the summer with Sarah's parents on the Cape, a respite that gave Sarah and Eli time together, and Sarah time by herself. When the boys came along, twice a year Eli would take them camping for a weekend. They'd load up a rented SUV with tents and backpacks, sleeping bags and coolers, more food than they could ever eat and more gear than they'd ever use, fishing poles and firewood, mountain bikes and flashlights and tarps and special bags to keep the food away from bears. Sarah would help them pack. She'd carry bags to the car. She'd stand on the steps, cheerfully waving goodbye, and then, once they were gone, she'd do an exultant jump in the air, thrilled at the thought of three entire nights where she would have the house all to herself.

The pandemic had stolen those precious days and hours. Even when everyone was tucked away in their bedrooms, Sarah could feel them, as if their presence had a physical weight, or a sound. It was the constancy of it, the unending-ness. She felt crowded and edgy and half-crazy; every time she turned around there was someone standing too close to her, speaking too loudly, needing something. *Mom, have you seen my sweatshirt? Mom, can we have chicken with mashed potatoes for dinner? Mama, do you know where my phone charger went? Sorry, Mrs. D., but we're out of toilet paper on the fourth floor.* Every request, no matter how polite, clawed at her with sharp nails. Every breath of air in the house felt stale and flat, like it had already been in and out of someone else's lungs; every surface she touched felt sticky. And she knew, from her friends, that she wasn't the only woman feeling that way. They were all trying to do too much, for too many people, in too little space, trying to manage their jobs and their kids' schooling, the meals and the housework and their working-from-home partners or spouses while they clung to sanity with their fingernails. As the months went by, Sarah thought that, if there wasn't a true end coming soon, there'd be a wave of women leaving their marriages, just as there'd already been a wave of women leaving the workforce. They'd log on to Expedia en masse; they'd buy themselves one-way tickets to the most deserted parts of the world with no plans to ever come home.

When Ruby and Gabe moved out, Sarah felt a measure of relief. When the boys began in-person school again, she told herself that things were getting better. Then Eli had declared 2021 the Year of Buying Nothing and launched a major purge. "We're at the stage of our lives where we need to start getting rid of things, not acquiring more," he'd announced, with a significant look in the direction of Sarah's side of the closet, where the racks and shelves were, admittedly, quite full.

Sarah's job at the music school had no dress code. If she'd wanted to, she could have worn jeans and blouses, or even T-shirts and sneakers to work. But Sarah loved clothes. She loved finding new boutiques and discovering new designers; she loved the feeling of buying the perfect azure-blue necklace to wear with a new navy-blue dress, and a pair of vintage leather riding boots to pull the look together. Even the clothes she didn't wear made her happy. She'd brush the sleeve of the pale-pink cashmere sweater she'd worn on her second date with Eli and feel, again, the first flush of infatuation; she'd flick past the black gown she'd worn for her last recital and feel a bittersweet pang. She loved the challenge of putting together an outfit, searching out each individual piece, shopping her closet, combining old and new. Getting dressed was its own kind of creativity, and it satisfied her in the same primal way she imagined gathering a perfect sheaf of wheat or an unblemished handful of berries might have delighted her hunting and gathering forebearers.

Eli, who treated his suits and ties like a uniform, didn't get it. He'd read a book about Swedish death cleaning and joined a Buy Nothing group on Facebook, and various upcycling and barter groups online. He donated their belongings, and gave things away, and when there were items he couldn't donate or trade away, he'd simply leave them on the sidewalk. Which meant that every week or so, Sarah would walk outside of their building to take Lord Farquaad for a stroll and discover some cherished belonging on the stoop with a TAKE—FREE sign taped to it somewhere.

At first, Sarah had been fully on board with this project. They did have too many things; the house was getting too full. She'd helped Eli excavate Ruby's child-sized desk from where it had been sitting, ignored, in the back of their basement for the past ten years, and donate it to a family shelter. She'd been fine giving away the bread machine, a wedding gift she'd used once before deciding that she preferred baking bread from scratch. She'd collected boxes of board books and chapter books that the boys no longer read; she'd had Ruby help her perform a merciless edit on her closet, getting rid of anything that didn't fit or that she hadn't worn or that was not attached to some specific pleasant memory. "Do not let me backslide," she'd told her stepdaughter as they'd filled three contractor-sized trash bags, and Ruby had whisked the discards out of the house, never to be seen again.

It was fine that Eli wanted them to pare back, to reduce, reuse, and recycle. It was not fine when she'd find that he'd gotten rid of something that she actually did use, or wanted to keep. She'd had to wrestle her old leather bomber jacket, purchased in college, with a small KEEP YOUR LAWS OFF MY BODY pin still attached to its lapel, away from some hipster girl with a pink bob and a pierced nose. "But it's vintage!" the girl had wailed, which hadn't made Sarah feel good about herself or the state of women's reproductive rights in America. That had been bad, but not as bad as the morning she'd walked outside to discover her beloved Le Creuset Dutch oven sitting on their stoop. She marched upstairs in high dudgeon, the vessel clutched to her chest. Eli had blinked at her, perplexed.

"You still use that?" he asked. On his face was Sarah's least favorite expression, the one where his forehead was furrowed, mouth slightly agape in a way that made him look slightly concussed. "I thought it was just taking up space on the stove."

Sarah didn't want to explain to him that his *taking up*

space was her *making the kitchen more attractive;* that, while he saw a pot, unused and extraneous, she saw her history. She didn't want to explain to him, again, since he'd clearly forgotten, that the Dutch oven, with all of its chips and scratches, had belonged to her parents, that it had been one of their wedding gifts, and that even if Sarah only used it a handful of times each year—for their Chanukah brisket, or for matzoh ball soup, when it was her turn to host Passover—it had meaning for her. It still, as they said, sparked joy. Its rich red-orange color lifted her mood a little every time her gaze happened upon it; when she ran her hands along its smooth enameled curves, she thought about her mom, and the holidays they'd spent together. She'd tried to explain this to Eli, who'd listened, nodding along, promising to do better. "Sorry," he said. "I won't do it again. I'll ask before I get rid of anything else."

That, it emerged, was a lie. As the spring progressed, every few days, Sarah would look for something—her set of two-pound hand weights, the ceramic vase she'd bought in Mexico the year they'd gone to Tulum, the blue-and-white teacups from Chinatown, or her *Collected Shakespeare* from college—and discover it wasn't there. "I don't understand," Eli would say. "I thought we agreed about this." He'd draw himself up proudly. "I got rid of all my dental textbooks."

"Eli." Sarah sounded as weary as she felt. "Nobody wants dental textbooks. They were just taking up space."

"Right! That's why I got rid of them."

"I can get rid of things," Sarah said. She'd hold up her Shakespeare collection, or her teacups. "But not this thing."

"So not *any* things," Eli would say, and Sarah would have to press her lips together to keep from saying truly hurtful things, things she could never take back. She didn't understand what had happened, or why Eli not only no longer saw their belongings, but no longer saw her, either—who she was, what she liked and used, what was meaningful and what was not. Which made her feel okay about lying. It was easy to do. Eli was smart, but not especially observant when it came to women's clothes or accessories. "Are those new?" he'd ask, peering at her earlobes or staring severely at a dress.

"This old thing?" she'd say, or, touching her earrings, she'd say, "I've had these for a million years," knowing that Eli wouldn't be able to tell for sure whether she'd owned something for decades, or had bought it the week before.

She could have kept lying. She could have endured the new austerity, the Buy Nothing group, the compost bin he'd set up on the kitchen counter, and the hipsters she'd find hovering by her front door every few mornings, their faces hopeful above their masks. She could have lived with the stories she'd been forced to invent to counter his relentless attempts to purge their lives of everything she loved. She could have made herself endure it.

But then there were the flip-flops.

"I need to tell you something," Eli had said, years ago when they'd first started dating. They'd been in a restaurant, and he'd reached across the table to take her hands.

Sarah looked at his serious expression and felt a prickle of unease. Had something bad happened to a patient? Was he sick? Or was he going to tell her that Annette had come back, that he had to give his ex-wife another chance, that Ruby deserved her real mother?

She swallowed hard. Eli was already so dear to her, with his high forehead, his curly hair, and his sweet smile. Eli was wonderful, and dating was awful. There'd been guys she'd liked who'd never called, guys she hadn't liked who had called (and called and called, and then had showed up at her apartment or her office, refusing to take no for an answer). And, of course, there'd been her first boyfriend, who'd broken her heart so completely that it had taken her a full year before she'd allowed another boy to even hold her hand.

She sat back, bracing herself. And then Eli had gravely announced, "I have plantar fasciitis."

"What is it? Is it bad?" she'd asked. It certainly sounded bad.

"Well, it's uncomfortable," Eli allowed, with a modest look suggesting that he was a nobly enduring, with barely a word of complaint, agony that would have reduced a lesser man to writhing and groans. As soon as she got home, Sarah had looked up his condition. *Plantar fasciitis: an inflammation of the tissue connecting the heel bone to the toes. Treatments*, she read, *include physical therapy, shoe inserts, steroid injections, and, rarely, surgery.*

"It's a man thing," Marni told her, when Sarah called. "Men don't get headaches, they get migraines. They don't get colds, it's always double pneumonia. So Eli doesn't have sore heels, he's got plantar whatever. Just indulge him."

Sarah had. Over the years, she'd heard her husband talk about his condition so often that her brain automatically shut down at the sound of its name. Then, at a dinner party on the Cape, one of Sarah's mother's friends turned out to be a fellow sufferer. She'd told Eli about the flip-flops she'd started wearing. "They changed my life," she'd said with her hand on her heart. Intrigued, Eli had pulled out his phone and ordered a pair on the spot. The flip-flops, made in China and back-ordered for months after a mention in *Runner's World*, hadn't arrived until March, right before the lockdowns began. They weren't cheap, but they looked that way, a pair of ugly, plastic-soled shoes, gray on the bottom, spongy white on top, with a black strap that went between the wearer's toes. They made the usual flip-flop slapping sound when Eli walked, which might not have been annoying in smaller increments, or at a lower volume, or in the summertime, when the sound was part of the aural landscape of the season. But, in the midst of a pandemic, in a house with hardwood floors, the sound of Eli slap-slapping his way through his days had become maddening, especially because it turned out that Eli was a pacer who walked when he was talking on the phone. From dawn until bedtime, Sarah would hear the *ssh-slap, ssh-slap* sound of his flip-flop'd feet. She'd sit at her desk, back stiff, fingers on the keyboard, her entire posture telegraphing the fact that she was working, or thinking, or busy, or she'd lie on the bed, curled around her book, when she heard his footsteps coming her way.

"Just getting my book!" he'd announce as she'd hunch close to her own book or her phone or her computer screen, trying not to lose her train of thought, her body language silently announcing *Leave me alone.* When the pandemic began, she'd asked him not to interrupt her; to just come and go quietly if she was in the middle of something, and he'd nodded and agreed. Maybe he'd forgotten his pledge, or maybe it ran counter to his nature, but Eli seemed as incapable of not talking to her upon arriving as he did of remembering to wipe out the sink's bowl after he finished shaving. "Just plugging in my phone!" he would call, or "Just grabbing a sweater!" or "Just going out to get Lord Farquaad's food!" Every time her husband came slap-slapping his way into the bedroom, she'd feel her stomach muscles clench and her heart start beating faster and her fingers itch with a desire to slap him. ("Please, you think you've got it bad?" asked Tasha, her assistant, when Sarah had complained on a work Zoom. "I learned that my husband's a circle back guy." She'd lowered her voice to what Sarah thought of as a business-casual baritone. "Uh, Bob, can we circle back on that?" Then Carole, one of the teachers, shared that her husband cracked his knuckles, and Justin, who taught the trombone, confessed to daily bickering with Timothy his sax player husband over where he and Justin could each empty their respective spit valves, and about the reed parings Timothy left on the floor.)

"You don't really think he's cheating, do you?" Marni asked as they turned the corner, crossing the sidewalk where the park became the city.

"I don't know." Sarah felt wretched. "I don't know what I think. Maybe it's not that, but there's something going on."

"If you want my advice—" Marni looked sideways, waiting for Sarah to say that she didn't. When Sarah said nothing, Marni touched her shoulder. "Just ignore it. Whatever he's doing that's driving you nuts, just ignore it. You don't want to end your marriage over the small stuff." She sighed. "Or at all, if you can help it."

Marni was speaking from experience. She'd gone back to work six weeks after the birth of her second daughter and had fallen in love with her new editor, a single man five years younger than she was. It might have been nothing more than an unrequited crush or harmless flirting, except the editor, Jeff, enthusiastically returned Marni's affections. He swore she was his soul mate, the only woman he had loved or could ever love. Marni and Jeff had carried on an affair for six months. Then Marni had gotten pregnant, and, because she believed that she and Jeff were meant to be, she'd told her husband that she was leaving him. Her husband, Jonathan, had begged her to stay, to go to counseling with him, to think of their children. He'd even promised to raise the baby as their own, but Marni was resolute.

"In my defense," she'd say, when she was telling the story—and Marni told the story a lot—"I was hormonal. And exhausted. Jonathan wasn't helping with the girls. And Jeff was promising to marry me at the time." Eventually, Jonathan surrendered and agreed to the divorce. And then, to no one's surprise, once Marni was single, available, and seven months pregnant, Jeff had reconsidered. When Marni emerged from that terrible whirlwind of a year, she had no husband, no boyfriend, a new baby, and barely any job, because when the magazine's publishers learned of the affair, they'd reassigned Jeffrey and demoted Marni, changing her status from staff writer to freelancer, lopping thirty thousand dollars off her salary, and taking away her benefits, too. Jonathan, meanwhile, lost fifteen pounds, acquired a wardrobe of dark-rinse jeans and V-necked cashmere sweaters, and began dating beautiful women in their twenties. Five years later, Marni, now the single mother of three girls, was still struggling to rebuild her life, her savings, and her self-esteem; trying to get back to where she'd been before Hurricane Jeff. She loved her daughters, but she was transparent about how hard it was for her to do alone, and her example was never far from Sarah's mind: *End your marriage and you and your children will suffer.*

Sarah had taken that lesson to heart. Ever since her wedding, she had never come close to thinking about walking away. Eli was a good man. He'd never cheated, or done any of the other objectionable things her friends' husbands had done, like quitting his job and announcing he wanted to become a rodeo clown, or gambling away all of their money, or getting fired and not telling his wife and continuing to put on a suit and tie and leave the house every morning at eight a.m. so she'd think he was still working. Eli had been the foundation upon which she had built her life and her family. And now it was like learning the foundation was made of soap bubbles, like an anchor that had looked substantial so was really just Styrofoam painted to look like iron. The pandemic had been awful. She'd hoped things would change once the vaccines were available and the world went back to something that looked like normal. But nothing had changed. Eli was still distracted and distant. He barely listened when she spoke. When they gathered in the family room to play board games or watch TV, he'd have to be reminded when it was his turn, or he'd get up after twenty minutes and go drifting through their house like a ghost. *A ghost on noisy flip-flops*, Sarah thought.

She'd held on for as long as she could, telling herself that marriages went through rough patches, and that the one she and Eli were currently enduring would end. But finally, in January, during a stretch of days where it felt like the sun never came out after she'd had to listen to Eli give a lecture on the anatomical structures of the tongue, delivered while holding his phone and flip-flopping up and down the hall, she'd decided that she had to do something.

She would have called her brother, who'd already sensed that something was wrong, but poor Sam had troubles enough of his own, and she didn't want to sound churlish or petty, complaining about her husband to a man who'd lost his wife. If her father had been alive, she might have asked his advice, and the idea that she couldn't, that he wasn't just away or unavailable but gone, forever, had hit her again and left her red-eyed and sniffly. So, instead, one morning right after Eli had left the house, Sarah had reached for the bat phone and called her mom.

"Hello?" Veronica had said, sounding slightly out of breath. When the phone had been ringing, Sarah had pictured her mother rooting through one of her tote bag–sized purses, groping for her phone. Sarah and her mother spoke every Friday night, after Shabbat dinner, and two or three afternoons a week, Sarah would dial her mom's number as she walked the boys home from school and let them tell their *safta* about their day. She never called Veronica first thing in the morning.

"Hi, Mom."

"Sarah? What's wrong?"

She hadn't been surprised that all she had to say was hello for her mom to sense that there was trouble. Sarah imagined she'd be the same with her own children, when they were grown and gone.

"Nothing, nothing. Everything's fine," Sarah had said. Her mother waited. "It's just—well. I've been thinking about renting a studio. Just to have a little space."

"A room of one's own," her mother had said, in a noncommittal tone.

"The house is fabulous. I'm so grateful. I'll always be grateful. But, with Ruby and her boyfriend here, and the boys doing virtual school, it's just feeling a little crowded."

Her mother hadn't responded. Sarah had made herself continue. "I think if I had a little space—like a studio—I could move my piano there. That way, I wouldn't bother anyone, and they wouldn't bother me. And I could have some privacy again."

She had waited for her mother to point out that Ruby and Gabe wouldn't stay forever, that the boys would eventually go back to school, and Eli had already returned to his office. She hadn't been sure if Veronica remembered that, in addition to the baby grand piano that had been in the house in Cambridge and was now in Park Slope, Sarah also had a fancy electronic keyboard, a birthday gift from Eli. It sounded almost like a real piano, and it had all kinds of features, allowing her to record herself as she played, or add drums, or bass, or, if she felt inclined, a bossa nova beat. Best of all, she could play it with headphones on.

"Did you ever feel like you needed some space for yourself? Away from us?" she had asked, and swallowed hard. "Away from Dad?"

Sarah had expected an immediate "No." Instead, her mother had sighed. "You don't remember, but before you and Sam were born, I spent a lot of time in New York."

"When you were writing," Sarah had said.

"When I was publishing," Ronnie had said. Sarah wasn't entirely clear why that distinction was important, but before she could ask, Ronnie had said, "Have you talked to Eli? I'm sure he'd get the boys out of the house, if that's what you needed. They're always welcome up here, you know. You are, too." Sarah had heard, or thought she did, the faintest hint of criticism. Her mother, she knew, wanted them to spend their entire summers on Cape Cod, or at least visit more frequently.

"I just—" Sarah had closed her eyes, knowing if she answered, if she said the words out loud, it would all become real. "I just need a little time by myself," she had said, her voice almost a whisper. *Maybe if I go away, I'll remember why I loved him*, she thought.

Her mother had waited, but Sarah had said all she was ready to say. She wasn't going to tell her mother how she felt like she was living with a ghost and not a partner, not a husband or a father, and certainly not a lover, because she couldn't even remember the last time Eli had reached for her in the night, bringing his lips to the back of her neck and kissing the spot just below her ear; the last time they'd played one of their games.

"I hope you're giving Eli a chance. You can't just expect him to guess what's wrong," her mother had finally said. "Men aren't mind-readers. If you don't tell him how you're feeling, he might not be able to figure it out."

Except, once, he could have, Sarah had thought. *He used to listen to me and notice how I was feeling. He used to pay attention. He used to care.* "I've tried to tell him," she had said. Except how could you tell your husband that every single thing about him was annoying you, that his indifference was making you feel like you didn't matter, and that you couldn't remember why you'd wanted to be with him in the first place? "I've tried," Sarah had said. "I have."

"Well," her mom had said. "If it's what you need, you should do it. And don't beat yourself up. From what I've read, there're lots of women locking themselves in their closets, or their bathrooms, or their basement storage units to get a little peace."

That afternoon, Sarah booked a room at a hotel that was an easy walk from the house. That night, after dinner, and the bedtime rituals of kisses and glasses of water and a chapter of *Captain Underpants*, she'd faked a phone call and told Eli that Marni was having a childcare emergency and that she was going over to help. "I'll spend the night if it gets too late," she had told Eli, who'd just nodded without looking up from his phone.

She'd grabbed the bag she'd packed before Eli's arrival from the closet and hurried along the slushy streets, barely feeling the cold air on her cheeks. When she had unlocked the door, pulled off her mask, and taken in the sight of the king-sized bed with its smooth covers and crisp pillowcases, the freshly vacuumed floor, the bottle of water on the bedside table, she had felt something inside of her unclench and loosen, like a too-tight bra that she'd finally unhooked. She had slipped off her shoes, put on her pajamas, washed her face, and brushed (but not flossed) her teeth. Those ablutions completed, she had settled her head on the pillow, closed her eyes, and fallen into the deepest and most peaceful sleep she'd enjoyed in months.

The following week, she had gone on virtual tours of four different apartments, all of them convenient to the music school. The timing had worked in her favor: during the pandemic, people had fled the city in droves. Rents were low, inventory was high, landlords were waiving security deposits. It felt, to Sarah, like the world wanted this to happen. Within a week, she had signed a lease for a beautiful, high-ceilinged studio with a small kitchen and a black-and-white tiled bathroom, and arranged for a contact-free key transfer.

Starting in February, every day or two, instead of taking lunch at her desk, Sarah would go to her new apartment. On the weekends, she'd tell Eli she was meeting Marni for a walk, or going to the music school for a few hours, to work in her office while the building was empty. "Can you handle the boys?" she'd ask, and he'd say, "Of course," in a distracted tone suggesting there'd be a surfeit of screen time in Dexter's and Miles's immediate future. She couldn't bring herself to care. Once she'd reached Manhattan, and turned down the street that led to her new place, she'd feel her pace quickening, her chest loosening until she could take deep, cleansing breaths. She'd unlock the building's heavy front door, climb the three flights of stairs, and stand on the threshold, unmoving, appreciating the emptiness. She would sit on the hardwood floors, in the center of her own four hundred square feet, sometimes with her eyes closed; sometimes looking out the window, or at the blank walls. For an hour or two, she would inhale that stillness, the air that had been breathed by no one but her. She'd buy fresh flowers every few days, extravagant bouquets of hydrangeas or lilies, and set them on the counter of the tiny kitchen. She'd listen to music, recordings of the pieces she'd pushed herself to master as a teenager: Bach's harpsichord concerti, Chopin's nocturnes, Debussy's arabesques. With the music in her ears, she would let herself imagine living here. A single bed, against the wall. A couch, just big enough for her. A television, a table; two barstools at the counter. A different life.

She told no one, not even Marni. A home for one, for her alone. *A room of one's own.* The thought thrilled her and scared her, but as the weeks went on, she found herself more thrilled than scared.

Slowly she began to furnish the place: a single bed, and linens, and pillows. A couch, a table, a television set. She had rented a piano and had it delivered during her lunch hour, telling herself that she wasn't moving her keyboard from home because she didn't want to have to move it back again, not because she didn't want Eli to know what she was doing, and she'd play for hours, filling the empty room with music. She would keep the keys in her pocket, on a heavy fob of scrolled silver in the shape of the letter *S*. During the day, she'd find her fingers seeking the cool silvery surface; tracing the shape of the letter, transmitting the sensation of respite and relief from her skin to her brain. Her heartbeat would slow; the tension in her chest would loosen, and she'd feel a measure of peace, the calmness she needed to go on.

"Call me if you want to talk later." Marni reached down to squeeze Sarah's hand. The sun was fully risen, and the park was emptying out, the bikers and the joggers doing their cooldowns, the sidewalks full of people on their way to work or bringing kids to school. Sarah sighed. It was time to go home.

By the time she'd made it through the front door of the brownstone, whatever peace she'd felt from the exercise and her friend's company had burned away, replaced by the resentment that was constantly present, seething right beneath her skin. Sarah took off her sneakers by the door. She was walking by the living-room couch when something stirred.

"Shit!" she yelped, as the blanket-covered lump rolled over and her brother-in-law's sleep-rumpled head emerged.

"Oh, hey," Ari said, yawning. "Sorry. I had, um, an appointment in Williamsburg last night, and it ran late. Hope it's okay that I crashed here."

Sarah rolled her eyes. She knew exactly what Ari meant by "appointment." She'd already had to tell Eli to speak to him after Dexter had asked her if Ari was a doctor, and when Sarah had said, "No, what made you think that?" Dexter had reported that Ari had told him he'd had a late-night appointment with a lady who'd needed her vitamin D.

"I just hope you're being safe," she said, hating the scolding school-marm's way she sounded.

He gave her a lazy grin and ran one hand through his disheveled hair. "We kept our masks on."

Shaking her head, Sarah walked past him, adding Ari's intrusion to the list of things she'd make Eli answer for. She washed her hands in the kitchen and started up the stairs. She'd meant to walk, but found herself stomping as she approached the bedroom, with her pulse hammering in her throat. *I'm going to say something*, she thought. *I'm going to tell him that if things don't change, he'll have to leave. I can't keep going like this.*

She opened the bedroom door. Eli was in the closet, standing in front of his tie rack, in suit pants and an undershirt. His feet were bare, shoulders were slumped, his posture defeated, and on his face was a look of such aching despair that Sarah's first impulse was to go to him, wrap her arms around him, to hold him and tell him that whatever was wrong would be okay, that they'd figure it out together.

At the sound of her footsteps, Eli turned. She could see him gathering himself, smoothing his face into a semblance of calm. But she'd already seen how miserable he'd looked. Was he sick? Could that be it?

"Eli," she said.

He gave her a rueful look, then turned his face to the floor. In a low voice, he said, "I know."

She stared at him, stunned into silence. "What?" she asked. "You know what?"

"I know Ari's downstairs on the couch." He took a breath. "I know I've been a terrible husband. I know I've been ignoring you. I know ..." His voice cracked. Sarah felt the surprise of that admission hitting her body like pellets of hail. She felt, again, that yearning to cross the room, to take him in her arms and comfort him, but before she could start moving, Eli turned back toward the ties.

"Why?" she asked, her voice sharp. "Why have you

been ignoring me? What's going on?" She crossed the room and put her hand on his shoulder, feeling him stiffen under her touch. "Can't you tell me?"

His shoulders rose as he inhaled. "Not now."

Sarah felt her face get hot. "Why not?"

"I can't," he said, in a leaden voice. She slipped her arm around his waist and leaned against him, inhaling his familiar scent, his comforting warmth. She squeezed him. Eli did not put his arm over her shoulders and squeeze back.

"Just wait until the wedding's over," he said. "We can talk about everything then."

"Are you having an affair?"

His eyes widened in shock. "No," he said, sounding startled that she'd even think it, and his denial sounded heartfelt. But there was something going on. His posture, his expression, all of it looked guilty.

"No?" she asked. He shook his head mutely.

"So what is it, then? I don't understand. Why can't you tell me what's wrong?" she asked. She could hear herself, sounding loud and raw and pained.

"I can't," he said, in a strange, muted voice. "I'm sorry, Sarah. But I just can't."

"Eli." She tried to sound reasonable. "You're my husband. We're a team. You can't just check out of this marriage and not even tell me why!"

Eli didn't respond. She waited, giving him a chance, staring at him, mentally begging him to say something. When it was clear he'd said all that he meant to, she let go of his waist and stepped back. "Eli, I got an apartment," she said in a rush. She saw the words, not him, saw his body sag. "It's just a studio, near the school. I rented a piano. I just—I need—" She waved her hands, angry to the point of speechlessness.

"I know." His voice was a hollow echo of itself. He looked, and sounded, like a pale, thin facsimile of her husband, his voice holding none of the familiar warmth, his expression showing no concern. *Fight for me*, Sarah thought. *Fight for us. Tell me I can't go. Tell me you'll do better. Tell me what's wrong.*

Instead, what Eli said was, "I understand."

"Well, I don't," Sarah snapped.

Instead of an answer, all she got was another sigh. "Do what you have to do."

He selected a tie and left the closet, gathering his shirt and his suit jacket and his wallet. Then he slipped his feet into his goddamn fucking flip-flops and went slap-slapping out of the room without a backward glance, leaving Sarah alone, furious and bewildered, her thoughts right back to where they'd been that morning. *He's having an affair.* That thought was followed, almost immediately, by more despairing ruminations: *But I love him*, and *How can he do this?*, and *Oh, God, what am I going to do now?*

ELI

~~~~~~~~~~

It happened on a Friday night in 1999, when Annette was pregnant and miserable, right after they'd moved back to New York. They'd had a horrible fight. Annette had accused him of sabotaging her birth-control pills in an attempt to force her to have a baby that he knew she never wanted, to live a life she would hate. Eli had looked at her as she'd yelled at him, wondering where the shrieking harpy with matted hair and dark circles under her eyes had come from, and what she'd done with his competent, curious, up-for-anything wife.

"I'm leaving," Annette had screamed. She'd thrown handfuls of clothes into a duffel bag, ignoring Eli's attempts to comfort her. "I'm going to my sister's. Don't call me," she'd said, and slammed the door behind her.

Eli had gone to a bar, with nothing more in mind than having a few beers, watching a ball game, trying to calm down and come up with a plan, even though he was starting to realize he was in an unwinnable situation. All he could do was hope that Annette would look at her baby and fall instantly in love, and just as instantly into happily contented motherhood ... and that was feeling increasingly unlikely. Eli had been on his second lager when he'd seen the woman, standing in a corner, in a black leather jacket and a top so tight he could make out the edge of her lacy bra beneath it. She was gorgeous, lushly curvy, with dark hair falling in waves down her back and dark-red lipstick on her mouth. Eli could see her in profile, lit by the glow of the jukebox, and he'd stared at her, helplessly enthralled. Eventually, the woman turned, as if she'd felt his gaze like a weight on her hair and her body. She'd spun slowly and had given him a saucy smile. Then she came sauntering toward him, hips swinging, until she was close enough that he could smell her perfume, musky and sweet. Annette never wore perfume. Or lipstick. Eli could barely breathe. He loved Annette, he had promised to spend his life with Annette, Annette was having his baby, but, oh, God, this woman. He wanted to devour her, to rip off her clothes and throw her down on the bar.

She looked at him, and he saw, in her eyes, that she knew everything he was feeling. She'd touched his arm, then his knee. "Hi," she'd said, and had run her tongue slowly across her glossy red lips, flashing her white teeth in a smile.

Five minutes later they'd been wrapped around each other in a dark corner by the restrooms. When the woman had slipped her tongue into his mouth, sucking at his lower lip, then biting it lightly, Eli felt like he'd been swept away by a wave of warm honey, slow-moving and sweet and irresistible. He cupped the woman's chin and touched her face. Her skin was so soft, and the smell of her perfume was all around him, and he stopped thinking about his wife, or the baby on the way. *Maybe she's a prostitute*, his mind said, but his thoughts felt foggy and dim, his sensible instincts very far away.

Somehow he'd paid their tabs and gotten the woman out of the bar, down the block, into the lobby of his apartment building. As soon as they were in the elevator, they'd fallen on each other like desperate, starving animals. Eli backed her into a corner and pressed her mouth against his, kissing and kissing her, like her mouth held the last bit of oxygen on earth. He breathed her in, and her mouth held his last breath. He licked at her, tasting her lipstick, and, oh, God, he could feel her body, her breasts pressing against his chest, the soft pressure of her belly and thighs against him. He thought he would die if he couldn't get inside her.

He pulled his mouth free long enough to suck in a breath as the woman gasped, "Don't stop," and wrapped one hand behind his neck, pulling his mouth back down to hers.

When they finally got to his apartment, he'd yanked off her jacket and ripped—literally ripped—the woman's shirt off her body, a thing he'd never done before. Buttons clattered on the floor. Her breasts were warm in his hands, her nipples already hard, as firm and sweet as berries. She tugged his pants open and Eli pushed her back against a wall, and she was wrapping her legs around him, gasping, almost sobbing, one word, over and over. *Yes, yes, yes,* she panted into his open mouth. When he'd tried to pull away, realizing that he didn't have condoms, she'd pulled him right back to her. "Don't worry. I'm safe."

That was when he'd had the briefest instant of clarity, a few seconds when it seemed like he was outside of his own body, looking down at himself, his briefs around his knees and some woman who was not his wife in his arms. "Wait," he'd tried to say. But the woman had taken his hand and pressed his fingers between her legs, against that slick, welcoming channel, and Eli had been lost. He'd gripped her shoulders and slid inside her in one delirious push, surrounding himself in her warmth, thrusting hard and fast, like the world was ending, like this was the last thing he'd ever get to do.

Afterward, they ended up on the floor, Eli flat on his back and gasping, the woman curled against his side.

"So what's your name?" she asked, in a lazy, amused voice.

Eli was hit with a wave of such paralyzing guilt, such awful, utter, all-consuming blackness, that he'd been, for a moment, unable to breathe. He'd felt his chest spasm, and he'd managed to force out a single moan.

"What?" asked the woman, rolling toward him. Her dark hair hung over her shoulder. "What is it?"

Eli couldn't speak. He managed to shake his head, a negating side to side.

"No, what?" asked the woman. A hint of a smile curved her full lips. "No, you don't have a name, or No, you don't want to tell me?"

"I've never done anything like this before. I'm married," Eli croaked. "I have a wife. She's—"

". . . not here," said the woman before he could say *pregnant*. "And as far as I'm concerned, it's her fault, for letting someone as handsome as you walk around on his own."

Handsome. Unbelievably, Eli felt himself stirring again, as the woman slid her hand across his chest, then down, down, down.

"I can't," he muttered.

"You already did," the woman pointed out. She removed her hand—*Don't*, Eli kept himself from gasping, *don't stop.* She got to her feet and stretched, with her arms extended over her head, standing on the tips of her toes. Her back arched, thrusting her breasts up. From the floor, he could see every inch of her: her toenails, painted dark red; the juicy, rounded curves of her calves and thighs and belly; the soft black curling hair between her legs; her breasts, tipped with sweet dark red nipples; and, oh, God, she had hair under her arms, gorgeous curling thickets of hair. Eli felt his mouth fill with saliva as he got to his feet. He reached out and touched her there, stroking with a single fingertip. She was so soft. He bet she smelled delicious. He wanted to bury his face there, to sniff, to lick, to kiss, to bite.

She looked up at him from underneath her long, curling lashes. "You got a bed in this place?"

He managed a nod. She arched an eyebrow.

"Think you could show me?"

He nodded again, then bent and scooped her, every warm, soft, sweet, fragrant, delectable, irresistible inch of her, into his arms. And if the first time had been incredible, the second time was a revelation.

The hair under her arms and between her legs was just as soft as Eli knew it would be, and its smell was the smell of sex itself, dirty and sweaty and intoxicating. Even better was the way this woman talked, murmuring the hottest, filthiest, most explicit commands in Eli's ear, telling him what she was going to do to him, asking him to do things, telling him how all of it felt. *Lick your finger. Now slide it inside of me, slow. Ohhh, like that, just like that.* Her eyes had glinted with a devilish light as she'd grabbed his wrist, pulled his hand toward her mouth, and slipped his slick finger between her lips, sucking her own juices off Eli's skin. *Deeper*, she said. *Harder. More.*

Eli thought his head was going to explode.

They'd had sex—no, Eli thought savagely, they'd fucked—three times that night. The last time he'd taken her from behind, on her hands and knees, with the warm weight of her ass smacking loudly against his thighs as he thrust and thrust. "I feel like an animal," he managed to gasp. The woman turned her head, looking at him over her shoulder. Her white teeth glinted as she smiled.

"Baby, we're all animals," she'd said. Then she'd pushed herself upright, up on her knees, with Eli still inside her. *Yeah, like that, like that. Faster. Faster faster faster. I want to come while you're inside me.*

After the third time, they'd fallen onto the sex-stiffened sheets, and both of them had slept. When he'd opened his eyes again, it was after eight o'clock, the apartment filled with early-morning light.

Eli stared at the clock. In that first moment of awareness, he hadn't remembered what he'd done, and his first conscious thought was to wonder why his thighs felt so sore. Then he looked down and saw the woman, still asleep, hair tumbled over Annette's pillow. Guilt crashed over him like a collapsing building. He must have made some kind of noise, loud enough to wake the woman, who yawned and stretched and slowly opened her eyes.

"Good morning, handsome," she said. Then she'd dropped her eyes, from his face to his chest to his morning erection. "Mmm," she'd hummed. The sheet had slipped down to show the curve of her breast. When she saw where he was looking, she'd brought her hand down, cupping her own breast, pinching her nipple, making it hard. She slipped her other hand under the covers, gliding it along his thigh until she found his erection and squeezed. "Looks like somebody's glad to see me."

"No," he said, and sat up straight. "No, you have to go."

She'd looked at him curiously for a moment. Then those lush lips had frowned, and her pretty face settled itself into a mask of indifference. She'd swept out of the bed, curvy bottom flashing, bending down to snatch her clothes off the floor and sashay into the bathroom, slamming the door behind her. Eli got dressed and collected two hundred dollars—all the cash he had. He'd never paid for sex, and had no idea how these transactions were conducted. When the woman emerged, he said, "We didn't—I mean, we never discussed—" Wordlessly, he thrust the money at her. She looked at it, then at him, indifference replaced by hurt.

"I'm not a prostitute," she snapped.

"I'm sorry," he blurted, feeling embarrassment in addition to shame. "A gift, then." He held the folded stack of bills. She looked at him again, then snatched them, slipping them into her pocket, and walked out the door with her head held high.

Eli had gone to the bathroom, where he stood under scalding-hot water until there was no hot water left. Then he stood under the cold water until he was shivering and his lips were blue. He forced himself to endure it, resting his head against the tiles as the icy water beat down.

His own father had cheated on his mother, endlessly, almost compulsively. Eli had sworn to himself that he'd be different; a different kind of man, a different kind of husband. And yet there he'd been, not even three months after his own wedding, buried between a strange woman's legs. He was so disgusted with himself he wanted to vomit, or scrub until his skin came off. *Never again,* he told himself. *Annette can never find out, and I'll never do this again.* He'd called Annette's sister's number three times that day. No one picked up.

And then, that night, somehow, he found himself back at the bar. The woman was waiting for him, as if they'd made plans to meet; standing by the jukebox with hair cascading down her back in those glorious waves, that sweet dark-red lipstick on her lips. As he walked toward her, she gave him a wink and a slow, knowing smile. She wore a dress that night, a tube of jersey fabric that clung to every inch of her, riding the curves of hip and waist and bosom. "No buttons," she'd explained, as they grabbed at each other in the elevator. "I can't have you wrecking every piece of clothing that I own." Five minutes after they'd walked through the door the woman was lying back on the bed and Eli was kneeling on the floor with her legs resting on his shoulders and his face between her legs. She tasted like honey and salt, Eli thought as he licked her, like candied apples and the sea.

"What's your name?" he asked, after she'd thrashed and keened her way through her first two orgasms.

She'd opened her eyes, and he'd watched the calculations that were surely taking place behind them. "Jane," she'd said very softly. "Call me Jane." It was clearly an alias. Maybe she, too, had something to hide, a boyfriend or a husband at home. Eli waited for her to ask his name again, or even to make a joke about how he could be Tarzan, but instead, she'd worked herself down the bed, down his body, and then her mouth was full, and he wouldn't have been able to answer her, even if he'd wanted to.

For the next two nights, they were together. They did not exchange histories, or confidences; they didn't talk about their pasts or their futures. He didn't know where she lived, or how old she was, or what she did for a living, and she didn't ask him a single thing about himself. It was nothing but chemistry, the alchemy of bodies coming together in a seemingly unstoppable way.

On the third morning, the last morning, he'd propped himself up on his elbow and looked down at her. Her skin was lit gold by the morning sun. Her full lips were parted, each exhalation stirring the fine hairs on her forearm as she breathed. She was gorgeous, Eli thought; the most beautiful woman he'd ever touched.

She opened her eyes and gave him that now familiar smile, but for once, for the first time, Eli didn't feel an answering surge from his traitorous body. The fever had broken; the infection was over. His voice was steady when he spoke.

"I can't see you again. I'm sorry."

Jane had stretched, one long, languorous shudder working its way from her curled toes to her fingertips. She had gotten out of bed, gathered her things, and walked toward his door, hips swaying their clockwork sway. At the door, she'd turned and winked at him, a see-you-tonight kind of wink. But Eli had finally found his strength. He hadn't gone back to the bar that night. Instead, he'd taken the sheets and pillowcases to the laundry and washed them in hot water, and cleaned the apartment, scrupulously wiping down every surface the woman had touched. The next day, after class, he'd gone out and gotten dozens of yellow tulips. Annette's favorite. Then he'd driven to Annette's sister's house, handed his wife the flowers, told her that he loved her, and brought her home.

"How are you?" he'd asked as she'd clambered into the car.

Instead of answering, she'd just given an unhappy shrug.

Two weeks later, Eli walked outside, on his way to the subway, and to his morning's first class. Jane had been sitting on the park bench across the street, wearing her leather jacket and a sad look on her face.

Eli's heart dropped. A part of him wanted to run. Instead, he made himself walk toward her, schooling his face into stillness. Her dark hair was gathered in a limp ponytail. Her nails and her lips were unpainted, and there were dark smudges under her eyes.

"What's going on?" Eli asked, his voice brusque, almost rude. She looked up at him steadily. He felt his heart sink even further.

"I'm pregnant."

Of course, he thought. All the times they'd had sex, for three nights, in pretty much every position, on basically every available surface of the apartment, including the bathroom counter and the breakfast bar. There'd only been that first, brief conversation about birth control. *Don't worry. I'm safe*, the woman had said and Eli had believed her. The bagel he'd eaten that morning, in his sunny kitchen, waiting for the water to boil so he could bring his wife the tea she hated but had to drink instead of coffee, felt like it was going to erupt out of his mouth. Had he really thought he'd get away with this? Had he actually imagined there would be no consequences for cheating, for having incredible, illicit sex with another woman while his wife was unhappy and suffering?

The woman's voice was hard-edged when she spoke. "And don't even ask if it's yours, because I haven't been with anyone else."

Eli hadn't planned on asking. He pinched the bridge of his nose with his thumb and forefinger, scrubbed one hand through his hair, and forced himself to breathe as he imagined Annette finding out, and leaving, and taking the baby with her, leaving him stuck, raising a child with this woman about whom he knew nothing, not even her last name.

"I'm not going to keep it," the woman said coolly.

Eli felt the breath whoosh out of him. The woman's mouth had a bitter twist. "So don't worry. You don't have to look like your whole life just went down the shitter."

He nodded. "What do you—how much is—"

"Six hundred dollars," she said.

Eli swallowed hard. Part of him wondering if she was scamming him, if this was what she did—sleep with strange men for entire weekends and then show up telling them that she was pregnant. But another part saw those dark shadows beneath her eyes, saw the ragged, chewed thumbnail on her right hand, and believed her. And knew that six hundred dollars was a small price to pay.

"Wait here."

He'd jogged into the lobby and taken the elevator up to the apartment, calling some excuse in the direction of the bedroom, where Annette was still in bed. In the kitchen, he'd rifled through the mail until he'd found the check his grandparents had sent him and Annette for their wedding, and another from an aunt in Arizona. The woman had walked with him to the bank branch, waiting on the sidewalk while he went inside. "Hundreds okay?" asked the teller, and Eli had nodded, watching as she'd slipped the crisp bills into a white envelope. He and Annette had talked about buying a new couch with some of the wedding money, hoping to replace the sagging, cat-clawed Ikea sofa that the previous tenant had left behind. Maybe she wouldn't remember, Eli thought.

Back outside, he handed the woman the envelope. She folded it in half and slipped it into her purse.

"Do you want me to come with you?" he asked. "When you have it done?"

She'd looked startled. Then she looked sad. "No." Her voice was glum, her posture defeated. "I'll take care of it at home. Back in California." She made a sad, scoffing noise and tugged at the end of her ponytail as she shook her head. "New York hasn't been so good to me."

Eli felt another stab of guilt. It wasn't the city, it was him. Him, and probably other men, who'd treated her like she was disposable, an object for their pleasure. "I'm sorry. Really, I am." He'd pulled one of his business cards out of his pocket—he'd just gotten them, for when he'd start seeing patients at the school's clinic—then the pen he'd taken from the bank. He wrote his home number on the back of the card.

"Here," he told the woman. He'd handed it over and watched as she'd read it. "That's me. Eli Danhauser. That's my number, if you need to reach me." He'd tried to smile. "Or if you need your teeth cleaned."

"Thank you." She put the card in her purse, gave him a wavering smile, and touched his hand. "You're a good guy."

I'm not, he thought. *I definitely am not.*

She'd turned, walking away, the ruffled red skirt of her dress swishing against her thighs. Eli watched her go, feeling almost faint again as he thought, *I got away with it. I think I actually got away with it.*

And after that, Eli had been good. He'd kept to his promise never to stray again. As the summer went on, he'd go hours without thinking of Jane, or whatever her real name was. Then hours became days, days became weeks, then months of not thinking of what he'd done. And then, on the subway, he'd see a flash of long, wavy hair or he'd see a woman in a red dress with a leather jacket on the sidewalk, or, standing in line at the coffee shop, he'd catch a whiff of a familiar perfume, floral and musk, and the memories would come slamming back into his body, leaving him feeling battered and breathless. Maybe he'd been possessed, he'd think, shaking his head, or maybe it had just been something he'd needed to get out of his system, a poison he'd had to expel before he could settle into being a good husband, a good father, a good man.

Annette had left when Ruby was just six months old. Eli had been a single father, and then he'd met Sarah, and had fallen in love, and they'd become a family of three, then four, then five. He'd blinked, and had become, somehow, middle-aged, with silver hairs in his beard and a bald spot he couldn't see but, still, knew was there. He'd lived decades of his life believing he'd gotten away with those few nights of madness. He'd been thoughtlessly happy, with no sense of a sword hanging over his head. Then the pandemic had arrived, and Ruby had come home. And she'd brought Gabe.

Eli would never forget the afternoon he'd met his daughter's intended. He'd been coming down the stairs to make himself a snack, and he'd walked into the kitchen and seen a dark, sleek head leaning against his daughter's curls. The young man had looked up, and he'd had exactly the same slant to his eyebrows that Eli remembered, precisely the same tilt to the corners of his lips, and the same wide, dark eyes. For a moment, it was like time had spun itself backward, and he was twenty-nine again, gangly and clueless, a married man, but still mostly a boy. Eli stood, paralyzed, in front of the refrigerator. He could barely move, could barely breathe.

"Daddy, this is Gabe," Ruby had said. "He's going to be staying with us for a while."

The boy had walked over to him, hand extended. Even his fingernails were the same shape as the nails of that long-ago woman. A dozen tiny, ineffable things that all added up to a single, inescapable conclusion.

The mug that Eli had grabbed, one with the words WORLD'S BEST DAD hand-painted on its side, fell out of his hands to shatter on the terra-cotta floor. Ruby had made that mug for him, years ago. Sarah had taken her to one of the paint-your-own-pottery shops that had been popular back then, to help her make a Father's Day gift for Eli. *Hashtag irony*, Eli thought dimly.

"Oops!" he said, his voice too loud.

"Oh, no!" Ruby had cried, and bent down to gather the shards. Gabe had given Eli a friendly smile. Eli made himself shake the boy's hand.

"So, Gabe, where are you from?"

"Los Angeles," he said.

I'll take care of it at home. Back in California. Eli kept himself motionless, remembering that Jane, or whatever her name really was, had been set on having an abortion. He couldn't be sure. Even if, through some terrible coincidence or joke of Fate, this boy really was her son, that didn't necessarily mean that Eli was his father.

"And how are you finding New York City?"

"I love it here." The boy gave his daughter a fond look. "It hasn't broken my heart yet, Ruby says."

Ruby took Gabe's hand and came to stand beside him, so that they were hip to hip and thigh to thigh. Eli swallowed hard. "Gabe did *The Bacchae* with me last fall. And he sings in an indie rock band."

Eli nodded. Eli smiled. He felt like a windup toy, going through the motions he had to make, behaving the way he knew he had to behave.

"So are you a senior? Like Ruby?"

"Yep. Not at Tisch, though. I'm in CAS. The College of Arts and Sciences."

"So you're twenty-one?"

"Yep." He gave Ruby a squeeze. "Ruby's five months older than I am. My old lady," he said, and kissed Ruby's forehead, right above her glasses.

Eli cast his mind backward, scrolling through the calendar, adding nine months to the date of his hookup, trying to remember precisely how pregnant Annette had been when she'd gone storming off to her sister's.

"And you're a native Californian?" he asked Gabe.

"Yep. Born and raised."

"Any brothers or sisters? What do your parents do?"

"Daddy," said Ruby, "can we skip the third degree? Or at least save it 'til dinnertime?"

"It's fine," said Gabe, with an easy smile. An easy, familiar smile. "No brothers or sisters. It's always just me and my mom."

"And what does she do?"

"Dad." Ruby's tone had sharpened.

"She likes to sing," Gabe said. "But she's a nurse." Singing and nursing meant nothing to Eli, who could remember exactly how Jane had tasted, how she'd smelled, the filthy things she'd whispered in his ear while they were in bed, the tiny cooing noises she'd made, but hadn't bothered to ask about her job or her hobbies.

He made conversation with his daughter and this boy, all the while with that numbness spreading through his body, up to his hairline and out to his fingertips. As soon as he could escape, he'd gone to his office, opened his laptop and started searching for Gabe. Gabe's account was private, but, later that night, he approved

Eli's friend request. Eli scrolled through hundreds of pictures—Gabe at college, Gabe at home, Gabe at parties, on beaches, on stage—until he finally located a picture of Gabe with a woman he presumed was Gabe's mother. It was a shot from a high school graduation ceremony. Gabe, in cap and gown, had his arm around the woman Eli was almost positive was the one he remembered from long ago.

Almost but not completely positive. Her hair was shorter, her face looked older . . . but was it still, essentially, the same face? A big part of him said *yes*. A small, increasingly desperate-sounding part, said *no*. Another part of him still clung to the hope that even if his mother was Jane, Gabe probably had a different father . . . and the biggest part, shrill and terrified, was saying that he had to find out if Gabe and Ruby were using reliable birth control, because Ruby getting pregnant would be a nightmare, but Ruby getting pregnant with a boy who turned out to be her half-brother would be a tragedy beyond all imagination. Another part, a cool, mocking part, had questions. Like, had Eli really imagined he'd gotten away with it? Had he actually thought his sin would go unpunished? Well, the joke was on him. He thought of something that he'd once heard Ruby say: Karma might not always be fast, but that bitch is always on time. And now she'd sprung her trap. Eli would be forced not only to confess to his long-ago transgression, but also to break his daughter's heart. He could imagine the look on her face, her eyes wounded behind her glasses. *You cheated on my mom?* And Sarah. What would Sarah think of him when she found out? *I think we need some time apart*, he could imagine her saying, her voice cool. She'd turn away from him, leaning forward, so that her hair would obscure her face. *I think you should move out for a while.* He'd lose his daughter. His wife. His home. Everything.

Eli plodded through the rest of the year, numb and shamed and frozen. Part of him—most of him—argued, persuasively, that Gabe couldn't be his. Gabe's mother's name was Rosa, not Jane, and if Eli actually was Gabe's father, Gabe would have been born six weeks early (of course, Eli couldn't think of a subtle way to ask Gabe if he'd been born prematurely. Ruby was already suspicious of all the invasive, personal questions he'd asked). Part of him thought that the worst was true, that he'd been the one to get Gabe's mother pregnant and that, instead of an abortion, she'd had a baby. In this tormented, divided state, one part of his brain insisting that it couldn't be true and another part whispering that it was, Eli existed through endless days and even longer nights. He made conversation and ordered groceries; he washed dishes and folded laundry while he collected the evidence, piece by piece, evidence that, maddeningly, wasn't enough to prove anything. He learned that Gabe's mother had briefly lived in New York, trying to make it as a singer when she'd been young. "She didn't have a lot of support," Gabe said. Gabe had been born in California, although whether his mom had gotten pregnant there or in New York, Gabe couldn't say (and Ruby had shrieked at Eli for even asking. "Dad, how is that possibly any of your business?").

"Yes, Ruby's on the Pill," Sarah had told him when he'd finally brought himself to ask. "No worries there." Frowning, she'd said, "Do you think we should make Gabe sleep in one of the boys' rooms after all?" Eli shook his head. *Too late for that*, he thought.

He tried to tell himself that young love hardly ever lasted. Once the disease loosened its grip and the world opened and Ruby and Gabe realized that there were other people in it, reality would wake them up (with a hard slap to the face, Eli thought, and not a kiss), and they'd figure out that they were too young to promise each other forever.

Then the vaccines came. The schools and the offices opened, closed, opened again, as the world stutter-stepped toward its new normal. Instead of breaking up, Ruby and Gabe moved in together, leaving Eli to spend most nights sleepless, staring at the ceiling, one part hoping and praying that his daughter wasn't lying in bed next to her half-brother; another part saying that he just needed to be patient, and that eventually they'd break up, and a third part, cool and smirking, telling Eli that he was well and truly fucked, that he'd skated under karma's notice for a good long while and now he'd finally be getting what was coming to him.

RONNIE

~~~~~

So you're sure?" asked Paul Norman, the real estate agent, as he re-capped his pen and put it in his breast pocket. Paul's hair was more silver than light-brown these days, and his tanned face had seams around the eyes and mouth, but he was just as handsome as he'd been almost forty years ago, when he'd sold her and Lee their summer place.

"I'm sure," Ronnie replied. "I love it here, but it's just too much house for me."

Paul nodded. Ronnie had already given him the tour—the new decks and hot tub, the new outdoor shower, the guesthouse. He'd made notes and snapped pictures, murmuring to himself as he worked. From her spot on the couch in the living room, Ronnie watched as he walked to the windows and stood there, in his white linen shirt and light-blue pants, with his hands in his pockets, looking down at the water. The sun was just starting to set, painting the sky tangerine and saffron, limning Paul in a haze of gold. That had always been her favorite thing, walking up to the third floor just as the sun was setting, raising the blinds to watch its show.

From the look on his face, Paul had found it just as enthralling as she had. "This view," he said. "It never gets old."

"No," Ronnie said quietly. "It never does."

Paul nodded at the couch, and the stack of books on the coffee table. "This must be your spot, right?"

"I read here," said Ronnie. "In the mornings, and then when the sun goes down." That was one of her favorite places, but she also loved the little desk in the pantry, where, beneath a shelf full of cookbooks, she played solitaire on her laptop and paid her bills. She loved her bed; the way she could lie there and hear the ocean through the windows, and the outdoor shower, with the cutouts in its door that let her stand under the spray and catch glimpses of the sea.

Her eyes were stinging. She turned away, hoping Paul wouldn't notice, and was relieved when he flipped to a fresh page on his pad and pretended to be busy. "I don't suppose you remember when you had the roof done?" he'd asked.

Ronnie did. She gave him the date, and told him about the neighborhood association, the home-alarm system, and the septic tank, and accepted his condolences on Lee's death. "I know we sent something—"

"Olive oils and vinegars from Atlantic Spice," Ronnie said. "They were lovely."

"But I wanted to tell you in person. Your husband was one of the good guys."

"Yes." Ronnie swallowed hard. "He was." She cleared her throat. "I usually have a glass of wine right about now." This wasn't true—Ronnie had never developed a taste for the stuff, and, on the rare occasions that she drank alone, she went straight to the tequila—but she wanted to be a good hostess. "Would you like one?"

Paul gave her a smile. "If you're offering—"

She went to the kitchen to find a bottle and collect two glasses. While she was pouring, Paul walked along the shelves that lined the living-room wall, inspecting the rows of books, eventually finding two that she'd written. Ronnie cringed, the way she always did when confronted with the evidence of her previous life. The books' covers looked dated, the fonts out of fashion, the illustrated covers gaudy, the foiled titles garish. Paul picked up one, then the other, and hefted them in his hands.

"Can I ask you a question?"

She nodded, knowing what was coming.

"Why'd you stop writing?" he asked.

Ronnie gave what she hoped looked like an indifferent shrug and kept her tone light. "Ran out of stories." That wasn't the truth, and she hadn't ever stopped writing. Just publishing. And she'd never told another living soul why.

Veronica Levy had grown up in Boston, the daughter of a bank manager and a stay-at-home mom who lived a quiet, middle-class life in a quiet, middle-class suburb. She understood, from a very early age, that suburban respectability was attainable and desirable. Fame was not. While her high school classmates were sneaking out of their houses to go to rock shows at the Avalon or the Tea Party, when they were wailing into hairbrushes in front of their bathroom mirrors, imagining themselves as famous singers, Ronnie was happy to stay home, sitting in their knotty-pine-paneled den, watching TV with her parents. While her sister was rolling joints on top of her guitar case and taping an almost life-sized poster of Eric Clapton to the wall of the bedroom they shared, Ronnie was quietly nurturing other dreams—different, but just as impractical. Veronica Levy wanted to be a writer.

Not a famous writer, insofar as such things existed. The famous female writers Ronnie knew of came in two categories. There were the poets—the depressives and the suicides. Then there were glamorous bestselling novelists like Rona Jaffe and Jacqueline Susann, who went on talk shows to trade barbs with Philip Roth. Veronica could not see herself in either category. Her ambitions were more modest and included staying alive. She would publish short stories in literary quarterlies, and maybe even *The New Yorker*. She'd also get her PhD so she'd be able to support herself as a professor. Combined, these two pursuits would guarantee her a quiet, contemplative, academic life; a life spent in the company of stories and storytellers, in the land of language and words. It was all she wanted; all she'd wanted since her fifth-grade teacher had read her class "The Road Not Taken" by Robert Frost, and every word, every pause, every image, had echoed through her and made her heart feel like a struck gong.

Her parents didn't know what to make of her. The Levys had taken pains to give their girls the recommended allowance of art and culture. They had a subscription to the Boston Symphony, and they dutifully brought Suzanne and Veronica to the city's museums. Once a year, there was a trip to New York City for a Broadway show and the Museum of Natural History, but the idea of a child making a living at the arts was utterly foreign, and more than a little frightening.

Ronnie had gone to Smith, where her parents had allowed her to major in English ("she can always pick up a teaching certificate," she overheard her mother tell her dad). After she graduated and announced her intention to pursue a PhD in literature, her parents had exchanged a glance. "Ronnie, are you sure that's practical?" her mom had asked gently.

"I'll teach," she told them, and watched their faces

sag, almost comically, with relief. Those expressions warned her to say nothing more. Better not to tell them about the handful of stories she'd placed in the literary quarterlies and chapbooks and the small magazines, the rejection letters she was already beginning to collect from *Harper's* and *The Atlantic*. Better not to tell them how she dreamed of publishing a book of poems, or a short-story collection, or even a novel, and making her living as a writer.

By the time she was twenty-five and had completed her master's, Ronnie had been rejected by the editors of every prestigious publication still in existence. A few of them took the time to include encouraging notes along with the "Sorry, but this isn't right for us" form letters, and it was enough to keep her going. In her apartment in Cambridge, she piled them all up, all the rejection letters, attached to all the poems and stories she'd written over the years, the ones where she'd tried to sound like John Cheever and the ones where she'd tried to sound like John Updike and the ones where she'd tried to sound like Kurt Vonnegut or Raymond Carver, only Jewish, or Philip Roth or Saul Bellow, only female.

The summer after she completed her dissertation, on the tension between atheism and a yearning for God in the works of the British poet and novelist Stevie Smith, Ronnie put her stories—hundreds, maybe thousands, of typed pages!—in a plastic milk crate. She put the milk crate in her closet, and gently shut the closet door. Then she pulled out the two-hundred-page lined notebook she'd bought at the drugstore and, in neat cursive, she began to write the story of two sisters, a story loosely based on her grandmother Shirley, and her grandmother's sister, her great-aunt Anya, and their life as immigrants in

America. Her plan was to complete the book, then pay someone to type it, but before that happened, she went on a first date with one of her sister's boyfriend's buddies, a shy, thoughtful law student named Lee Weinberg.

They'd gone to the movies—a double feature of *Jaws* and *Rosemary's Baby*—then out for dinner at a hole-in-the-wall restaurant that served Szechuan food so hot it made your eyes water. "You order," Lee said, so Ronnie got them dumplings, glistening and fried; crispy, salty egg rolls; and a dish called four-cup chicken, studded with red peppers. Lee's glasses fogged up after his first bite, and his forehead started to sweat, but he kept going, gamely. Ronnie was impressed.

"Suzanne tells me you're a writer," Lee said.

"Aspiring," said Ronnie, and patted her lips. Lee poured more tea from the metal teapot into her cup. Casually, he said, "You know, my aunt's a literary agent."

Ronnie's heart began to beat faster. She hadn't known that. Suddenly, Lee Weinberg was looking a lot more appealing, steamy glasses or not. "Really?"

"In New York City." He named several reputable writers his aunt represented, and asked, "What's your book about?"

When she told him—two sisters, their marriages, and, eventually, their daughters and sons; the tension between tradition and modernity, the old world and the new, Lee listened while attempting to maneuver a dumpling onto his plate. After his third try at grasping it with his chopsticks, he'd shrugged, stabbed it through its center with one chopstick's tip, and plunked it in the dipping sauce. "What books would you compare it to?" He smiled, showing even white teeth. "I know that's a question my aunt always asks."

Ronnie ran her fingers over the tablecloth, thinking that this was where things got tricky. As much as she'd wanted to be a respected, literary writer, she was starting to suspect that she was something else. "It's commercial," she'd said, her voice low, as if she was confessing something terrible. "Like Jacqueline Susann, or Judith Krantz." Her grad school classmates would have laughed, or denied knowing who those writers were, even if they privately devoured those sprawling, dramatic, breathlessly plotted books, hiding the cheap paperback covers behind more respectable fare.

Ronnie had never set out to write that kind of book, even though she'd happily read dozens of them, along with horror and romance and mysteries and every other kind of fiction. She'd simply failed at writing the kind of book she thought she'd wanted to write, the kind the critics would appreciate and future English majors would someday study. Attempting to change the kind of voice in which you wrote, or the subjects that interested you, she'd finally decided, was like trying to change your blood type. Instead of trying to turn herself into the kind of writer she would never be, she had decided to write in her own voice and tell the story that kept talking to her, urging her on; the one that made her both a writer and a reader, eager to see what would happen next.

Lee Weinberg spooned fried rice onto his plate. "Would you like me to ask my aunt if she'd meet with you?"

Ronnie considered. How would she feel if Lee's aunt rejected her? How beholden to him would she be if, somehow, it did work out, and his aunt took her on as client and actually sold her book to a publisher? How would she feel if she didn't try at all?

"Yes," she said. "I'd be very grateful."

The next day, Ronnie went into her closet and gathered the short stories that had garnered the most encouraging rejection letters. She sent them to Lee's aunt, along with a note introducing herself, and explaining that she'd also written a novel. Two weeks later, Alice Weinberg called, inviting her to the city. Ronnie tucked the notebook that held the only copy of her now-completed novel into her handbag. She took a train from Boston to New York City, and walked uptown to Alice's office in Midtown Manhattan, across from St. Patrick's Cathedral. For the length of the trip, she'd readied herself for the rejection she was certain was coming. She only hoped the woman would be encouraging, maybe offering suggestions for how to improve her work, or other places she could submit it. Still, when she'd found herself in the middle-aged woman's office, sitting on the other side of her desk, after she'd glimpsed her short stories sitting in a neat stack, she couldn't keep her heart from swooping madly, or from sinking, precipitously, when Alice Weinberg leaned forward and said, "May I speak frankly?"

"Of course." Ronnie had worn her best dress for the meeting, a peasant-style frock in a red and gold paisley print, with an empire waist and dangly ties at the collar. The dress had felt fine back in Boston, only now, compared to Alice's chic black dress, it looked gaudy. Plus she realized that the sleeves had been made for a woman with a more delicate frame, and the elastic at their ends was biting into her forearms and leaving dents around her wrists.

As Ronnie tugged at first one cuff, then the other, Alice rested one hand—manicured fingernails with a diamond solitaire, gold bracelets gently clinking together on an unmarked wrist—atop Ronnie's short stories. "These are fine, and you're definitely a writer. Your prose is very clear. Workmanlike. In a good way," she'd added, even though her lip had curled—unconsciously, Ronnie was sure—as she spoke that word "workmanlike." "But I don't feel like any of these have your heart in them." She'd looked at Ronnie, her expression not especially hopeful. "Lee mentioned a novel? Why don't you tell me about that?"

Looking back, Ronnie would never know what gave her the nerve to hand over the notebook. Maybe it was the compliment, the words "you're definitely a writer," from someone who could say so with authority. The praise, even following so closely on the heels of criticism, left her feeling like she was flying.

"It's a first draft. It's really rough," she said, almost stammering, as Alice leafed through the pages.

"Tell me about it. Give me the pitch in a sentence or two."

Ronnie felt whatever courage she'd briefly conjured slipping away. The notebook looked like something a sixth-grade girl would scribble on in the cafeteria, not something the almost-graduate of a prestigious academic program would produce. It wasn't even typed! The longer Ronnie stared at it, the more she began to feel like a fraud. Worse: a fraud who'd handed over some essential part of herself—a piece of her heart, a chunk of her liver—and needed to get it back if she was going to survive.

With a great effort, she stilled her fidgeting hands and started to speak. "It's about two sisters, how they grow up, their marriages, and the different paths their lives take. It's the story of two Jewish girls becoming American women." There was more to the book than that—readers would meet their parents, in flashbacks, as they made their way out of their respective shtetls, toward Berlin and one another, in addition to the sisters' daughters, the generation to inhabit the new world— but the part readers would remember (assuming, someday, there'd be readers) was the two young women, the men they loved, the lives they built.

Alice gave her a polite smile, slipping the notebook into a gorgeous leather satchel that Ronnie knew probably cost more than a month's rent back home. Ronnie thanked her for her time and made a hasty retreat. A week later, Ronnie was blow-drying her hair when Alice called. Wrapped in a towel, her hair hanging damp on her shoulders, Ronnie clutched the receiver, hardly believing what she was hearing.

"No, really, Veronica. I loved it. I couldn't put it down! I have some notes, of course. But that's totally normal. I'd like you to do a polish and then I'll read it again, but bottom line I think what you have here is extremely commercial, and . . ." She paused. Ronnie held her breath. "I really think I can sell it."

"Okay," Ronnie had said. She had no idea what, exactly, she was agreeing to. The only thing she knew for sure was the way her classmates and her professors would sneer at the word "commercial." *Oh well*, she thought. Maybe she'd get an advance, and that would insulate her from their scorn.

Two weeks later, she was once again on a train to New York City, this time in business class instead of coach. Her agent—two words Ronnie had been slipping into every sentence she could—had paid for the ticket. Alice was that confident that she'd be able to sell the book Ronnie had agreed to call *The Summer Sisters* (Summer being the surname that Rosie, the fictional matriarch, uses to replace Shulevitz when she reaches New York City).

Lee had come to the station to see her off. He looked her over, in the new clothes she'd bought for the occasion: a gray fedora, a pair of lavender-colored suede boots, impractical and lovely; high-waisted, men's-style trousers, a button-down white blouse with a patterned vest on top. "This is a new look," he said, in a tone that was mostly approving, and slightly puzzled.

Ronnie didn't tell him that the clothes were less an outfit and more of a costume, a disguise. Which felt appropriate, insofar as she felt herself disguised as a novelist, pretending to be a thing that she really was not. She leaned forward to kiss Lee goodbye. She could feel him holding her; wanting to keep her there, lingering on the platform; hoping she'd kiss him again. All the while, the percolating, buzzing excitement inside of her was propelling her forward; urging her to hurry onto the train, to get moving, to get to New York City as quickly as she could before someone else claimed her prize.

Alice had reserved her a room at the Algonquin, which delighted Veronica. She imagined Dorothy Parker sitting at the bar each time she walked past it. What followed was a dreamlike, bewildering, joyful three-day blur of meetings in offices at publishing houses and long, boozy lunches, drinks and dinners with editors who praised Ronnie's talent and called her a genius and promised her that her novel would be a huge bestseller, that they'd need to build bigger warehouses to store all of the copies of her books. "They're exaggerating," Ronnie said to Alice, as they took a Town Car back to Ronnie's hotel.

"Some," said Alice, and smiled. "But not entirely." She squeezed Ronnie's hand. "Enjoy the ride, hon," she said. "This only happens once."

By the end of her second day in the city, three publishing houses had made offers. Ronnie called her parents ("You wrote a novel?"), her sister ("Am I in it? You can put me in it; just make me ten pounds thinner"), her best friends, and Lee, laughing and crying, hardly believing her good fortune. With Alice's assistance, she chose the house where she'd be edited by a young woman about her age; where they offered her a contract for two books, not just the one she'd written. "You want people who are going to build a career, not just publish a book," Alice counseled. Veronica signed the contract. Then she went back to Boston and stowed the first chunk of money in a savings account at the First Bank of New England, where her father worked. In August, she defended her thesis; in September, she began her first semester as a teacher. *The Summer Sisters* was scheduled to come out the following spring, right after Mother's Day, which, Alice told her, was the ideal time for a summer book to go on sale. Ronnie started work on her next book and resumed her academic life, the one she'd thought of as her real life.

"Most first novels flop," her agent told her bluntly. "Even the ones acquired for a lot of money. Even the ones with lots of advertising and publicity money behind them. This could be an exception, but I don't want you counting on it."

"In other words, don't quit my day job?" Ronnie asked.

Alice smiled. "Exactly right."

It was easy enough to put her suede boots back in her closet and her fedora on a shelf; easy to stop acting like a novelist, which was what Ronnie felt like she'd been doing. As the school year progressed, she'd get the occasional reminders of what was to come—a cover for her to approve; early, starred reviews in the trade publications to squeal over—but, for the most part, the idea that she was a soon-to-be published author felt like a fantasy. Her students, her lesson plans, the books she assigned, the lectures she wrote, and the papers she stayed up late to grade: those things felt real. So did her romance with Lee Weinberg, who was wooing her with great determination. Lee took her for long walks in the Public Gardens, and to a Red Sox game at Fenway Park. They went ice skating, on a frozen pond in his hometown in Connecticut, and afterward Lee built a fire in the fireplace, brought her a cup of hot cider, and tucked an afghan made of soft wool around her. "This is wonderful," Ronnie said, as Lee came to sit beside her. Her legs felt pleasantly sore from the skating, unused muscles tingling as they warmed. She settled her head on his shoulder, making a pleased noise as he put his arm around her and pulled her close. "I want to make you happy," he said, murmuring the words against her temple, pressing them into her skin.

The Summer Sisters was published in 1979, and it landed with all the splash that Alice and Ronnie's editor, Emily, could have hoped for: a review in *Time* magazine and one in *Life* and one in *Ladies' Home Journal*. The *Boston Globe* hailed her as a hometown hero in a profile that took up most of the Sunday paper's feature section, and the paper's book critic pronounced the novel "the must-have beach accessory for this summer."

The *New York Times* critic was more than a little condescending—he called the book "glib" and "melodramatic," words Ronnie knew would live in her memory forever—but it was a long review that featured a full-color picture of the book's cover, and a smaller shot of Ronnie, and both Alice and Emily assured her that even a mixed review would interest the readers Ronnie wanted—namely, women. "If Gary Holt had raved about it, it would have been the kiss of death," Alice explained, over martinis in the Algonquin's bar. "Gary Holt is not your audience. *Mrs.* Gary Holt is."

"And her sister, her daughters, and every one of her friends," Emily added, and lifted her own martini for a toast.

If iPhones and the internet had existed when Ronnie made her debut, the tools that let people track one another's every move; that made everyone immediately reachable, eternally findable had been around, she wouldn't have been able to compartmentalize her two lives so effectively. In New York City, in her hats and her vests and her tall suede boots, she was an author, and she felt like an author, whether she was posing for publicity shots, or giving interviews to reporters, or doing readings and signings at the 92nd Street Y. In Boston, in her paisley skirts and peasant blouses (which eventually gave way to kilts and cardigans and penny loafers), she was a professor and, eventually, a wife. In Boston, with Lee, she was Ronnie. In New York, with Alice and Emily, both of whom were single, she was Veronica. Maybe that was what had gotten her in trouble, she would think: that sense of being split, of inhabiting two identities, of being two different women in two different worlds, more or less at the same time.

On a day in March 1982, two months before her second book, *After Dawn*, was scheduled to come out, Ronnie took the train to New York City. The weather had been miserable the previous week, cold and gray with intermittent sleet, but that morning she'd smelled spring in the air. Just as the train pulled into Penn Station, the sun broke through the clouds. She emerged onto Thirty-Fourth Street and lifted her face to a sky that was brilliantly blue.

She walked uptown to her publisher's office and found Emily, her editor, hanging up the phone, bouncing on her toes, practically vibrating with delight.

"Guess who wants to buy the film rights to *Summer Sisters* . . . and just guess how much they want to pay?" She broke into a dance, shimmying her shoulders, like the news was too big for her to hold still. "Guess!"

Ronnie shook her head, speechless. Emily leaned close and whispered a name and number in her ear. Ronnie drew back, shaking her head in disbelief.

"No way."

"Yes, yes! Congratulations, Veronica!"

The publisher, a silver-haired man who seemed, at sixty-five, impossibly old to Ronnie, had ordered champagne, and that night they'd gone to Elaine's to celebrate. Alice promised she could get them in. "Maybe we'll see Woody Allen!" In her high-heeled boots and her newest jacket and fedora, with two glasses of champagne already inside her, Ronnie would have said yes to anything.

Woody Allen hadn't been there. But Elliott Gould had, and so had Bernadette Peters. Ronnie thought she glimpsed Liza Minnelli in the ladies' room, and she got a look at Elaine herself, holding court from her table in the corner. The first sip of her martini was sliding down Ronnie's throat like nectar from a glass so icy that her fingers felt chilled when she gripped it, when someone tapped her shoulder. "Veronica Levy?"

She turned. The man was movie-star handsome, with a strong jaw and a head full of thick dark-blond hair. Ronnie felt herself staring. Then Emily was on her feet, grabbing the man's hands and kissing his cheek, and Alice was saying, "Veronica, you remember Gregory Bates?"

Gregory Bates was Emily's colleague, another editor at the publishing house. Veronica had met him in passing when visiting the office and been struck by his good looks.

"Come have a drink with us!" Emily said. A moment later, Gregory was installed at their tiny high-top table. More champagne in a bucket of ice arrived at the table, and they were toasting Ronnie's film sale, her brilliant future, her brilliant book.

By the time the second bottle arrived, the four of them were throwing out casting suggestions for *Summer Sisters*, with Gregory insisting, absolutely straight-faced, that Jane Fonda should be cast as both Jenny and Jill. "She should at least play one of the sisters, but both would be even better," and when Ronnie asked how they'd pull that off, Gregory had said, very solemnly, "Wigs," and she'd laughed so hard that tears had been streaming down her cheeks.

By last call, two bottles of champagne were upside down in their ice buckets, and empty glasses covered their table. Alice had announced, with a dignified hiccup, that she needed to get home to her cat, and Emily had a breakfast meeting the next morning, and then it was just Veronica and Gregory.

"Can I call you a cab?" he asked. Veronica still felt wide-awake, tingling with booze and excitement, enthralled with all the good news. She knew she'd never sleep. At least, not anytime soon.

"I think I'll walk," she said, and Gregory had offered to escort her, even though he lived, she'd learned, on the Upper West Side.

"Where are you staying?" he asked, and when she told him she was at the Algonquin he'd smiled and said, "Of course."

Outside, the morning's rain had returned as a luminous mist that filled the air, obscuring the city's grit and dirt. The streetlamps glowed like moonstones in the fog, like echoes of the full moon overhead. When Gregory offered her his arm as they crossed Fifth Avenue and entered the park, it seemed rude not to take it, and when they reached the hotel, it seemed rude not to invite him up for a nightcap. Gregory called down to the bar to order a pair of old-fashioneds, and Ronnie went to stand by the window and look down at the city, so different from Boston, or from any other place in the world. She imagined she could feel the ground vibrate beneath her, all that coiled energy, all that striving, all the people dreaming dreams of fame and glory.

When the drinks arrived, Gregory handed her a glass and stood beside her. "It's something, isn't it?" he asked, his voice low.

She turned to him. The dim, pearly light from the street cast his face in shadow. All she could see was his profile—the broad shoulders and firm chest, the angles of his jawline and the straight line of his nose. And what she thought was, *This is my reward*. As much as the champagne and the movie deal and the money, she had earned this man, this night, through her determination and her hard work. When she put her hand on his cheek and drew his lips down to hers, Veronica felt like a queen, claiming the spoils of a plundered land.

They kissed, chests pressed together, one of her hands cupping the back of his head, one of his hands gripping possessively at her bottom. Lee was always so gentle and respectful, touching her with something close to reverence, always watching her face, touching her body, gauging her reactions, and making sure she liked what he was doing. Gregory was as intent on his pleasure as hers, and somehow, Veronica found that fiercely arousing. When he bit at her tongue, then her neck, with a sound somewhere between a groan and a growl, she grabbed him as hard as he'd grabbed her, pulling him toward the bed, where Gregory knelt and pulled off her boots. He raised her foot, pressed a kiss to her instep, and began kissing and licking his way up her leg. "Veronica," he whispered, and slid his hand up her thigh.

"Now," she said, imperious as an empress, as he pulled them off. She propped herself on her elbows, watching as he unbuckled his belt. "I want you inside of me now."

She tried not to think about how different he was from Lee, with his curly hair and his sloping shoulders and his gentle eyes, gray-blue behind the glasses that he'd worn since he was eight years old. She told herself that she wasn't cheating, because she was not the woman Lee knew. There, in Boston, she was Ronnie, a sister, a daughter, a PhD candidate, and soon, she suspected, a fiancée; a bride, a wife and a mother. There, in spite of her achievements, she would be Mrs. Levy; another woman driving carpools in a wood-paneled station wagon, carting cut-up oranges to soccer games, bringing banana bread to the bake sale. She'd seen it happen to her friends, fellow PhD students, some who'd published their work. Put a ring on their finger and, through some dark magic, they turned into wives and mothers, and instead of talking about Elizabethan poetry or symbolism in Shakespeare's sonnets or how the market economy had shaped post–Civil War America, it was all teething and toilet training and which towns had the most desirable school districts.

Veronica wasn't ready for that. She wanted to be what she was in the city: a bestselling author, a woman who'd been paid two hundred thousand dollars to write books and would make even more from the film adaptation, a woman who was ambitious and accomplished and hungry for everything the world could give her. She loved Lee, she wanted a life with him in Boston; children, a house, family vacations, all of it. But, before she succumbed, didn't she deserve a little time to be the star of her own life? Didn't every woman deserve that—a few days or months to feel remarkable?

She and Gregory met four or five times over the next year. Veronica was scrupulous about not inventing excuses or lying to Lee. Every time she told him she had to be in New York for work, she was telling the truth. He'd see her off at the train, and kiss her goodbye, and then, somewhere between Hartford and New Haven, she'd slip her Ronnie skin and turn into Veronica.

She and Gregory would meet for drinks, sometimes with Emily or Alice or Gregory's other colleagues, other editors or agents or authors, New York people who made conversation about books and authors, who read novels and poetry and did not just use their *New Yorkers* as ornaments for their coffee table, set dressing that would signal certain values to any visitors. She and Gregory were careful not to look at each other too much, or to touch, although sometimes, Gregory would let his fingertips linger on her shoulders as he pulled out her chair, or trail against the back of her neck as he helped her on with her coat. Sometimes they'd go to dinner, at restaurants Gregory chose, Greek or French or Italian, and, once, sushi, which Veronica had never eaten before. Gregory fed her bits of slippery fish from his chopsticks.

They would eat, and talk about books that they'd read; other authors Gregory was working with or books that he'd acquired. At some point, under the table, his foot would brush her ankle; his fingers would touch her hand as he poured her more wine. Sometimes she'd want him so desperately that they'd end up in the ladies' room, kissing frantically, groping each other with other patrons banging on the door. Once, they hadn't been able to make it back to the hotel. Gregory had backed her into an alley, pushing her against the rough brick wall, shoving her skirt up around her waist as she wrapped her legs around him and closed her eyes.

Veronica knew that Gregory dated other women. Gregory knew that Veronica had a boyfriend in Boston. It didn't stop them, or even slow them down.

As things with Lee became more serious, he started to plan for holidays and weddings months in advance with the unspoken assumption that they'd be attending as a couple, and ask her about the various suburbs they might theoretically live in someday. Ronnie knew that she should end the affair. She wanted to be with Lee, wanted the life she would have with him. Maybe things weren't as glamorous in Massachusetts, or as exciting; maybe she herself was different there—less extroverted, happy to let someone else be the center of attention—but she was comfortable with Lee, who was steadfast and loyal. He would always love and care for her. She couldn't say the same for Gregory . . . but still, she couldn't bring herself to give him up.

Whenever she was in New York, she could feel her Boston life, her real life, the life she wanted—at least with most of her heart, most of the time—beckoning, waiting to consume her. She knew that, at the very least, she should feel guilty about what she was doing. Lee, she knew, was scrupulously faithful to her, even surrounded by young, comely paralegals and secretaries. He'd been shy in high school, a boy who preferred reading Isaac Asimov novels to most sports, and he'd been, he told her with a wry expression, shorter than his five-foot-three-inch mother until his junior year. Now he was taller, solidly built and pleasant-looking, with a law degree and a successful practice, and still charmingly oblivious to the women who flirted with him, the way his secretary would smooth his tie or a waitress would brush her arm against his as she set the check down on the table. He'd be, she knew, a good husband and father.

And yet, for almost an entire year, the affair continued. She kept seeing Gregory even after she and Lee moved in together, to an apartment on Beacon Street, right near the Charles River, and began planning a wedding for the following year. She didn't stop, and she didn't feel guilty. Maybe she would have, if she'd taken up with some man in Boston, a fellow academic, or a friend's husband, or a stranger she'd met on the T, but of course Ronnie would never do such a thing; she would never dare. Veronica was a different creature. Veronica dared.

In the end, it was Gregory who'd ended it. They'd

been at the Algonquin, where it had started. In bed, Gregory had leaned down, gently brushing a lock of Veronica's hair behind her ear.

"This has been wonderful, but we need to say good-bye." She felt the shock of it rocketing through her, and opened her mouth to ask him why when he said, gently, "I'm getting married in the spring."

Veronica swallowed hard. It made her a hypocrite— why was it okay for her to have someone else, but wrong if Gregory did? Why was it wrong for him to be getting married when she was, too? Her face felt frozen as she made herself ask, "Who is she?"

"No one you know." He caressed her thigh idly, one fingertip tracing the line where her leg met her groin. "She's a girl I've known forever. Her parents know my parents. We all summer together in the Hamptons."

Ah, thought Veronica, feeling bitterness twisting in her heart. Of course he'd marry someone else who used "summer" as a verb. Probably this girl Gregory had known forever was pretty and petite and blonde. All at once, Veronica felt plain and unlovely; her nose too big and her skin too dark.

"You're right," she said, and moved away from him. "It's time to stop."

Gregory reached for her, his hands unusually gentle, his voice tender. He held her face in his hands, the skin of his palms warm on her cheeks. "I'll never forget you."

They'd made love one last time, slowly. Gregory had kissed her body, touching her, like he was trying to memorize her shape, and the smell and feel of her skin. He'd been inside of her, rocking slowly, holding her thighs, pulling her body as closely against him as he could, when Veronica had gasped, and frozen.

"Condom!"

"Oh, shit." Gregory had pulled out of her, gotten on a condom, and they'd finished. Afterward, he'd fallen asleep, while Veronica had lain awake beside him, counting backward to the date of her last period, trying to convince herself that she'd be okay. They'd always used condoms, even the time in the alley. They'd always been careful. Surely she wouldn't find herself in trouble because of this one brief lapse, she thought. Surely not.

Three weeks later, she missed her period. "It's fine," Lee said, holding her as she cried, and, of course, not understanding why she was crying. "Look. You'll go to the doctor. Maybe it's a false alarm. And if it's not . . ." He held her face in his hands, which only made her think of Gregory. She'd swallowed hard as Lee said, "We were going to get married, anyhow. This just accelerates the timetable a bit." Sick with shame, hating herself for deceiving this good, kind man, Ronnie had nodded. He'd been the one to call her doctor, and, after, he'd brought her a warm washcloth and tenderly wiped the tears off her face.

"I don't deserve you," she'd sniffled.

"Of course you do," said Lee.

It will be his baby, Ronnie told herself a month later, when the doctor confirmed what two weeks of nonstop nausea had already suggested. *Whatever the truth of it is, this baby is going to be Lee Weinberg's son or daughter.* Gregory had dark-blond hair, thick and straight. Lee's hair was brown and wavy. Gregory's skin was pale; Lee's was darker, and it tanned easily in the summertime. Gregory was almost six feet tall, broad-shouldered and narrow-waisted and graceful; Lee was a few inches shorter, with a tendency to stoop. Their faces and features were completely different—different noses, different cheeks, different foreheads, different chins. None of it mattered, Ronnie told herself fiercely. There was only the tiniest chance that Gregory was the father, and, even if it was true, this would be Lee's baby. Lee would believe it. He had, Ronnie thought sadly, no reason to doubt her.

Then, at her six-month appointment, the doctor heard two heartbeats. "Twins!" he said, slapping Lee on the back. Lee's face lit up with delight as Ronnie lay on her back, her legs still in the stirrups, frozen in shock, paralyzed with shame.

"We always said we wanted two," Lee told her, down in the parking garage, as he hurried around the car (they'd already bought what Ronnie had dubbed the Inevitable Volvo) to hold the door open for her.

"Yes," Ronnie said. She felt numb. She felt like her guilt was right there on her face, like Lee could see, and Dr. Sanderson could see, and astronauts in outer space could see what she had done.

The next morning, after Lee had gone to work, she called a gynecologist; not the one she used, a stranger whose name she'd pulled from the phone book at random. "Twins with different fathers?" the woman repeated, after Ronnie had introduced herself and said that she was researching a new novel. "It's rare, but it does happen. Some months, a woman releases two eggs instead of one. If both of them end up being fertilized within a day or two, and then both successfully implant, you've got two babies with different dads. Of course, it's much more likely that one man fathered both babies."

Ronnie hoped the woman couldn't hear the tremble of her voice. "So let's say the twins have different fathers.

Would her husband be able to tell right away? As soon as the babies were born?"

"Well, for example, if the fathers are different races, that would make it pretty obvious," the doctor said dryly. "But beyond that, unless you did genetic testing, you wouldn't be able to tell. If the babies don't look too different, and if the husband has no reason to suspect that he's not the father, your main character wouldn't have much trouble pulling the wool over his eyes." Ronnie felt sick. When the doctor paused, Ronnie was certain she was going to say *This isn't a theoretical question, is it? Why don't you tell me what's really going on?* but instead, the doctor said, a little shyly, "Love your books, by the way."

Ronnie thanked her and promised to send her a signed copy of *After Dawn*. She hung up the phone and sat at the kitchen table, with one hand resting on the ledge of her belly. Maybe both babies were Lee's. Maybe both of them were Gregory's. Maybe each man had fathered a baby. Should she try to find out the truth? And what would she do with that information, assuming that she could obtain it? *Break my husband's heart*, she thought.

Ronnie decided to wait and see. Assuming the babies did not look obviously, visibly like they had different gene pools, she would keep quiet. The truth would only hurt Lee. She tried to tell herself that she wasn't lying, that the woman Lee had married had never cheated on him. That woman, the one who'd let Gregory shove her skirt up around her waist and fuck her against the rough brick of an alleyway, was someone else, someone Ronnie felt like she'd barely known (and, she thought, someone she wouldn't have liked much if she had). And if the babies clearly did have different fathers? She decided to cross—or burn—that bridge when she came to it.

Then Sam and Sarah were born. They didn't look like Lee. They didn't look like Gregory. They looked like babies, pink-faced and toothless, both with tiny button noses and faint, sketched-in eyebrows. Both of them had the same fine brown hair, both had eyes the same dark-blue shade, although Sarah's eyes had lightened to a changeable blue-gray, while Sam ended up with hazel eyes. As they grew up—Sarah, confident and assertive, with blonde hair that shaded to light brown as she got older; and Sam, quiet and shy, dreamy, with Lee's curls, happy to let his sister push through the world on both of their behalf—Ronnie had some strong suspicions about their paternity. But she never did any testing, not even when the technology for doing so became more accessible. After that last night in New York, she never got in touch with Gregory, or googled his name, after Google became a thing. She never told Lee of her suspicions, as the years went by and the kids grew up. It was her secret to keep; her burden to bear. Lee had been their father in every way that mattered, and if biology told a different story, he never needed to hear it.

The few times Ronnie had to go back to New York, she went wearing the armor of motherhood, depending on it—plus its attendant exhaustion—to keep her chaste and untouched. Emily was also married by then. Their long, boozy lunches and the late nights out came to a natural end, replaced by breakfast meetings and coffees. She'd never set foot in her publisher's office again and conducted her business with her agent over the phone. As time went on, Ronnie decided that the woman she'd been, the author, who'd swept through New York City in those high suede boots, hadn't been a good woman. It was more than just what had happened with Gregory. There was also the anecdote she'd lifted, almost unchanged, from a friend's life and used in *After Dawn*, and the way she'd ignored the now former friend's hurt look when they'd run into each other at a dinner party, and how, two weeks later, when the woman sent her a letter, Ronnie had shoved it into the back of a drawer, unread. There was the way she'd listened to her sister's dating stories, feigning interest, only because she wanted to glean details from them to use in her fiction. The time she'd used a particular detail about the way that Lee chewed and given it to the villain in her second book, and how she would encourage her friends to go on second and third dates with guys who were clearly jerks, only because their tales of depradation and heartache lit up the novelist part of her brain. The way she'd started accepting things like first-class plane tickets and pricey hotel rooms and expensive meals as her due; forgetting to be grateful, forgetting how lucky she was. The way she'd sneered at a colleague who'd asked to be introduced to her agent. "God, can you imagine what Alice would do to me if I sent her Martha's manuscript?" she'd laughed to Lee, who'd looked startled.

"Maybe she's talented," he'd said mildly, and Veronica had pictured mousy Martha, in her shapeless sack-style dresses and her clogs, and, sneering, had thought, *Probably not*. As if she could tell, just by looking, who had talent and who didn't; who deserved luck and good fortune and who did not.

Veronica the author was arrogant and entitled, demanding and cruel. Saying goodbye to that woman would not be a hardship. Resetting her life, making her teaching and her children and her marriage her priorities, would be a good thing.

Veronica's last act as a published author was attending the premiere of *The Summer Sisters*. The movie still reappeared sometimes, late at night, on obscure cable channels. Ronnie would always flip right past it. She didn't stop writing, but after the babies were born, she'd never tried to publish another word of fiction. When Lee asked her, gently, if she'd quit because the sales of *After Dawn* had been disappointing—at least compared to her debut—or if she was sad that the movie hadn't been a bigger hit, or that nothing had come of the second book's option, she'd shaken her head. "I don't feel like I have anything left to say," she told him.

"Oh, I don't believe that."

"It's fine. I'm fine. I'm happy now," she assured him. The babies and her classes kept her busy. She loved her husband. She'd had her adventures—or, rather, Veronica had. Now Ronnie was relatively fulfilled; mostly content. She couldn't go back in time and change what she'd done. She couldn't make it up to Lee, because she couldn't tell him what had happened, not ever. What she could do was make a sacrifice. She could give up something that she loved and, in doing so, renounce the last vestiges of that other woman she'd been. She would stop being a novelist and be, instead, a wife, a mother, a professor of literature, a secret scribbler, accumulating stacks of pages that reposed in plastic storage boxes on the top shelf of her closet. She could refocus her energy and her ambition on her home life, and on teaching, and she could suffer, quietly, for the sin only she knew she'd committed. She would be like a medieval penitent with a girdle of thorns under her clothing. No one would know but her.

For almost forty years, Ronnie wore her thorns and wrote in private, and believed herself safe, trusting that what she'd done would stay, forever, between her and God. She'd written eight novels, each in its own plastic box, high on a shelf in the guest room, with instructions as to their disposal in the will she'd written years ago. Her kids had grown up; and Lee had died, without suspecting that Ronnie had ever been untrue. She'd had no reason to think that anyone would learn her secret. And now, thanks to faddish DNA kits and her idiot sister, her children, and their children, were all going to know.

She and Paul each had a second glass of wine as the sun went down and the darkness gathered and the wind rose, making conversation with the tall grasses, the rosebushes, the pine trees. They settled on a price, and Ronnie said she'd let him know when she was ready for the listing to go live. "We're having a wedding," she said, and Paul congratulated her and said, "I hope it's a beautiful day." She saw him out, and, instead of going to bed, she walked back upstairs slowly, standing in front of the big windows that looked out over the water, for once without noticing the waves or the starry sky. *After the wedding*, she told herself. *If Sam and Sarah find out beforehand, if they have questions, I'll get them to wait; I'll tell them we can't ruin Ruby's big day. We'll get through it, and then, when it's over, I'll tell them everything.*

PART
TWO

~~~~~~~

THE COURSE OF TRUE LOVE

INTERLUDE

A wedding, thought the house, with a small shudder that made her roof joists groan. A wedding! It should be one of her happiest occasions, but over the previous week, she'd heard what was coming after the last of the confetti was cleared. *Too much house* indeed! She was just the right amount of house, for a grandmother, and parents, and children and stepchildren; for cocktail parties and birthday cakes and rainy days of puzzle-solving and Scrabble. *You have hurt my feelings*, she wanted to tell the lady of the house, but she could sense that the lady would soon be having enough troubles of her own.

So: a wedding. The boy and the girl who'd grown up here were a man and a woman now. They would come. They'd see the problem with their mother. They would help. And then, she hoped, they would change her mind. They would realize all that she was, and all she had to give them, and they would decide that there was no better house in the world; that there was nothing to do but stay.

But first, she'd have to help them. Maybe help their children, too. Whatever obstacles they'd encountered, whatever kept them from being happy—and, by extension, from being here, with her—she would fix it. She'd clear the path; she'd smooth the way. She'd figure out how, and she'd fix it all.

RONNIE

~~~

Ronnie started off in the laundry room, gathering a basket of sheets and pillowcases and holding it against her midsection as she set off, with a line from *A Midsummer Night's Dream* bouncing around in her head: *I am sent with broom before / To sweep the dust behind the door.* The wedding was still over a month away, but she knew, from experience, that setting the big house in order would take time, and she wasn't moving as fast as she used to these days. Better to start early, she'd decided. Her plan was to begin at the bottom of the house and work her way up to the top, determining who would go where. Once she had the sleeping arrangements figured out, she could start to think about meals, and pre-wedding activities, and, most important, the thing that she was dreading: what she'd say to Sam and Sarah when the wedding was over.

There were two bedrooms on the ground floor, one with a single queen bed and a bathroom where, long ago, the mothers' helpers used to stay. The other was a spacious room called the dorm, with three twin beds, each with a trundle. She'd put Sam and Connor in the smaller room. Connor could share a bed with his stepdad, or he could sleep with Miles and Dexter in the dorm, which, Ronnie supposed, he would probably prefer.

She put fresh linens on the beds, then climbed the stairs slowly, thinking as she walked. Normally, she'd put Sarah and Eli and Ruby in the guesthouse. Sarah and

Eli would take the bedroom, with its king-sized bed, and Ruby would get the Murphy bed that pulled down from the guest house's living-room wall. She'd loved that bed as a kid, Ronnie remembered, picturing Ruby pulling it down, then folding it back, watching as the wood on the bed's base blended in almost invisibly with the wall. "It's like magic!" she'd said.

But Ruby was the bride now, which meant that she should have the entire guesthouse. Ruby and her husband-to-be could sleep in the bedroom and keep the living room free for whatever beauty ministrations Ruby and her bridesmaids intended for her big day. Ronnie wasn't sure what Ruby's plans were, if she'd arranged for people to help with her hair and makeup, if she even planned on having bridesmaids, or wearing a traditional wedding gown. When she'd offered to help, Ruby had refused. "Don't worry about anything, Safta," Ruby said. "I've got it all under control." *Typical Ruby*, Ronnie thought. Ruby, like her stepmother, had always been a competent girl, making her own arrangements because she didn't trust anyone to do it as well as she could. Ronnie was musing that it was nice to be a guest in your own home, and how she'd get to be surprised by Ruby's dress, when her phone rang. She set down her laundry basket and pulled her phone out of her pocket.

"Speak of the devil," she said to Ruby. "I was just thinking about you!"

"What were you thinking?" Ruby asked.

"About how much you loved the Murphy bed when you were little."

"Oh, right," Ruby said. Sarah could picture her, her ringlets, her pale skin, and her smile. "It was like magic!"

"That's what you'd say." Ronnie stretched from side

to side. She'd woken up with her back feeling stiff again. "Did you set up any hair and makeup?"

"Yep. Called a salon in P-town. They're sending two people Saturday morning." Ruby paused.

"So, listen," she said. "I need a favor."

"Sure. What's up?"

Ruby inhaled. "Gabe's mother's coming out."

"To her son's wedding? I should hope so," Ronnie said.

"His mom's bringing her sister, Gabe's aunt Amanda," Ruby continued. "And the thing is . . ."

Ruby paused. Ronnie waited.

"They'll probably get a hotel," Ruby said, her voice rising, almost imperceptibly, on the word "probably." "Except I just went online, and everything's sold out. There's nothing left. No hotels; no Airbnbs."

Ronnie didn't reply, but what she was thinking was that if Gabe's people hadn't booked something already, there would be exactly a zero percent chance of them finding a place. At this point ahead of a normal summer, everything would be booked, from the budget motels to the high-end bed-and-breakfasts, and in a world still coming out of a pandemic, when everyone was extra-desperate to travel and could only do it domestically, it was even worse.

"But just in case . . ." Ruby's words came in a rush. "Maybe, if Gabe and I stay in the guesthouse, his mom can crash on the Murphy bed for a night or two."

"His mom and his aunt?" Ronnie permitted a little doubt to season her voice. "Do you really want other people in the guesthouse with you the night before your wedding?"

"It'll be fine," Ruby said stiffly.

"And they'll be okay sharing a bed?" Ronnie was

already trying to remember what had happened to the air mattress she'd used one year when she'd hosted Thanksgiving and couldn't get out of inviting her sister and brother-in-law and their kids, who were, of course, too cheap to spring for hotel rooms.

"I think they're close." Ruby made a scoffing noise. "Except I think his aunt's maybe kind of a bad influence. That's what Gabe says."

"Well, that's a not uncommon family dynamic," said Ronnie, thinking of her son-in-law and his brother, and about her own sister, who'd convinced her, many years ago when they were both teenagers, to shave off her eyebrows. They'd never completely grown back, either, she thought, with a prickle of irritation. "I'm giving you the entire guesthouse. Anyone you want to stay there is fine with me," Ronnie said.

"Thank you," Ruby said fervently. "Seriously, Safta. Thank you so much for all of this."

"Of course." Ronnie said goodbye, put her phone back in her pocket, and picked up her laundry basket again. She hadn't wanted to ask Ruby if her biological mother, Annette, was planning on coming to the wedding. She still couldn't understand a mother leaving her child. She tried not to judge. Maybe Annette had suffered from postpartum depression, or she'd had some kind of mental health problems. Maybe Annette had just known that she was poorly equipped to be a parent. Better, if that was the case, to leave the job to someone who could do it, someone who genuinely wanted to be a mom, Ronnie thought. And things seemed to have worked out well for Ruby. Her father doted on her. Sarah loved her and had been happy to step into the role of stepmother. Being raised by a single father for so many years, with a mother out of the picture, hadn't seemed to affect Ruby as dramatically as it could have. Perhaps it was even at the root of her drive. Ruby had always done well in school; she'd had plenty of friends; she'd chosen her career and worked toward it with unwavering focus and unrelenting determination. And now Ruby would be a wife. Ronnie shook her head in wonder, hardly able to imagine the girl she'd met as an eight-year-old becoming someone's wife. She set fresh linens on the guest-room bed and sat down on the bench at its foot to catch her breath and call her daughter.

"Annette? I know that Ruby invited her," Sarah said. Sarah sounded distracted. But that was probably to be expected, with the wedding so soon, and with managing the boys' complicated schedule. "She told Eli that she's going to try to make it."

"She's going to try to attend her only child's wedding?"

Sarah sighed. "I know, Mom. I don't understand it, either."

"I'm asking because I need to know if I should save her a bed."

"Annette can take care of herself." Ronnie could picture her daughter, walking at her typically brisk pace, shoulder-length hair swinging. "She'll probably pop a tent in the backyard."

"Well, that would work for me. I've got a nice one in the garage. Are you still planning to come up on Wednesday?"

"Thursday, I think. We'll leave first thing in the morning, probably get to you by midafternoon."

"That's great. Do you know how long you'll be staying?" Ronnie kept her tone perfectly neutral, without even the hint of an accusation, but, still, Sarah managed to hear one.

"Just until Sunday. I'm sorry, and I wish it could be longer, but Miles has soccer and Dexter's got nature camp and they both start first thing Monday."

Nature camp in New York City, Ronnie thought, *instead of letting your kid experience actual nature on Cape Cod.* Oh, she'd never understand Sarah, not as long as she lived.

"I understand. Tell the boys I can't wait to see them." She waited to see if Sarah wanted to keep talking. Some afternoons, the conversation would range from Dexter's obsession with turtles to Miles's scathing book reports ("In my opinion, this book is bad and boring and I do not know why it's for sale," was how his assessment of his last book had begun), or the most recent show that Ruby had stage-managed, or the postponed trip that Sarah and Eli were planning on taking, when the world allowed for travel again. If Ronnie caught her at the right moment and gave her time, Sarah would start with the family news and work her way to whatever was bothering her. But ever since their talk about the studio she'd rented, Sarah hadn't been chatty, and that morning was no exception.

"Love you, Mom, but I've got a million things to take care of. We'll see you soon." Sarah hung up the phone, leaving Ronnie to wonder. Sarah had not been herself lately, Ronnie thought as she made her way across the deck to the guesthouse. Ronnie had been on the brink of asking Sarah, a dozen times, *What is going on?* She'd been ready with advice on the necessity of working at a marriage, the importance of putting your head down to get through the hard times and not throwing love away. She'd even considered calling Eli herself, asking him the same questions. In every instance, she'd managed to keep her mouth shut. *Every marriage is a mystery,* as her own mother would say. If Sarah needed her help, she would ask for it. Trying to pull Sarah close to her would only send her further away.

Ronnie settled her basket in her arms and got back to work. Halfway to the guesthouse, she had to pause, because she'd developed a painful stitch in her side. It was disheartening. Ronnie could still remember when she could trot up and down the six flights of beach stairs with a baby on each arm. *Oh, well*, she thought, setting down her basket, raising her arms over her head and bending from side to side. She could see her reflection in the guesthouse window—widelegged cropped cotton pants, one of Lee's old undershirts, bare feet. Wisps of hair had escaped from her bun, and without underwire and shapewear her middle looked thick, without a noticeable waist or bustline. *You're lovely*, Lee used to tell her. Right up until the end, even on the days when all she saw were ruin and sag. *You're lovely*, he would say; *still my beautiful bride*, and his conviction made it true.

Ronnie picked up her basket and continued on, balancing it on her hip as she pulled the sliding door open. The guesthouse had once been Sam and Sarah's private domain. They'd play house. Ronnie smiled, remembering Sarah, at five or six, sitting importantly at the diningroom table with a stack of paper in front of her. *Bring me a coffee*, she'd tell Sam, with an imperious tilt to her chin that would send her mother's reading glasses sliding down her nose. *Then take the kids to the beach. I am VERY BUSY doing my writing.* Poor Sam would scurry to obey, filling a mug up with water and saying *I'm going to be late to work!* while Sarah ignored him, scribbling on the pages with a red pen or pretending to take calls from the dean.

I was a good mother, Ronnie told herself. She'd stopped smiling, the memory giving her an unpleasant twinge. She didn't like the idea that all that Sarah remembered was a parent too busy or distracted to notice her. Was that why Sarah never brought her boys out here for long? Was it that all she remembered from their summers in Truro was a mother too busy to give her the attention she needed?

Ronnie shook her head. What was done was done. She couldn't change the past, or what her daughter felt. Head down, she walked back to the house, barely noticing the sound of the waves, or the warmth of the deck beneath her bare feet, as she thought.

If Sarah and Eli weren't going to be in the guesthouse, they'd have to be in the guest bedroom, on the other side of the hall from Ronnie's bedroom. It was a smallish room, with a queen-sized bed, and for a minute Ronnie considered giving up her own room, and her larger bed, so that her daughter and her six-foot-tall son-in-law could have more space.

She decided against it. Giving Sarah the master bedroom could serve as a reminder to her twin about what he'd had and lost—or, worse, it would give Sam evidence that Sarah was Ronnie's favorite (Sam was actually her favorite, but that was a secret she'd be taking to her grave). Ronnie liked her space and her privacy and disliked the thought of having to move her clothes, and her makeup and her medications, not to mention the Poise pads she'd started to occasionally require. The bedroom still held the ghost of Lee's scent; the strongest echoes of presence. If the upstairs couch had been Ronnie's domain and the guesthouse had been Sam and Sarah's hideout, this room was Lee's fiefdom. There was a small office set up in front of the window that faced the pool and the meadow, and there was a round cushioned seat, big enough for two, on the deck that overlooked the bay. *Dad's tuffet*, the kids had called it. On summer afternoons, Lee would head out there with a book, and most of the time she'd find him dozing, the book open on his chest and his glasses askew. Sometimes, she'd look out the bedroom window and imagine that she could still see him there, stretched out on the tuffet with the breeze ruffling his hair and a glass of ice water beside him.

This house is full of ghosts, Ronnie thought, and wiped her hands on her legs. Sometimes, she almost thought she could hear the house itself talking to her; telling her that Lee was still there, that he hadn't left her; telling her that Sarah and Sam were still little, that they hadn't grown up and left her behind.

Ronnie shook her head at her own folly, telling herself she was turning into a foolish old woman. She forced her brain back to the present, reviewing her decisions. Sarah and Eli in the guest bedroom, Sam and Connor and Miles and Dexter downstairs, however they decided to configure themselves; Ruby and Gabe in the guest-house, with Gabe's mother and aunt there, too, unless she could work some magic and find them a hotel room. Best of all, she could tell Suzanne and Matt that there was no room at the inn, and she wouldn't even be lying. Perfect.

Ronnie showered and dressed and drove into Provincetown. She had an appointment at noon for her annual physical at the clinic on Shank Painter Road. Once that was done, she'd go to the Stop & Shop to start stocking the kitchens, and to talk to the people at Wildflowers. Cherry blossoms, she thought dreamily. Was the end of June too late for cherry blossoms? Maybe they could cover the banister in pink and white blooms, and build centerpieces of blossoming branches.

But Ronnie never made it to the supermarket that day.

"An MRI?" Ronnie asked an hour later, hearing the paper of the examination table crinkle underneath her. "Really?"

"Really," said Dr. Dominguez. Usually in perpetual motion, hurrying from one patient to the next, the doctor had spent a long time lingering over Ronnie's belly, pressing here, prodding there, rattling off a series of questions: Any unexplained weight loss? Any fatigue? Nausea? Loss of appetite? Blood in her stool? Now, she kept her gaze on Ronnie's, making an unnerving amount of eye contact.

"And right now? It has to be right now?"

"Yes," Dr. Dominguez said. Her tone was soft; her eyes, cool and gray behind her glasses, gave nothing away, but her doctor was not an alarmist.

Ronnie licked her lips. "Did you—why do you think—"

"There's a mass." Her voice was low and steady, and Ronnie shut her eyes, thinking that this couldn't be good.

Two hours later, Veronica was sitting in the waiting room at Hyannis Hospital. Two hours after that, she'd been admitted and was lying in a bed with an IV in her arm, pumping her full of she wasn't entirely sure what. There was an endoscopy scheduled for later that afternoon and, in the morning, should the blood tests and the endoscopy reveal what the doctors thought they would, a consult with an oncologist.

"Is there anyone you'd like us to call?" asked the nurse.

Ronnie shook her head. "Not yet," she said, her voice a little faint. Whatever was happening to her, whatever lay ahead, all of it could wait. She wasn't going to spoil Ruby's day. *After the wedding*, she told herself. There'd be time enough to deal with whatever was coming, to tell whoever needed to hear.

SAM

〰〰

I s this a good time?" Sam asked when Sarah answered his call. It was nine thirty in the morning in Los Angeles, twelve thirty in New York. Sam had already dropped Connor off at school and put in his hour at the gym. "I wanted to ask if you'd figured out when you're heading to the Cape?" Sam hoped he sounded casual, like a man with nothing to hide. "I'm looking at tickets, and Connor wants to know how long Dexter and Miles will be there."

On his phone's screen, Sarah's glance slid sideways. "The wedding's on Saturday. We'll get there on Thursday. Mom's already leaning on me to have the boys stay for a few weeks. 'Leave them with me! I'll take care of everything!'" she said, imitating Ronnie's tone. "But the boys have to be back to start their camps Monday morning. I'm trying to figure it out," she said, and sighed. "Maybe I'll have Eli take them back and I'll stay with Mom for a while."

Sam frowned. This didn't sound normal. "Does Eli have time to do all the picking up and dropping off?" Sam had only one boy to care for, and Connor wasn't nearly as busy as his cousins, but even soccer practice and games once a week got time-consuming.

"Eli can figure it out," Sarah said, with uncharacteristic asperity. "He knows how to hire a sitter, same as I do."

"Okay," Sam said. "What's wrong?" He looked at

the screen, at the poster over his sister's shoulder. "And where are you? Is that your office? Did you redecorate?"

Quickly, Sarah shifted the phone so that all Sam could see was her face and a blank white wall. "It's—well. Actually, I rented a studio. The rents are super-cheap right now. Everyone left the city during the pandemic, and landlords are practically giving places away. And with Ruby and Gabe in the house, it was feeling so crowded, and I just thought . . ." She stopped talking and sighed deeply. Then she shook her head. "I don't want to dump my stuff on you. You've got enough going on."

"Connor and I are fine," said Sam, who was quietly relieved that Sarah wasn't going to ask about the length of his own stay on Cape Cod. "Dump away."

"Things aren't good," Sarah said. "With Eli."

"Hang on." Sam carried his phone from the kitchen to the living room and took a seat on the couch. "What do you mean, 'aren't good'? What's going on?"

"I don't know," she said. "I don't know, and he won't tell me. He's been tuning me out for months, ever since the pandemic started, and I thought things would get easier when he went back to work and the kids went back to school, but it's only gotten worse."

"Do you think—" Sam started. Then he stopped, because he wasn't sure what to suggest. All the possibilities he could think of—Eli using drugs, Eli having an affair, Eli involved in some kind of financial scandal, Eli in trouble at work—seemed equally improbable. Rock-steady, rock-solid Eli, who'd been Sam's role model as he'd taken on the responsibilities of being a stepfather? It was impossible to imagine him making the kind of misstep that would have Sarah sounding so glum. "What do you think it is?"

"I don't know!" Sarah said. "I just don't know." She rubbed at her forehead. "I'd assume that he was having an affair, except I don't know when he'd have time. He's under my feet every minute of the day." She shuddered. "I feel like I'm going crazy."

"The flip-flops?" Sam guessed.

"I want to burn them," Sarah said darkly. "Except then the house would smell like burning plastic and he'd probably just buy new ones."

"Could it be related to money?" asked Sam.

Sarah shook her head. "I checked. Everything's where it's supposed to be. He hasn't taken anything out of our savings, or our retirement funds." She raised her shoulders in a helpless-looking shrug. "I don't know. Maybe it's online gambling. Or porn."

"Watching it or making it?" Sam asked.

Sarah gave a startled bark of laughter. "Good God. Because people are lining up to watch middle-aged periodontists have sex. That would be a very niche market, am I right?"

"You'd be surprised," mumbled Sam.

Sarah gave him an imploring look. "I thought—I don't know—maybe he'd talk to you."

"I'll try," Sam said. "It's, what, five weeks until the wedding? I'll see him in person and ask what's going on."

"Thank you," Sarah said, her voice pitched low. "It's been . . ." She bent her head. Sam saw her swipe her eyes, and could barely hear her when she said, "I've been trying to decide if I should just ask him to move out."

Sam felt his face sag in surprise. Sarah and Eli's marriage had always felt as reliable as anything he could imagine; as solid as their own parents' union had been. "It's that bad?"

Sarah nodded sadly. "Something's got to change. Eli knows he's been awful, and he won't tell me why. He told me he won't even talk about it until after the wedding, and I agreed. I thought maybe he was asking me for time because he wanted to fix whatever's going on. Or end it. Whatever 'it' is." She raised her hands, then let them fall into her lap. "The whole time we were dating, he made me feel like I was the most important person in the world. And now it's like he can't even see me. If I walk into a room, he walks out of it. If I cook dinner, he chews it like it's cardboard. I can't remember the last time he gave me a compliment, or looked at me like I mattered to him."

"Ouch," Sam murmured. He knew, maybe better than anyone, that Sarah needed to be seen. She was like their mother that way, comfortable at the head of a classroom, or onstage, performing, drawing from the energy of an audience or the admiration of a partner.

"He barely talks to me. He looks right through me, and he won't tell me what's going on, or why he's acting this way, and I have no idea how to help him, and . . ." Sarah closed her mouth and raised her chin. "I don't want the boys thinking that this is what marriage is supposed to be. Or Ruby, either, for that matter. I don't want any of them believing that a husband, or a wife, can just check out emotionally, and the other person just endures it."

Sam nodded. "I'm sorry," he said.

Sarah sniffled. "I wish you were still here."

"I'll see you soon," he promised. He told her to call him if she needed him, and that he'd do his best to talk to Eli, and ended the call feeling sorry for his sister, puzzled about his brother-in-law and glad, again, that she hadn't asked him about his plans, or how he was doing, or if there was anything new in his life.

After Saul Barringer delivered his ultimatum, and Sam had cleared it with Connor's father. ("Yeah, sure, man, whatever works," Jason said, after Sam made his pitch. "I mean, I'd take him, but they say that the road ain't no place to start a family, right?") Sam had packed them up and brought Connor to New York for the summer.

Sarah and Eli had welcomed Sam, and their sons had been thrilled to have Connor staying in their house. Dexter was almost seven, and Miles was five, and Connor fit neatly into the boy-pack, a loyal (and extremely tractable) car in what his sister sometimes called the Testosterone Train. "I am going to pretend they're my big brothers," Connor told Sam, with a delighted expression on his usually somber face, and Sam felt his own heart lifting. He might have screwed up any number of things in his life, but at least he didn't need to second-guess his choice to get Connor away from his grandfather.

Sam rented a desk in one of the neighborhood's many shared workspaces and tried to re-gather the strands of his professional life. Every morning, he and his sister would drop the boys off at the day camp they attended. Then Sarah would take the subway to the music school, and Sam would head to his temporary office, ending his day in time to pick up the boys and escort them all back to Sarah's for a snack. The boys would play or read until dinner. Sam would help with the cooking, and Connor and his cousins would set the table ("Dexter only gets to do the silverware because he always drops the plates," Sam overheard Miles telling Connor), and they'd go around the table with Sarah and Eli asking each of the boys about the best and worst part of their day.

Sam and Connor stayed in the attic, which had been Ruby's domain before she'd gone off to college, Connor spent most of his time on the third floor, where Dexter and Miles had their bedrooms. After three weeks, Connor asked Sam if he could have a sleepover in Miles's room. Miles had bunk beds, and he'd generously offered his step-cousin the lower bunk. ("Sometimes I have nightmares," Sam heard Connor explaining in his gravelly voice. "That's okay," Miles had answered, before lowering his own voice to a whisper and saying, "I used to wet the bed.")

Sam watched over Connor carefully, worrying about the boy's bad dreams, and his extremely limited diet. Connor had always been picky, but after Julie's death, his selections narrowed to a tiny list of foods: chicken nuggets, carrot sticks, macaroni, peanut butter (never crunchy) on bread (always white), grilled-cheese sand-wiches, cheese sticks, and ice cream.

Sarah told Sam not to worry. The pediatrician said, "I promise you, he isn't going to starve. Keep offering him fruits and vegetables, and just be patient with him."

Sam did his best. He paid careful attention while his sister and brother-in-law gave him an introductory course in the parenting of little boys. Sarah took Sam to Old Navy and talked him through the bewildering particulars of kids' clothing sizes. ("How is a 6 differ-ent from a 6T?" Sam asked, and Sarah leaned close and stage-whispered, "*No one knows.*") Together, Sam and Connor picked out a new backpack, shaped like a stego-saurus, and a duvet cover with a dinosaur print. After his first day of camp, Connor joined his cousins for a play-date in Prospect Park, then, a week after that, an invitation to a classmate's birthday party arrived. It seemed like Connor was making friends and settling into the rhythms of a new house. When Sam tentatively asked his sister if she knew of any children's therapists, Sarah had smiled and said, "This is Park Slope. I bet I'd have an easier time telling you the kids who aren't in therapy than the ones who are," she said.

"Really?"

"Really. Personally, I think Connor's doing fine."

Sam sipped his coffee. "Sometimes I hear him crying in the bathtub," he said.

Sarah made a face. "Sam. His mother died. Of course he's going to sneak off and cry. And have bad dreams, and pitch a fit if you accidentally give him crunchy peanut butter." She looked at her brother fondly. "I get that it's probably hard to imagine what he's going through. You and I had the most normal childhood in the world."

"And I still did some crying in the bathtub," said Sam, remembering being eight years old, when the older boys hadn't let him join their ice hockey game, or twelve, when Missy LoPresto had broken up with him the day after agreeing to be his girlfriend because she'd decided she liked Craig Shepard better.

The therapist Sarah eventually found was named Ava Bidwell, and her office was just a few blocks from Connor's camp, conveniently close to an ice-cream parlor. Sam and Connor would share a dish of vanilla with caramel sauce after Connor's appointments on Wednesday afternoons, until that particular taste and texture became the taste of mental health. After they'd finished their treat, they would walk back to Sarah and Eli's brownstone together, with Connor's small hand secure in Sam's larger one.

By the end of August, Dr. Bidwell pronounced Connor ready to face the world—"or at least try whole-wheat bread." Sam brought Connor back to California. Maybe, someday, they would move East for good, but for now, he wanted to at least keep Connor in the neighborhood he knew and send him back to the school he'd attended before Julie had died.

He found a Craftsman bungalow with a guesthouse in the back, and he and Connor spent two eight-hour days at Ikea, where they bought a kitchen table and a couch and an entertainment unit and bunk beds like Dexter and Miles had. Sarah helped him equip the house, sending him links to furniture websites and places to buy rugs and towels and dishes and glasses and the thousand different things he'd need. Sam found Connor a new therapist, and got him signed up for a soccer team, and a kids' cooking class that met on Saturday mornings. "Okay?" he asked, after he'd clicked the final buttons for enrollment.

"I guess," Connor said. He turned away, then looked over his shoulder as he asked, almost casually, "Only can't I just stay home with you?"

Sam scooped him up, deposited him on the dark-blue couch they'd picked out together, and sat down beside him. "I know that you're scared."

"I'm not!" Connor said unconvincingly. "I just like it at home. I have all my dinosaurs." Back in Brooklyn Sam had helped him put together a collection of plastic models: a triceratops and a spinosaurus, a brachiosaurus and a T. rex.

"I know," Sam said. "Tell you what—if you do two soccer practices and you don't like it, you don't have to keep doing it."

Connor considered this. "Can I bring my dinosaurs to practice?"

"How about you can bring one? And maybe we'll keep it in your backpack until practice is over." Connor considered, then nodded his assent. Sam dropped him off at the first practice, praying it would go well, watching as Connor edged toward a cluster of boys. "Do you like dinosaurs?" he heard Connor ask. Three small heads had nodded. Sam felt like pumping his fist in exultation as Connor ran over, round face flushed.

"Sam, can you get my backpack? They want to see my spinosaurus!" He felt himself grinning as Connor grabbed the beast and raced away.

Sam stayed vigilant as the school year progressed, watching Connor for signs of trouble. He mourned Julie. He thought of her constantly as he filled the house with furniture, realizing that the new bed was one they'd never share; the new TV was one she'd never watch with Connor sitting between them for the hundredth viewing of *Toy Story*. He grieved for her, even as their time together started to take on the quality of a dream. If they'd ever fought, he couldn't remember; if there'd been things he hadn't liked about her, he couldn't recall. He kept plodding forward, keeping all his attention on Connor, determined to honor his wife's memory by giving her son a stable childhood and a happy home. In October, he'd called Jason, who hadn't been in touch since they'd returned from Brooklyn.

"Hey, listen, if you could just, you know, hang on to him, that would be great," Jason said, as Sam was almost sure he would.

"I'm not going to ask you for child support," Sam said.

"Good, because I know I'd been kind of running be-hind, but, here's the thing—"

Sam cut him off. "I don't need money. I just need to know if you want Connor in your life. Because, if not, I'd like to be his legal guardian."

Sam could hear Jason thinking, weighing what he wanted and what Sam would think of him if he asked for it. "Look, it's not that I don't like the little guy," he began. "It's just—look, I told Julie this. I never wanted a kid. I wasn't ready. She said she'd take care of everything."

"And she did," Sam said. "So will I. You just need to sign the papers."

Jason paused, then said in a grown-up version of Connor's rasp, "I feel like shit, you know? I'm not a bad person."

"Of course not," said Sam. He asked Jason for his address, sent the papers he'd had drawn up via certified mail, and showed them to Connor when Jason returned them.

"So now you're my dad?" He looked at Sam solemnly, right in the eyes.

"Yes," Sam said. "Now I'm your dad."

Connor threw himself at Sam, wrapping his arms around his waist. "Good," he said. "Good." Then he'd pushed his hair out of his eyes (*Got to get him a hair-cut*, Sam thought). "Can we make another dinosaur this weekend?"

For the entire first year without Julie, Sam didn't even think about dating. Getting meals on the table, doing his job, keeping Connor on track—all of that was enough.

Sam and Connor made it through the holidays, the first Halloween without Julie, the first Thanksgiving and Chanukah (which Connor had never celebrated) and Christmas (which he had). In the spring, Connor turned to Sam one night after dinner as he was clearing the table and Sam was washing the dishes and said, "Sometimes I can't remember Mom's face." His voice was grave. "And I feel sad, because it means I'm forgetting her."

Sam went to him and gave him a hug. "We'll never forget her," he said. "And I can show you lots of pictures any time you like."

Connor looked at him shyly. "Do you ever have trouble remembering how she looked?"

Sam kissed his cheek. "No," he said. "I see her every time I look at you."

Just over a year after that terrible afternoon, the day of the cops and the salmon, which Sam and Connor had never eaten again, Sarah began suggesting it was time for Sam to get back out there. Even though Sam felt no impulse to meet someone new, and no idea where he'd find the energy for dating, he agreed with his sister, because it was always easier to agree with Sarah than to argue. When she'd ask if he wanted to meet a nice woman she knew from college, or a woman she'd met in a Pilates class who'd been transferred to California, Sam would say yes, and would dutifully go on dates . . . but the first and second dates never became third dates, or led to anything like a relationship. "You're not ready yet," his sister pronounced. Sam figured she was right. He was still mourning Julie, still processing the way his life had been upended. He was also still holding a gigantic grudge against Connor's grandfather, who was alive and well and had, if his boasting could be believed, become a father again at the age of ninety-two. ("Isn't he bedridden?" Marcus asked when Sam relayed the news. Then he considered, shrugged, and said, "Maybe being in bed all day just means he's halfway there.")

Sam's realization that something had shifted started to dawn during a phone call one Friday night in early spring. Sarah had been telling a story about how one of Ruby's friends had gone viral for writing Drarry stories.

"Drarry?" Sam repeated.

"Ah, you and Connor haven't dipped your toes into the wonderful world of Harry Potter yet, I presume?" Sarah asked.

Sam admitted that they hadn't, and Sarah explained that the hero and one of the villains in the story were named Harry and Draco, and that people—young women, mostly—wrote stories where the two of them were actually in love. "So Drarry is their ship name."

"Ship name?" Sam was lost.

"Ship like relationship," said Sarah. "Draco plus Harry is Drarry. Hang in there," she'd said cheerfully. "I'm sure by the time Connor's a teenager there's going to be completely new slang to figure out."

Later that night, moved by a whim he didn't consider too deeply, Sam typed "Drarry" into his browser and went tumbling down a rabbit hole of smut. There were thousands of stories; maybe tens of thousands. Some of the stories were silly, or poorly written, or anatomically improbable, even if the lovers were both wizards (which, of course, meant they contained any number of terrible "magic wand" puns), but some were well-written and funny and sexy. Sam poked around the website, impressed and a little shocked by the multitude and creativity of pairings, and the worlds from which they came. Harry Potter was just the beginning (Sam would have called it the tip of the iceberg if the phrase "just the tip" hadn't already started to sound perverted). If you wanted to read about Sherlock Holmes and Dr. Watson getting it on, you could. If you wanted a fifty-thousand-word novella about Captain Kirk and Mr. Spock making sweet, same-sex love in a villa in New Orleans, it was there. Sam worked his way deeper and deeper into the archives, until he looked up from a story about Frodo and Sam sixty-nining beside the Cracks of Doom and realized two things, both of them shocking. The first was that it was two o'clock in the morning. The second was that he had an erection.

Tentatively, Sam palmed his crotch, rocking his hips forward, pressing into the warmth of his hand, thinking, *What on earth?* His sex drive had dwindled to practically nil in the months since Julie's death, a phenomenon Sam ascribed to a combination of grief, antidepressants, and parenting a little boy who'd frequently start the night in his own bed and finish it in Sam's. Maybe it wasn't weird that he'd find himself turned on by any kind of X-rated fiction, whether it involved men and women, or men and men, or a pair of male teenage wizards.

Or maybe, suggested a voice in his head, *this is what's been missing, all those years. This is the thing you never knew about yourself, the blank space you could never fill in. This is what will make the rest of your life make sense.*

Sam closed his computer. He changed into his pajamas, brushed his teeth, and lay in bed, staring up into the darkness, wondering. Was he gay? Was he bi? Was he—oh, God—into hobbits? A hobbitsexual? Was that a thing? And if he was gay, how could he have missed it? Unless he was the stupidest person in the world. Which, at almost three in the morning, seemed like a real possibility.

He wasn't worried about being judged or shunned. His parents were admirably open-minded; his best friend wouldn't care. His sister would just be happy for him ... and certainly few people in Los Angeles would be shocked by a gay man, even one as late-blooming as Sam.

I'll keep an open mind, he decided. That week, he found himself noticing men in a way he hadn't before. The swell of a mailman's calf as he pushed his cart down the sidewalk; the solid span of a neighbor's chest beneath his golf shirt while he watered his lawn; that one of the other dads in the park had very nice eyes. A month after the night of the hobbits, Sam downloaded the app that every gay man in America seemed to use. He set up an account, first hesitating over a screen name (he settled on SamIAm37), then agonizing over how to identify himself. Gay? Bi? Questioning? *Thirty-eight years old and just realizing that maybe I'm into dudes because I read some Harry Potter fan fic?* What was the shorthand for that?

He finally clicked *questioning*, then moved on to his next hurdle: the profile picture. Plenty of men used their faces. Others displayed body parts, abs or chests or asses. And when you started perusing the profiles themselves—oh, yep, there they were. The dick pics. After lengthy consideration and a few experimental selfies, Sam posted a full-body shot of himself on a hike with Connor (he made sure viewers wouldn't be able to see Connor, and that they would be able to see all of his body, in the interest of not misleading anyone, or sending anyone home disappointed).

Sixty seconds after his profile went live, his notifications started chiming.

Hey sexxxy, said Queers4Fears.

Hi daddy, wrote MarcosPolo, while TomTom83 just used the waving-hands emoji.

Haven't seen you before, said someone called—oh, God—DadBodFanboi. Who was, according to the app, a terrifying 0.1 mile away from Sam, a piece of information that prompted Sam to jump up from his desk, racewalk across the room, and yank the blinds down, as if DadBodFanboi might have been crouching in the oleander right under the window.

Sam immediately disabled his geographical tag and changed the settings to show that he was offline. But he kept scrolling. Young men, older men; men who identified as gay and queer and bi and pan and poly; bearded men with bellies; clean-shaven men with eyeliner; a panoply of men, an endless buffet.

You can do this, Sam told himself. He found a man whose profile said he lived in the Valley and who was a few years older than Sam; a man who'd used a picture of his face and not a body part to introduce himself to the world. The man's name was Tim. He was more pleasant-looking than handsome, in a baseball cap that could have been covering a bald spot and a plaid shirt that did not look like it was disguising a six-pack. After long moments of agonizing, Sam typed, *Hi.*

Hi yourself, Tim wrote back. *Looking for company?*

Well, thought Sam. At least "company" was less explicit than some of what had already been proposed. He typed, *No. At least, not yet. I'm very new at this—it's my first time using this app, actually. I've only ever been with women, but . . .*

He paused, and Tim jumped into the silence.

You're curious?

Yes, Sam typed gratefully. *I don't want to lead you on . . .*

No worries, said Tim. *If you need someone to hold your hand, I've been out since I was thirteen and could probably use the karma points. Want to jump on the phone?*

Sam agreed. Ten seconds later, his phone lit up, and a warm male voice was on the other end.

"Sam?"

"Thank you for doing this," he blurted. His palms and the small of his back were sweaty and he felt like he couldn't quite catch his breath. "This is probably ridiculous, someone just figuring out he's maybe attracted to men at my age."

"Sexuality's complicated." Tim sounded cheerful and perfectly unfazed. "Don't feel ashamed. People figure out they're into all kinds of things at every age. Some people never manage to figure out what they like at all."

"That's . . ." Sam tucked his phone under his chin to dry his hands on his jeans. "That's sad."

"It is," Tim agreed.

"And I always thought that people who were gay— well, at least men who were gay," Sam amended, "they figure it out early."

"Some do. Maybe most do. But not everyone."

Sam braced himself for questions about when he'd known, and what he'd known, and, inevitably, how he'd known. He was trying to figure out how to spin the Harry Potter piece of his gay origin story, but Tim seemed to sense his discomfort.

"So what do you do?" he asked.

Sam told him. He learned that Tim managed an upscale Italian restaurant in Beverly Hills, that he was the middle of three children, that his older sister and younger brother were both fine with his sexuality, and that his parents, after some initial resistance, had come around. Tim had been with his partner for fifteen years, which comforted Sam, as did the news that their parting had been amicable. "And so here I am, back on Grindr," Tim said, his voice good-natured. "Do you want to meet? Grab a drink? No pressure," he added. "If you decide you don't want this to be romantic, we can just talk."

In the interest of full disclosure, Sam told Tim that he was widowed, that he had sole custody of a stepson, and that he also was on antidepressants, which could make orgasms elusive. "I'm really selling myself," he concluded, and Tim laughed and said, "At least you've got your teeth." He paused. "You do have your teeth, right?"

Sam assured him that he did, and they agreed to meet at a coffee shop that Saturday, when Connor would be at his cooking class.

For the next three days, Sam was anxious and distracted. He couldn't decide if he was actually going to go through with this. When he decided that he was, he had no idea what to wear. He wanted to ask Sarah, but he knew he wasn't ready for that conversation, so he finally settled on his newest jeans and a button-down that Julie had once told him brought out the green in his eyes. On Saturday morning, he made sure Connor got out of bed on time. He fed the boy breakfast and got him into the car a half hour before they normally left, just in case there was traffic.

"Are you okay?" Connor asked, as Sam fidgeted, drumming his fingers on the wheel. "Is something wrong?"

"No, no. I'm just . . ." Just what? "I'm meeting someone new while you're in class."

"Making friends is scary," Connor said solemnly, and unzipped the backpack he carried with him everywhere, rooting around, finally producing his stegosaurus. "Here. You can take him. If you need something to talk about, just ask if the other boy likes dinosaurs."

Sam thanked him. He slipped the dinosaur into the glove compartment, sent Connor off to class, and got to the coffee shop ten minutes ahead of time, approaching the door with his heart fluttering madly, a little bird trapped in his throat. He got a coffee, found a table, and watched the entrance, feeling his armpits prickling, trying not to panic; telling himself that he had nothing to be afraid of, that it was just a conversation with a man, like thousands of conversations with hundreds of men that he'd had in his life.

A few minutes later, Tim arrived, greeting Sam with a wave and a smile. He wore jeans and a plaid shirt. Without a baseball cap, Sam could see that his light-brown hair was thinning, and that his teeth were a little crooked, but when he smiled he was very appealing. *Could I kiss him?* Sam wondered. *Could I kiss any guy? And why am I assuming that he'd even want to kiss me?*

"You made it," Tim said, offering his hand.

Sam swallowed hard as he tried to tell if the touch of the man's hand made him feel anything. "Did you think I wouldn't show?"

Tim's eyes crinkled at their corners. "I figured there was a chance. What can I get you?"

Sam indicated his coffee. "I'm fine for now."

"Okay. Be right back." He got in line. Sam's heart thumped even harder. Was he supposed to offer to buy the drink? What was the etiquette here? Had he screwed things up already?

"You look," Tim observed as he came back with his coffee and took a seat, "like you're about to pass out."

Sam exhaled in a rush. Tim patted his shoulder. "Breathe," he said. Sam felt relief, but no particular spark at the touch, and wondered if he'd been wrong about the whole thing.

"So," said Tim. "You grew up in Boston, right? How'd you end up in LA?"

Sam told him his story—UC Berkeley, Marcus, Julie, and Connor, and what his life was like now. Tim told him about his year in art school in Miami—"my misspent youth"—before he'd gone into hospitality. They talked about sports, and their favorite hiking trails in Los Angeles, and then, somehow, a pleasant half hour had passed. Tim was easy to talk to, with a sharp sense of humor and that appealing smile. The longer they talked, the more relaxed Sam felt. When Tim asked if he wanted to walk a little—"there's a park nearby"— Sam checked the time, then agreed.

As soon as they'd made it outside, he felt his fears returning. The sun felt too bright, and the world felt crowded. Moms pushed double-wide strollers; kids ran up and down and over an elaborate wooden climbing structure, chasing each other in games of tag. Tim and Sam sat on a bench. "So," Tim said, "what do you think?"

"About . . ."

Tim put his hand on Sam's shoulder, eyebrows raised. Sam could feel the weight of the other man's palm; the press of his fingers. "Can I kiss you?"

Sam hesitated, thinking. Then he told himself not to think, to just try, for once, to feel. He nodded. Tim's palm slid up to Sam's jaw. Sam felt his face cupped in a hand that was bigger and stronger than any hand he'd ever felt there before, and then Tim was kissing him. Sam could feel the familiar sensation of warm lips and the novelty of stubble, the way Tim smelled like male sweat and some subtly spicy cologne. He felt the other man's lips move against his; then Tim pulled away, with a teasing crinkle around his eyes.

"So? What's the verdict?"

Sam found that he was smiling and that his knees were wobbling. He was feeling the strangest rush of contradictory emotions, fear and arousal, confusion and excitement, all at the same time. His belly was full of butterflies; his feet were shuffling, antsy, ready to run. Tim sat, regarding him calmly, waiting for an answer. "Huh," Sam managed. "Wow."

Tim smiled and thumped him on the back. "Welcome aboard, baby gay."

Sam and Tim quickly realized that they were going to be friends and not lovers, and Sam's next attempt at meeting someone, a few months later, was considerably less successful. When Connor agreed to spend a Saturday night with the one babysitter he liked, Sam and Tim had gone to a dance party, an underground bash held in what was literally a bar's basement. Sam had presented his proof of vaccination, gotten his hand stamped, then stood in a corner staring as, less than a foot away, men in underpants made of less cloth than their face masks and body glitter were gyrating on platforms. *This is how men our age meet each other?* he yelled to Tim, hoping the other man could read lips.

Tim assured him that, indeed, this was how men their age met each other—"especially the ones who don't like the apps." He swore that Sam's age wouldn't be a problem, and that, in fact, the world was full of men looking for daddies (Sam cringed), bears, and silver foxes. Sam did not believe he fit into any of those categories. He wondered what animal he was. A frightened groundhog? An extremely shy otter? Definitely something that was timid. Something hairy, for sure, because while he didn't object to some judicious trimming, Sam wasn't up for anything involving hot wax. At least, not yet.

At the club, the bass notes were making his fillings shiver. "I'll get us drinks!" Tim shouted, and Sam nodded and went to stand in the corner, where, for fifteen minutes, he marveled at the beautiful boys in Speedos and N95 masks, waving their arms and singing along to Lady Gaga, delighting in the night, in the music, in their own freedom. He realized, too late, that he was staring when one of the beautiful boys approached him.

"Wanna dance?" Before Sam could answer, the boy had grabbed his arm and dragged him out on the dance floor, where, in his jeans and New Balance sneakers, Sam felt as conspicuous and ungainly as a fire hydrant plopped down in a field of lissome, waving reeds. He did his best to move with the music. The boy spun around, waving his arms in the air before attaching his backside to Sam's midsection, leaving a smear of glitter on Sam's polo shirt.

When the song changed, the boy grabbed Sam's hand. "Wanna go outside?" he mouthed. Sam scanned the crowd frantically, looking for Tim, but his friend had disappeared, and the boy was tugging him insistently toward the door. Sam followed him out into the night and down into a parking garage. His ears were still ringing from the music. The night air was soft around them, and everything felt dreamlike, not quite real, as the young man unlocked a car and climbed into the back seat. Sam climbed in beside him. The boy pulled off his mask and fell on him, like he was a zombie and Sam the last meal he'd ever eat. His mouth was on Sam's neck, then his ear, then back at his mouth. His tongue demanded entry, pressing and prodding and finally plunging as he slipped one of his hands up Sam's shirt and tweaked his nipple. Sam squirmed away, trying not to giggle, because that had been Sarah's particular torture, when they'd been little and Sam had displeased her.

"Ooh," the boy breathed.

"Ow," Sam said. The young man was undeterred.

"Hey," Sam managed, as he felt fingers on his zipper. "Hey, could you—"

Too late. The boy wrenched his zipper down, and then his mouth was on Sam's startled, but not entirely disinterested, penis. The young man was good at this, taking Sam's entire length down the warm tunnel of his throat, his tongue making practiced swoops along the way. All of that would have been fine if the suction hadn't been so insistent, quickly becoming just short of uncomfortable. "Hey, um … could you … could you please …" There was no way, Sam was realizing, that you could complain about a blow job and not sound ungrateful. He squeezed his eyes shut and concentrated as hard as he could on his favorite snippet from Pornhub. There was an older man, maybe in his fifties, with silvery hair and a beard, and a younger man, dark-haired and slender. The older man had attended to the younger with an attention just short of worshipful. He'd undressed the young man tenderly, telling him how handsome he was, how beautiful, and then the young man had undressed the older one, revealing a mat of springy gray chest hair, caressing him slowly. For a long time they'd just kissed, lingeringly and lovingly. It was like a scene from Greek mythology, like Narcissus twined around a statue of Zeus. That was what Sam wanted, that, not this platinum-haired Hoover-throated sex demon who still had Sam's now mostly flaccid penis down his throat and showed no signs of letting go.

Finally, finally, the boy pulled off with a wet pop. "Hey, you need a pill?" he asked. "I can . . ."

"No." Sam's voice sounded sharper than he'd intended. He tried again. "No. I'm sorry. I just—I was—" He started over. "I don't think this is what I want. Right now. I mean, maybe if we got to know each other a little better?"

The young man was staring at him, his expression as puzzled as if Sam had started speaking in tongues. "We could go out to dinner," Sam said. "Or a drink? Or we could—"

The young man smiled, not unkindly, and touched Sam's cheek. "You want a relationship," he said. Which was true, except he said "relationship" the way Sam would have said "incurable herpes." "That's cool. Good luck." He patted Sam's cheek again, then turned and hopped nimbly out of the car, heading back toward the party, leaving Sam to sit there, amused and dumbfounded, trying to understand this new revelation, which was that he was interested in men, but not just to have sex with. He wanted someone to love. And now, maybe it was already too late. Maybe he'd missed his chance. He had wasted his twenties and most of his thirties being oblivious, and now it was just never going to happen.

After the wedding, Sam thought, tucking himself back into his pants and climbing out of the car. After the wedding, Sarah and Eli and the boys would go back to New York, and Sam and Connor would stay on in

Truro. Maybe he'd try telling his mother his news and see how that went over. Then, at night, after Connor was sleeping, he'd go to Provincetown, one of the great gay meccas of America.

He pictured himself, with a fresh haircut and a Tim-approved outfit, walking along Commercial Street, locking eyes with someone handsome and kind and funny and interesting. He would look at this man, and the man would look at him, and just like that, they'd know. No awkward groping, no confusion, no strange mouths on his genitals. Just the faceless, gorgeous man of his dreams, who would see Sam, and know him, and desire what Sam desired, and want the same things for himself.

Sam snorted to himself, thinking that this was as much of a fairy tale as anything Walt Disney had ever put onscreen. Love didn't work that way. Sex didn't, either. But, Sam decided, in the handful of weeks between now and his niece's wedding, he would allow himself to hope.

SARAH

~~~~~~~~

Six weeks before the wedding, on a gorgeous day in May, Sarah and Eli and Ruby had an appointment at a caterer's showroom. Ruby and Gabe made a list of their favorite dishes, and Diana, the manager of a restaurant in Provincetown called Safe Harbor, had helped them craft a menu for the wedding night. After the ceremony, waiters would circulate with passed appetizers, including options for Ruby's vegan friends, and there'd be a raw bar with oysters and fresh shrimp. For dinner, the guests would enjoy salads of fresh local greens, with candied pecans and goat cheese from one of the nearby dairies, then grilled striped bass and rice pilaf or beef Wellington, Ruby's old favorite, with sour cream whipped potatoes. There would be a selection of cheeses, then miniature desserts, and, at midnight, a truck serving hot doughnuts to the revelers. Diana, who had once been Sarah and Sam's babysitter for the summer, and who'd lived, for a time, in a cottage that Sarah's mother owned, had flown down from Boston to show Ruby tablecloths and napkins, china and crystal—"All the stuff you need to see in person," Ronnie said—and have her sample wedding cakes.

Sarah was glad to be out of the house; happy to feel useful to her stepdaughter, delighted, as always, for a reason to wear something that wasn't a hoodie and pajama bottoms. She'd chosen a cream-colored silk blouse with lavish ruffles at the sleeves, slim-fitting black twill pants, and, for a pop of color, pointy-toed pumps in hot pink. Her favorite necklace, a rough chunk of topaz on a fine-link gold chain hung around her neck, a gold cuff brace-let sat on her wrist, and she'd dabbed perfume behind her ears.

Once, Eli would have looked her over with approval, or even pulled her back down to bed and made them both late for work. But it had been weeks since the last time they'd made love, and Sarah couldn't recall the last time Eli had paid her a compliment, which was, some-how, even sadder. That morning, he hadn't even been there to see her. "If you won't tell me what's going on, I think you should sleep somewhere else," she'd said, after that morning where she'd found him almost crying in front of his tie rack. She'd hoped an ultimatum would finally get him talking. Instead, he'd just given her a sad nod, gathered his blankets and pillow, and moped his way to the attic. He'd slept there ever since.

Ruby, on her lunch hour, bounded into view right on time, with an enormous black iced coffee in her hand and a clipboard tucked under her arm.

Sarah looked at her stepdaughter, feeling her heart expand, and her anger at Eli evaporating instantly re-placed by a fierce and protective love. Ruby wore a red T-shirt, denim overalls, and black Keds. A few curls had escaped from her ponytail to bounce around her cheeks. Sarah opened her arms and hugged her hard. She adored her sons, and loved being a mother of boys, but there was something special about a daughter, and Ruby had been that to her. Together, they'd seen musi-cals ("Too much singing," Eli would grouse), and had gone thrift-shopping and watched hours of trashy reality TV. They'd made dozens of trips to museums and hundreds of batches of chocolate chip–studded pancakes. The two of them were the family's early risers, and they'd spent many Sunday mornings together, frying bacon and mixing batter in the quiet kitchen, in the hush of a city still sleeping.

"Have I told you how lucky I am to be your stepmom?" Sarah asked, with her arms still wrapped around Ruby.

Ruby stood on her tiptoes, rocking back and forth as Sarah held her. "I'm lucky to have you, too."

They were both a little teary when Diana came out of the building and stood blinking owlishly in the sunshine. She wore a black pantsuit, a white T-shirt underneath, and the same Keds as Ruby's on her feet. Her dark hair was pulled back in a low bun, and the corners of her eyes crinkled as she looked at Sarah.

"My goodness," she said. "You're a grown-up!"

"It happens to the best of us," Sarah said, studying what she could see of Diana's face and trying to connect it back to the girl who'd been a teenager during her summer in Truro. She knew that eventually, her mom had sold Diana the cottage on the dunes, which had undergone two additions and was now barely a cottage at all. Sarah's sense was that something had happened to Diana that summer on the Cape, and that Ronnie felt responsible somehow. Sarah thought that Diana looked like an accomplished professional, the owner of one of the most acclaimed fine-dining spots on all the Cape, and Sarah could see a diamond wedding band on her left hand. If she'd had troubles, Diane seemed to have put them behind her.

"You're my bride?" Diana asked, and when Ruby

nodded, she'd bumped Ruby's elbow, then Sarah's. "Come on in! Everything's ready." She looked around. "Are we waiting for a third?"

"I think your dad got stuck at the office," Sarah told Ruby as Diana led them through the high-ceilinged room, where two tables were waiting. She'd reminded Eli of this appointment before she'd left the house, and she'd texted him another reminder an hour ago.

"Now, this is the gold damask with the sheer overlay, and then we have the maize linen with the crimson runner. I wanted you to see them both in the sunshine," Diana said.

Ruby touched the edge of the first tablecloth, then looked at Sarah. "Should we wait for Dad before we decide?"

"I'm not sure he's going to have strong opinions, but I'll call him," Sarah said, and thought, *I'll kill him. If he's forgotten about this, if he lets Ruby down, I will kill him.* While Ruby and Diana talked through the merits of the different shades and fabrics, Sarah called Eli, and when her call went straight to voicemail, she did her best to sound calm. "Ruby and I are here with Diana. I hope you're on your way."

Thirty minutes later, Ruby had decided on the table-cloths, and on the china and crystal and flatware. The three of them sat at the first table, and Diana pulled up photographs of the Cape house on her iPad to take them through what she called the run of show.

"Such a beautiful house," Diana murmured as the first picture popped onto the screen—a shot taken from the living room, looking out at the deck and the water. "So, I'm thinking cocktails in the living room, an hour before sunset. Then we go out to the deck for the ceremony, and then . . ." Diana swiped, and Sarah heard Ruby sigh happily at the image of a long table, running the length of the deck, draped in a shimmering pale-gold tablecloth. Votive candles twinkled in the twilight, and low bouquets of orange and gold roses stood at regular intervals. "When it gets dark, we'll have fairy lights on a trellis." She swiped again, showing Ruby another picture, and Ruby sounded awed when she said, softly, "It's so beautiful."

"I do love a decisive bride," Diana said with the corners of her eyes crinkling.

"That's our Ruby," said Sarah, as she texted Eli, again, while Diana sent the pictures to Gabe and to Veronica.

"Now for the fun part!" Diana hurried away and came back with a tray bearing dozens of slivers of different flavors of cake. She'd just poured them glasses of water when Eli finally arrived. His hair was disheveled, and his expression was confused. "Did you start without me?"

"You're almost an hour late," Sarah said.

Eli frowned, shaking his head. "It was entered in my calendar for one o'clock. I don't know what happened."

"Never mind," Sarah said, trying not to glare. "You're just in time for dessert."

Eli sat, and Diana passed around the first sample. "This is our classic yellow cake with buttercream frosting."

Eli chewed, swallowed, patted his lips with his napkin, and said, "Tastes like a winner to me."

"It's good," said Ruby, looking thoughtful. "Just maybe a little . . ."

Sarah said "boring" at the same instant that Ruby said "basic." They laughed together. Diana nodded. Eli looked puzzled.

"How about chocolate? That's your favorite, right?" he asked his daughter. "Chocolate cake with chocolate icing?"

"Yes, Dad," Ruby said, rolling her eyes. "When I was six."

Eli frowned. "You don't like chocolate anymore?"

"Let's try this one," said Diana, reaching for fresh forks. *The poor woman*, Sarah thought. She'd probably navigated through hundreds of dysfunctional family quarrels. Then the thought hit her like a poisoned dart. Were they a dysfunctional family? She'd never thought of them that way. Blended, yes. Dysfunctional, absolutely not. She felt herself drooping and tried to sit up straight, to look cheerful, to smile, for Ruby's sake. "Here we are," Diana said. "Lemon pound cake with a raspberry buttercream filling and coconut frosting."

They ate their samples, sipped ice water, debated the merits of fondant versus buttercream, and discussed how many layers made sense. Or, rather, Sarah and Diana and Ruby debated and discussed. Eli kept his eyes down, shoveling cake into his mouth like he was being paid by the forkful, chewing and swallowing and barely saying a word. "They're all good," he said, when Ruby asked, and he didn't seem to notice her wounded expression, which, of course, made Sarah want to hurt him. *Ruby is your only daughter, and, God willing, this will be her only wedding. How can you do this to her?* After fifteen minutes, he pulled out his phone, poked at its screen, and muttered something about an emergency root canal. "Sorry," he said, reaching for his briefcase. "Time and toothaches wait for no man!"

Sarah and Ruby watched as he walked to the door. When Diana gathered the forks and plates and whisked them away, Ruby looked at her stepmother.

"Is something going on with Dad?"

Again, Sarah made herself smile. She wouldn't worry Ruby, not with her wedding so soon. "He's watching his little girl grow up," she said. "I think all fathers struggle with that."

Ruby nodded sagely. "Gotcha," she said. She gave Sarah another hug, shook Diana's hand, and went bouncing back to the subway.

Sarah walked slowly uptown, back to work, trying to put the unpleasantness with Eli out of her mind. Outside the school, she pulled on her mask and walked up the stairs, past a class of preschoolers carefully making their way down, one step at a time. Every day the building was full of little kids from nearby preschools who'd come to bang on bongos and shake maracas and rain sticks, dance and stomp and learn about rhythm and melody and how to make music. Sarah was glad to have them back; was lucky to be there herself. After a year of dealing with the difficulties of virtual lessons—the glitchy platforms, the overloaded internet, the digitally clueless instructors, and the kids who had to share their tablets or smartphones with parents or siblings, everyone had been delighted to resume in-person study, even if it meant uncomfortable masks, endless hand-washing, and sanitizing the keys on twenty pianos eight times a day. *I'm lucky*, Sarah told herself. No one in her family had gotten sick. She hadn't had to watch a loved one being hospitalized or, God forbid, dying. Everyone was healthy, and there was a wedding coming up. *Lucky*, she thought, and walked inside.

At five o'clock, Sarah was walking to the subway, with her mask looped around her wrist. Part of her mind was on an upcoming (please God in-person) fundraiser, which would be held outdoors in Gramercy Park. One of their wealthy donors had a key. Part of her was, as always, trying to solve the puzzle of what was wrong with

Eli, simmering with anger that he wouldn't just tell her. Yet another part was trying to figure out how she could smuggle a new dress for Ruby's wedding into the house without attracting Eli's attention or censure ("More clothes? Really? You've got so many dresses!"). It was so unfair, she was thinking, when she heard someone come up behind her, and a familiar voice calling her name.

"Sarah? My God. Sarah Weinberg?"

She didn't answer. Instead, she just stopped, right in the middle of the sidewalk, and closed her eyes. It seemed that her body had recognized his voice before her brain did; as if something deep inside of her, on a molecular level, remembered it. Remembered him. For a minute, she didn't want to turn around. She didn't want to look and see what twenty years had done to her first love. She didn't want him seeing what those years had done to her.

She heard him moving toward her; that familiar, sure-footed tread. When she'd known him, the summer they were both eighteen, Owen had been an athlete, a standout soccer and lacrosse player. Once, she'd dared him to swim butterfly across the length of Slough Pond. She'd tread water in the shallows, watching the graceful rise and fall of his torso and arms. He'd been maybe fifty yards from the shore when he'd taken a deep breath and slipped beneath the surface. She remembered his dark head popping out of the water, his wet hair clinging sleekly to his skull, his face, beaded with water, inches from her own.

On the sidewalk, Owen touched her shoulder. Sarah turned and opened her eyes. In that first glimpse, it seemed that he hadn't changed at all. He'd filled out some since he'd been a teenager, gotten more solid. His skin was rougher, more wrinkled, and there were threads of silver in his dark hair, but his face, his smile, his eyes . . .

"Sarah," he said. "Wow. Hi."

Sarah's heart stuttered. She felt unbalanced; flushed and dizzy, and she could tell that he knew what she was feeling. It had always been like that between them. He'd always known. *Don't ever play poker*, he used to tell her. *Everything you're thinking, it's right there on your face.*

She cleared her throat. "Owen. My goodness." She tried to draw the armor of *wife* and *mother* and *successful professional* around her even as her traitorous mind jumped to think of what else had happened on the day of the dare. *I'll bet you can't make it the whole way across swimming butterfly*, she'd said, and Owen had given her his easy smile, and said, *If I do it, what's my prize?*

Sarah curled her toes hard into the soles of her shoes, hoping the discomfort would bring her back to the present, away from herself at eighteen and the memory of gleaming young bodies in the water. She smoothed her hair and cleared her throat again. "I didn't know you were in New York." She hadn't known anything about him. They hadn't spoken since that summer had ended, and he'd dumped her via email and, in spite of her entreaties, had refused to call or write and tell her why.

"And you've been here how long? Since college?"

"Since college," Sarah confirmed. "How about you? Do you live here now?"

She longed for the answer to be yes. She also feared it. Owen that close; Owen in her city, with Eli barely making eye contact with her these days, was a dangerous situation.

Owen rolled his shoulders, a gesture she remembered. "For the next six months. I'm on assignment."

"Doing what?"

"I'm an FBI agent."

"You are?"

"Want to see my badge?" When he reached into his back pocket, his shirt and jacket pulled tight against his chest. Sarah forced herself to look at his face as he pulled out his wallet and showed her his badge, then extracted a business card, which had his name—Owen Lassiter— and the FBI's logo. She ran her thumb over the embossing, with the sensation of the air being too thin, of the world subtly tilting. When she and Owen had been teenagers, they'd told each other their secret ambitions, their most grandiose hopes and unlikeliest dreams. Sarah told him now she'd wanted to be a concert pianist, even if she'd already put that dream aside, unwilling to hang her whole future on the vanishingly slim possibility that she was talented and hardworking enough to rise above the rest of the would-be stars. Owen had wanted to be a writer, a journalist like Sebastian Junger or Jon Krakauer who would travel the world, covering wars and disasters and sporting competitions. "But I'll probably end up in law school," he'd glumly concluded.

"The FBI," Sarah said to Owen. It made sense, she realized. Owen had always loved superhero movies and westerns, and maybe his chaotic childhood, his multiply married parents, might have drawn him to the black-and-white dichotomies of law enforcement. She couldn't stop looking at him, comparing the man on the sidewalk to the boy who lived in her memories. "No law school?"

"Yes, law school. But no office job, thank God." He gave her a grin. "This is a lot more fun." He smoothed his tie, his eyes on hers. He was looking at her, she thought, like he knew exactly how she looked without her clothes. Which he did. Although her body, after two kids, was a long way from the body he'd remember, Sarah thought, and spared a moment of anger at the idea that she'd ever found flaws in herself when she was eighteen.

"What about you?" asked Owen. "Music?"

"Music school administration," she said, and hoped it didn't sound as pathetic out loud as it did in her head. "I like it. I used to teach, but it turns out what I really like is developing a curriculum and doing outreach in the community. Figuring out how to make lessons and instruments accessible to anyone who wants them. And there's the fundraising—" She made herself stop talking.

"I always thought I'd see you onstage," Owen said. Sarah felt her heart expanding, her face heating with embarrassment. She shook her head.

"You were so good," said Owen.

She waved the compliment away. "I wasn't."

"You were, though."

"Agree to disagree," Sarah said, and wondered, for the hundred thousandth time, how far she could have gone if she hadn't given up, if she'd just kept trying.

"Do you live nearby?" Owen was still looking at her, pleasantly but intently.

Sarah felt her palms start to itch. *It's not fair*, she thought, looking at his face, already tanned, his hands, the dark hair on his wrists. Why does he still have to be hot? Couldn't he have looked old, or completely unappealing; couldn't he have shown up with some disfiguring rash or a really unfortunate mustache? Except she suspected that even an Owen with pustules or weird facial hair would still look good to her. He would still be the first boy she'd ever loved.

"I have a studio here, but I live in Brooklyn. Park Slope." She made herself lift her chin, forced herself to say the rest. "My husband and I have two boys, plus a step-daughter." Then, without her planning on it, her biggest question—really, her only question for Owen—slipped out of her mouth. "You never came back to Cape Cod." When they'd parted, at the end of the summer, they had planned on staying together, or at least trying to, even though they were going to different colleges. Sarah had a Motorola flip phone back then and Owen, without a phone of his own, was going to call her as soon as he had his dorm phone number. But he'd never called. Instead, a week after they'd started college, he'd sent her a two-sentence email, telling her he'd met someone, at Duke, presumably during orientation ("Orientation!" Sarah had wept to her mother. "He couldn't even wait for classes to start!"), and that he wanted to break up. *It's for the best*, he'd written. *We should both be free.* She'd cried. Then she'd emailed, begging him to call her, thinking that, maybe, if he heard her voice, he'd remember how much he loved her, and how much she loved him. When Owen hadn't called, or written back, Sarah had been devastated. She didn't want her freedom, or some boy from BU or MIT or Harvard. She wanted Owen. And Owen, clearly, had no longer wanted her.

For the entire school year, she'd held out hope, ignoring the boys who did want to date her and waiting for summer to come. She thought that as soon as they saw each other, the Cape would work its magic again, and Owen would remember that he loved her. But that hadn't happened. She'd never seen Owen again. Not on Cape Cod, or anywhere else.

A pugnacious-looking woman with a pug on a pink leather leash came toward them, bugling "Excuse me!" as she approached. Owen and Sarah stepped to the far edge of the sidewalk, where Owen shifted his weight from foot to foot. "I owe you an explanation, but it's a long story."

"I'm not in a rush."

He smoothed his tie again. "The short version is that Sass and Anders got divorced. Then Sass got married again, and her new husband hated Cape Cod. He said you never saw anyone who mattered there. He had a place in the Hamptons."

"I'm sure your mom liked that." Owen's mother, Ballard Moreland Lassiter Renquist, known, for obscure reasons dating back to her childhood, as Sass, had divorced Owen's father when Owen was five, and had married Owen's stepfather when Owen was seven. Owen's biological father, meanwhile, had been on his third marriage by the time Sarah met Owen.

"How are your parents?" Owen asked Sarah, as the traffic surged by them, taxis honking, pedestrians blank-faced and exhausted as they made their way home at the end of the day. "How's your brother?"

"Sam's good. He's out in California." No point in getting into Sam's situation now, how he'd gotten married and had then been widowed and was now a stepfather. "And my mother's well." She swallowed and wondered how long it would hurt to say out loud. "My dad died just over a year ago."

"Oh, no. I'm sorry," he said. "I know how much you loved him."

Sarah nodded, not trusting herself to speak. She was remembering how Eli had tended to her after her father's death, bringing her plates of toast and cups of tea, rubbing her back, keeping the boys occupied when Sarah had stayed in her bedroom and cried. Her father had loved Sam, of course, but he and Sarah had enjoyed a different bond. There was something special about a father and his little girl, especially if she was his only daughter. She'd seen it with Eli and Ruby. It had been one of the things that made her love her husband.

Owen's gaze returned to her left hand. "So you're married."

"For thirteen years." Owen raised his eyebrows. Twenty-five wasn't young to be a bride in most of the country, but it was among her friends and, probably, his, too. Before he could comment on it, Sarah hurried to change the subject. "How about you?"

He put his hands in his pockets and shook his head. "No one could ever live up to you," he said. His tone was teasing, but his expression was serious, and Sarah had stood there, not knowing what to say.

When Sarah had been little, she'd had a fantasy of being constantly observed; watched by an invisible but surely vast audience as the star of the story of her own life, a story that someone else had already written and that it was her job to perform. Here's Sarah on her first day of school, walking into her new classroom. Who will be her friends? Here's Sarah on soccer-team tryout day; here she is at her piano recital; here she is in the cafeteria at school. With every new development in her life, she would imagine an audience watching, with approval or shock or delight. When she performed in front of an audience for the first time, at her first recital, she felt, instead of stage fright, a click of recognition. *Ah*, she thought, looking out at the assembled faces as they waited for her to begin. *There they are.*

Even as she imagined the audience, Sarah also pictured herself as an observer; that she was both the star and someone waiting to see how the action would unfold. *Oh*, she'd think to herself, *so that's what happens next*.

Was this, then, what happened next? *Sarah leaves her joyless marriage to reconnect with her old flame?* Or was this a test? Was she meant to renounce Owen and recommit to her family, to her boys and to Ruby, who loved her and needed her?

"Hey," Owen said. He reached for her hand, then seemed to think better of it. "Are you rushing off somewhere? Do you have time for a coffee?"

Sarah imagined her audience; invisible and attentive, watching and waiting for her decision. "Not today," she said. A refusal, then, but not an absolute one. She'd closed the door, for now, but she'd left it unlocked.

Owen nodded at the business card. "Well, now you've got my number. Give me a call if you want." He took a step toward her, close enough for her to appreciate, once more, the otherworldly blue of his eyes, and brushed his lips against her cheek. She smelled what must have been cologne or aftershave, layered over the scent that she remembered, the one that was just soap and Owen's skin.

"It was good to see you, Sarah."

"You, too," she'd said, and she'd walked to the subway, then home, with her heart pounding, her fingers returning, over and over, to the spot on her cheek where he'd kissed her.

Sarah Levy-Weinberg had heard about the Lassiters before she'd met them. Her mother referred to them, and to all the families with houses in the woods of Wellfleet and Truro, as the Pond People. She'd heard her parents discussing them at parties, when talking she and Sam would sneak out of their beds and up to the kitchen.

They'd ease the sliding door open and tiptoe onto the half-moon-shaped deck, where they would watch, and hear, the grown-ups below them, gathered around the glowing turquoise rectangle of the pool. *WASPs. Snobs. Anti-Semites.* "They think they own the Outer Cape, and they don't like it when people like us show up," she'd heard her mom telling her aunt Suzanne, who'd crinkled her nose and said, "Are you sure they just don't like you?"

Sarah first encountered the Pond People when she was seven. It was the first summer she and Sam had managed to swim all the way across Gull Pond, with her mother swimming with them, encouraging them, letting them tread water and catch their breath while they held on to her shoulders. Every few strokes, Sarah would lift her head and squint at the shoreline. In the distance, through the reeds, she could see a house. At first it was just a blur, but as she got closer, she could see it in more detail: a one-story building with a shingled roof and red paint, set on a little rise behind the shore, with a splintery wooden dock sticking out like a stubby finger into the water. Sarah swam and swam for what felt like forever, and the reeds and the house shoreline never seemed to get nearer, until finally, in tiny increments, she could feel the water growing warmer, could see it changing color. First she felt the tickle of reeds against her feet, and then, a few strokes later, she could just brush the sand on the bottom with her toes. A minute later, Sam came up behind her, gasping and splashing.

"Rest for a few minutes," said their mom, who wasn't out of breath at all. "Then we'll start back."

Sarah felt, before she saw, that there was someone watching them. She looked past her mother's head and she saw a boy on the shore. He seemed to be about her age. He was barefoot, dressed in faded blue swim trunks and nothing else. His skin was deeply tanned. His hair was dark brown, almost black, and he was staring at them. No—he was scowling at them.

"Good morning!" her mother called, her voice loud and cheerful as she waved hello. The boy's scowl didn't change. "This is private property!" he called, in a carrying voice. Behind her, Sam was paddling noisily, breathing hard, as the screen door slammed and a woman's voice called, "Owen? Is someone there?"

Beside her, Sarah's mother rolled her eyes. "Are you ready?"

Sarah wasn't actually ready, and her mom ended up towing her and her brother the final two hundred yards or so back to the public beach. After she'd dried off, and her brother was flopped, facedown and panting, on a towel in the sun, Sarah asked her mom, "Why did that boy say it was private property?"

"It's not," her mother said absently. She was sitting in her folding chair, in her wide-brimmed sunhat and her big sunglasses, already engrossed in her book. "The shoreline might be, but the water itself isn't anyone's property."

"So why'd that boy say it was?"

"He's been misinformed," her mother said. She closed her book, her finger marking her place. Sam didn't lift his head, but Sarah could tell that he was listening. "Bottom line is, you're allowed to swim in any part of the pond you want to. It isn't theirs, no matter what they say."

The next time Sarah saw the boy was later that summer, in Wellfleet, at an ice-cream parlor in the center of town. This was their Sunday-night tradition: they'd go out to dinner somewhere (Moby Dick's or PJ's, if the kids prevailed; Ciro & Sal's or the Abbey in Province-town, if Ronnie and Lee had their way), and they'd always stop somewhere for a cone for dessert. Sarah and Sam had just joined the line when Sarah spotted the boy, almost at the window, standing with a slender woman dressed in an oversized men's shirt, the sleeves rolled up, tied at the waist above a pair of white jeans. The woman's hair was streaky blonde, twisted in a knot at the nape of her neck. She wore sunglasses, even though the sun was almost down, and a swipe of bright-pink lipstick, which caught Sarah's eye. Her mother never wore makeup in the summertime. There was an older girl, too, who seemed to be maybe eleven or twelve, with dark hair in a ponytail, shoulders hunched in a forest-green sweatshirt. Sarah recognized the boy's scowl. When she got close enough to see his face, Sarah added to her impression brilliant blue eyes, a color between azure and turquoise, the bluest eyes she'd ever seen.

"Three skinny cones," the woman said to the girl behind the counter, in a husky smoker's voice. Her lipstick, Sarah saw, matched the rubber thong of her flip-flops.

"Can I get a sundae?" asked the girl.

"You don't need hot fudge," said the woman, without looking at her daughter. "What does *Mere* always say? One minute on the lips, a lifetime on the hips?"

Sarah could feel her own mother's disapproval as the girl stared down at the ground, chewing on her bottom lip. Once they were at the front of the line, Sarah's mother said, in a voice louder than was necessary, "Sam and Sarah, you can get anything you want."

Sam's eyes were wide. Before their mom could change her mind, he ordered a hot-fudge sundae, and Sarah got a black-and-white frappe with whipped cream and a cherry, which she drank so fast she ended up with an ice-cream headache, her stomach unsettled from all the sugar. She'd looked for the boy at the metal tables where people sat with their desserts, and on Main Street, and in the parking lot, but he and his family were gone.

Sarah didn't see the boy again that summer, although sometimes, on her trips across the pond, she'd see other people around the red house with the peeling paint. She spotted the woman and the girl, once, on the porch. Another time she saw the woman and a man her father's age. The woman's hair was loose, and she was smoking a cigarette, gesturing with her free hand. The man stood in front of her, his body menacingly close. Sarah could tell, without hearing a word, that they were fighting, and she wondered where the boy was and if he was listening.

Her next sighting came years later, when she was fourteen. She swam across the pond on a Saturday morning in late August and there was the boy, shirtless again, dragging a net on a pole through the water. A big yellow dog sat on the sand beside him. The boy's skin was the same deep nut-brown it had been the first time she'd seen him, and he wore another faded bathing suit, this one red. He'd gotten taller, and his shoulders were broader, his forearms lean and corded with tendons that shifted beneath his skin as he moved the net. She could see a dusting of dark hair on his calves.

He lifted his head as Sarah approached. She kept her distance, treading water, waiting to see if he'd yell at her. Instead, he just looked out across the water, his face expressionless.

"What are you trying to catch?" she finally called.

He looked down at the net as if surprised to find it in his hands. "I don't actually know," he said, and shrugged.

"I just found this in the boathouse . . ." He raised the pole and lifted the dripping net up and out of the water, so that Sarah could see a hole in the netting. "It's ripped." Before she could ask why he was wasting time dragging a torn net through the water, the boy said, "I was bored." He smiled, and it transformed his face, turning it from sullen to almost painfully handsome. He waded out into the pond until he was knee-deep in the water, which reflected rippling sunlight into his bright-blue eyes. Sarah could hear the water lapping at the shore, and the sound of raised voices; a man's deep voice, a woman shouting shrilly back.

The boy glanced over his shoulder, looking uncomfortable. "Do you know how to canoe?" he asked.

"Um, yeah," said Sarah, who'd been on dozens of canoe trips through the marshes in her years at Audubon camp.

"Want to go?"

"Okay." Sarah walked slowly out of the water. That summer, she'd been newly aware of her body. She braced herself for the kind of scrutiny she'd gotten familiar with at school, but the boy just set the ripped net and pole down on the sand and handed her a folded, threadbare towel. "My name's Owen," he said.

"I'm Sarah." The towel felt warm from being left in the sun. Sarah wrapped it around her waist as the boy set off.

"Cool. C'mon. We'll get the canoe." He whistled, and the dog got to its feet, following them as Owen led her past the house, with its scabby paint and splintery wooden railings and the sounds of fighting still through its opened windows, to a boxy one-room concrete structure with the right side of its shingled roof almost completely caved in.

"This is the boathouse," he announced.

"What happened?" Sarah asked, looking uneasily at the roof.

"Tree fell," Owen said nonchalantly.

"Is it safe?" she asked.

Owen scratched at a mosquito bite on his arm. "I guess so. I mean, the roof hasn't fallen in so far."

Inside, the only illumination came from a single lightbulb on a string. Owen tugged it, and Sarah peered around the cobwebby dimness. She could make out a pair of canoes, a few paddles, a bicycle missing its front wheel, and a tennis racket that needed restringing. A volleyball net sagged against the wall next to a few rusty metal-legged beach chairs. At Owen's direction, Sarah helped lift one of the canoes and carry it out to the beach. Sarah considered asking for a life jacket, which her mother always made her wear, then decided not to. The dog, whose name was Hopper, leaped into the center of the canoe and sat there, looking dignified and a little bored. Owen held the canoe steady as Sarah took the seat at the back of the boat. He towed the canoe out until he was knee-deep in the water before gracefully jumping up and in. He dipped his paddle, first left, then right, and Sarah matched her strokes to his as they started gliding toward the opposite shore.

Sarah learned that Owen lived in Westport, Connecticut, and he attended boarding school in Rhode Island. His parents were divorced, and both were remarried, and he spent every summer with his mother, Sass, and his stepfather, Anders, on the Cape.

"Me, too," she said. "I mean, not the divorce part. But we're here all summer."

"Do you live in Wellfleet?"

"Truro." Sarah couldn't see his face, but she could

watch his back and arms and shoulders, the play of muscles beneath his skin. It was a hot day. The sky was cloudless and blue, with a breeze stirring the tops of the tall pine trees that circled the pond. A Sunfish with a yellow-and-white sail tacked across the water, a few other canoers paddled along the shoreline. On the public beach on the other side of the pond, little kids were splashing around in the shallows, while older kids sunned themselves or cannonballed off the raft.

"Do you have brothers or sisters?" Owen asked.

"One brother. He's my twin. But I'm older." Even at fourteen, that felt important to mention. "And you've got a sister, right?"

"How'd you know?"

"I saw you in Wellfleet at the ice-cream place."

Owen nodded. "I saw you in P-town once. I go to sailing camp there."

"I didn't know there were any camps in P-town."

"Yup." Owen didn't seem like he was going to say any more, and Sarah found herself babbling to fill up the silence.

"My mom called you guys the Pond People." As soon as it was out of her mouth Sarah wished she hadn't said it. It had sounded funny when her mother used the term. Out loud, to an actual Pond Person, it just sounded insulting. She was about to apologize when Owen turned around, grinning.

"Pond People. That's pretty good."

"And I guess we're the Bay People."

"Ha," Owen said, sounding less amused. He turned around again, giving Sarah his back. "No. You're the rich people."

That shocked her into silence, as if "rich" were a curse

word, something you couldn't say out loud. She'd never thought of her family as rich, although she guessed that probably they were. But if Owen went to boarding school and sailing camp and spent his summers here, wasn't he rich, too? And if that was the case, why did his house look like it was falling down?

"I don't think my parents are really rich. My mom's a professor, and my dad's a lawyer," Sarah said. When Owen didn't volunteer any more information, Sarah asked, "What do your parents do?"

"Well." Owen paused, seeming to gather himself. "My real dad's a stockbroker. He lives in Manhattan. Anders is between jobs at the moment." From the clipped way he spoke, Sarah guessed that Owen was quoting someone. Probably his mother. "And Sass doesn't work. Well, she does house stuff. And she gets married. I guess that's her job."

Sarah barely knew where to start. She could understand that *being* married might count as a job, the same way being a mother was, but how did getting married qualify as work? "You call your mother by her first name?" was what she finally decided to ask.

Owen dipped his paddle smoothly in and out of the water. "Her real name is Ballard Moreland. Then she was Ballard Moreland Lassiter, and now it's Ballard Moreland Lassiter Renquist. But everyone calls her Sass." He backpaddled to steer them around a fallen log.

"Oh," said Sarah. "How about your sister?"

"She's sixteen. She's working on the Vineyard this year. Her name's Eliza, but everyone calls her Bump."

"Why Bump?"

"Because she used to bump her head against her crib when she was a baby."

"Do you have a nickname?"

"Yup."

Sarah waited for a few strokes. "Will you tell me what it is?"

"Nope."

"Oh, come on!" Sarah used the edge of her paddle to flick water at him.

Owen turned around. He splashed her back and gave her a smile that made her heart do strange, swoopy things. "Someday. Maybe."

For the rest of the afternoon, Sarah and Owen paddled around the pond, talking. Sarah learned that Owen was fourteen, like she was. She learned about his favorite food (pizza with sausage and onions), and which TV shows he liked (*ER* and *Law & Order*). She found out his favorite musicians (Outkast and Eminem) and what he was planning to do with the rest of his summer (attend sailing camp in P-town, then go back to school a week early, when lacrosse practice began).

When Sarah told Owen that she'd taken piano lessons since she was six and that her current teacher was on the faculty at the Berklee College of Music, he sounded impressed.

"Are you really good? I guess you must be."

"I practice a lot," said Sarah, which was true. It was also true that she was beginning to wonder if she was good enough to be a concert pianist. When she was little, her teachers had been effusive, telling her parents that she had innate musicianship, that she was gifted. Now they said that she needed to apply herself; that if she was serious about making a life as a musician, she needed to practice at least three hours a day and, ideally, even more than that, at least six days a week. That kind of schedule didn't leave time for anything besides sleep and homework, and Sarah wasn't sure if she loved music enough to persist, to give up everything else and devote herself completely to the piano.

The first time they approached the public beach, Sarah called to her mother, who walked down to the shore, peering at them from underneath the hand she'd raised to her brow. "New friend?" she called, and Sarah felt her face get hot.

"Mom, this is Owen. Owen, this is my mom."

"Hi," said Owen with a wave.

"Nice to meet you, Owen. Sarah, you should put on more sunscreen," said her mom.

"I'm fine," she said, and wished her mother hadn't made it sound like she was still a little kid.

They'd gone paddling off, waving every time they came close to shore. After their fourth circuit of the pond, Veronica stood up and pointed meaningfully at her wrist, where a watch would have been if she'd worn one.

"I think I have to go." Sarah didn't want to leave him, didn't want this day to end, but could already feel her skin of her shoulders tightening with incipient sunburn. She'd pay for her refusal to put on the sunscreen her mom had offered. *Worth it*, she decided.

Owen paddled them up to the shore, until Sarah could feel the bottom of the canoe scrape against the sand. He held the boat steady with one hand and extended his other one out to her. She took his hand and climbed down, unfolding her legs, which had gotten stiff during the hours they'd been on the pond. "This was fun."

Owen nodded as he stood in the water, scratching Hopper behind his ears. She wondered if she should ask for his phone number, or propose a plan for the weekend, but before she could decide, Owen said, "See ya," and pushed the boat back into the water, hopping into it and paddling away.

On Sunday, then Monday and Tuesday, Sarah swam across the pond and waited, treading water, across from the red house ... but she never saw Owen, or anyone else, and she was too shy to walk out of the water and knock on the door. On Wednesday, Sarah's dad drove her back home, to Boston, and two days after that, they went to the Berkshires, where she'd be attending music camp at Tanglewood for the last two weeks of her summer vacation. She didn't see Owen again for the next three years, and in that time she met other boys, boys whose smile or touch made her heart beat faster. But she never forgot about Owen. At odd moments of her day, or in her bed at night, she would find herself remembering his smile, his brilliant blue eyes, something he'd said, the muscles flexing and tendons flickering in his legs as he'd hopped into the canoe.

Sarah spent her last year of high school trying to decide if she'd go to a conservatory, aiming at the small chance of fame and fortune, or if she'd take the more reasonable path of a liberal arts degree. Her parents left it up to her, telling her they'd pay for her education no matter where she decided to go. Her teacher encouraged her. "You have enough talent to do this," Mr. Ascarelli said. "All you have to decide is whether or not you've got the drive. And you have to decide if you'll have regrets for the rest of your life if you don't try."

She'd asked him about his classmates from Oberlin, where he'd studied. "Well, let's see," he said, removing his eyeglasses and polishing them on his sleeve. "One of them recorded three CDs by the time he was thirty and has performed with orchestras all over the world. Another one works on Broadway, playing keyboard in the pit for different musicals. He was even onstage for a while, with *Cabaret*, where the ensemble was part of the show." He sighed and put his glasses back on. "And I've got one who gives lessons out of her house in Texarkana to little kids. And one plays music in the cocktail lounge on a cruise ship," he'd added. This hadn't helped Sarah make up her mind.

Back and forth she went, all year long, as January 15, the deadline for applications, approached. She'd finally decided on Wellesley. "If you hate it, or if you miss music, you can always change your mind," her mom said, right after Sarah had submitted her application. "Nothing has to be forever."

She'd been accepted. Her parents had sent in a deposit. That summer, Sarah, at her mother's insistence, got a job as a maid in a hotel in Provincetown, down the street from the shop where Sam sold penny candy to tourists. (Her mother was a great believer in the value of working in the service industry. "You'll learn how to deal with customers, and with a boss, and you'll give waitresses good tips for the rest of your life.")

At the end of June, Sarah had been walking down Commercial Street at the end of her shift when a male voice had called her name. She'd turned, and there was Owen, taller, broader through his chest, in khaki shorts, a dark-blue T-shirt, and boat shoes.

"Sarah!"

She'd smiled at him. "Do you know, this is the first time I've seen you with a shirt on?"

He looked down at himself, then did a model's spin. "So what do you think?"

"Blue is definitely your color."

"Are you here for the summer?" he asked.

She nodded.

"Want to go canoeing again?"

Sarah tried not to smile as widely as she wanted to, tried not to show how delighted she was that he'd remembered her, and wanted to see her again. "Sure."

Owen told her how to find his house from the land, instead of the water. "Turn left off Route 6 right before Moby Dick's on Rose Road. There's a dirt road on the right-hand side. It's pretty bumpy and rutted, but if you go slow, you'll be fine. Just follow it around until you see the Camp."

He told her he was also working, as a counselor at the Provincetown Yacht Club, the sailing camp he'd attended, and as a bar back at a restaurant with an expansive outdoor deck right on Commercial Street, a place that did a booming business from brunch, which began at ten a.m., through last call at two in the morning ("the food's not great, but they've got cheap drinks," Owen said). Between their jobs, Owen and Sarah didn't have a lot of free time that overlapped, but whenever they did that summer, they would kayak, or ride their bikes along the path into Eastham or Orleans, or walk the paths through the dunes, gathering cranberries and wineberries and wild blueberries. They swam in the pond, and in the bay, and in the ocean. At night, they'd build bonfires on the beaches and roast hot dogs and clams and ears of corn. Their romance unfolded, slowly and sweetly, each milestone marked in Sarah's mind: the first time they held hands, the first time Owen kissed her, and the first time she felt his hands on her breasts as she lay on a towel on the cooling sand, with a bonfire warming her face and the wind whispering through the dune grass.

Two weeks after their reunion, Sarah brought Owen

home for dinner on the Fourth of July. She led him past the pool and through the front door. She pulled the sliding door shut, calling, "Mom! We're here!" and walking upstairs to the kitchen. When she realized Owen wasn't behind her, she turned around to find him standing perfectly still, with his eyes closed and an expression suggesting he'd just seen the face of God.

Sarah raised her eyebrows. "What?" she asked.

"Air-conditioning," he whispered back ecstatically. Sarah saw that he was standing right over one of the vents. It had been hot and humid all week, the temperature soaring into the upper eighties every day, rarely dipping below seventy degrees at night. Every evening, heat lightning would illuminate the sky in flashes, but the rain never came, and the weather never broke. Sarah was used to the air-conditioning. From his expression, she could see that Owen, clearly, was not.

Then her mom called, "Come on up! Dinner's ready!" and Owen left his spot over the vent and came upstairs, where he joined the rest of the guests, two other families that had homes near theirs. Sarah watched as he introduced himself, shaking her mom's hand, then her dad's. At sunset, everyone gathered in the living room. Sarah's mom pressed a button to roll up the blinds, kept down during the day so the room would stay cool, and they sat on the couch for the ritual of oohing and aahing at the sunset. Her dad grilled steaks and Vidalia onions; her mom steamed corn and served her watermelon and feta-cheese salad. Owen spread his napkin on his lap. He cut his steak into slivers and talked to Sam about sports, and answered all her parents' questions, telling them he was going to Duke, where he planned to study history and play lacrosse, where he'd live with other freshmen on the East Campus, in a house called Pegram. Sarah could see him looking around, at the bookcases that lined the living-room wall; at the paintings on the walls, at the gleaming kitchen. She guessed it was different from his house, if the insides matched the outsides, and wondered how her house looked to him, whether he thought it was pleasant or ostentatious.

At the end of the night, Owen and Sarah walked down to the beach and sat together on a blanket, watching as the waves came foaming gently onto the sand. Owen was in a quiet mood, staring out at the sea, stroking her hair almost absently.

"What?" she finally asked. "Is something wrong?"

He shook his head and gave her a tight-lipped smile that was nothing like his usual easy grin. "I was just thinking how long it's been since I sat down at a table for an actual meal where nobody yelled at anyone or threw anything."

Sarah was startled. "Do people throw things at your house?" she asked, then thought of something worse. "Are they not feeding you?"

He squeezed her hand. "No, no, there's food. There's just not, you know. Meals, with vegetables and side dishes, and setting the table. And it's less about the throwing things than the yelling." He sighed and picked up a piece of driftwood and used it to trace patterns in the sand.

"So, um, what are meals like?"

Owen shrugged. "My mom doesn't eat much." He gave another tight smile. "She says it's harder to get a buzz on if your stomach's full."

Sarah must have looked shocked. Was Sass an alcoholic? Before she could figure out how to ask, Owen shook his head at her expression.

"It's not that bad. Anders and I fend for ourselves. There's frozen pizzas, and chicken nuggets. And most nights, somebody's grilling on the beach. We're scavengers." With that, he grinned, baring his teeth, grabbing Sarah by the shoulders, rolling her onto her back, nibbling at her neck in a way that always made her shiver. Sarah closed her eyes, holding him tight, and it wasn't until later, after Owen had gone home and she was alone in her bed, that she thought about what he'd said, and what he hadn't said. She'd never been introduced to anyone in Owen's family; had never been invited to a meal; had barely spent any time at the Camp, which was what Owen called the collection of three buildings where the Lassiter clan stayed in the summertime. The largest building, called Papa Bear, was the house with scabrous red paint. It had a kitchen and a living room, two bedrooms, and a screened-in porch. Mama Bear was a one-room cabin, with, Owen told her, a double bed and a set of bunk beds crammed inside. Baby Bear, the smallest building, hardly had room for a twin bed and a dresser. It was still the spot Owen and his sister preferred—and the only building where Sarah could claim to be familiar with the inside as well as the outside.

"But why?" Sarah asked after Owen showed her where he slept. "Don't you get claustrophobic?" She would have felt like she was sleeping in an elevator if she had to spend a night there.

Owen had shrugged. "It's farther away from the big house," he said. *And the fighting,* Sarah thought.

In addition to the Three Bears, there was the boat-house, its roof still unrepaired, slumped in on itself like a toothless mouth. There was also a bathhouse, which boasted a single toilet and an old-fashioned sink in a cinder block enclosure. The bathing facilities consisted of a showerhead nailed up on a tree, with a flimsy plastic curtain hung on the tree's branches, in a gesture toward privacy (Owen had told her that his mother got up early and took a bar of soap and a container of shampoo into the pond, where she took her bath. "Is that okay for the pond?" Sarah asked, and Owen had shrugged and said, "I don't think Sass is much of an environmentalist"). The whole setup was very different from the Levy-Weinberg house, where there was a pool and a hot tub, where each of the four bedrooms had its own bathroom, where there was a caretaker employed year-round and a handyman on call, where every meal featured all four food groups and where anything broken was immediately repaired or replaced.

Finally, in the middle of August, Owen brought Sarah to a bonfire on the beach. That was where she met his mother at last. Sass gave Sarah a cool, limp-fingered handshake, her lips, painted the same shade of hot-pink lipstick that Sarah remembered, lingering over the syllables of Sarah's last name. "Sarah Levy-Weinberg. You're Veronica Levy's daughter?" Sass turned to one of the other women Sarah had been introduced to—there'd been, she remembered, a Mimsy, and a Bunny, and a woman named Laurence—and said, "Veronica Levy, the novelist," in a tone that turned "novelist" into what sounded like an insult.

Eat before you go, Sarah's mom had told her. "If it's like any WASP party I've ever been to, there's going to be oceans of booze and not a thing to eat." Once Sarah escaped from Sass, she walked down the beach, weaving through the clusters of people, looking around. On a card table, draped in a plastic tablecloth that flapped in the breeze, she saw plastic bags of tortilla chips and potato chips, a plastic jug of cheese balls, and a container of onion dip. There were jars of salsa and honey-roasted peanuts, and a paper plate with hamburgers and hot dogs. So not a complete absence of food, but there definitely wasn't as much as there would have been if her parents were hosting, and the card table that held the booze did seem extremely well stocked. Most of the party crowd was clustered around it, squeezing chunks of lime into plastic cups of gin and tonic, or opening beers. Sarah could hear Sass's shrill laughter. She saw Owen's mother with her head thrown back, throat exposed, streaky blonde hair blowing in the night breeze, her hand resting lightly on the forearm of a man who wasn't her husband as she talked.

Owen got Sarah a burger, a handful of salt-and-vinegar potato chips, and a soda, doctored with a shot of rum, and they sat on the sun-warmed dunes to slap at the mosquitos. When the fire was burning low, he led her into the darkness. They lay down together, and, without a word, he turned to kiss her. Usually, Owen talked to her—*Can I kiss you?* he'd murmur into her ear. *Is this okay?* That night, he was silent and intent, his hands possessive, almost fierce. When they broke apart, he pulled back to rest his forehead against hers, gazing into her eyes. Sarah knew what he was asking, and she nodded, thinking, *Yes. Please.* Whatever she could give him—love, comfort, even just a distraction—she would.

They had felt inevitable. Everything they'd done, everything they'd told each other, as they'd progressed from kissing to making out to everything-but. Finally, on the Wednesday before Labor Day, when they'd both be going home, and then to college, Owen had taken Sarah to Slough Pond, and she'd dared him to swim the butterfly across it, and he'd said, *What will you give me if I do it?* Once he'd won the bet and carried her out of the water, he'd spread his towel on the pine needles, laid Sarah on top of it, and stripped off her swimsuit with something like reverence, kissing up from the arches of her insteps to her ankles to the soft, ticklish flesh behind her knees. Kissing and nibbling, higher and higher, until her thighs fell apart and she found her hands fisted in his hair. "Show me," he'd whispered. "Show me what you like." She'd been so ashamed. She'd always imagined this part happening in a bed, in the dark, not out here, in the bright midday sunshine, where anyone could come down the path and see, but Owen had been insistent. "Don't worry," he'd murmured in her ear. "No one can see us. And no one ever comes here. Do you trust me?"

Sarah had nodded.

"Then show me. Let me make you feel good."

Face flaming, she'd squeezed her eyes shut, letting one hand slip down her belly, letting her fingertips stroke, first gently, then faster. Owen, it turned out, was a quick learner; or maybe this was a thing he'd already learned, with other girls. She would have dwelled on that thought, only Owen's fingers and lips and tongue soon had her in a state where she couldn't hold on to any thought at all. When she'd cried out, at the height of her pleasure, a blue jay had burst from the tree above them, chattering and scolding as it flew off. Owen had laughed and wiped his face. Then he'd pulled a condom out of his pocket and looked at Sarah.

"Okay?" he'd asked, his eyes steady on hers. "We don't have to. Not unless you want to."

"Yes," she'd said. "I do. I want to. Please."

She hadn't regretted it. Not any of it. Not even the night before she'd left, when she'd ridden her bike to the Camp to say goodbye to Owen. She'd been walking down the rutted road toward Papa Bear when she'd heard Sass, her voice bright and cutting, talking to one of her friends.

"Is he still seeing that girl?" the friend had asked. Sarah held herself still, trying not to move, not to blink.

"For now," said Sass, in her drawling voice. Sarah saw a bluish curl of cigarette smoke snaking through the ripped screens. "He's *besotted*." Sass sounded amused at the idea of her son being besotted with Sarah, who held herself perfectly still. Part of her wanted to make noise, to call out a greeting so Sass would stop talking. Another part, a more persuasive part, wanted to hear more.

"And her mother's a novelist, right?" asked the friend.

"Uh-huh. Hasn't published anything in years, but she must have done quite well. Owen says they live in one of those . . ." Sarah could imagine Sass gesturing with her cigarette, her bright-pink lip curled. ". . . showplaces up on the dunes." The word "showplaces" was freighted with just as much scorn as "besotted" had been. The friend said something Sarah couldn't hear, to which Sass replied, "Well, those people know how to hold on to their pennies." She'd laughed a tinkling, breaking-glass laugh, and said, "Maybe Miss Weinberg will be the one to save us all."

Those people. Sarah's hands had felt icy; her lips, still swollen from Owen's kisses, had stung as if she'd been slapped. Was that why Owen was with her? Part of her wanted to deny it, utterly and completely. Another part remembered the first thing Owen had told her about his mom; how she treated getting married like it was her job. Maybe he'd inherited his mother's worldview.

Maybe he did see Sarah as a means to an end, the one who would rescue his family.

Fiercely, Sarah told herself to forget what she'd heard. She'd gotten moving again, striding down the path, making as much noise as she could, calling Owen's name, and Owen had come running out of Little Bear, smiling just for her. They'd spent the afternoon at Ballston Beach, riding the waves, then they'd gone to the drive-in, then back to the beach. As midnight and Sarah's curfew approached, they'd made love again, with the sound of the wind and the waves in their ears and hundreds of stars burning in the sky above them. "I love you," Sarah whispered, so low that Owen could pretend he hadn't heard. He'd put his thumb beneath her chin, lifting her head for a kiss, and she'd thought her heart would burst wide open when he'd said, "I love you, too."

The next morning, Owen went home. "I'll email you my phone number as soon as I get to school," he'd said. Only, instead of a phone number, five days into her tenure at Wellesley, she'd gotten a breakup letter. Or, rather, a breakup email, from Owen's AOL account. *I've met someone here and I want to be with her. I'm sorry, but it's for the best. We should both be free.*

She'd written back immediately, begging him to call, to explain it to her, to give her a chance, but he hadn't, and she didn't have a number to reach him at school. After two days of crying, she'd called information in Connecticut, thinking she'd reach Sass and beg for Owen's number. But when she'd tried, a computerized voice told her there was no such listing: not for Owen's mother or his stepfather or any combination of their many first and last names. The same voice gave her the same bad news when she'd tried to find a listing for the family camp on the Cape. She'd held out hope for nine months, but when she'd finally come back to Cape Cod after her freshman year, when she'd made her first trip across the pond that summer, the Camp was abandoned; the buildings razed, nothing left where they'd been but holes in the ground. Owen, and his entire family, had disappeared.

That night, Sarah lay in bed with the brownstone silent around her, trying not to think about those summers. The boys were sleeping, one floor above her; Eli, presumably, was one floor above them, tucked into Ruby's old bed.

Sarah rolled over onto her left side and shut her eyes. She flipped to her right side, then onto her back, where she stared helplessly at the ceiling. She counted backward from one hundred; she played scales in her head, from C major to A-flat minor. Finally, she swung her legs out of bed, earning an irritated look from Lord Farquaad, who'd been snoozing on Eli's side of the bed, which, in Eli's absence, he'd claimed for himself.

"Apologies, Your Highness," she muttered, and grabbed her purse off the chair. Owen's card was in her wallet, tucked in deep, behind ticket stubs from shows she'd seen with Ruby, receipts from the dry cleaner's, and loyalty punch cards from the place she'd gotten her manicures before the pandemic. She typed in his number and tapped out a text. *I'd love to get that coffee sometime this week.*

When she woke up the next morning, to the sound of the boys getting themselves dressed overhead, there was a text waiting. *Thursday afternoon any good? Can you meet at the Guggenheim? I could use some culture.*

Sarah felt the strangest tangle of emotions—hope and sorrow and guilt and excitement, all twisted together, as she tapped her answer. *YES.*

ELI

~~~~~~~~~

In the month since his banishment, Eli had developed a routine. He'd wait until he heard the soft chirp of their home alarm, the front door opening and closing as Sarah left for her morning walk. Then he'd collect his belongings and slink down to the bedroom before the boys could wake up and see him. On a Monday morning, he'd just finished shaving when his brain informed him that there was less than a month until Ruby's wedding, and he found himself gripping the sink and groaning out loud.

"Eli?" He hadn't heard Sarah returning, but he could hear her now, through the bathroom door, sounding worried. "Everything okay?"

He put on his hearty, jolly voice. "Fine!" he called as he opened his eyes and stared at his reflection in the steamy mirror. He still looked, to his own eyes, normal, and not like a man who moved through his days a single heartbeat away from a scream. "Everything's fine!"

But of course, nothing was fine, and he was, he knew, running out of time to come up with a solution. That morning, at work, he waited until his office manager had gone to lunch, then opened an anonymous browser on her laptop (too afraid to use an anonymous browser on his own) and googled "DNA Paternity Tests." Judging from the bloom of ads and links, Eli wasn't the first person to do a search on this particular subject.

He chose a link at random and clicked. Beneath a picture of a beaming white man embracing an adorably chubby-cheeked toddler was text reading, "If you choose the private test option, a painless buccal swab (mouth swab) collection kit will be sent directly to you for sample collection in the privacy of your own home."

Great, he thought, and imagined handing Gabe the kit—after dinner, maybe, while they were all together, him and Sarah and Dexter and Miles and Ruby and Gabe, watching a movie. *Hey, Gabe, mind giving me a few epithelial cells? Oh, no special reason. Just curious.*

Okay, then. He'd find an excuse to go to Gabe and Ruby's place. He'd take Gabe's toothbrush. Except how would he know which one was Gabe's? Fine. He'd take both the toothbrushes. He'd take all the toothbrushes. He'd show up with replacement toothbrushes. An early wedding gift! He'd bring a bottle of champagne, and he'd ask them the last time they'd replaced their toothbrushes, and he'd give them the new ones and leave with the old ones. Maybe he could even give Ruby a blue toothbrush, for her something blue! Except, of course, Ruby would be suspicious. And Eli had never been good at lying to his daughter.

There was, of course, an obvious solution: Tell Sarah the truth. Tell Ruby the truth. But then Eli imagined his daughter, her face flushed with anger, mouth turned down, hair disordered and frizzy, because when she was anxious she'd take it out of its bun, then rewrap it, then take it out again, over and over. *You cheated on Mom when she was pregnant with me?* Then he pictured Sarah, the way she went pale when she was upset, the way her chin jutted out and her back got very straight. *You have another child?*

Maybe he could wait until Shabbat, keep track of the silverware that Gabe used, and send in his fork or his spoon. Would that work? Could the labs find the DNA in the midst of particles of roast chicken and gravy?

"Fuck!" he hissed. His office manager, who'd just come through the door, stared at him, her eyes very big behind her glasses. Eli made himself smile. "Lost at solitaire," he said, and she'd nodded, still looking concerned.

The even more obvious solution was to just ask Gabe's mother to tell him the truth. *Did you and I have sex in New York City? Did you have a baby instead of an abortion? Am I Gabe's father?*

Except Gabe's mother had turned herself into something like a ghost.

"No, my mom doesn't do social media," Gabe said when Eli asked, casually, if his mom had announced their engagement on her Facebook page. Eli had already looked on Instagram and LinkedIn and Twitter and couldn't find her anywhere.

But Rosa had an email address. Everyone had an email address. She had a phone number, too, which Gabe was happy to provide when Sarah insisted that they FaceTime his mom and introduce themselves. Eli's heart had almost stopped when Sarah proposed it. Then he realized maybe it was a good thing. Maybe he'd see Gabe's mother onscreen and know, for sure, that she wasn't the woman who'd called herself Jane. Or maybe she'd see him, and recognize him, and reach out on her own, and they'd figure out how to fix things together.

Eli made sure to be in front of the camera, completely visible during the call. He'd even tried to grow the goatee he'd worn back then, because Rosa would have remembered him with facial hair, except, with five days' notice, he hadn't been able to produce more than a sad, straggling mustache and a few wisps of beard. "Could you please shave?" Sarah had asked, the night of the phone call. "Please? You'll have plenty of time to grow a beard before the wedding, but right now you look homeless."

"You're not supposed to say that," Dexter called from his spot in the living room, where he and his brother were building a Lego Death Star.

"What's that?" Eli asked.

"Homeless. We learned that in school. You're not supposed to call people that. You're supposed to say 'housing insecure.'"

"Got it," said Sarah, leaving Eli thinking, not for the first time, how in the end, he'd probably have kids who could instruct him on the seventy reasons he should be driving an electric car but couldn't find their own state on a map.

Eli had shaved. He spent the entire afternoon and evening before the call feeling like he was going to vomit, or scream, or scream and vomit at the same time. When the table was cleared and the FaceTime began, he braced himself for the sight of his old lover again, preparing for Rosa's wide eyes, her look of recognition, the horrified expression on her face that would match the horrified way that he felt. But when the call finally happened, it was more bad news.

Rosa was Jane. Eli saw it immediately. Her hair was still dark; her skin still that glowing golden bronze that Eli remembered, and she had the same dark brows, the same dark-eyed, direct stare. "Hello, Rosa!" Eli said, into the camera of Gabe's phone. "It's wonderful to meet you!" He saw—or, maybe, he just thought he saw—her eyes widen incrementally, her mouth fall open for just an instant. Then that look of recognition, if it had been recognition, was gone, and Rosa was saying, "It's nice to meet you, too. Thank you for making Gabe feel so welcome."

"Of course," Sarah said. "Gabe is a sweetheart. We've enjoyed having him."

"Yes," Rosa said quietly. "Gabe's a good boy."

Sarah said that they were all looking forward to seeing her. Rosa said, again, how grateful she was that they'd given Gabe a home during the pandemic. Sarah praised Gabe's kindness with Dexter and Miles—"Not to get ahead of ourselves, but he's going to be a wonderful father." Eli's stomach lurched as Sarah and Rosa smiled at each other, as more pleasantries were exchanged; more plans were made, and, finally, the call concluded.

Later that night, Eli quietly asked Gabe for his mother's number—"just so Sarah and I know how to reach her." But when he called, the calls went straight to voicemail.

He tried texting. *Hi, Rosa, this is Eli Danhauser, Ruby's dad. I'd love to talk to you for a minute.*

Nothing.

Rosa, it's Eli Danhauser again. Please call me when you can.

Nothing.

Rosa, it's Eli Danhauser. I really need to speak to you. Please call. It's important.

Nothing.

Maybe she's avoiding me, he thought, then laughed at himself. Obviously she was avoiding him. She'd recognized him, and her response to the horrible truth was to stick her head in the sand, an impulse Eli completely understood. Still, he kept trying. He called early in the morning. He called late at night. Rosa never picked up.

Days—miserable, frantic, clenched-fisted days—sped

by, tipping into weeks, with the two voices constantly arguing in his head: *He's my son. No, he isn't. I'm Gabe's father. No, I'm not. It happened. No, it didn't.* Some days he'd wake up calm, thinking, *What are the chances? What are the chances that some stranger I slept with half a dozen times twenty-two years ago, a stranger who told me she was going to have an abortion didn't have an abortion, and had a son instead, and the son grew up and came to New York City and fell in love with my daughter? Are the chances one in a million? One in a billion?* Then he'd remember that people did win the lottery, even when their chances were infinitesimal. It happened sometimes. People got lucky, or in his case, unlucky.

Then it was June. Almost every morning, Eli would come up with a new idea, or revisit an old one—*steal a toothbrush! Ask to borrow a hairbrush! Tell Gabe breast cancer runs in the family, and that we need to screen him for the BRCA gene!* For a few hours, the idea would seem watertight and foolproof. Then doubt would creep in, and he'd find a dozen holes in the scheme he'd dreamed up, and end up back where he'd started, completely and utterly fucked.

There was only one more thing that he could think of, a Hail Mary pass, a high-risk, last-ditch maneuver. Only a desperate man would ever consider it, but Eli was desperate and completely out of options. And so he called his brother. "Sure," Ari said without even asking what Eli wanted with him.

Eli arrived at the diner where they'd agreed to meet right on time and secured a booth in the back. Ari sauntered in, ten minutes late, an ironic fedora cocked over his forehead. He looked handsome, happy, and relaxed. Eli hated him for it. As his brother slid into the booth,

smiled at the waitress, and asked for a cup of coffee—
"light and sweet"—Eli realized that this was a historic
occasion: the first time in their lives that he had been the
one to come to his brother for help.

"What's up?" Ari asked.

Eli swallowed hard. As succinctly as possible, he explained what he needed, without exactly saying why.
"Gabe says he has no idea who his father is, and I just
want to make sure that it's no one we need to worry
about."

Ari narrowed his eyes. "Worry about how?" he asked.
"Like, if his father's a mobster or something?" He
smirked. "Could Gabe be the son of Son of Sam?"

"I want to make sure there aren't any genetic issues,"
Eli said, and hoped his brother wouldn't push. Which,
of course, Ari did.

"What, like cancer? Or, what's that disease that Jewish people get?"

"Tay-Sachs," Eli said, tight-lipped. He and Sarah
had both been tested, he remembered, before Dexter
had been conceived.

"But that's not what you're really worried about, is it?"
Ari's grin grew feral. "What are you thinking? That this
kid is, what? Related to Ruby? Related to us?" His smile
got wider, turning even more greasy and sly. "Related to
you, my good brother?"

Eli forced his fingers not to drum and his knee not to
bob up and down. He met Ari's gaze steadily. "Annette
and I had broken up," he lied, "and I hadn't met Sarah
yet. But yes, I, uh, think that I knew Gabe's mother."

"Knew biblically," Ari amplified. He had the nerve to
look pleased with himself, instead of being sympathetic.
"No condom?"

Eli kept his eyes on the table. "It happened very fast," he muttered at the Formica.

"I'm not surprised," Ari murmured. Eli ignored him.

"She told me she was getting an abortion," Eli said.

"Yeah, they usually do," Ari said. "You gave her money?"

Eli nodded. Ari shook his head in fake commiseration.

"Okay, so she scammed you. But you were free and single. Just tell the kid you were going through a ho phase, ask him for a swab, and you're done."

"Have you done this before?"

Ari smirked. "No comment."

Eli shook his head. "I can't. What if he tells Ruby? Or Sarah? Can you imagine how awkward that would be?"

"How's it going to be less awkward if I'm the one asking?" Ari inquired. Eli didn't answer. He just waited for his brother to figure it out. Eventually, Ari did.

"Oh. I get it. He's supposed to think that I'm the one who banged his mom." He raised his eyebrows. "Is she at least hot? Because I have my reputation to think of."

"She's very pretty," Eli muttered. "But he doesn't even need to think that either of us were, uh, involved with his mother. He doesn't have to know about this at all." He reached into his pocket and showed his brother a copy of the key to Ruby and Gabe's apartment. Sarah, God bless her, had insisted that Ruby give them an extra key in case of emergency.

Ari, still smirking, stirred his coffee slowly and said nothing. Eli looked into his brother's eyes. "Ari, I've never asked you for anything," he said, and hoped Ari heard what he wasn't saying: *And you've asked me for plenty.* "If you could do this one thing, I'd appreciate it. You can think of it as your wedding gift." A mean, petty part of him couldn't help but add, "That way you won't have to buy them anything."

He saw the hurt move across Ari's handsome face, quickly replaced by a mask of indifference. Eli felt the shameful stab of a memory: he and Ari, as little boys, playing in the park on a cold, wintry afternoon, while their parents fought in the car. *Let's pretend we're Lost Boys*, Eli had said, urging Ari away from the sound of their father shouting and their mother crying, because their dad had cheated on her again. Let's pretend we have to get away from Captain Hook. Once, he'd been proud to be his brother's protector. When had it turned into this detestable chore?

"Sure thing. You got it," Ari said, his face expressionless. "One DNA test, coming right up." He held out his hand. "Just give me the key."

Eli handed over the key, plus the swabs and collection kit he'd ordered online and the envelope to mail it, and texted his brother the pertinent details.

"Do you know when Gabe's out of the house?" Ari asked.

"Friday nights," Eli said. "They'll be at our place for Shabbat dinner."

"Guess I'm not invited," Ari said in a low voice before sliding out of the booth and off into the night.

Eli tried to be optimistic. Maybe this would work. Maybe the whole thing would go smoothly.

He shouldn't have been surprised when it didn't.

"Yeah, you're all set," Ari said, after four days had elapsed, and Eli broke down and called him.

"Great. That's great. I'm really grateful."

"Three 'greats' in one sentence," Ari observed. "I guess you are."

"Tell me where I can meet you, and I'll pick it up."

There was a pause. Eli's heart sank. "Well. I've been thinking," Ari said. "There's a few things I want to discuss."

Eli stifled a sigh. He'd been ready for this. "How much?"

Ari's voice was affronted. "What?"

"How much do you want?" Eli asked.

"I don't want your money," Ari snapped.

Well, that's a change of pace, Eli thought. "So what, then?"

"Meet me tonight at eight o'clock in Prospect Park by the boathouse."

Eli agreed. That night, after dinner, he leashed Lord Farquaad, put on a WFMU T-shirt, shorts, and his miracle flip-flops, and made sure he had his checkbook in his pocket. Although Ari was probably using Venmo or Cash App, or whatever the most up-to-the-moment grifters preferred.

For once, Ari didn't keep him waiting. When Eli got to the appointed spot his brother was sitting on a bench, his face tilted toward the setting sun. That night, the ironic hat was a porkpie, and he wore a dark-blue shirt and what Eli assumed were fashionable sneakers. A few of the women and some of the men walking by gave his handsome brother approving glances. *Don't be fooled*, he thought about telling them. *He's basically the essence of uselessness in the shape of a man.*

"Hi, Ari," he said.

His brother nodded at him. "Hey, dog," he said, and bent to greet Lord Farquaad, who growled and crowded behind Eli's knees.

Eli took a seat. "So, what's up?"

"I did what you wanted. I went to Ruby and Gabe's place, and I got a toothbrush, and I mailed it in. Here are the results." From his pocket, Ari removed a Ziploc bag. Eli could make out a folded sheet of paper and the outline of a toothbrush inside of it. With a superhuman effort, he kept himself from reaching out and snatching it out of his brother's hand.

"So can I have them?" Eli finally asked.

"I asked Ruby when Gabe's birthday is," Ari said.

Eli stared. "What's that got to do with anything?"

"I told her," Ari continued, "that one of my old girl-friends does astrology, and she'd do their charts as a wedding gift." He paused. "And then I did a little math." He sat back, smirking at Eli. "He's, what, four and a half months younger than Ruby?"

"I'm surprised you remember Ruby's birthday," Eli said coldly.

If Ari heard the implied criticism, he chose to ignore it. "I looked it up. And I realized that you and Annette were still together when Gabe was conceived. Still married," he amplified, as if Eli might have forgotten, and pointed at his brother. "That's the part you don't want Ruby knowing about."

Eli didn't speak, couldn't speak. He could do nothing but sit still on the splintery park bench and absorb the consequences of his own idiocy. Why, why had he thought he could go to his brother for help? Ari Danhauser had never done anything altruistic in his life. He always, only, ever looked out for himself.

"What do you want?" Eli finally asked.

There was what felt like another endless pause. "Do you know I've been in therapy?" Ari finally asked.

"Recently?" Eli knew his parents had started sending

their bright, troubled younger boy to therapists right around the time he'd refused to be bar mitzvahed, but as far as Eli knew, Ari had never taken therapy seriously, or gone of his own free will.

"Yeah," Ari said, and rubbed his hands along his shorts. "I, uh, met someone, and I decided it was time."

"Good for you!" Eli said, and tried to find the generosity to mean it. If Ari could actually, finally grow up; if he could find a job and stop hitting Eli up for money, it would be a good thing. A great thing.

"Are you familiar," his brother inquired, "with the term 'identified patient'?"

Eli indicated that he was not. He refrained from telling his brother that he didn't want to learn new therapeutic terminology, he just wanted the results of the DNA test.

Ari cleared his throat and adjusted the angle of his hat with one graceful, long-fingered hand. "An identified patient," he began, in a lecturing tone, "is a dysfunctional family's scapegoat. The other family members project their issues onto that person, and he or she gets blamed for everything. Which means that the other members of the family never have to face their own issues, or deal with their own shit. And," he concluded, "the identified patient is never allowed to get better. Because if that person did get mentally healthy and stopped being the scapegoat, it would expose the real problems. The stuff the rest of the family doesn't want to talk about, or face up to, or fix."

Eli pinched the bridge of his nose and tried to make himself count to ten in his head before responding. He only made it to six.

"Ari. I don't know how to break this to you, and I can tell it's going to come as a tremendous shock. But nobody is inventing your problems. They're real."

"Oh, right," Ari said sarcastically. "Of course. You're the golden boy, and I'm the fuck-up. You're Mr. Perfect, and I'm Calamity Jane. You're the one who gets straight As, and I'm the one who sells Dad's coin collection to pay off his gambling debts."

"That actually happened!" Eli shouted.

"Yeah, and do you know why?" Ari asked. "Because you, and Mom, and Dad, all treated me like screwing up was all I could ever do."

The hair on the back of Eli's neck started to prickle. "Why are you telling me this now?" he asked.

For a moment, Ari didn't answer. "I'll give you the results. But I want you to tell Mom and Dad," he said.

"What?" Eli blurted.

Ari had an unpleasantly smug look on his face. "I want you to tell them that you cheated on Annette while she was pregnant, and that you knocked up some other lady. I want them to know that you're not as perfect as they think you are. And," he concluded, eyes gleaming with malice, "I want you to do it at the wedding. Promise me you'll do that and you get this." He waved the Ziploc tauntingly in front of Eli.

"And what if I don't?" Eli managed to ask.

Ari shrugged. "Then I take this home, and I flush the results down the toilet, and you figure it out yourself."

Eli tried to count to ten again and kept himself from saying—from shouting—all of the things he wanted to say. Things like *Fuck you* and *That's never going to happen* and *I'd die first*. In his mind, he grabbed Ari, roaring, and lifted his brother over his head and threw him into the pond. In reality, he sat very still, afraid to move, afraid to speak.

"Pick your poison," Ari said softly.

Eli clenched his fists. "You're going to therapy, right?" he asked. Before Ari could nod, Eli asked, "What does your therapist think of this scheme? Is she on board?"

Ari looked startled and hurt. Then he smirked. "Do you see what you're doing here? You're making me the problem. Again."

"You are the problem! You're blackmailing me. On the eve of my daughter's wedding."

Startled, Ari said, "It's tomorrow?"

"I meant that figuratively," Eli said, raking his hands through his hair. "Look. I'm not dismissing this whole identified patient thing. Maybe you're right." Eli did not, of course, think that Ari was right, but he could see his brother nodding, and could tell that Ari's posture had relaxed. "You want things to be different, right?" Eli asked. "You want Mom and Dad to see us as both good and both bad, instead of me as all good and you as all bad."

Ari was nodding more vigorously. "That's it. That's it exactly. I want a reset." His eyes shone. "I think this family needs it."

"Okay, then. Fine. I promise. I'll tell them. I'll tell them at the wedding. I'll stand up, in front of everyone, only instead of making a speech congratulating the happy couple and welcoming Gabe to the family, I'll say that I slept with his mother. Is that what you want?"

Ari nodded. "Yes," he said. "That's what I want."

"Fine," Eli snarled. He held out his hand. Ari shook it. Then he handed over the bag. Eli tore it open, unfolded the page, and sat there, motionless, paralyzed, feeling his world crashing down around him. DNA PATERNITY REPORT: INFORMATIONAL USE ONLY, read the heading. There were rows of numbers, lists of alleles collected, and, at the bottom, the result: *99.9999 percent positive for paternity.*

Ari, reading over his shoulder, said, "Oh, my, oh my."

Eli slumped against the bench. His jaw sagged. His hands fell open. The Ziploc bag dropped to the ground, disgorging the remainder of its contents: a small, plastic-wrapped blue toothbrush topped with the likeness of Grover from *Sesame Street*.

Eli stared down at the toothbrush. "Ari," he said, after what felt like forever, "is that the toothbrush you took?"

Ari looked down. "Yup."

"That's not Gabe's toothbrush. That's Dexter's."

Ari stared at him. "What was Dexter's toothbrush doing at Gabe and Ruby's place?"

"He and Miles had a sleepover last weekend." Eli shut his eyes.

"Well, how was I supposed to know this wasn't Gabe's toothbrush?" Ari demanded.

"I don't know!" Eli shouted back. "Maybe because there's a *Sesame Street* character on top of it?"

Ari shrugged. "Oops."

Eli got to his feet and started toward home with the dog plodding behind him. After a moment, Ari scrambled after him.

"Hey, man, I'm sorry. Really. Honest mistake. Want me to try again?"

Eli shook his head. "There's no time." In a few days, they'd all be leaving for the Cape. His only hope, the only thing left to do, was to get Gabe's mother alone and make her tell him the truth, and hope against hope that the boy she'd given birth to eight months after they'd been together had been fathered by someone who was not him.

Ari was following him, still talking, but Eli wasn't listening. *Before the wedding,* he told himself. *I've got to find out, for sure, before the wedding, because if it is what I think, and the worst is true, I cannot let my daughter marry this boy. I'll have to figure it out somehow. I'll have to find some way to stop it.*

ROSA

〰〰〰

"Mami, are you okay?" Gabe had asked.

She fixed a smile on her face and hoped he'd be able to hear it. "I'm fine. I'm so excited for you!" Gabe had wanted to FaceTime, but she'd bargained him down to a phone call. "I'm getting my hair done next week, before I fly out, and I don't want you seeing your old mother like this," she'd said. Gabe had assented, but had heard something in her voice that had concerned him, and his kind, probing questions—"Is everything all right? Is there anything I can do?"—made her want to scream and cry and rake her own face with her fingernails. *I don't deserve him*, Rosa thought.

"I'm fine," she'd assured him, and he'd promised her, again, that she had nothing to worry about. "Ruby's father and stepmom are good people. They'll like you. It's going to be fine."

"Sure," said Rosa, knowing that Ruby's father, whether a good person or not, was not going to like her, that it was not going to be fine. She thought back to the beginning of the pandemic, when Gabe had told her he was moving in with Ruby, that Ruby's mom had found him a job, remembering how grateful she'd been that her son was safe. She'd called Ruby's mother to thank her, to offer to contribute to the expense of feeding and housing him. Sarah Danhauser had waved away her offer, saying, "Please. We should be paying you. Gabe's a delight. He cooks, he cleans, he's friendly first thing in the morning, and Ruby's brothers adore him. We're lucky to have him here. He's a wonderful kid. You should be proud."

Rosa had been so glad that her son had found a safe harbor, that he'd found not just a girlfriend but a family, with other boys, and the kind of father who could show him, however belatedly, what a father should be. It was ironic. Because, soon, she'd be face-to-face with that father. That good man. And he would know that Gabe had been raised by the kind of woman who'd mislead a man about being pregnant just to get a few hundred bucks.

We're lucky to have him here, Sarah had said. *You should be proud.*

Proud, Rosa thought, as a sob caught in her throat. Oh, if only she could be proud! If only she'd behaved honorably; if only she'd told the truth, if only she'd done the right thing when there was still time!

She tried to smile, to sound normal, as Gabe went over the travel plans. Rosa and Amanda had tickets from Los Angeles to Boston. Gabe would meet them at the airport, in a rental car, and the three of them would drive up to the Cape together. "The house is incredible. I can't wait for you to see," Gabe told them, and explained that they'd all be in a guesthouse, with Gabe and Ruby in the master bedroom, and Rosa and Amanda in the living room. "We tried to find a hotel, but there wasn't anything within an hour's drive that weekend," Gabe said. "I'm sorry."

Rosa couldn't breathe. She felt like a giant's hand was gripping her chest. Her knees felt trembly; her belly was a knotted ache. "Don't apologize," she told her son. "I'm just happy I'll be with you. That's all I want."

Meanwhile, Eli Danhauser was frantic to reach her. Every time she turned her phone on she found another spate of texts and emails from him—*please call, it's important, we need to talk.* The last time it had happened she'd gotten so dizzy, so sick with disgust and regret that she'd turned the phone off and thrown it onto her bed, like it was a snake that had bitten her. Then she'd deleted her email and text apps from her phone. It didn't mean his messages weren't still coming, but at least she wouldn't have to see them, and have her mistake thrown in her face.

Gabe talked, and Rosa let herself imagine how it would go: the plane ride (she pictured Amanda throwing back those miniature bottles of vodka and flirting with whatever men were nearby). The airport in Boston, where she'd never been. Seeing Gabe, for the first time since the pandemic. She'd run to him and hug him, so hard she'd probably leave bruises; she would bury her face in the space between his ear and his shoulder, letting the smell of his skin surround her. The last time she'd seen him, he'd had a new, short haircut, and his clothes had smelled of a different detergent from the one she used, but beneath it all, he was still Gabe, her beloved angel boy. She would hold him, and he'd smile down at her. *Let me have this*, she would think. *I won't have it for very much longer.*

SARAH

On Thursday afternoon, Sarah played hooky, slipping out of work early to meet Owen in front of the Guggenheim. They spent two hours in the museum, looking at the Picasso prints and the Frankenthaler watercolors, at Owen's favorite Matisse sculpture and Sarah's favorite Degas paintings. Then they'd gone to a café, where they'd lingered over drinks, asking each other polite questions, learning the contours of how the other had spent the last twenty-plus years.

Owen had talked about the Guggenheim Collection in Venice, where it turned out he'd spent a semester abroad. "There's this one sculpture of a man on horseback with, um, an erection. Only the pope was a great friend of Peggy Guggenheim's, so the sculptor made the penis detachable."

"Handy," said Sarah.

"Yes," Owen had deadpanned. "But is it art?"

Sarah had listened, and stolen looks at him, appreciating the way his blue button-down stretched against his shoulders, the economy and grace of his movements. He'd always been comfortable in his body, at ease in his skin. Eli, she knew, had shot up six inches between junior high and high school. He walked with a permanent stoop, the result of the years he'd spent bumping his head on doorframes and ceilings that weren't sized for a man of his height. Eli was still sometimes oblivious to the way his body occupied space. Owen always seemed to know exactly where he was.

"I'm glad I ran into you, because there are things I want to tell you," he said. "Things I should have told you a long time ago."

"Are these things I'm going to want to hear?" Sarah asked, feeling her heart start beating hard.

"I think so," Owen said. "I hope so, anyhow." He ran his hands over his close-cropped hair. "I wasn't honest with you, back then. And you deserve to know what was really going on."

She held herself very still, hoping none of what she was feeling showed on her face. "Okay," she said. "I'm listening."

Owen rolled his shoulders and began to shred his paper napkin. "You remember what the Camp was like, right?"

Sarah nodded. She had lots of memories of the Camp: the peeling paint, the single toilet, in its cinder block enclosure; the way Owen's tiny cabin had smelled of mouse, and was so small that when you were lying in bed you could touch both walls with your outstretched arms. She remembered the boathouse, full of abandoned and broken things, with its roof caving in. Back then, she'd been charmed by some of the Camp's idiosyncrasies and oblivious to the rest. She hadn't cared where she was, as long as she got to be with Owen.

"I know your mom thought that it was a performance, right?" Owen asked. "Rich WASPs pretending they were poor, just for the hell of it." His voice had a hard, ironic edge.

Surprised, Sarah asked, "Did she say that to you?"

He raised his eyebrows. "You told me she called us

the Pond People. Remember?" Sarah cringed. "And I might have done a little eavesdropping the first night I came over for dinner."

"Exotic," Sarah murmured, hoping she and her mother hadn't hurt teenage Owen's feelings. "My mom said you guys thought it was exotic, and amusing, to live that way."

Owen made a scoffing noise. "Maybe it was fun, for some people. Maybe some of them were just pretending to be broke. But we weren't. We were the actual item."

Sarah sat very straight, waiting. Owen went on.

"Our house—our real house in Connecticut—was just like the Camp. It was enormous, and drafty, and nothing worked right. It was falling down around our heads." He gave her a tight-lipped smile. "But it didn't matter, because it was big, and in the right zip code, and it looked fine from the outside, if you didn't look too closely."

She stared at him. "Wait. Hang on. I thought—"

"I know what you thought." Owen sounded unhappy. "You thought Sass was an heiress, and that Eliza and I were rich, and that Anders was . . ." Owen tilted his head back, staring at the ceiling, like he was reading a quote written there. "The wealthy scion of a prominent banking family. Right?"

Sarah nodded. Not only had that been what she'd thought, but it had also been what the *New York Times* had said, in Sass and Anders's wedding announcement, which she'd seen in a photo album, on the sagging shelves in the Camp's living room that held more board games than books.

But that hadn't been the only thing convincing her that Owen came from old money. "You went to private school. You and your sister."

He nodded. "My great-grandparents set up a trust to pay for that. We got financial aid, too. Sass couldn't touch that trust." His eyes were fixed on the table and the napkin. "Believe me, she tried. And as for Anders, he might have come from a prominent banking family, but when my mother married him he was unemployed, and he wasn't speaking to his father. My mom thought she'd married into wealth, and when she found out she hadn't—that Anders's grandfather had money, and his father had money, and his brothers had money, but what Anders had was some kind of bullshit degree as a life coach, and no clients—she was furious. She started cheating on him on their honeymoon."

"No," Sarah breathed.

"Yes," said Owen. "With the golf pro at the resort in Bermuda, I think. At least, that's what Anders would say when they were fighting." He folded his hands. "Sass hoped that Anders would get it together, or that his father would forgive him, and let him join the family business. And she didn't want anyone knowing what was going on."

"Oh, God." Sarah was thinking back, her mind shuffling through the minutiae of Owen's life that she'd collected over that summer, rearranging that evidence to tell a different story. She remembered how all of Owen's clothes were frayed or faded; how his swim trunks hung low on his hips because they were missing their drawstring (not that she'd minded, back then); and how one of his sneakers had a hole in its sole. He'd always seemed to have enough money in his pocket for the minimal expenses of their dates, but back then, their most expensive night out entailed the purchase of two tickets to the drive-in and two lobster rolls. At first, Owen had insisted on treating, but Sarah had worn him down, telling him that she was a feminist, insisting that she wanted to pay her own way.

She remembered feeling charmed by his nonchalance, finding his family's indifference to the material world endearing. At eighteen, it had compared favorably to the way her own family lived—the single thin, frayed towel that Owen brought to the pond versus the stacks of plush fabric softener–scented beach towels that her mom kept piled on the pool deck, for family and guests; the nicked and weathered butcher-block counters of the Camp's kitchen versus the brand-new granite countertops and state-of-the-art appliances in their house. The Lassiters had an ancient toaster with a fraying electrical cord, a wedding gift to Sass's own mother that sometimes shot sparks when you plugged it in. The Levy-Weinbergs had a fancy new toaster oven. Owen's mother collected cosmos and catmint, seagrass and hydrangeas, and made charming, casual arrangements that she stuck in empty jam jars that still wore the remnants of their labels and rode an elderly three-speed Schwinn with balding tires and an ancient wicker picnic basket bungee-corded to the rear rack. Sarah's mom hired florists and drove a minivan. At Owen's house, they kept the windows open, the patchy screens admitting flies and mosquitos to be cursed at or slapped away. At Sarah's house, her mother could control the temperature with the touch of a button and used a remote control to raise or lower the blinds.

Owen's people would swim in the pond or the ocean in the cool morning hours, nap during the heat of the day, and eat, and drink, late into the night, by the glow of the bonfires they'd light on the beach. Members of her family bent the climate to their will; shutting out the sounds of the wind and the sea with double-paned glass, installing a swimming pool, with its bright, chlorinated water, instead of being content with the bay or the ponds.

Now, here was Owen, telling her that the choices she'd found so charming were not quirks or idiosyncrasies but plain old poverty. It was unsettling. She felt terrible for assuming, and for romanticizing; a little uneasy about what else she'd missed or gotten wrong. And she still didn't understand how Owen had vanished so completely, like he'd erased himself from her life and somehow managed to take his house with him.

"So Sass and Anders got divorced, and the Camp got sold," she said. "You could have told me that's what was happening. Why didn't you call me? Or email me? Even if we weren't still going out, we could have been friends."

"You wouldn't have wanted to hear from me."

"Well, maybe not right away, after being dumped by email. But eventually . . ."

He shook his head. In a soft, toneless voice, he said, "You wouldn't have wanted to hear from me because I lied to you." Sarah just looked at him as Owen said, "I wasn't at Duke. I didn't get in."

Sarah stared across the table, shocked into silence. Over the summer they'd spent together, Owen had spoken in elaborate detail about the campus, about the lacrosse team's preseason and its coach. He'd told her the name of his dorm and the name of his suitemates and teammates, the classes he was going to take and how he was already planning to sleep outdoors in a tent in K-ville, named in honor of Duke's famous basketball coach, in hopes of getting tickets to the games.

Sarah shook her head. "I don't understand."

Owen sighed, the memory of old disappointment darkening his features. "Believe me, neither did I, at the time. My guidance counselor said I was a sure thing."

"And you were a great lacrosse player!"

Owen made a scoffing noise. "Good. Not great. Definitely not as good as I led you to believe."

"Weren't you All-State?"

"In Rhode Island," he said, shamefaced. "It's not a very big state."

"I . . ." She licked her lips and rubbed her hands against her thighs. "I don't know what to say. So it wasn't that you'd met some other girl?"

He shook his head. "All summer long, every day, I'd wake up and think, *Today I'm going to tell her the truth.* But I couldn't." He shook his head. "You were this perfect, shining thing. You were so talented, and you were going to be a famous pianist—"

"—and you can see how well that turned out," Sarah said, and hoped she sounded wry, not bitter. Hoping, too, that her face didn't show how the words *perfect, shining thing* were ringing through her, making her feel trembly and flushed.

"I was embarrassed," Owen said. "I felt like a failure, and a fraud and a liar. Probably because I *was* a liar. But, more than that, I didn't want you thinking . . ." He paused, tilting his head toward the ceiling again. "I wanted you to think I was what I pretended to be. A rich, preppy kid on his way to play lacrosse at the Harvard of the South. That's who I wanted to be." He lowered his head and looked at her. "Because that's the boy you were in love with."

"No," Sarah said. She reached across the table and

touched his hand. "I was in love with you." She felt herself blush at the words, but how could she not have said them? She'd loved Owen the way she'd never loved any boy or man. There was nothing as pure or as passionate as that kind of first love. And, she thought, nothing as devastating as that first breakup.

Owen smoothed his cropped hair with both hands. "In my family, lying was a way of life. I was just keeping up the family tradition."

"Where did you go?" Sarah asked. "You did go to college somewhere, right?"

"University of Vermont," said Owen, and gave her a crooked smile. "I did a lot of skiing. It wasn't so bad. After Sass sold the Camp, there was some more money. Then, after she got married again, and moved out of Westport, there was even more."

Sarah said nothing. She was remembering how she'd felt, the summer after her freshman year, swimming across the pond, hoping to see Owen, and, instead of his house, seeing nothing but a hole in the ground. How it had felt hearing that automated voice in her ear, telling her there was no listing for any Lassiters anywhere.

"The house was a teardown, but the land itself was worth a good bit of money. It got us back on our feet." He looked up, his brilliant blue eyes finding her gaze. "But I couldn't tell you what was really going on. And my mom . . ."

He paused. Sarah waited, realizing that this was the first time Owen had called Sass his mom. "The Cape was a huge part of her identity. She'd gone there as a kid, and it meant a lot, that she'd been the one to inherit the place from her grandparents. It killed her, having to sell it." He was quiet for a minute, smoothing the shreds of his napkin with one long-fingered hand. "She had kind of a breakdown that year, after she and Anders split. I think losing the Camp—losing her place—was worse than losing her husband." He gave Sarah his rueful smile again. "It's hard to play it off like you're part of the landed gentry when you don't have any land."

Sarah shook her head, still feeling unsettled and bewildered. "I can't believe I didn't know."

"You weren't supposed to know." Owen's voice was patient. "That was the whole point. No one was supposed to know." He steepled his hands on the table. "And none of it excuses blowing you off the way I did."

Sarah nodded. She could still picture the email, the sting of that handful of words that she still knew by heart: *I've met someone here and I want to be with her. I'm sorry, but it's for the best. We should both be free.* She could also remember her pulse beating hard in her throat as she'd swam across the pond to the opposite shore where the Camp had been, and found no house at all. There'd been a bulldozer where the boathouse had stood, and a crane, a bunch of workmen standing around a hole in the ground, smoking cigarettes and tossing their butts into the dirt. Sarah had been gaping when one of the men had noticed her. "You lost, sweetheart?" he'd asked, his expression just short of a leer. "This is private property." *Private property*, Sarah thought, remembering the first time she'd heard Owen Lassiter's voice. Without saying a word, she had turned around and swum back the way she'd come.

Owen looked down. "I was ashamed. I didn't want you knowing the truth about me. About us. About any of it."

"You know that it wouldn't have made a difference.

I didn't ..." She took a sip of water and patted her lips dry. "I didn't care about money, or your family. I cared about you."

"But you didn't know who I was. Not really." He lifted his gaze to meet hers. Up close, she could see faint wrinkles around his eyes, a few strands of gray in his eyebrows, but his eyes were still that brilliant, aching blue of a perfect summer day. "And I'm sorry. You deserved the truth. I just wish ..." He paused, drumming his fingers on the table. Sarah felt her mouth go dry. She was barely breathing, fingers twisting in her lap, heart fluttering, knowing what was coming. "I wish we'd had a real chance," he said. "Because I've never been as happy with anyone as I was with you that summer."

She looked across the table at the first boy she'd ever loved, saying nothing, not trusting herself to speak.

"Are you happy?" he asked gently. "I—I thought about you so much, after we ..." His voice trailed off, and he gave a wry smile. "Well. After I dumped you. I hated that I'd hurt you, and I'd always hoped that you were happy."

Am I? Sarah asked herself. Not lately. And here was Owen, looking at her like she was the only woman in the world.

Ever since she'd texted him—no, Sarah thought, ever since she'd seen him—she'd been deciding what would happen next, how far she'd let herself go. She'd spent almost fifteen years with Eli and had never once considered cheating. She'd never even been seriously tempted. And Owen was so handsome, and it had been so long, and he was looking at her with an intensity that made her feel like she was melting, like she'd spill right out of her seat.

"Do you have any plans right now?" she asked him.

He met her eyes and shook his head.

"Come with me," she said, and Owen got immediately to his feet, without asking where they were going, like he'd follow anywhere she led.

They were mostly quiet as they walked through Central Park to her studio. Sarah unlocked the front door and led him up the stairs, aware of his closeness. She opened the door to her place, now furnished: her single bed against one wall, her piano against the other, the two windows overlooking the street, a bouquet of white hydrangeas on the coffee table. Owen looked around and nodded like he was confirming something he already knew.

"This is exactly the kind of place where I imagined you living."

"It is?" she asked, thinking how different the studio was from the brownstone, which was bright and warm and colorful, full of furniture and art and toys and books and people. Here, the walls were painted white. There was just a stack of sheet music on the piano's lid, a single framed poster from the Spoleto Festival on the wall, the white flowers on the kitchen's tiny counter, and the white down comforter on the bed.

"Like an artist's garret. Just you and your music." He gave her another knee-wobbling smile, then nodded at the piano. "Will you play for me?"

"Oh, I don't—"

"Please?"

She'd only played for Owen once in their time together, that first night he'd come for dinner. She'd been reluctant. Part of her didn't want him to think she was showing off, and another part couldn't wait to dazzle him.

"Play one of your recital pieces!" her mother had called

from the kitchen, and Sam, lounging on the couch, had popped his head up to say, "She's really good."

She sat at the keyboard, played a few scales to warm up her fingers, and decided on one of the first recital pieces she'd ever learned, something that even a nonclassical-music lover would appreciate: the first movement of Beethoven's Opus 79 in G Major. "The Cuckoo Sonata," so-called because it imitated the call-and-repeat of a songbird. It was bright and playful, and had some showy moments where her left hand would cross over her right. Sarah had adjusted the bench, then her posture, then struck the first three chords. By the third or fourth measure, she'd closed her eyes, and by the time she reached the first repeat the room and her family and her boyfriend had all ceased to matter, the room had disappeared, and it was, as ever, just Sarah and the music, Sarah and the song.

When the final note had died away, she'd opened her eyes. Her parents stood together, her dad with his arm around her mom's waist, both of them beaming at her. Sam applauded. Owen had looked stunned.

"Oh my God," he'd blurted.

Sam had sat up. "Toldja," he'd said. Sarah had brushed off their compliments, feeling proud and shy. Later, on the beach, Owen had kissed her with something like reverence, and said, "You never told me you were that good."

In her studio, with the sounds of the city coming through the windows, Owen took her hand and led her to the piano. "Please," he said. "I've waited so long to hear you play again."

Sarah struck the first notes of "The Moonlight Sonata," knowing that she was lost. She might have been able to resist Owen's good looks and charm, she could have made herself immune to flattery, or the way hearing someone else's confession could soften you. But the way he looked at her, that combination of tenderness and awe, like she was special, and talented; some rare and beautiful creature he couldn't believe he was allowed to touch—that, Sarah could not withstand.

She played him pieces she thought he would know, a Brahms lullaby, a Bach concerto and Mozart's Piano Sonata 16, which made him smile. This time, instead of losing herself in the music, she found herself aware of Owen: his presence, his warmth, his eyes on her.

When she finished, she pushed back the bench and got to her feet. Owen was standing behind her, with that same look of amazement on his face; a look that said *You are the most incredible thing. You astonish me.* When he opened his arms, Sarah did not hesitate. She walked into his embrace, fitting herself against him like a puzzle piece into its space, like a key into a lock, like every cliché about long-lost lovers who are meant to be together. She was the one to put her hand on his neck and draw his lips down to hers; she was the one who unbuttoned his shirt, then led him toward her single bed. *I deserve this*, Sarah told herself, remembering all the times Eli had ignored her or looked right through her; all the times he'd come slap-slapping down the hall in his infernal flip-flops, or tried to give away the things she loved.

"Kiss me," she whispered, pulling him close. Then his arms were around her, his mouth on hers again. Sarah closed her eyes, savoring the sensations that threatened to overwhelm her, the feeling of adult Owen superimposed over Owen at eighteen. Then Owen's face had been boyishly smooth. Now-Owen had stubble that rasped her cheeks. Then-Owen had been more passionate than skilled; enthusiastic with his tongue and his hands. Now-Owen was a much more skilled kisser. *Much more skilled at everything*, Sarah thought as he unhooked her bra, one-handed, and eased his other hand up her skirt. But then, when he touched her between her legs for the first time, he gave a soft groan, just as then-Owen had done, all those years ago. He'd sounded like she was a marvel, like she imagined the old explorers had sounded when they'd finally sighted land. Now-Owen hummed a pleased sound against her neck as he slipped his fingers inside of her, then pulled them out, stroking delicately along the edges of her most private place, and it was so good that Sarah gasped out loud. She reached for his belt, then his zipper. Part of her wanted to show him that she, too, had grown up; that she, like him, had learned things, but part of her—most of her—just wanted him naked and inside her.

Owen scooped her up and set her gently on the bed, then lay down beside her. They kissed and kissed, and Sarah let her hands explore the thicker tangle of hair on his chest, the play of muscles beneath the warm skin of his flanks, the strong length of his legs. Finally, she urged him onto his back. She gripped his erection, giving it a single, slow stroke, twisting her hand as she went, making him gasp, before she straddled him, settling her knees on each side of his hips. In the dimness of the room, his eyes were open wide, his pupils large and dark, taking her in.

"Wait," he said hoarsely, just before she slid down, drawing him inside of her. "Do I need . . ."

She shook her head. She'd had her tubes tied, after Miles. Two boys plus Ruby was all she'd ever want, she thought.

Now a part of her cried out for the years they hadn't had, for the babies they'd never make. She slid down, taking him inside of her, and regret and comparison and every other conscious thought left her mind, until all that was left were bodies, fitted together in the gathering twilight.

When it was over, Owen fell asleep, curled against her, one leg slung over hers. Sarah lay on her back, looking up at the ceiling, hearing the day winding down. She could hear more of the traffic outside her window than she could in Park Slope; a neighbor's voice in the hallway, a burst of laughter from the sidewalk below. Sarah stared up into the shadows, hearing Owen's voice: *This is exactly the kind of place where I imagined you living.*

This was a life she could have had; maybe the life she should have had, instead of what she'd had at twenty-five. As a new wife and the step-parent of an eight-year-old. A studio room instead of a brownstone; a home with no space for anything but her piano, a life with no room for anything but her music. A half-sized refrigerator, a two-burner stove. Less a home than a touchdown pad, a place to land between engagements in Leipzig and Paris and London. Or, she supposed, between cruises on the ship where she'd play in the cocktail lounge. No children to distract her, no day job to eat up her time. Nothing but music and the man who loved her; the comfort of his body, the balm of his attention. If she and Owen had stayed together she could have had that life. More likely, Sarah thought, she would have spent her twenties at parties and happy hours and on first dates, having her heart broken, feeling increasingly frantic as the finish line loomed.

So she'd chosen Eli, jumping into marriage and a ready-made family, fast-forwarding right through her twenties. Sometimes, it had felt like she'd walked into a movie that had already begun. While her friends were trying to get pregnant, were enduring miscarriages or struggling with babies, she was dealing with a bratty eight-year-old; while they'd been applying to kindergartens she'd been pregnant and planning a bat mitzvah. She hadn't been unhappy, but an older husband and a stepdaughter had meant she was always a little out of step with her peers. Did that mean she'd chosen incorrectly? Were there lessons she should have been learning, experiences she should have been having in those first years she'd spent as Eli's wife and Ruby's stepmother? Could she wish her boys away, or wish she'd never known Ruby, never made it through all of Ruby's scorn and rejection to the reward on the other side?

In the near-dark, with Owen breathing steadily beside her, no answer came.

Sarah lay awake, thinking, until it was seven o'clock and she knew she'd need to either text home with some excuse or leave immediately. She was trying to edge herself out of the bed when Owen sighed, pulling her close, kissing her neck. "What are you thinking?" he asked.

Sarah shook her head, knowing that she had too many thoughts to sort through, and certainly too many to say out loud. The only thing she knew for sure was that she wasn't sorry. Maybe, later, there'd be guilt and regret, but for now, there was only the delicious high of new love (or, she supposed, new old love), the surging chemicals that made her feel like she'd never need to eat or sleep again.

"When can I see you?" Owen asked.

Sarah got out of bed and began gathering her things: skirt and underwear, bra and blouse and shoes. She started to get dressed, reassembling herself as a wife and a mother. "I'm going to be busy for the next few weeks. My stepdaughter's getting married. On the Cape, as it happens."

"Congratulations," Owen said. "When do you leave?"

"Three weeks," she said. "The wedding's Fourth of July weekend."

"Huh. Really? I'll be on the Cape then."

She turned around to look at him. He held his hands open, grinning.

"It's still my favorite place in the world. I go for two weeks every summer. I stay at the same Airbnb in Wellfleet. It's near where the Camp used to be." He got up, crossed the room, embraced her. "You don't have to see me," he said. "But I'll be there, if you decide that you want to."

Dismayed, Sarah shook her head. "It's Ruby's wedding," she said. "I can't—I won't ruin anything."

"Of course not." His tone was indulgent, and his fingers were tracing patterns on her back and her bottom. "I'm just saying, maybe you get to slip away for an hour or two. I could make a picnic. We could go for a swim. You'll need a break from everything, right?"

Even as she shook her head, Sarah was imagining it: being with Owen in the water again, swimming across the pond. His blue eyes, fringed with dark, wet lashes. How it had felt to kiss him there, their bodies cool, their lips warm.

"Maybe," she whispered. Owen kissed her, then pressed his finger against her lips, like he was fixing her conditional assent in place. "I'll keep my phone on. I'll be waiting."

PART
THREE

~~~~~~~~

MET BY MOONLIGHT

*A*nd so here they were, thought the house. The mother, and her children, and their children. Other adults, some of them strangers, some familiar. One, who'd been a girl, now all grown up. How good it felt to be full again! she thought. How good, to welcome people, to hold them, to do what she'd been built to do. How good it was to feel little feet, trotting up and down her stairs; how good to hear them, splashing in the pool. The hum of conversation, the smells of good things to eat.

You can't leave me, *she thought,* to the woman, whose step had gotten slower; who'd started crying in the shower, and alone, in her bed at night; whose scent now included a new, unsettling note that the house recognized with sorrow. *You can't go yet. We have work still to do. We have to fix this. We have to fix them. You need me, and I need you. You need this, all of the people you love around you, and you need me for it to happen. Don't leave,* the house pleaded, *in words no one could hear. And, when the woman didn't answer, she knew it was time to act.*

WEDNESDAY

SAM

~~~~~~

Sam and Connor left Los Angeles early on a Wednesday morning and landed in Boston at just after one o'clock, which became just after four o'clock, a change that confused and delighted Connor. "But how did we lose three hours?" he asked, his voice plaintive. "Where did they go?"

Collecting their luggage and their rental car went smoothly, and traffic was light. "If this were a Saturday," Sam said, as they crossed the Bourne Bridge, "we'd be sitting here for hours." They stopped for lunch in Chatham. Connor had fish and chips, and Sam enjoyed his first oysters of the summer. By eight o'clock, they were pulling into the driveway of the Levy-Weinberg home, and Veronica was waving from the second-floor deck, backlit by the setting sun.

"Hi, Mom," said Sam, bounding up the stairs to kiss her, hoping he didn't look as startled as he felt by her appearance. He hadn't seen his mother in person since his dad's funeral, before COVID and the lockdowns, and in the intervening months she seemed to have sped through the remainder of late middle age and gone straight to old. Her skin had new wrinkles; her hair was as fine as dandelion fluff, and she moved with the slow, careful gait of an invalid. As he walked up the stairs behind Connor, he wondered what he'd missed, and how it had been for her, alone on the Outer Cape, which emptied out from October to May. Had she been sick? Had she been lonely? Was he a terrible son because he hadn't come to visit?

Veronica bent down to Connor's eye level to greet him. "Hi, Connor, I'm Sam's mom. We've met before, but you might not remember."

Connor was prepared. He was the kind of child who always liked to know what he'd be doing, and where, and for how long, and with whom, and so Sam always let him know the schedule. During the last half hour of the car ride, Sam had briefed him on the wedding guests, and how all of them were connected. "You were there when Sam and my mom got married, right?" he asked Veronica. "I remember. But I was a little kid then," Connor said, with all the scorn an eight-year-old can muster for his five-year-old self. Sam saw his mother hide a smile when Connor extended his hand for a shake, and gravely shake it. Connor looked up at Sam and said, "Can we go in the pool now?"

Sam convinced him to have dinner first. Veronica had hot dogs and sausages waiting. They ate on the picnic table on the deck and had chunks of watermelon for dessert. Veronica told Sam that his sister was on her way. "Sarah decided to bring Ruby up tonight, and Eli and the boys will come tomorrow." Sam agreed to let Connor have a quick swim before bedtime. "I'm not even tired!" Connor said, his words immediately belied by an enormous yawn.

"Well, it's only dinnertime in California," Ronnie

said, which launched another conversation about time zones.

"One quick swim, then bed by nine," Sam said.

"Nine thirty?"

"Nine fifteen." Sam dug Connor's bathing suit out of their bags and was handing his stepson a towel when Sarah and Ruby pulled up the driveway. Sarah got out of the car, then opened the back door so that Lord Farquaad could escape. The dog shook himself off, strutted across the driveway on his stumpy legs, and peed disdainfully on a rosebush before making his way up to the pool.

Sarah opened the trunk and handed Ruby a garment bag, which she carefully draped over her arms. Her wedding dress, Sam figured.

"Can I help?" he called.

"No, we've got it," his sister called back. "We'll be right up." Sam watched as Ruby ceremoniously carried her dress up the stairs and into the guesthouse, with Sarah behind her, pulling a wheeled suitcase, with a duffel bag over her arm. A moment later, everyone was on the pool deck, exchanging hugs and greetings.

"Where's the lucky guy?" Sam asked.

"He'll be up tomorrow," Ruby said. "His mom and his aunt are flying into Boston, and he's going to rent a car and drive them up."

"I can't wait to meet him," said Sam. Ruby gave him a distracted smile and said, "I've got to make some calls."

"Watch this," Ronnie called. She flicked on the pool light and smiled at Connor's approval when the water lit up, brilliantly turquoise.

"I love Cape Cod!" Connor shouted, and cannonballed into the water.

Sam smiled. This had been one of his favorite spots,

out on the pool deck, which always smelled like the lavender that grew in the bed by the fence; where the boards always held the warmth of the day's sun. At night, the underwater lights would cast a cool, eerie glow. The crickets would chirp and the frogs could croak and the spill of brilliant stars would shine in the sky.

Ronnie and Sarah went upstairs, talking in low voices. Lord Farquaad established himself under a lounge chair, tucking his legs underneath him, resting his snout on the still-warm deck and looking, for all the world, like a furred baked potato. Sam watched his stepson, and the time.

"Nine fifteen," he called.

"Five more minutes? Please?"

"Okay," said Sam, and thought of his father, who'd always been the nighttime lifeguard. Ronnie liked to go to bed early, tucked under the covers with a book, but Sam had liked to stay up late, and his dad would indulge him, sipping his after-dinner coffee by the pool, sometimes tossing weighted rings that Sam would dive for.

"Five minutes are up!" Connor groaned, but paddled to the edge of the pool, where Sam stood, waiting with a towel. "Come, let me bundle you," he said, the same words he used after every bath at home, the ones his father had used with him. When Connor was wrapped, head to toe, like a boy-sized burrito, Sam scooped him into his arms and carried him downstairs. He gave him his Spider-Man pajamas and watched as he brushed his teeth.

"This is a good place," Connor said.

"And you haven't even seen the beach yet."

"Can we go now?" asked Connor. "Just for a minute? Just to look?"

"We'll go tomorrow." Sam patted Connor's hand. "Don't worry. We have lots of time."

THURSDAY

~~~~~~~~

The next morning, Sam left Connor sleeping and went quietly to the kitchen. He poured himself a cup of coffee, slipped through the sliding doors, down the stairs, and walked along the beach, thinking, and trying not to think, about what he might do that night. Connor was still asleep when he got back. He showered and went back upstairs. His mother and sister were out by the pool deck, in the shade of an umbrella, sitting at a table set next to the hydrangeas, which were in glorious bloom, boughs drooping with big, showy blooms in blue and pink and purple. Ronnie and Sarah turned identical gazes on Sam as he approached.

"Where's Connor?" asked his mother. She was wearing one of her typical summer outfits: cropped linen pants and a long-sleeved T-shirt, both of which seemed too big for her. Her hands were veined, age-spotted and thin-skinned, the hands of a grandmother, not a mom. Although, Sam supposed, she was a grandmother now . . . the same way he was middle-aged.

"Still sleeping. Where's Eli?" he asked his sister.

His mother and sister exchanged a look. "We decided

to take two cars," Sarah said. "He and Ari and the boys are on their way up now."

Sam pulled his chair closer to his sister. "What's going on?"

"Nothing," Sarah answered, too quickly. She wore a white sundress, damp at the back and the shoulders from her shower-wet hair. Her feet were bare, toes freshly painted, and she seemed fidgety as she spun, with one hand, her coffee cup on the table. Her other hand, Sam noticed, rested on her pocket, through which he could see the outline of her phone. Maybe she was worried about Eli and the boys, he thought, or expecting a text from the car.

"When will they be here?" Ronnie asked.

"No idea," said Sarah. "All I know is that Eli's doing all the driving because Ari's license is currently suspended." She sighed. "Also, there's a bench warrant for him in Connecticut."

"Why?" Sam asked.

"I don't want to know." Sarah shook her head. "I think your assignment, should you choose to accept it, will be to keep Ari away from the pot dispensaries."

"They have those here?" Sam asked.

"Oh, sure," said Ronnie. "There's one in Wellfleet called the Piping Plover. I liked the name so much I went in to compliment them, and they gave me a sample!"

"Jesus, Ma," said Sam.

"Well, I didn't *take* it," Ronnie said primly.

"Throw it away," said Sarah. "The absolute last thing I need is Ari getting high." She sighed, and wrapped both hands around her mug.

"How are you doing?" Ronnie asked. "Has planning this been stressful?"

Sarah shook her head. "It's not that. It's ..." She

shook her head again. Sam watched his sister carefully, wondering if she'd tell Ronnie what was troubling her. Finally, Sarah just said, "Eli's been a little moody."

Good job, Sam thought, feeling glad that his sister had broached the topic and relieved that the focus was off him.

"Maybe it's the wedding," Ronnie suggested. "His little girl is getting married. It's a big thing for a father."

"I don't know." Sarah's voice was low. "God knows I'd never say this to Ruby, but I think this wedding is a mistake. She hasn't known Gabe that long, and she's so young."

"So maybe that's it," Ronnie said.

"I don't know!" Sarah said. She drew a shaky breath. "I'd assume that he was having an affair, except I don't know when he'd have time. He's under my feet every minute of the day." She shuddered. "And he's got those plantar fasciitis flip-flops." Sarah pointed at her mother. "I blame you for those, by the way."

Ronnie looked bewildered. "How are his flip-flops my fault?"

"Because your friend was the one who told him how great they were."

"Ah," said Ronnie. "A thousand pardons." She reached across the table and patted Sarah's forearm. "I don't know what's going on with him. But Eli loves you."

In a leaden voice, Sarah said, "Sometimes people change."

It struck Sam that he wouldn't get a more perfect segue, or a better moment for his big reveal. *You know how you think you can know someone, and then they surprise you? You know how you think you know yourself? Well, guess what I just figured out!* He opened his mouth, unsure of how to start. Which, of course, was the moment that Eli's car came crunching up the driveway. As soon as the car stopped, both back doors popped open, and Dexter and Miles raced out of the car. Ari ambled out after them, wearing rumpled khaki cargo shorts and a T-shirt from a half marathon that Sam was almost positive that Eli, not Ari, had run.

"Hello, hello," Ari called, giving a genial wave, as Eli started to remove what looked like a dozen bags and suitcases from the trunk. Connor, still in his Spider-Man pajamas, hurried out of the house to greet his cousins. "You guys. You guys, guess what? There's a beach here! And a pool! And a shower, and the shower is outside!"

"We KNOW!" said Dexter, who was trying to run and talk and take off his shoes at the same time. Eli came thumping up the steps with a tote bag in one hand and a canister of sunscreen in the other, calling, "Children! Do not even think about going in the water until you bring your things inside!"

Sarah almost jumped out of her chair. "I should go get some wine for dinner," she said. "Do we need anything else from the package store? Or Stop & Shop?"

"Toilet paper," Ronnie said. She reached for Sarah's hand. "But hang on, okay? I want to talk to you two about something."

Sam and Sarah exchanged a worried look. "Nothing bad," Ronnie said quickly as Sarah took her seat. "Just, now that you're both here, in person, I figured it was a good time." Ronnie smoothed her fingertips over her eyebrows. "I spoke to Paul Norman a few weeks ago. We agreed that it's the right time to put the house on the market." Before either of them could reply, Ronnie continued, "I'd planned to leave you both the house in my will. I hoped you'd want to come here with your own kids, so they could spend their summers together." She smiled sadly. "But I think that was my vision of summer, not yours." She touched her eyebrows again. "I was going to tell you after the wedding, only there's a couple who want to see the house on Monday, after the wedding. They're only up here until the end of next week, and Paul thinks that they're serious buyers, so . . ." She clasped her hands at her chest, sighing.

Sam tried to hide his shock, realizing that he couldn't imagine his mother living anywhere but here. He didn't spend much time at the Cape house, but he felt comforted knowing it was there; that he had a home, a place where they would have to take him in. He murmured something about how much he'd loved it here as a kid, how he wished he lived closer, how he and Connor would be here all the time if he did.

"Where will you go?" Sarah asked her mother.

Ronnie shrugged. "I've got time to figure that out."

His sister's expression was rueful and chagrined.

"I know," she said. "I know we should have spent more time here. I know Dex and Miles are overscheduled. I know I'm turning into That Mom. I should just give them time to hang out on the beach and collect seashells, instead of taking them from cello to Hebrew school to Krav Maga." She buried her face in her hands and shook her head. "I know."

Ronnie put her hand on Sarah's shoulder. "Honey, I promise I'm not trying to make you feel guilty. You're a wonderful mother."

Sarah continued as if her mother hadn't spoken. "But every parent I know is like that. You have to give your kid every possible opportunity, and if you don't, you're failing them. You can't not try."

"It's okay," Ronnie said firmly. "Really. It's okay. I understand. I'm just so glad everyone's here, together. And I—" She looked like she wanted to say more as Dexter and Miles and Connor, appropriately swimsuited and sunscreened, came thundering across the deck.

Ronnie got to her feet. "Wait! Stop! I haven't seen you creatures in one entire year! How about a hug for Safta?" Miles and Dexter ran to hug her, and over the din of the dog barking and Ronnie exclaiming how much the boys had grown, Sam almost didn't hear his sister when she said, "I am a terrible human being."

Before Sam could wonder at that, or come up with an answer, Sarah was on her way down to the driveway. "Let me get the lobsters in the fridge," she said. "Then I'll head out. Sam, can you watch the kids?"

Sam said that he could. When Sarah had gone down to the driveway and Ronnie was up in the kitchen, he walked to the edge of the deck and studied his brother-in-law, watching as, one story below him, Eli pulled grocery bags and tote bags and a set of golf clubs from the trunk. His brother-in-law looked the way he always did, maybe a little bit thinner. His hair was neatly trimmed, his clothes clean and relatively unwrinkled. His wedding band winked in the sunshine. He seemed fine. But, of course, who knew better than Sam that you could keep a secret, one that completely altered your sense of yourself and the world, and not have any of it show, not even to the people who knew you best?

After lunch, and an hour spent unpacking, Sam and Sarah took all three boys down to the beach.

"So," Sam said, when the boys were taking turns pushing each other around on the paddleboard. "Enjoying the guilt trip?"

Sarah shook her head. She'd pulled her hair back in a ponytail. It made her look young, even though she'd traded her bikinis for a conservative swimsuit with a skirted bottom, the kind of thing their mother had once worn. "She's right, though. I bet the boys would be happier here, doing nothing, than they are in Brooklyn, doing everything." She wrapped her arms around herself and stared up at a parasailer, gliding over the bay. "I know I'd be happier if I were here."

"You know, I can work from anywhere," Sam said. "If you ever did decide to try a whole summer here, Connor and I could come for a while. We could ask Mom to hold off for a year or two. I bet she'd do it."

"Maybe," said Sarah. She looked sad and remote. "I don't know." She slid the elastic off her ponytail, staring down at the water. "It feels like everything's changing, you know? Everything, all at once."

It was another near-perfect opening. But Sarah already looked so glum, Sam was reluctant to drop another bomb.

"Agh!" yelled Connor, running backward through the knee-deep water as fast as he could. "There's a crab! A giant big one!"

"Did it pinch you?" asked Sam.

"No, but I can see it!"

Sam waded into the clear shallows, where he saw a large crab, waving both of its claws in the air as it attempted to scuttle away.

"It's more afraid of you than you are of it," Sam reassured his stepson. Together, they watched as the crab skittered sideways and buried itself in the sand.

"I like how they do that," said Connor.

Sam put his hand on the boy's shoulder. "Stick

with me, kid," he said. "Tomorrow, we'll go out at low tide and I'll teach you how to find clams with your feet."

After an hour, Connor's nose and cheeks were looking pink. Sam herded the boys up the beach stairs and into the outdoor shower to rinse off. When the kids went back to the pool, Sam took his own shower, changed into khaki shorts and a polo shirt, and went up to the kitchen. He helped his mother pick the meat out of the lobsters, while Ruby, her curls held back by a red bandana, sliced avocado, tiny heirloom tomatoes, crispy bacon, and hard-boiled eggs. Lobster Cobb salad was Ronnie's signature summer dish, and she served it with ears of corn on the cob and homemade garlic bread. It was their usual welcome-to-the-Cape meal, and the taste of it had always signaled the beginning of summer to Sam.

The boys shucked the corn and set the table. Ruby whisked the dressing. Just before sunset, they all took their seats at the long wooden table that stretched between the kitchen counter and the living room's couches. Ronnie and Sarah wore sundresses, and the boys were in T-shirts and shorts, with their faces flushed from the sun. Everyone's feet were bare, and everyone looked relaxed and happy as Eli passed a bottle of white wine around the table and the boys pleaded to be allowed to drink soda instead of water ("It's a special occasion!" said Dexter).

Ronnie raised the blinds for the traditional exclaiming over the sunset. Once the sun had dipped below the horizon and the ritual was complete, the platters were passed the length of the table, and everyone began to eat.

Sam kept his eyes on Eli during the meal, watching as his brother-in-law picked at his food and ignored his daughter's teasing remarks. Miles had to ask him twice to pass the water pitcher, and when Veronica asked if he'd prepared a toast, he'd looked like a kid who hadn't done the reading and who'd just learned there'd be a pop quiz.

"I'm working on it," he muttered.

"Don't worry," said Ari. "Eli's Old Faithful. He's never let anyone down." Sam was almost positive he saw Eli glare at his brother and Ari smirk in return, as his mom asked, "Sam, what's new with you?"

"Oh, the usual," he said. "Nothing to report."

Ronnie narrowed her eyes and looked him over, before giving a shrug so small that everyone else at the table probably missed it. Sam didn't miss it. His mother, he realized, had figured out that something was going on. He wondered if she had any idea what that something was.

Ronnie looked at Sam, then at Sarah, then at Eli, before lifting her wineglass. "To family," she said. "I'm so glad for Ruby, and so glad to have all of you here."

"To family!" the boys repeated, in a noisy chorus, and knocked their plastic cups together.

"To family," said Ruby, and clinked her glass against Ronnie's. Sam looked at his step-niece, remembering her sitting at this very same table, when she'd been holding a plastic cup instead of a wineglass. *Sunrise, sunset*, he thought. There was a lump in his throat, and his eyes felt hot.

"To family," said Ari.

"Family," Eli said very softly.

"Family," said Sarah, giving Eli a look that was both pointed and frightened.

"To family!" said Sam, and glanced discreetly at the time, thinking that in only a few hours, he'd slip away from all this and into the gaudy, spangled spectacle that was Provincetown after dark.

SARAH

~~~~~~

From the moment she'd arrived on the Cape, Sarah had tried to keep busy. If she was constantly in motion, occupied with important, wedding-related tasks, her mom couldn't engage her in the conversation she was dreading: *How's that new studio working out? How are things with Eli? And by the way, how's your marriage these days?* She'd unpacked all her clothes, hanging the light blue linen dress she'd bought for the wedding only after making sure she'd removed all the price tags. She'd cut off the conversation on the pool deck with her brother and her mom as quickly as she could, feeling almost weak with relief at the sound of Eli's arrival. Maybe her mom thought that she wanted to avoid Eli, or maybe she thought Sarah just needed some time to take in the news that the house was going on the market. Ronnie could think whatever she wanted, as long as she wasn't there, asking Sarah questions that Sarah didn't want to answer.

So she'd fled. She'd gone to the liquor store for wine and champagne, and then on to the grocery store for toilet paper, for fruit and cheese and crackers. She lingered in the aisles, inspecting poison-ivy remedies and frozen dinners, staring at Owen's texts. *I'm here waiting. Let me know if you've got any time.* He'd sent a picture—a thirst trap, Sarah was pretty sure the kids would call it—a shot of his legs, in board shorts, as he sat on a towel in front of the sun-dappled pond.

Part of her thought, *I can't.* Another part thought, *I could.* She could make up some excuse, invent some errand, even simply tell the truth: *I'm going to the pond for a swim.* The boys would be happy to stay home with Sam and with Connor, and with Ari doing his Fun Uncle shtick. No one would miss her. Eli certainly wouldn't. She'd typed, and erased, a half-dozen responses to Owen before finally deciding to go home, to be a good daughter, a good stepmother, a good wife. At least for now.

Back at the house Sarah had set the table and washed the dishes and swept the kitchen floor. After the lobster Cobb salad had been decimated, she'd volunteered to put the boys to bed, but when Sam said, "I got it," she had gone out on the deck, to listen to the ocean and let the evening breeze cool her cheeks. Less than a minute later, she heard the door slide open behind her, and knew that the moment of reckoning had arrived.

"How are you?" Ronnie asked, and touched Sarah's arm. "Everything okay?"

Sarah kept her face expressionless, cursing her mother's empathy. "I'm fine."

Ronnie leaned on the railing, mimicking Sarah's posture. "This is all making me think about your wedding," Ronnie said. "I couldn't believe you were old enough to be someone's wife! I could still remember you and Sam playing on the beach. Remember how you used to tell Sam he had to pay you a toll to get up the stairs?"

Sarah nodded. *The toll is three hermit crabs*, she'd announce imperiously, or *You have to pay me six slipper shells*, and poor Sam would grab a bucket and run back down the stairs to collect them.

"Your father was a wreck," her mother said. "He was

so worried he'd start crying under the chuppah and that he wouldn't be able to stop. How's Eli doing?"

"Eli's fine." Sarah heard how angry she sounded. In truth, she had no idea how Eli was handling things, because Eli had stopped talking to her . . . and, ever since her night with Owen, she hadn't been able to bring herself to care. She ordered the groceries, she went to work, she picked up Ruby's wedding gown, and made calls to triple-check on the flowers, and all the while her body was tingling and her mind was pre-occupied, full of blissful thoughts of Owen Lassiter. She barely ate; hardly slept. She felt like a teenage girl with a crush . . . because, of course, she'd been a teenage girl with a crush the first time she'd fallen for Owen.

"And you're okay?" her mother asked.

"I'm fine," Sarah said, before deciding to give her mother a small piece of truth. "Honestly, I guess I was a little hurt that Ruby told you about the wedding before she told me. I know you guys are close, and I think it's great, but . . ." She shook her head, ashamed at herself for being petty, for finding her mother's happiness a threat to her own. "I'm probably being stupid."

"No, I get it," said her mom. "I'm sorry if I hurt your feelings. I wish I'd told you as soon as she'd told me." Sarah looked at her mother, surprised by how shrunken she seemed, how fine her hair looked. She'd only seen her mother for a week the previous summer, and only after they'd all been tested for COVID and quarantined two weeks in advance, and then another two weeks after they'd come home. In less than a year, Ronnie had lost weight, and, Sarah thought, height, too. There were new pigmented spots on her face, new bags beneath her eyes, and Sarah could see, clearly, the shape of her skull through her hair.

"Ruby loves this place as much as I do." *As much as you and Sam didn't*, Sarah heard her mother say. "When she called and said she wanted to be married here, I was just so happy we'd have a chance to all be together."

"It shouldn't have bothered me," Sarah said. "And, for the record, I always loved it here, too. It's just, with the boys, and everything they've got going on, it's complicated." As she spoke, she discovered that she was angry at her mother, angry in a way she'd never let herself acknowledge. Ronnie had pulled it off perfectly. She'd had a life as an artist, and had then been able to comfortably, happily set that life aside. Ronnie had never strayed during her happy marriage, because Sarah's father had never given her a reason to look elsewhere for love and affection. She'd given her children idyllic summers in this unspoiled, perfect place. Even in her anger, Sarah wished that, in spite of the complications, she'd let the boys spend more time here during the summers; that she'd allowed them to take a few months off from their music lessons and language classes and spend lazy, unstructured hours reading or swimming or exploring or daydreaming, as she and Sam had done.

But the truth—one that she'd barely acknowledged, even in the privacy of her own brain—was that she hadn't loved it here. Not after what had happened with Owen. For years, every place she saw, every food she tasted, the sight of the Wellfleet Drive-In's marquee or a whiff of fried onion rings as she drove past Arnold's brought back a memory of something they'd done together and made her ache. Everything felt tainted; everything had hurt. She'd been glad when she'd fallen in love with Eli; glad of the path that life with him offered. Glad, too, that the path had led her away from Cape Cod, from Ronnie's scrutiny, and maybe even her disappointment, that Sarah hadn't stuck with her music. Eli's parents had a place at the Jersey Shore, a two-and-a-half-hour drive instead of a six-hour one. It gave her an easy excuse not to make the trip to Massachusetts.

"You don't need to apologize. I understand," her mother said, but Sarah felt like she had to keep trying to explain. Maybe to Ronnie, maybe to herself.

"I've got friends who rent places in the Hamptons, or who stay with their parents out there, and that's doable. But getting up here . . ."

"I know it's a haul," said her mother. She smiled a little. "Did I ever tell you I was in the Hamptons once? For a film festival, when *The Summer Sisters* came out."

Sarah, who'd only ever heard a handful of her mother's stories about her writing life, shook her head.

"I don't know what it's like there these days, but when I went there, I'd never seen such awful traffic leaving the city in my life," Ronnie said. "And then, at the screening, I remember feeling like I was twice the size of every other woman there." She laughed a little. "Twice as big and maybe one-sixteenth as fashionable. And I'd never been skinnier or better dressed." She shook her head, her expression regretful. "I wasn't in a hurry to go back. The Outer Cape is much more my speed."

"Is it hard being here?" Sarah asked. "Without Dad?"

Ronnie hesitated. Her shoulders slumped, and Sarah felt guilty for bringing up something that was clearly still painful. "I miss him. Sometimes I still feel like he's just away, you know? Not dead, just at the hardware store buying lightbulbs, or at the library, getting a new book." She sighed and added, "But this was always much more of my place than his."

"Really?" Sarah knew, of course, that her mom had spent every day here in the summertime, while her father had only come for two weeks' vacation, and then on weekends. But she had memories of her dad in Truro: showing her and Sam how to build bonfires, wading with them out to the sandbar to kick a soccer ball around during low tide; clamming in the summer and oystering in the fall, teaching Sam and Sarah how to drive when they were thirteen in the Corn Hill Beach parking lot at twilight after making them swear not to tell Mom.

"Oh, Lord," Ronnie said, laughing a little. "You don't remember? Your dad got sunburned if he even thought about the sun. He wasn't much of a swimmer. He didn't like seafood. He got seasick on any kind of boats, including kayaks and canoes."

Sarah was bewildered. "He went fishing with us!" She could picture her dad, in his Red Sox ball cap and aviator sunglasses, with a stripe of zinc on his nose. They'd catch striped bass, and eat fillets for weeks, cooked in the oven, with mustard and bread crumbs, or grilled.

"He'd take Dramamine."

"And he was always on the beach."

"In a hat," Ronnie said. "And a long-sleeved shirt, and a face full of SPF fifty." Ronnie was staring at her daughter, eyebrows drawn. "You really don't remember?"

Sarah shook her head, imagining she could feel the ground wobble under her feet. "If he hated it here, he did a good job of hiding it."

"He didn't hate it." Ronnie's voice was patient. "But I was the one who loved the Cape, and he was willing to indulge me." She curled her fingers around the railing, her gold wedding band catching the light of the moon. "Maybe because it was my money that paid for the place."

Sarah felt like she'd been walking briskly down a flight of stairs where one of the steps was missing; like she'd set all her weight down on empty air instead of a solid surface. Her mother had never spoken to her about her marriage, and they'd never talked at all about money.

"Was that an issue for him?" Sarah asked, choosing her words carefully. "That you bought the house?"

Sarah expected immediate refusal. Ronnie, instead, gave her a sigh. "He was proud of me," she said. "He was proud that I was successful. But . . . no, I don't think it was easy for him, the years I was making more money."

"Is that why you stopped writing?"

"I stopped publishing," Ronnie said. Again, Sarah wondered at the distinction, as her mother said, "And that wasn't the reason, but I think that maybe it did end up making things easier."

"So Dad was jealous of you." Sarah's voice was flat. She could feel anger building, a tension in her chest. Lee Weinberg was dead. Couldn't Sarah be allowed to remember him as a good man, the good father she'd loved?

"Aren't you ever jealous of Eli?" asked her mother. Sarah began to shake her head, when a memory struck: a morning in the winter when Dexter was one and a half and Miles was a newborn. Eli had taken two weeks off for paternity leave, but as of that morning, the leave was over. He'd gotten dressed in his suit and tie and was heading off to work, leaving Sarah at home. She'd had a nanny who came five days a week, and a cleaning woman who came twice a week, and Ronnie would be there that weekend. Sarah knew she was one of the lucky ones. She was ashamed of feeling so overwhelmed. And still, she could recall being angry at Eli, who'd be able to spend his day having conversations with other adults, who wouldn't have his bathroom breaks interrupted, who'd be able to sit down for a meal with a napkin on his lap and both hands at his disposal, who could go for as long as he wanted without anyone pawing at him or sucking at him with grasping hands and sticky fingers and surprisingly strong toothless mouths. "Marriages can survive a little resentment," Ronnie said. "Marriages can survive a lot of things."

What's the worst thing your marriage survived? Sarah thought. She'd never asked her mom that kind of question, but, in the darkness, with the wind erasing their words almost as soon as they were spoken, she felt as if she could. "Anything you want to tell me, Mom?" She kept her tone light, but her mother surprised her again.

"Oh," said Ronnie, with her lips curved into that thin, ironic smile. "Well. I guess the statute of limitations has expired." Sarah held her breath, fighting down an urge to slap her hands over her ears as her mother said, "Once, a long time ago, there was another man."

Sarah heard herself gasping, her mother's words lighting her up with shamed recognition. "No."

"Yes," said her mother. "In New York."

"And what happened?" Part of her wanted her mother to have virtuously walked away from the other man. The idea of her beloved father being betrayed made Sarah furious. But part of her wanted it to be more complicated; because that, she acknowledged, would assuage her own guilt.

"I gave him up," her mother said. "Or, really, he ended

things. And I decided I wanted to be with your father. I realized, in the end, it wasn't even about the other man. It was about how he made me feel. Who I was when I was with him. I decided that I didn't want to be that version of myself." She smiled thinly. "I didn't like her very much."

Sarah swallowed hard. "Did Dad know?"

Ronnie shook her head. "I never told him."

"And this other man . . ."

Ronnie raised her hands, palms open, to the sky. "We didn't keep in touch, and I never went looking for him, even after Google."

"But this other man—he was in New York?"

"He was. He was one of the people I met when my first book came out."

"And is that why you stopped . . ." Sarah almost said *writing* and, at the last minute, corrected herself. ". . . publishing?"

"That's one of the reasons," said her mom. She tilted her head. "Part of it was about punishing myself for what I'd done. And avoiding temptation, of course. I knew that I wanted to be married to your dad. I wanted to be a mother." She gave Sarah a wry look. "Even though you don't remember it that way."

Sarah bit her lip, flushed at the memory of how she'd complained about the babysitters and the mother's helpers who'd cared for her and Sam while her mom worked. She pulled off the elastic band securing her hair in a ponytail and wrapped it around her index finger, so tightly that the flesh at her fingertip turned red, then white. "Do you remember Owen?" she asked.

"Owen Lassiter," Ronnie said in a dry voice. "How could I forget?" Her mother, of course, knew Sarah's whole history with Owen. How desperately, foolishly in love she'd been; how they'd planned to stay together in college, and how he'd dumped her. Sarah waited, braced for questions, or sardonic commentary on the Pond People, but, again, her mother surprised her. "Poor Owen."

"Poor Owen?" Sarah's voice rang out, loud and indignant. "He dumped me, remember?"

Ronnie drummed her fingers on the railing. "You probably don't remember this, but for a while, twice a year the local paper would print a list of who was in arrears for their property taxes. And how much they owed."

"So you knew." Sarah tried to keep her voice expressionless, but she still sounded like she'd been punched, her voice breathless and faint. "You knew his family was broke."

Ronnie nodded, looking a little surprised. "I did. But how did you know?"

Sarah felt her face get hot. She curled her bare toes into the deck. "I ran into Owen recently, in the city," she said. "We had coffee. He told me he hadn't been honest with me about—well, a lot of things."

"About how he wasn't at Duke?"

Sarah stared at her mother, once again shocked into silence. Ronnie gave a small, shamefaced shrug. "One of my former colleagues was in their English department. I asked her to keep an eye out for him. She was the one who told me he wasn't enrolled."

"And when were you going to tell me?" Sarah asked.

"I wasn't," said Ronnie. "It was his story to tell. I didn't see the point."

"You didn't think I deserved to know he was lying to me?"

"I figured he had his reasons. I didn't want you thinking I was spying on your boyfriend." Ronnie's voice was maddeningly serene. Sarah scraped her hair back into its ponytail, twisting the elastic punishingly tight. She found herself wishing, pointlessly, that her mother had told her more: told her which path to follow when she couldn't decide whether or not to pursue her music. Told her the truth about Owen. Told her that her own marriage hadn't always been perfect, hadn't always been easy. But that would have made Veronica Levy a different kind of person; certainly a different kind of mother. A mother who hovered and directed and micromanaged; a mother who cleared every obstacle out of the way before her child could come close to stumbling, who'd never let her kid struggle to figure it out for herself. A mother very much like Sarah herself.

Through her guilt and confusion, it was hard to form a question; hard to speak. "Why'd you feel sorry for Owen?" Sarah made herself ask.

Her mother's expression was hard to read in the dark. "I remember the way he looked, every time he was over, like he'd never seen people eating at a table or speaking kindly to each other. I know he hurt you, in the end, but he always made me feel sad. Sad, and lucky." Her voice cracked, and Sarah looked and saw a tear sliding down her mother's seamed face.

"Mom? What's wrong?"

Ronnie wiped her face, shaking her head. "Oh, it's just that weddings make me cry. And I love having all of you here. I just wish—" Her voice cracked again, and she pressed her hands to her eyes.

"What?" Sarah asked. "You wish what?"

"Nothing." Ronnie shook her head and straightened her spine. "I just want you to know that, as long as I'm here, you and the boys are welcome, for as long as you want to be here." And Sarah, still stunned by her mother's revelation, and relieved that Owen was no longer the topic of discussion, that she hadn't blurted out a confession she wouldn't be able to unspeak, found herself promising that she'd look at their schedule, and see if she and the boys could stay for another few weeks, once the wedding was through.

RUBY

~~~~~~

After eating enough lobster Cobb salad to prevent comment, after helping Sarah clean the kitchen and her brothers find their pajamas, Ruby went to the guesthouse and pulled the door shut behind her. Her wedding gown, still sheathed in its clear plastic garment bag, was hanging on the back of the bathroom door. Her white satin shoes with their sparkly blue crystal buckles were underneath it. In the twilight, in the breeze, the shoes and the dress looked like a ghost bride, an invisible woman, facing her. Taunting her.

Ruby's phone hummed. She pulled it out to see Gabe's text. *Got my mom and Aunt Amanda. Hitting the road. See you soon!*

She pocketed the phone without responding and turned away from the wedding dress. A vase of pink peonies stood on the kitchenette counter, and two extension cords were coiled neatly beside it. A makeup mirror, lined with lights, was set up on a vanity in the bedroom, and in the bathroom Sarah had found two plush terrycloth bathrobes, one monogrammed BRIDE, the other monogrammed GROOM. *I'm so happy for you both*, read the card in the BRIDE robe's pocket. *Love you always. Safta.*

Ruby knew if she looked in the miniature refrigerator she'd find flavored seltzer, Greek yogurt, and Rainier cherries, because her grandmother knew all her favorites. She knew, too, that the bed had been made with her favorite brushed-flannel sheets, and that Safta had purchased the hazelnut-flavored coffee that she liked. Tomorrow morning the florist was coming to do a walk-through. Tomorrow afternoon the musicians would stop by to drop off their amps. The caterers had already left boxes of plates and crystal wineglasses in the garage; the cleaning crew had already ensured that the house was spotless. Every possible hitch that Ruby had imagined—*are you crazy, you can't get a wedding dress in just four months!* Or *Sorry, all of our musicians are booked!* or *I've called every single caterer and no one's free on such short notice*—had either failed to materialize or just been artfully, charmingly, negotiated by her stepmother and her *safta*, so that Ruby could have what she wanted. Or what Ruby had thought she'd wanted.

I can't do this, Ruby Faye Danhauser thought to herself. She said it out loud, to the empty guesthouse: "I can't do this," and, with the words still ringing in the air, she sat down hard on the edge of the bed. The windows were open. Ruby could smell, and hear, the ocean, along with bonfire smoke, and the sound of music, conversation, laughter when the wind gusted. Someone was having a party, down on the beach; she pictured people her age, laughing and happy. Maybe they were passing around a bottle, or a joint. Maybe they were flirting; maybe there were old couples breaking apart, new relationships sparking to life. All her happy peers who hadn't gotten themselves stuck; young men and women who hadn't played Houdini, wrapping themselves in chains and locking themselves into a box with no hope of escape. She could hear the murmur of female voices from the deck. Her stepmother and her *safta*, probably talking about last-minute details, making sure everything was perfect. Her wedding dress rippled in the breeze.

Ruby for sure, her dad used to call her. Her first-grade teacher had written *Ruby is an extremely focused and hard-working student. Her drive and determination will surely help her succeed* on her report card . . . and what kind of kid gets described as driven and determined when she's six years old? Ruby buried her face in her hands and groaned. All of her teachers had said versions of the same thing. No matter what she'd tried, whether she had any talent or not—school and soccer, drums and Hebrew lessons—it was always the same thing. *Ruby is focused. Ruby is driven. Determined. Single-minded.* A little scary—that last, from her drumming teacher, an amiable stoner named Scoot. Ruby had overheard him say that to her dad once, that he'd never seen a kid practice as hard as Ruby; that he'd never seen anyone so set on mastering a skill. *She just keeps bashing away at it*, Scoot had said, shaking his head in what could have been admiration or could have been fear. *That's my Ruby*, her dad had said fondly. *She knows what she wants and she works for it.*

When she'd seen her first Broadway show, she'd sat, leaning forward, entranced, as the story unfolded. It had been *Phantom of the Opera*—super cheesy, super unfashionable, super easy for her eventual Tisch classmates to trash. But when the very first organ chords came thundering through the theater, Ruby had felt electrified. Her skin had prickled with goose bumps. She'd almost been afraid to draw a breath. In the second act, the Phantom was singing, in front of a stand holding sheet music, with a candelabra flaming beside him, and one of the pages had caught on fire. Ruby wasn't sure if it was part of the show or not, and as she watched, as the Phantom kept singing, a man dressed all in black, wearing a headset, hurried onto the stage. He'd deftly snatched the burning page, given it a brief pump of something chemical from a bottle in his pocket, and ran into the wings. It had all happened so smoothly, and so fast, that Ruby wasn't completely sure that she'd seen it. After, she'd asked her father about it, and her father, it emerged, hadn't even noticed.

"Oh, one of the stagehands, probably," he'd said after Ruby recounted, what had happened, how disaster had been so narrowly and gracefully averted, and had asked about the man who'd come running. "It takes a whole lot of people to make a show like that happen, and we never even see most of them."

Ruby had been enthralled at the idea of *backstage*; the notion that there were people the audience would never see, people who didn't sing or dance or act who still were a part of the performance, invisible but indispensable as they helped the story unfold. As soon as she'd figured out that those were jobs and that when she grew up, she could have one, that was what she'd wanted to do with her life, and she'd never wavered. She'd never wavered about anything big, until this. Until now.

With her face buried in her hands, her eyes squeezed shut, Ruby felt like she was pretending to be a little kid again; a kid who thought that if she couldn't see anyone, no one could see her. She whispered, again, "I can't do this," and started to cry, a great, scalding flood of tears that made her throat ache.

Still crying, Ruby stood up, on legs that felt as heavy and immobile as the pillars of Stonehenge, and found a pen and a pad in the kitchen. "Gabe. I'm sorry. I can't do this. I thought I was ready but I'm not. It isn't you, I promise." she wrote, knowing that she couldn't begin to encompass all the ways that Gabe was wonderful, how he was sweet and considerate, how he'd filled their apartment with plants and made them grow and bloom; how he'd made her feel cherished and cared for. Somehow, still, that wasn't enough. Or it was enough, only it wasn't what she wanted right now. For one of the few times in her life, Ruby was unsure, and that sensation of not knowing her own mind was terrifying. "I'm so sorry. I never meant to hurt you." More inadequate words, lying there limply on the page, but what else was there?

She signed her name. And then, because she was a gutless coward, she folded the piece of paper, wrote Gabe's name on top, left it on his pillow, and walked out the door.

She planned to take a bicycle out of the garage, to ride it, by the light of the moon, out to Route 6, and make her mind up there. There were buses that ran from Truro to Hyannis, there were planes that went from Hyannis to New York City, and from New York she would return home, to Brooklyn, or go anywhere in the world. She hurried down the steps and over to the side door that led to the garage, but when she pulled the handle, the door refused to budge. Frowning, Ruby worked the doorknob back and forth. She could feel it turn, but when she pulled again, the door was unyielding.

"Shit," she muttered.

Ha! thought the house.

Ruby walked through the courtyard to try to open the big garage doors and found that all of them were locked. Or maybe they'd only respond to electronic clickers and not hands. *Fine,* thought Ruby. If she couldn't ride, then she'd walk.

She took off, head down, moving quickly, down the steps, up the driveway, and out to the road that led to the beach, and Route 6. Provincetown was one way; Boston was the other. Her heart was beating too hard, her eyes stinging. She didn't see the car as it slowed and pulled up beside her; didn't notice the window roll down or feel the driver's gaze upon her. Then she heard a woman's voice call her name.

Ruby turned. And there, as if she had conjured her out of the ether with the force of her own longing, was her mother, the mother she hadn't seen since before COVID. Ruby wiped her eyes, then squinted to confirm that it was, indeed, Annette, sitting behind the wheel of a rental car, wearing a white peasant top with flowers embroidered on its bodice and an incongruous straw sun hat on her head.

"Ruby?" asked Annette. "Is everything okay?"

Ruby armed tears off her face. "Oh, Mom," she said, and couldn't go on.

Annette pulled onto the shoulder and put the car in Park. She got out and wrapped her arms around her daughter, pulling her close. They stood together, for a long moment, mother and daughter on the side of the road. When another car's headlights swept the pavement, Annette led Ruby around the back of her car and opened the passenger's-side door.

"Hop in."

Ruby looked at her mother, wide-eyed, tears trembling on the tips of her eyelashes. "Where are we going?"

"Wherever you need to be right now." Annette put the car in gear and pulled smoothly out onto the road. "We can go get fried seafood, or we can Thelma and Louise it."

Ruby wiped her eyes. "I don't want to drive over a cliff."

"So we'll drive to an airport," said her mother. "Or we'll just drive. Whatever you need. Just let me take care of you. Let me help."

ANNETTE

~~~~~

Annette Morgan—once, briefly, Annette Dan-hauser—knew what the world thought of her. She had flouted a primal directive; broken a central rule. She had walked away from her child. Not to mention a man who loved her; a man who'd loved them both.

Annette had always understood the consequences of her choices. She'd known, when she left, that she would spend the rest of her life paying the price, and the price would be punishingly high. *Do you have any children?* New friends and lovers, well-meaning coworkers, strangers who'd struck up a conversation with her; all of them would ask, in a dozen different languages. *Do you have kids?* Annette had tried, at first, to simply say *No*. She'd birthed a child, of course, but she'd never had one, and while that distinction might have been lost on most of the world, it was meaningful to Annette. Ruby had never truly felt like she belonged to Annette. Ruby belonged to her father, Eli; and to Eli's parents. Eventually, Ruby had belonged to Eli's new wife, and to Sarah and Eli's sons; to Sarah's parents, who served as honorary step-grandparents. Ruby belonged to the family that Eli and Sarah had built together. Ruby had a place in the world, and it was a good place. Things had worked out for the best.

But you couldn't always say all of that, Annette had found. Not to well-meaning strangers or curious colleagues or the person on the mat beside yours in a yoga class. At least, a woman couldn't. The world made space for men who left; who walked away from wives and children, sometimes more than once. Maybe the world had to make room for those men because there were so many of them; men who put themselves, or their careers or their dreams or their desire to sleep with other people, ahead of their spouses and children. The world forgave them. It gave them second and third chances. Women were not offered any such grace. A divorced man who'd moved out of the family home, to a different town or a different state or even a different country, could still be regarded, in some circles, as a catch. A woman who did it was a monster. Annette thought sometimes that even women who hurt their children got more sympathy than ones who decided to leave them. People would murmur sympathetically about postpartum psychosis; friends and neighbors would give interviews about how much that poor mother had loved her kids. *She must have snapped*, a neighbor would say. *She just cracked*, a friend would announce. A weeping husband would say, *This wasn't her; she would never, ever do a thing like this in her right mind.*

Annette wondered about that; about all those mothers, snapping and cracking, bending and breaking. Sometimes, she'd think that there had to be more women like her; that she couldn't be the only one. She looked for them, the women who, like her, had held their babies in their arms and looked down at those dear, tiny faces, the womb-crumpled ears and off-kilter noses, and felt . . . nothing. No, worse than nothing: bone-deep terror, a certainty that they would make nothing but mistakes and cause nothing but pain, and an overwhelming desire to run. Other women who would sit at home with that new baby in their arms and watch the clock counting the hours until a boyfriend or husband or babysitter came to rescue them, because they could feel their very souls shriveling and dying as the minutes dragged by. Women who gagged at the smell of a dirty diaper; women who longed for sleep the way they'd desire the most sumptuous meal, the very best sex. Women who always felt like imposters; women who never automatically looked up when a childish voice called, "Mom." Surely, Annette would tell herself, there were more women like her out there. No matter how alone and isolated she felt, she couldn't possibly be the only one.

Annette had always known that she could never be a mother. She had never lied. She told Eli, all along, that she never wanted to get married or become a mother or settle down in a suburb, and Eli, the duplicitous, self-centered creep, had sworn to her that he felt the same way. Eli had grown up in a suburb of Long Island, with a dad who commuted to the city and a mom who stayed home and tended her children. Annette had grown up in a suburb of New Jersey, with a dad who commuted to the city and a mom with a part-time job at a boutique. Neither Annette nor Eli wanted that life for themselves. Together, they'd watched their classmates, marching in lockstep from the altar to the delivery suite and then to the better suburbs of the tristate area, in that order. *Not for us*, Annette would say. *Not for us*, Eli would agree. Eventually, it emerged that when Eli said *Not for us*, he'd really meant *Not right now*; that when he'd said *Never*, he'd meant *I won't want any of that until I turn thirty, at which point I will want all of it; everything that you and I say we despise.*

Annette hadn't planned on telling Eli when she'd gotten pregnant. She was going to take care of it herself. They'd been in the States, which was lucky, subletting a studio in Brooklyn. Annette had been waitressing, per usual, at an Italian restaurant in Williamsburg, and Eli had found work with a master carpenter. He would come home fragrant from wood shavings, telling her about the Brazilian mahogany floor he'd installed at a gut renovation on Court Street, or the tiger maple escritoire he and Pete were refinishing. Eli's parents would take them out to dinner, which meant free food and nonstop interrogation. Stan and Judy would start out with subtle hints during the appetizer ("Haven't you gotten all this wanderlust out of your blood?") and move on to direct questions with the main course ("You're not going to do construction for the rest of your life, are you?" "If you apply to dental school now, you could start in September!"). By the time dessert and coffee arrived Eli's mom would practically be in tears ("This is not what I wanted for my sons. First Ari, now you!"), and his dad would be tight-lipped and glaring. After those meals, Eli would be quiet and moody, and in the days that followed, Annette would catch him staring at some kid's braces, or hear him sighing longingly at the sight of an overbite.

Annette knew that a pregnancy would tip the precariously balanced scales. If Eli found out, she'd lose the life she wanted and end up stuck with the life that everyone wanted her to have. He'd notice if she took the necessary funds out of their joint checking account, but she had her tips, and she had friends, and they could loan her the money. Eli would never have to know.

Except it turned out that Eli was paying attention to her cycles. He'd known that she'd missed her period; he'd dug the pregnancy test out of the kitchen trash can. On a Friday night, Annette came home from work to find him waving the urine-soaked wand at her, his attitude somewhere between exultant and furious.

"When were you going to tell me?" he asked.

"I wasn't," she answered.

"You can't have an abortion," he said.

"I can," she said. "It's already scheduled."

Eli had looked shocked. Then he'd begged her not to do it. He'd yelled that it was his baby, too. Then he'd cried. Over the weekend, he'd painted her a picture of a life they could have, the two of them plus a baby, which, in his descriptions, sounded no different from an adorable doll, easily transported, no impediment to their travel, no trouble at all. They could buy a sailboat and travel around the world, dropping anchor anyplace Annette had ever dreamed of. They could raise chickens on a farm upstate or build birdhouses in Montecito or lead bike trips around azure-blue Lake Atitlán in Guatemala, only please, please, don't kill our baby.

"It's not a baby," she'd said, irritated and nauseated and exhausted after an eight-hour shift on her feet.

"Don't tell me she's just a clump of cells, because she isn't. She has her own DNA. Her own fingerprints." Eli had started referring to the embryo as "she," just to be extra aggravating.

"It's a parasite," Annette said. "It's alive, yes. It's its own thing, fine. But it can't live without me."

"She has her own heart."

"Which is pumping my blood, and which can't beat without me."

They'd gone round and round, Eli insisting that what was inside her was a child, *their* child; Annette just as certain that what was inside of her was more like a possibility; a set of circumstances that might, or might not, come to pass. And who was he to even voice an opinion? None of this was happening inside his body. "If you really believe that what's inside of me is an actual person, you should sit shiva every time I get my period, because maybe there's a fertilized egg in there that didn't implant, or didn't survive, and, according to you, that's a person, too," she said.

For hours they'd fought, with Annette saying it was her body and her choice and Eli saying that the baby was half his. Annette had shouted; Eli had pleaded. Finally, Annette had locked herself in the bedroom while Eli stood in the hallway, still making his case. "I swear I'm not trying to trap you or tie you down. We'll get married, and I'll go back to school, just so we'll have health insurance, and my parents will help us out. You have the baby. And if you aren't happy—" She could picture him, drawing himself upright; could picture the look of stoic, long-suffering nobility on his face. It made Annette want to puke. Or maybe that was the quote-unquote baby. "If you aren't happy, you can go."

"Do you promise?" she'd asked, and he'd said that yes, of course, he did. "You have my word."

Seven and a half months later, she'd given birth to a tiny, squalling, red-faced baby girl. They'd cut Annette open, after a day and a half of labor. She'd been half-dead from exhaustion, still shivering from the shock of the surgery, when they put Ruby in her arms. Annette had cradled her daughter. She'd gazed down at Ruby's tiny face. She'd caressed the downy curve of her skull with one fingertip; she'd held the baby to her breast. And she'd felt nothing.

Five days later, they went home to a new apartment, a spacious two-bedroom place on the Upper West Side that Eli's parents had been more than happy to pay for, as soon as Eli had enrolled at the Columbia dental school. Eli was enthralled with their new baby, instantly besotted. He had been the model of a solicitous husband and proud new dad, installing the car seat in the sedan his parents had bought them, putting together the crib and the changing table and the bookcase full of brightly colored board books. Except Eli wasn't playing a part. He wasn't pretending. He'd happily hold Ruby for hours, rocking her, singing to her, gazing into her eyes. He'd bathe her, tenderly sponging her dimpled limbs, sudsing each minuscule finger and toe, carefully clipping her teensy fingernails, so she wouldn't scratch herself. When Ruby cried in the middle of the night, Eli would spring out of bed, instantly awake, with Annette trailing blearily after him, groggy and disoriented. *What does my princess need?* Eli would croon, scooping Ruby into his arms. *What can we do for you, little miss?*

He wasn't pretending. Neither was Eli's mother, who'd walk into their apartment with her arms extended, like she couldn't wait an extra second for the feel of her granddaughter. They all felt it, whatever it was that new parents and grandparents were meant to feel. And Annette felt nothing, nothing but an arid annoyance, permanent exhaustion, and a growing sense that she'd made a wrong turn, that this was not what her life was supposed to be. She was failing this child—and, just as important, she was failing herself.

She'd hung in for months, trying her hardest, waiting to feel what mothers were supposed to feel. Once she'd realized that those maternal instincts weren't there, she would scan the parks and the playgrounds, looking for kinship, for some other new mother with circles under her eyes collapsed on a bench, pushing a stroller back and forth with her foot and trying to finish reading a single page of a book or make a phone call or just drink her coffee in peace. She found other exhausted mothers, women who were overwhelmed and physically depleted. She found angry, frustrated mothers, upset by the lack of support from their spouses or their families. But, at some point in every conversation, each of those mothers would send a fond gaze toward the baby in the stroller, or curl her hand tenderly against the head of the baby strapped against her chest. *But I wouldn't have it any other way*, the other woman would say, *just look at her*, and her voice would get softer; the furrows in her forehead would smooth themselves out. She would smile, and her expression would resolve itself into a look of pure and tender adoration. Even the most un-showered, unhappy, exhausted of the mothers, holding the most unattractive baby, would look, for a moment, like a pietà, a Madonna gazing down at the baby Jesus, in awe of her own creation. Annette scoured her heart for that feeling. She waited for it to come. Eventually, she realized that love couldn't be forced, and maternal instincts didn't develop over time. Either you had them or you didn't; just like either you loved someone or you didn't.

Annette held out for as long as she could, until she'd finally come to the end of her reserves; when she felt she wouldn't make it one more day. She went to Eli, who'd looked furious and bewildered, as if they'd never had any of the prebirth discussions, as if he could not remember her objections and had never imagined that her departure was an actual possibility. Which, Annette realized, was probably true.

"You're leaving?"

"I tried," Annette said steadily, with her eyes on the bag that she was packing. She felt like Lot's wife, knowing that if she looked back, at Eli or at Ruby, she would change her mind. Not because she'd be overwhelmed with love, but because she'd be overcome by fear. The easy thing, she knew, would be to stay, to keep faking what she didn't feel. If she hung in there, no one would judge her, and no one would condemn her, and Annette knew that leaving would set her up for a lifetime of judgment and condemnation. She'd be marked as a transgressor; a woman who'd slipped the bonds of matrimony and motherhood, a prisoner who'd crawled through the tunnels and the muck to breathe the sweet air of freedom, the maternal version of Andy Dufresne. She'd be a target, all her life, for the rage and scorn of a world that hated women already, a world that didn't see them as entirely human, or truly worthy of respect. She'd be a screen upon which people would project their own issues with their mothers or their wives. And, she supposed, some women would look at her and see a door they could have opened. Those women would hate her more than anyone, because she'd done what they hadn't, because she was free and they were not. They would think it their job, even their holy obligation, to punish her, to make her pay.

"Ruby," Eli said, as if repeating her daughter's name would be the thing that kept her from going. "How can you do this to Ruby?"

Annette turned to face him with spine rigid and her hands clenched, so he wouldn't see that she was shaking. "Eli, you know I tried."

Eli was crying again. God. How many tears could one man hold? It was as if tears had replaced all the other fluids in his body; like he was a man made of tears. "Please," he blubbered. "Please don't go. Ruby needs a mother."

Annette kept her eyes on the wall just beyond Eli's left shoulder. "I have no doubt you'll be able to find her a great one." A nice-looking Jewish periodontist, even a divorced one with a young child, would have no problems attracting ladies. Eli would be fine. Ruby would be fine.

"My lawyer will be in touch." She lifted her old, familiar duffel bag and felt herself relax, incrementally, as she settled its strap on her shoulder. "Goodbye, Eli," she said. She pressed a gentle kiss against his cheek and pushed past him, out into the hallway, then down the stairs, then out onto the street, where she set down her bag and tilted her head back, eyes shut, just breathing. The air was sour, tinged with bus exhaust and grit, a faint whiff of dog urine. Annette could almost feel the dirt accruing in her pores, that greasy air leaving a film on her face. But in that moment, the air felt like the softest spring rain. Its scent was the finest perfume, and its taste was ambrosial, like clear water trickling down the throat of a woman who'd been crawling in the desert. When she lifted her hand, a cab pulled to the curb. The back seat stunk of body odor and cheap cologne. Annette sucked it down deep. She felt very light, as if she could float right out of the car. Warmth glowed in her chest like a small sun.

"Where to, miss?" asked the driver.

"Take me to the airport," said Annette.

"Ah, JFK? Or LaGuardia? We have many airports."

"Whichever one's your favorite," she said. She had settled her bag in her lap, like that was her baby, and as the driver pulled into traffic, Annette had held it against her like a shield; something to deflect whatever arrows came her way.

It took Eli longer than she would have expected to remarry, but when he did, Annette was pleased with his choice. She'd worried that, after her ignominious departure, Eli would find a woman who was, above all, compliant; someone who'd let him make the choices; a woman who wouldn't have a career and wasn't very smart. To her ex-husband's credit, Sarah Levy-Weinberg was educated and accomplished. She had a career she seemed to like, and, at the dinner where they'd met, when Eli started talking about his marathon-training plan and the orthotics he'd gotten for his running shoes—"I swear to you, they've changed my life"—Sarah had given him a fond smile, patted his arm in what was clearly spousal Morse code for *stop talking*, and said, warmly, to Annette, "I'd love to hear more about Barcelona."

Annette had expected judgment, but Sarah didn't seem to be judging. Instead, Sarah was grateful. Not in a desperate, pathetic, your-child-made-my-life-complete way, but in a way that felt real and sincere. If Sarah didn't understand Annette, if she resented or judged her for what she'd done, she kept it to herself.

At the dinner that Eli and Sarah hosted the night before Ruby's bat mitzvah, at Ruby's favorite dim sum restaurant, Annette stayed in the corner of the room and watched, marveling, as Ruby held ten-month-old Dexter in her arms, cradling him expertly, patting his back to coax a burp. Watching her daughter with a baby made Annette's heart do strange things. She put a few dumplings on her plate and found a seat at the very end of the table. She was surprised when Sarah's mother, Veronica, came and sat down beside her.

"I want to thank you," Ronnie said. "Lee and I are so grateful we've gotten to have Ruby in our life."

Annette was relieved to hear it. Especially since, according to Eli, Ruby at thirteen could be more of a pain in the ass than a gift. "She's very determined," Eli said. *Just like her mom*, Annette thought.

"You probably think I'm a monster," Annette said, her voice low. Instead of the reflexive denial she'd been expecting, Ronnie shook her head.

"Being a parent is hard. And it isn't for everyone. If you knew you couldn't be the mother that Ruby deserved, leaving was the best thing you could have done," she said.

"I worry she'll have abandonment issues," Annette said. "Maybe she won't be able to trust people. Or she'll think everyone's going to leave her."

Again, Ronnie seemed to consider before answering. "Every kid deals with something," she said. "Maybe their parents fight all the time. Maybe their fathers are never home. Maybe they've got a mom who drinks. There're a lot of things that can go wrong. Kids figure out how to handle it, and most of them grow up just fine." Ronnie gave her a close-lipped smile. "Although she may have some questions for you at some point. I'm sure you'll have your answers ready."

Annette bit her lip and wondered if there was anything she would be able to say; any way to explain how she'd felt and what she'd done that wouldn't leave Ruby believing that it had all been her fault; that Annette's defection had something to do with Ruby, and not with Annette. Annette sighed. Veronica nodded toward the table where Ruby was sitting, having an animated conversation with one of Eli's cousins, with Dexter snuggled in her lap. "Ruby has a place in the world. A good place."

Annette knew this to be true. Ruby lived in a beautiful home. She attended an excellent school. She had a father and a stepmother who loved her, two solid, stable adults to model solid, stable adult behavior. She had doting grandparents, a half-brother she adored, two tables full of giggling preteen friends from her school and her summer camp. And if she also had a crazy, selfish mother who'd cut and run, it could be worse. Like if she'd had an unhappy mother who'd stayed and made everyone miserable. Maybe Ronnie was telling the truth. Maybe Ruby, having endured this first, most primal wound, would be able to navigate disappointments, broken promises, and breakups and whatever other misery the world served her, with ease, because she'd already survived Annette. She would be, as the pop psychologists like to say, *resilient.*

For all the years of Ruby's life, Annette had been there for her daughter as well as she could. There were phone calls and birthday gifts; there were visits during winter break and for a month each summer, no matter where Annette was or what she was doing, except for the handful of times when she couldn't—the summer she'd been helping a friend in Aruba and a hurricane had stranded them there; the year she'd gotten a last-minute invitation to study Ashtanga yoga in India, and had called Ruby to say she'd wanted her to come, and had asked, but children weren't allowed.

"It's okay," Ruby had said, her voice leaden, and later Eli had called her, hissing, "I hope it's fucking worth it, Annette. Namaste."

Don't hate me, Annette begged her daughter in her head . . . but she hadn't said it out loud. Ruby probably despised her already. It might not be until Ruby was much, much older that she would be able to see her mother as anything but the villain of her story, and her father as the hero; when she'd be able to set aside her black-and-white thinking and appreciate the nuances and shades of gray. It might never happen, Annette admitted. Ruby might hate her until the day she died . . . but at least Ruby hadn't grown up with a mother who was miserable, a mother who'd taught her daughter, by example, that sacrifice and self-abnegation were what made a woman a good wife and mother. A little selfishness could be healthy. It could even save your life. That, she thought, was a message more girls and women could stand to hear, a thing that few were ever taught.

And she was glad, because now, finally, for the first time in Ruby's life, Annette had managed to be exactly where Ruby needed her to be at precisely the right time. Maybe it was a sign, she thought. The universe telling her she'd made the right choice.

"Where to?" Annette asked as she flicked her high beams on to light up the darkness.

"I don't know." Ruby's voice was faint.

"How about we just drive for a while?"

"Okay," Ruby whispered.

Annette squeezed her daughter's hand and pointed the car toward the highway.

SAM

~~~~~

After dinner, the boys had seen the distant glow of three separate bonfires from the living-room windows and had begged to go back to the beach. "Not tonight," Sam said. He looked at his watch, then looked around for his brother-in-law for backup, but Eli had wandered out to the deck, where he stood, staring out at the sea like an emo teenager.

"I promise, before the end of the week we'll have a bonfire, and I might even be convinced to buy you guys sparklers. We can roast hot dogs, and make s'mores, and stay up late. But not tonight."

"Listen to Uncle Sam," said Ronnie, and helped Sam herd the boys downstairs for face-washing and teeth-brushing. Sam got everyone into a bed. He read a chapter of *Captain Underpants* and turned off the light after delivering a final threat: "If I hear any more noise out of this room, no one is getting a malasada in the morning." That did the trick.

Sam lurked in the hallway until he was pretty sure that at least two of the three boys were sleeping. From the doorway, he could see Sarah's and Eli's cars in the driveway. He'd left his car up on the street, poised for an easy exit.

Finally, here was the moment he'd been planning since his arrival.

Sam was still on West Coast time, still wide-awake,

eager for the adventure he'd been imagining for weeks. But, suddenly, the idea of going to Provincetown to trawl for men—or even just to watch other men trawling for men—struck him as tawdry. Ridiculous, even. *Forget it*, he thought. He'd just brush his teeth, read until he felt sleepy, get an early start in the morning, and—

"Sam?"

He looked up to see Ronnie calling him as she leaned over the third-floor banister.

"Can you see if there are any lightbulbs in the closet?" she stage-whispered. "One of the bulbs up here just blew out."

Sam went to the utility closet, rummaged until he found a single lightbulb and a stepstool, and carried them both up the stairs.

"Oh, perfect," said his mom. Sam climbed onto the stepstool, unscrewed the burnt-out bulb, and, with his sister and his mother both offering suggestions ("Careful! It might be hot!" "Should I get the oven mitts?"), successfully replaced it.

"Try it now," he said. His mother flicked the switch. The new bulb lit up. Everyone cheered. An instant later, the bulb beside it burnt out with a loud pop. Everyone groaned.

"Were there any more bulbs?" asked Sarah.

"That was the last one," said Sam, and thought, *Maybe it's a sign.* "How late's the Stop & Shop open?"

"You're going to go out now?" asked his mother, as if he were still sixteen, with a brand-new driver's license.

"It's not a big deal," Sam said. "I'll pick up a bunch of bulbs, so we'll have them for the weekend." Five minutes later, Sam was back in his bedroom, with the credit card his mother had insisted on giving him in his pocket and his heart pounding hard. *I don't have to do anything*, he told himself, as he brushed his teeth and shaved with extra care and patted cologne onto his cheeks. *I'm not going to do anything*, he thought, as he pulled on a pair of khaki shorts and, after extensive consideration, a short-sleeved button-down seersucker shirt, in a dark-blue check, and slipped his feet into his loafers. *I can just look.* He could hear Tim's voice in his ear, telling him that no self-respecting (if extremely tentative and still entirely closeted) gay man would ever miss the chance to hang out in P-town. *You don't have to do anything*, his inner Tim assured him, as he drove along Route 6. *You can just see what it's like.*

Sam went to the Stop & Shop for the lightbulbs, then drove down Bradford Street and found a parking lot two blocks from the center of town, where he paid a shocking thirty dollars to park. "Have a delightful evening," the young person who handed him his ticket cooed with a wink of a glitter-dusted eyelid. Sam felt like he'd wandered into another world, a snow globe that some unseen hand had flipped upside down and shaken hard.

On a Thursday night in the summertime, Commercial Street was as packed as Times Square on New Year's Eve. There were drag queens, seven feet tall in their heels, resplendent in their wigs and their gowns as they called out to passersby and handed them flyers for their shows. There were men in pairs and in threesomes, men walking hand in hand, or with their arms around each other's shoulders, tall men and short men; clean-shaven men and hairy-chested, bearded men wearing T-shirts that said SAVE THE BEARS; men slender as ballet dancers, in teeny-tiny cutoff shorts and hot-pink tank tops, and men who were as burly as linebackers, with leather harnesses across their otherwise bare chests.

At first Sam tried not to stare, then he gave up and let himself look his fill. He walked until his feet were sore, then he bought himself an ice-cream cone, and found a spot on a bench outside of Town Hall, near the buskers and the itinerant poets with their top hats and their old-timey typewriters who'd write you a poem on the spot. He sat, and watched, remembering what he'd heard over the years: about what happened after last call at the bars, when the men who hadn't yet paired up would gravitate toward Spiritus Pizza. ("I've heard people call it the garage sale," Tim had said. "You know, when all the stuff that no one wants gets its price reduced.") Sam already knew about what went on underneath the deck of the Boatslip Resort, colloquially known as the Dick Dock, and along the sandy paths that passed through the dunes, but he was one hundred percent certain that he wasn't interested in public sex. He didn't think he was ready for any sex at all.

But he was still wide-awake, and his curiosity was far from sated. So he abandoned his bench and walked until he found a line on a side street that was snaking out of a club called Inferno and, for lack of a better plan, joined it.

Most of the men he saw were both younger and much more fit than he was. The handful of guys who appeared to be in their forties and fifties looked like bodybuilders, or like they were in the BDSM scene. One wore a leather cap; another was bare-chested and had steel barbells glinting from his nipples.

Sam suppressed a shudder, looking down at his seersucker shirt and his loafers—loafers!—in despair. What had he been thinking? Why hadn't he packed anything slightly less square? Why was he here? Unfortunately, the peak of this existential crisis coincided with his arrival at the front of the line. The bouncer, an extremely large man with a spiderweb tattooed on his face, looked Sam up and down.

"You law enforcement?" he rumbled.

"Am I—what? No!" Sam stammered.

"If you are, you have to tell me," the hulking man said implacably.

"I'm not. I'm just . . ." *Old. Clueless. Wearing loafers. Scared out of my mind.* Sam tried for a smile. "I'm not from around here." The doorman held out one meat-slab-sized hand. Sam stared for a minute before fumbling for his wallet. He gave the man his money and was waved inside, into what looked like one of Dante's circles of hell. The room was dark as a cave, except for the wash of red lights that lent the gyrating bodies an unearthly glow. Some of the men—most of them, Sam thought—wore nothing but underwear. Some wore jockstraps and a sprinkling of glitter. Nobody wore short-sleeved seersucker shirts or loafers. Everywhere he looked, men were grinding or kissing, or more. The leather daddy he'd spotted in line was standing in the corner, leaning back, a cigarette, or possibly a joint, dangling from his lips, one muscular arm folded behind his head, the other tangled in the hair of the boy kneeling in front of him, who was . . . Sam's eyes widened. Oh, yes, that was, indeed, a blow job in progress.

Quickly, Sam turned away, and bumped into a young man with dark hair, almost knocking him off his feet. "Sorry!" he shouted. The young man touched his arm, leaned toward him, and put his mouth close to Sam's ear. "We're in hell!" he shouted.

"I know!" Sam shouted back.

"Want to leave?"

Sam nodded before he had time to think and found himself being tugged through the mass of writhing bodies, toward the door. Outside, Sam closed his eyes, leaning against the building as he gasped in relief. The cool air caressed his cheeks; the silence was a blessed contrast to the noise of the club.

When he opened his eyes the young man was standing there, looking at Sam with concern.

"Are you okay?"

"I think so," said Sam. "Whew. That was a lot."

"First time?" the young man asked, his voice sympathetic.

Sam looked at himself. "What gave it away?" he asked. "Was it the loafers?"

The young man considered. "It was more the look of unadulterated terror," he finally said, and Sam surprised himself by laughing.

"Want to go for a walk?" the young man asked.

He's going to rob me, Sam thought. Except there was nothing in his pockets but the car keys and two folded twenty-dollar bills. He'd left his wallet and his mother's credit card locked in the car. *Or maybe he's after my kidneys. Maybe I'm going to be one of those people who wakes up in a bathtub full of ice with a bunch of stitches in his back. Tell him no*, Sam thought. *Just call it a night and go home.*

Except somehow, while Sam's brain was drafting a polite refusal, his head had made the decision to nod, and his feet were walking down Commercial Street. When the young man took Sam's hand, it felt like the most natural thing in the world. They made their way down a grass-lined path, toward the bay. Sam could smell the salt before he saw the water, glimmering blackly under the moonlight. The young man led him to a sandy spot under a deck. They sat down on the sand that still retained a hint of the day's heat. Sam could hear waves, and the sound of other people: male voices, music. The wind carried the scent of woodsmoke and salt water.

Sam looked down and saw that their hands were still linked, and it still felt good, not strange at all. In fact, *not* holding this young man's hand would have felt much stranger than holding it.

Again, he heard his inner Tim. *When it's right, you'll know.*

Sam cleared his throat. "Thank you for rescuing me."

"You're welcome," the young man said gravely. He raised his eyebrows and, at Sam's nod, scooched over the sand until they were sitting shoulder to shoulder, hip to hip. Sam braced himself for a repeat of what had happened back in LA, in the parking garage, but instead of lunging for his zipper, the young man used his free hand to touch Sam's cheek. He ran one thumb, feather-light, along Sam's left eyebrow. "Hi," he whispered.

"Hi," Sam whispered back. The young man traced Sam's cheekbones, his chin, his lips. Sam let his eyes slip shut. He wondered if he was supposed to do something; kiss the young man, or touch his face, but he felt like he wouldn't have been able to move if he'd tried. He was frozen; enchanted, stunned into immobility, just from the feeling of this man's body close to his, the warmth of his breath, his scent, and the feel of his hands on Sam's skin.

Warm fingers stroked the skin of his neck, then his ear, then delved down to touch his collarbone. A hand, strong and assured, gripped his chin, tilting his face. Sam opened his eyes.

"Can I kiss you?" the young man whispered.

I'll die if you don't, Sam thought. He nodded and shut

his eyes again. The boy's mouth tasted fresh and sweet, like apples, and his lips were warm and soft. Then his tongue slid against Sam's, and Sam's mouth was open, and they were kissing, gently at first, then more eagerly.

The young man's mouth was warm, utterly thrilling, and it was all Sam could do to keep from groaning out loud when he felt the young man's tongue flicker against his own, and the rasp of stubble against his cheeks. He reached out, blindly, catching the young man's shoulders in his hands, turning him and pulling him forward until he was more or less sideways in Sam's lap. *This*, Sam thought. *This is what I need.*

They kissed for what felt like an endless length of time, sometimes almost desperately, lips and tongues and teeth all crashing together; sometimes gently, almost sweetly. Sam kept one arm locked around the man's waist and the other one around his shoulders, holding him with a grip just short of desperate, thinking that there was nothing in the world that would make him let go, and that he'd never felt, or even imagined, anything like this, not ever. There was none of the awkwardness he remembered from previous encounters, no worrying about what went where or if he'd been eating onions that day or if he was moving too fast or too slowly or what he was supposed to do next. Everything he did, everything that happened, all of it felt completely natural, absolutely right. Sam raised his hands to cup the young man's face, the soft skin and strong bones. His brain had gone blank, every worry gone, replaced with a low hum of happiness, like bumblebees droning through the lavender in his mother's garden.

"Lean back," the young man whispered. Hypnotized, feeling almost drugged, Sam complied. He could feel the sand, firm and cool, against his back, and the young man's hands moving against him, smoothing and petting their way over his chest, reaching up under his shirt. Clever fingers reached down to gently tweak his nipple. When Sam gasped, the boy pulled away and sat on his heels, looking at Sam, his eyebrows knitted in concern.

"Was that okay?"

It was more than okay, Sam thought, *it was the most incredible thing I've ever felt in my life.* Already, this was better than any sex he'd ever had, either alone or with Julie or with long-lost Gracie Chen Cohen, better than anything he'd ever imagined.

The boy was still looking at him, a smile on his face. "Just tell me," said the boy. "We don't have to do anything you don't want."

"Okay," Sam croaked. His voice was hoarse and strange in his ears. *Yes*, he thought. *Please. Do anything. Do everything.*

He shut his eyes. A warm hand cupped his shoulder. Sam arched up, leaning into the touch. "Yes," he said, and leaned back, settling his hands lightly on the young man's hips, tugging him forward against him.

It went on and on, until Sam pulled back to look at the young man. His brain was still humming with that feeling of rightness and with wonder. *This easy?* Sam was thinking. *Can it really be this easy?* The young man's pupils were dark, blown wide, his mouth was swollen, his cheeks and chin abraded by Sam's stubble. Sam brushed his thumb over the boy's lower lip. "Are you okay? Did I hurt you?"

Smiling, the young man shook his head.

"We—we don't have to do anything else," Sam stammered. And then, because he couldn't stop himself, he blurted, "God, you're gorgeous."

The boy smiled. "You're very handsome," he said. He reached for the hem of Sam's shirt, and Sam raised his arms. When he returned the favor, pulling the shirt over his head, and the young man pressed himself against Sam's bare chest, there were no more thoughts, just the singing sensation of the boy's skin, Sam's hands sweeping over his back; the boy's glossy hair against Sam's cheek, the boy's scent, sweet and earthy, all around them.

Sam settled the young man on his lap again and let his hands go where they wanted, stroking and petting the silken skin of the young man's shoulders, the elegant span of his back, the bumps of his vertebrae, the jut of his collarbones. He raked his fingers through the silk of the young man's hair, then gave a gentle tug, hearing and feeling the pleased noise the man made against Sam's mouth.

Oh, God. Sam couldn't stop himself from groaning. He tugged the young man's hair, a little more forcefully, feeling the man writhe against Sam's chest, his body hot and slippery as an eel. Sam was thrusting his hips upward, helplessly, unable to stop himself, and the young man was gasping and sighing, shuddering each time Sam touched him. Sam had one hand holding on to the young man's hip, the other tangled in his hair, his mouth locked against the other man's mouth. He could feel pleasure gathering, surging up from the tips of his toes to the base of his spine, pouring down all the way from the crown of his head and his heart.

He opened his eyes in time to see the young man throw his head back, exposing the strong column of his throat. Sam didn't even think. He leaned forward, and licked, then bit. "Yes," the other man groaned, with a noise that sent a surge of pleasure roaring through Sam's body. *Yes,* thought Sam, as the boy gasped and shuddered against him. *Yes. This. You.*

After, they lay together; Sam with his back pressed into the cooling sand, the beautiful young man curled against him, with his head resting on Sam's chest. Sam stroked the other man's dark hair, fine and soft as silk. He wished he could see him in the daylight. He wanted to see his skin flush when Sam kissed his neck, and to see his eyes flutter shut when Sam touched him.

"Did you need that?" the young man asked, and kissed Sam's lips lightly.

Sam's own voice was gruff. "I guess I did."

They were silent for a minute, the young man snuggling in his arms, Sam holding him, lovestruck and dizzy.

"Look at the stars." The young man shifted so the back of his head was on Sam's shoulder and he was looking up at the sky. "Isn't that amazing? I've never seen so many stars in my life."

"The air's clearer up here. If you live in a city, there's always smog. Ambient light. But up here . . ." Sam gestured at the sky. "You get to see everything."

"Do you spend a lot of time in Cape Cod?" asked the young man.

"I did," Sam said. "When I was growing up. My parents have a house here, and we'd stay for the summers. How about you?"

"It's my first time." The young man wriggled against him with a breathy sigh that made Sam's heart clench. Sam ran one fingertip around the other man's ear, tracing the ridge of cartilage down to the softness of the lobe. The moon rode high and bright in the sky; the waves sang against the sand, and the scent of the fires and the ocean had been joined by the smells of sweat and sex.

"Where are you staying?" Sam asked.

The young man gestured vaguely in the direction of the road. "I don't know the names of any of the places yet."

For the first time in their encounter, Sam felt awkward. *Are you staying in a house? A hotel? A campground? Where do you live? What do you do? Are you here with someone? Do you have a boyfriend? A husband?* And, of course, the most basic question of all.

"What's your name?" he asked, then laughed at the ridiculousness of it. Here he was, a half-naked stranger in his arms, semen drying in his underwear, and he didn't even know this young man's name.

He felt the young man's weight shift as he turned his face away and heard him clear his throat. "Anthony," he said after a minute. "Call me Anthony."

"Anthony," Sam repeated. "I'm Sam." He cleared his throat. That sense of contentment and of wonder, of rightness, was still humming through him, singing sweetly in his bones. "I've never done this before," he said.

"Done what?" Anthony asked. "Made out with a stranger on the beach?"

Sam shook his head. "I've kissed two men. And, um, kind of fooled around with one." "Fooled around with," he decided, sounded better than "was attacked by." "But nothing like this. Not ever."

"Seriously?" Anthony's eyes widened. He didn't sound scornful or dismissive, thank God. Just surprised.

"I always thought I was straight. I had girlfriends in high school and college, and then I was married, briefly. And then my wife died." The young man made a murmur of sympathy, and Sam continued. "I was by myself, and I just—well, I guess I started to figure it out. Belatedly."

Anthony's expression hovered somewhere between amusement and disbelief, but his voice was gentle. "How?" he asked.

"How what?"

"How did you figure it out? Did you walk down the street and trip and fall on someone's dick?"

Sam was startled into laughter. "Do you really want to know?"

"I really do," Anthony said, and he sounded sincere. So Sam told him the story about fan fiction, and Drarry, and the hobbits, and how that had led him to gay pornography, which had led him to Grindr, which had led him to Tim, and the club, and the terrible parking garage hookup, and then to P-town and, finally, here, to this beach, with Anthony in his arms.

Anthony listened attentively. "Better late than never, I guess." Any sting the words might have carried was negated when Anthony snuggled closer to Sam, kissing his cheek, then nipping at his neck. "I'm glad I was your first," he whispered.

"I'm glad you were, too," Sam whispered back. He wanted to tell Anthony that what had happened had been a revelation, the best thing that had ever happened to him, a million times better than anything he could have ever imagined. What came out of his mouth was, "Can I see you again?"

As soon as he'd spoken, he realized he didn't know anything about Anthony, including whether or not he was a professional, a sex worker who trawled the clubs of Provincetown, looking for bewildered, terrified men to seduce.

Anthony rolled away from Sam and sat up straight, pulling his knees up against his bare chest. Sam waited, terrified, anticipating rejection until Anthony said, "I would like to see you. I'd like that a lot. Only it's a little bit complicated," he said.

"Are you with someone?" Sam asked, feeling jealousy pulse through him. He told himself he was being ridiculous. It was insane to feel his heart breaking at the thought of Anthony being taken. Sam had absolutely no claim on this man. He shouldn't feel devastated that someone else had a right to kiss that beautiful mouth and draw moans and shudders from between those lips.

Anthony shook his head. "No. I am completely single."

Sam felt a little faint with relief.

"But—"

An icy hand seized Sam's heart. "But what?"

The boy looked at him, then ducked his head. Sam lowered his voice.

"Whatever it is, it's okay," he said. "You can tell me." Sam brushed the hair away from Anthony's brow. He pulled him close, and Anthony came easily, his body warm and pliant. *I love you*, Sam thought, which was insane. He didn't know this young man; didn't know a single thing about him, not where he lived or what he did there; not how old he was or where he'd grown up. He didn't know anything, except how Anthony felt in his arms, how he tasted when Sam kissed him, how he sounded when he came.

Anthony settled himself against Sam's chest. "I just broke up with someone. Or, I guess, she broke up with me."

Sam's heart lifted, exultant. Anthony was single! Then he frowned. "Wait. Did you say 'she'?"

"I'm bi," said Anthony, the same way he might have

said that he was a vegetarian, or left-handed. *Kids today*, Sam marveled.

"Oh," Sam said, because he felt like he had to say something, and couldn't think of what that might be.

Anthony reached for Sam's hand and squeezed it. "I'm glad I was your first. I feel honored."

Sam pulled him close. *Come home with me*, he was thinking. *Spend the night in my bed. Show me everything. Stay with me forever.* Instead of saying any of that, he said, "How long are you here for?"

"A week. How about you?"

"Five days." Sam gathered his courage. "Can I—that is, would you want to . . . ?" *Can you feel this?* he thought. *Am I imagining it, or do you feel it, too?* There was just enough silence for Sam to feel the first thorny prickling of regret, the initial burn of shame. Then Anthony took his hand.

"Yes," he said. "Yes, I want to. I do." He snuggled close to Sam, looking up at him from under his long lashes. "I wish you could put me in your pocket and take me home."

Sam felt his heart expanding, like one of those thin discs of sponge when you put it in the water. He knew that repeat engagements weren't necessarily a thing when two men hooked up; knew, too, that being needy was rarely a turn-on, for either men or women, but he couldn't help himself. The last hours had been the most tender, romantic, sweetest time of his life, and he knew that if he didn't ask he would spend the rest of his life regretting it.

"Maybe tomorrow?" Sam said, trying to keep his voice light, trying to sound like he didn't feel his entire life balanced on a precipice, waiting to tilt toward sorrow or joy. "Can I see you tomorrow?"

He felt the boy still against him, could feel him gather himself. Then, all in a rush, Anthony blurted, "The thing is, the girl I just broke up with. I'm staying with her, and her family."

"Ah," Sam said, and tried to hide his disappointment. He mulled it over. "I see where that could be complicated. Does your ex know that, ah . . ."

"That I'm bi? Yeah. That I'm here?" Sam sensed, more than heard, the boy's sigh. "No."

"She wouldn't be happy," Sam guessed.

"There are probably some conversations I need to have," Anthony said carefully. "But . . ." He reached up to cup Sam's cheek. When he smiled, his eyes were dazzling dark stars. "You don't have a curfew or anything like that, right?"

Sam shook his head. His heart and belly both felt like they were fizzing with fireworks; his veins felt shot full of unadulterated joy. *How did I get so lucky?* he wondered.

Anthony rolled onto his back, pulling Sam down against him until they were chest to chest, belly to belly.

"Kiss me," Anthony whispered. Sam wrapped both of his arms around him, drawing him close, never wanting to let go.

ANNETTE

~~~~~~

Annette and Ruby drove for hours, up and down the length of Cape Cod; down to the Bourne Bridge and back again, sometimes talking, mostly silent. Finally, Annette brought Ruby back to her room at a hotel at the very end of Provincetown. Ruby sat on the edge of the bed, and Annette untied her daughter's shoes, the way she never had when Ruby was little. She put Ruby to bed, and tucked her in gently, and said, "Get some sleep. Things will look better in the morning." Ruby had looked up at her, with trembling lips and tear-glazed eyes, and said, "Will they? I don't think they will."

"I promise." Annette considered. "And even if they don't, there's always hot coffee and doughnuts."

Ruby managed a smile. "I'm here," said Annette, and touched her daughter's cheek. Ruby closed her eyes and, just as Annette guessed, was sound asleep almost as soon as her head touched the pillow.

Annette moved around the room as quietly as she could. She set Ruby's shoes by the door. She unpacked her toiletries and hung up the dress she'd bought, telling the saleswoman she was going to a wedding without saying she was the mother of the bride. She was shopping for a mother-of-the-bride dress, but she probably wouldn't have wanted a traditional mother-of-the-bride dress anyway, something floor-length, covered in sequins, with a bolero-style jacket, in some muted noncolor with a name like "greige" or "eggshell" or "horn." She was very happy with the dress she'd gotten, which was indigo-colored cotton, simply cut, with colorful embroidery at the neckline.

When there was nothing left to unpack or arrange, Annette sat in an armchair in the corner of the room with her legs curled underneath her and regarded her daughter. *Another runaway bride*, she thought, and wondered if it was genetic; if all of the women in her family got itchy feet at the notion of being wives and mothers. Her own mother had done, at best, an indifferent job. Vivian Morgan had always been more interested in her tennis games and her clothes and the parties she threw and attended than in her three children. When, in the midst of an argument, Annette had flung the eternal teenage-girl accusation at Vivian—*I don't know why you even had kids!*—her mother had rolled her eyes, taken a drag from her cigarette, and said, *Do you think I had a lot of options?*

Annette had had options—at least, more than her own mother. She could have defied Eli's wishes and gone through with the abortion. But then, no Ruby. And she couldn't bring herself to wish Ruby away. Not even with the misery that had followed Ruby's birth; not even with how that shame had dogged her, recurring every time she'd had to explain herself to a new lover who'd noticed her Cesarean scar, or to a friend who'd become close enough to deserve the truth. Ruby was an adult now, an actual person. A person whose company Annette enjoyed. And if Annette's unhappiness had been the price of that, the price of Ruby being and becoming who she was, happy and loved, with a family around her, Annette was not sorry she'd paid it.

Maybe this was progress. Her mother, she knew, hadn't wanted children, but had had them anyhow. Annette hadn't wanted children, and had had one, but she'd known enough to walk away so that Ruby could be raised by her father and her stepmother, a woman who, by every indication, had wanted kids. Maybe Ruby would be the bravest of them. Maybe she represented the final stage in the Morgan women's evolution; the one who would reject marriage and motherhood completely. Or maybe she just didn't want marriage now, or to this particular guy, and she'd do it when she was ready, and she'd be happy.

Whatever she decided, whatever she wanted, Ruby would have, God willing, many, many years ahead of her to get it. Years to make up her mind and change it; years to make mistakes, and fix them; years to try, and fail, and try again, and fail again.

Annette went to the bathroom, filled a cup from the tap, and set the glass of water on the bedside table, so it would be there if Ruby woke up. She smoothed Ruby's curls away from her forehead. On the top shelf of the closet, she found an extra blanket. She pulled the armchair up to the side of the bed and tucked the blanket around herself, and sat in the darkness, listening to her daughter breathe.

FRIDAY MORNING

ELI

~~~~~~~~~~

Eli Danhauser had lain awake through an endless, miserable night, on his back on the bed underneath the guest-room window, his entire body on alert as he listened for the sound of a car crunching up the driveway.

"I'm sorry about this," his wife had said, indicating the queen-sized bed that took up most of the space in the small room. They'd be sharing a bed for the first time in weeks, and Sarah was clearly not happy about it.

"It's fine," Eli said. He was remembering the first time Sarah had brought him to the Cape, to meet her parents, when they'd been glad of a tiny bed. They hadn't been able to keep their hands off each other; had barely managed to get dressed and make appearances at meals.

That night, Eli sat on the edge of the mattress with his back to his wife as Sarah undressed. He let her use the bathroom first, finding solace in the familiar, homey sounds of running water, a toothbrush clattering in a glass, his wife humming. He recognized the song: "Happy Days Are Here Again." It made him want to cry.

"Well, good night," Sarah said after she turned off the lights. *I love you*, Eli thought, but could not say. *I love you, and I'm so sorry that I'm going to disappoint you.* He'd listened as Sarah's breathing deepened, lying awake, the guilt chewing at his chest, gnawing at his belly. Waiting. It was torture . . . especially because the narrow bed seemed to have developed a declivity in its middle. No matter how hard he tried to stay in place, Eli found himself, again and again, sliding down the incline, rolling toward his wife's sleeping back as if pushed by an invisible hand, as if some force, or maybe the house itself, was trying to get them together again.

It was just after midnight when he finally heard the car arrive. Eli crept into the shower in the bathroom, which had a circular window, like a ship's porthole, cut into the tiled wall. He stood on his tiptoes to peer through the window, but all he could see was the treetops. Gingerly, he climbed on top of the toilet, balancing his feet on its rim so that he could see through the window and get a look at the driveway below.

Eli saw Gabe get out of the driver's seat and go to the trunk to pull out suitcases. A dark-haired woman got out of the passenger's seat. A second woman emerged from the rear of the car. The mother and the aunt, Eli figured. He couldn't see their faces. He watched as the trio collected their bags and carried them up to the guesthouse. Then he forced himself to go back to bed, where he lay, wide-awake, for the duration of the night. He could hear people coming and going; the sound of a car leaving in the night at about one in the morning, and the door opening and closing at just after six. *Probably Ari out tomcatting*, he thought. He didn't care. He was focused on his mission, Project Confront Gabriel's Mother.

At six thirty in the morning, Eli worked his way out of the bed and got dressed as quietly as he could. He went to the kitchen, where he brewed a pot of coffee, sliced pineapple and strawberries, piled muffins on a platter, and poured juice into a pitcher. By seven, he had the table set, the dishwasher unloaded, the floors swept, and the countertops clean.

"Eli?" Ronnie was standing at the top of the staircase, gripping the railing, looking startled. His mother-in-law wore a bathrobe, and her hair was uncombed.

Eli set the fruit on the table. "Good morning. Want some coffee?"

"Please."

He poured Ronnie a cup and brought it to her. "I can't thank you enough for doing this for Ruby."

"Oh, I'm the one who should be thanking you." Ronnie carried her mug to the table, where she sat in her usual spot. "I've loved spending time with Ruby, you know." She smiled fondly. "My bonus grandkid. Remember when she collected that shoebox full of toads? And I found it in her closet?"

Eli nodded, because he didn't trust himself to speak. What a gift it had been, he thought, that he and his daughter had found a place with Sarah and in this family. What a gift Ronnie and Lee had been, to him and to his daughter. How lucky he'd been.

He went back to the refrigerator to gather eggs and milk and butter, not wanting Ronnie to see his face as he considered the possibility that this might not be his family for much longer. Ruby would always belong here. So would Dexter and Miles. But not him.

"So what's new with you?" Ronnie asked. "You know, other than your only daughter getting married?"

Eli tried to sound normal as he discussed the patients who'd put off checkups and procedures, and the post-pandemic gum disease he'd been dealing with. He talked, even as most of his attention was focused on the staircase, body tense, heart knotted, as he waited for Gabe's mother to show herself.

He could hear the other houseguests, stirring on the house's lower levels; doors opening and closing, toilets flushing, the sound of the boys' voices and their pounding feet as they went racing along the deck. *Come on*, he thought, as he whisked eggs and pancake batter. *Come on, come on, come on!*

But the next guest to emerge in the kitchen was Ari, who came shlepping up the stairs, looking predictably bleary. He grunted a greeting at Eli, rooted around in the freezer for a bottle of vodka, and waved it at his brother, then at Ronnie. "Hair of the dog?" he asked.

"No thanks," said Ronnie.

"I'm good," said Eli, tight-lipped.

"Glad to hear it." Ari smirked and Eli thought, *I'll kill him. I will.* Finally, finally, he saw Gabe's dark head bobbing up the staircase. He tried not to be too obvious as he turned, wiping his hands on a dishtowel, looking at the women flanking his please-God-not-son/son-in-law. One of them wore a white halter top, gold hoop earrings, a big, wide-brimmed beach hat, and a dramatically patterned skirt in shades of bright yellow and pink and green that tied in a knot at her waist, and a pair of impractical pink shoes that laced around her legs, from her ankles to her knees, with pink ribbons. For a sliver of a second, Eli was almost weak with relief, because that woman was definitely not the woman he'd slept with all those years ago. Her lips were thinner, her face was more angular, her eyes were the wrong shape. Then he saw the other woman, the one slightly behind Gabe, wearing a gray sweatshirt and light denim jeans and plain, inexpensive-looking white sneakers. She wore no makeup. Her gaze was on the ground. Eli felt his heart sink, plummeting through his belly and right through the floor. Because that woman unquestionably *was* the woman. There was no doubt about it. Even with all the time that had gone by, Eli recognized the shape of her mouth, the arch of her eyebrows, a birthmark high on her left cheek.

Eli tried to look pleasant as he felt his last tiny bit of hope evaporate and the truth settle in. "Good morning!" he called. The first woman smiled broadly and clasped his hand in both of hers. "I'm Amanda," she said. "Gabe's auntie." Her teeth were the bright white that came from veneers, made even brighter by the contrast with her lipstick. "My God, look at this place!" she said, letting go of Eli and walking to the windows. "It's like living in the clouds!"

"Isn't it something?" said Ari, oiling back into the kitchen and pulling out a chair for Amanda, before proffering the vodka. "Hair of the dog?"

"Yummy," said Amanda, giving Ari a big smile.

Eli turned to the other woman. "And you must be Rosa. It's so good to finally meet you in person."

Rosa nodded politely, murmuring a greeting.

"A real pleasure," Eli said. He took her hand and held it a beat too long, watching as her gaze snapped to his. For a single, electric instant their eyes met. Then she dropped her head, looking miserable and ashamed.

"How do you ladies take your coffee?" Ronnie asked. Rosa didn't answer. Her sister said, "Strong and black, like my men." Ronnie laughed, but Rosa didn't. She looked just like Eli felt, and he hoped he was doing a better job of hiding his dismay than she was.

"I think," he announced, "that the father of the bride and the mother of the groom should have a little private time." Let them think that he and Rosa were talking about the intricacies of their respective families, or the logistics of the ceremony. Let them think they had to discuss the seating arrangements, or how to handle Annette when, and if, she showed up. "Rosa, can I show you the beach?"

SAM

~~~~~

At just after seven a.m., Sam parked his car on the cul-de-sac in front of his mother's house so he wouldn't crunch down the driveway and wake the house. He walked to the front door, beneath a gorgeous early-morning sky. He felt like he was floating, like he'd inhaled helium and moonbeams, and a puff of wind would send him soaring.

He'd left Anthony with his car, in a public lot in the West End at five in the morning, with the sky just starting to get lighter. "Can I have your number?" Sam had asked.

Anthony looked a little shamefaced. "I'm on Grindr," he said. "I haven't used it in a few years, but that would probably be the best way to keep in touch right now."

Sam must have looked dubious, because Anthony said, "I promise, I'm not lying, and I'm not cheating on anyone. It's just, with my phone . . ." He cleared his throat. "I'm on my girlfriend's family's plan. I don't know if that means she can see my texts or anything, but better safe than sorry, right?"

Anthony gave Sam his username, which was Ziggy-Stardust01, and grinned at SamIAm37. "I'll message you tomorrow," Sam said.

"Got it. Okay." He gave Sam another meltingly tender smile and stood on his tiptoes to kiss him. "I'll see you soon."

Sam kissed him one last time, and closed the car door, watching Anthony's taillights getting smaller and smaller, until they were twinkling red dots in the dawn. He walked back into town as the sun rose, turning the sky from pale gray to gold. Then, because he was already awake, he went to the Portuguese bakery, which opened at five a.m., and got a brown paper bag full of fresh malasadas. Finally, so full of joy that he wanted to shout it to everyone in the world, he drove home.

He slipped through the front door, easing the screen door shut behind him. In the bathroom, he brushed his teeth, even though he was tempted to keep the taste of Anthony's mouth on his lips and tongue. He could hear the sound of footsteps over his head and the low murmur of voices. Maybe his sister, or Eli, he thought, or Ruby and her intended, getting an early start to the day.

He turned on the shower, got out of his clothes, and spent a long time under the hot water. His neck and lips felt tender; his face felt flushed. He couldn't stop thinking about Anthony—the warm velvet of his skin, the sound of his voice, how his hair had felt between Sam's fingers. Once he was wrapped in a towel, his cheeks still stretched and aching from smiling, he couldn't help himself. He wiped condensation off his phone's screen and opened Grindr.

He found Anthony's profile quickly enough and smiled again when he saw that Anthony had used a David Bowie album cover instead of his own face or body. The green dot by his name was glowing, which meant that he was online.

Sam looked at his profile, then wiped the screen down again and peered at it more closely. There was the name that Anthony had given Sam, and the picture—

dark curls, dark eyes, the flash of a white smile—was unquestionably him. Except the location feature must have been broken, or confused. It said that Anthony was in Truro. Massachusetts. 02666. Less than fifty feet away from where Sam was standing.

Sam stared, feeling his mouth drop open, his wet hair uncombed and dripping on his forehead. Fragments of the previous night's conversation were coming back to him; tumbling into his brain.

In town for a week.

Just broke up with someone.

My girlfriend knows I'm bi.

Things had been moving really fast. She's probably just as relieved as I am.

He didn't want to believe it, but Anthony was the right age, in town for the right length of time, and, worst of all, in the right location—namely, less than ten yards away from Sam.

Sam put down the phone. Picked it up. Put it down. Picked it up again and tapped out a message to Anthony.

GO DOWN TO THE BEACH AND WAIT FOR ME, he typed. Then, just in case, IT'S SAM.

A minute later, the reply came. WHICH BEACH? WHERE ARE YOU?

CURRENTLY I AM ONE FLOOR BELOW YOU, Sam typed. GO DOWN THE BEACH STAIRS AT THE BACK OF THE HOUSE. WAIT FOR ME THERE. WE NEED TO TALK.

Bubbles indicated that Anthony—no, not Anthony, Gabe, as in Ruby's fiancé, Gabe—was typing. OKAY.

Sam gave him a five-minute head start, timing the interval on his phone. Then he eased open the screen door he'd just closed, walked around the house, and raced down six flights of steps. The young man—Gabe, Sam reminded himself—was waiting at the bottom. His eyes had gotten wide during Sam's descent. They got even wider as he inspected Sam's face.

"Oh, God," he said. "You're . . ."

"Ruby's uncle."

He kept staring. "No way. Does Ruby know that . . ."

"Nobody knows!" Sam grabbed the young man's shoulder harder than he'd meant to, clutching it in a panicky grip. "Not Ruby, or my sister. Or my mom. Or my son." *Who is probably awake by now*, Sam realized, with a sinking feeling. "I don't even know your name," he said. "Is it Anthony, or Gabriel, or what?"

"It's Gabe," said the boy. "Gabriel Anthony Andrews." He touched Sam's arm. Sam flinched, and Gabe pulled his hand back. "Look, I'm sorry," he said, in a soft voice. "I know this is super weird, but we didn't do anything wrong. I didn't lie to you about anything."

"Except your name," said Sam. "And that you weren't breaking up with a girlfriend, you were breaking up with a fiancée."

"Yeah," Gabe agreed. "Except for those things." He looked away, out at the water, then back at Sam. "But I want to see you again," he said. "I didn't lie about that."

Sam tried to steel himself against Anthony's—no, not Anthony—Gabe's charm, even as he felt himself yearning, swaying, ever so slightly, toward the other man's chest. "We can't have this conversation now," he made himself say.

"No," Gabe agreed, and looked at Sam from underneath his long, curling lashes.

Sam took a deep breath and tried to sort through his roiling emotions. Anger, chagrin, disappointment, shame. Lust—plenty of that. And hope, unfurling in his chest a small and tender flower.

"So, let me understand this," he said. "The wedding's off?"

Gabe nodded. "Ruby left me a note and said she couldn't go through with it."

"And is she okay?"

Looking shamefaced, Gabe said, "I haven't seen her yet. I thought I'd let her, you know, make first contact."

"So Ruby dumped you, by note, and she canceled your wedding and you haven't seen her yet." Sam heard his voice rising as he enumerated the events of the previous night, before he'd met Gabe in Provincetown. "What if she thinks you're furious at her? Or miserable?"

Gabe shrugged. "Ruby knows I'm not mad at her."

Sam shook his head, feeling sorry for his niece. And her parents—Eli and his sister. Did Sarah even know yet what had happened? "Who has she told?" he asked, his voice short.

"I don't know," Gabe said. "Maybe just me."

Sam put his hand on his forehead, wishing he'd slept even a little bit, wishing he had the mental capacity to sort through everything that had happened, and what it meant for Ruby, and for his twin sister, and for him.

"How old are you?" was what he finally asked.

"Almost twenty-three," Gabe answered. Sam covered his eyes with his fists and groaned. "My mom says I'm an old soul," Gabe said helpfully. "How old are you?"

"Old," Sam said. "Older than you."

"I like older men," Gabe said softly.

"We should go back," Sam said. Sarah and Eli needed to know what was happening; if they didn't already . . . but he could hear there wasn't quite as much force behind the words as he'd intended.

Gabe looked toward the stairs. Sam followed his gaze to the staircase, and the space underneath the landing, shadowed and semiprivate with its screen of hedges, a cozy nook just big enough for two.

No, Sam thought . . . but when he opened his mouth to say it, nothing came out. Gabe reached for his hand, and instead of shaking him off, telling him he was crazy, that this entire thing was insane, Sam let himself be pulled into the darkness, for the dizzying, bewildering pleasure of Gabe's mouth against his.

ROSA

Eli led Rosa out onto the deck, and they walked down the six flights of beach stairs in silence, Rosa in the lead and Eli close behind her, hurrying, making sure there was nowhere she could go but down. She thought she heard rustling in the bushes behind the last landing—male voices, low laughter—but Eli took her arm as soon as her feet hit the sand, and pulled her along, walking her quickly away from the house, toward an inlet where motorboats were roaring through the rock-lined channel into the open water. The sky was a clear, pale milky blue, and the beach was still mostly empty. Families were just starting to trickle out, children racing for the water, parents behind them, burdened by armloads of tote bags and towels and umbrellas.

When they were a few hundred yards away from the house, Eli stopped. He turned to her and said, "We've met before."

"Yes," said Rosa. Her voice was faint.

"In 1999," said Eli.

"Yes," Rosa said again.

"You—we . . ." Eli spluttered and finally said, "You came to my apartment. You told me you were pregnant. You asked me for money for an abortion."

"Yes," Rosa said, for the third time.

"I am guessing," Eli said, biting off each word, "that you didn't have that abortion. Which means that

Gabe . . ." Rosa watched his mouth working, like he was tasting something sour. "That Gabe is my . . ."

"No!"

He glared at her. Rosa made herself meet his gaze, even though she felt faint, sick with shame and weak-kneed with fear. "No," she said again, more quietly. "He isn't."

Eli grabbed her by the forearms, pulling her close. "What do you mean? How do you know?"

"I mean," Rosa said, "that I was already pregnant when you and I . . . met."

She watched him absorb the news, pupils getting big, face going slack. "What?"

Rosa sighed. "I was pregnant, and I was broke. I needed to find a man who looked like he had money, so he could pay for an abortion." She looked at Eli. "I found you."

Eli let go of one of her arms but kept his grip on the other as he started walking again. "Tell me everything," he said.

Rosa nodded and sent herself back in time; back to when she was just twenty-one and had never been more beautiful, or more afraid. She'd just learned that she was pregnant, and she knew she was in no position to provide for a baby. Worse, she knew what a baby meant: the end of her dreams. Sweet, dopey Benji had no money for an abortion and no one to ask, with a dead father, a mother even more devoutly religious than Rosa's, and two brothers just as broke as he was. Her choice was really no choice at all.

Find a guy, Amanda told her. Rosa took the subway to Manhattan with the explicit goal of seducing someone's husband. She found a likely-looking bar full of an after-work crowd, self-assured guys with expensive haircuts drinking top-shelf Scotch and yelling to each other about sports and how much money they'd made. Rosa stationed herself by the jukebox, telling herself that she'd know her mark when she saw him. A responsible man, a good guy. Someone who would feel guilty ten seconds after the sex was over; someone who would do anything to keep his wife from ever finding out.

She'd watched and waited, and then she'd seen Eli, with his curly hair, shoulders a little slumped, twisting his wedding band around his finger as he sat at the bar. It had been as easy as Amanda had promised. Rosa walked over to him, putting a little extra swing in her step. She touched his arm, she licked her lips, she tossed her hair, and saw hunger animating the poor guy's features, like he'd been starving and she was an all-you-can-eat buffet on legs. She wondered what his story was, this good-looking man with his blue-green eyes and his pale, freckled body; because it was very clear from the way he fell on her, first by the jukebox, then in the elevator, and then, finally, in his apartment, where he tore at her clothes and plunged himself inside of her, that this man hadn't gotten laid in a long time.

They'd done it up against the wall, the first time. When he'd managed to try to slow things down, she'd told him—cringing inwardly—that she was safe. When he'd tried to stop, she'd made sure he hadn't. *Are you proud of yourself?* a voice inside of her inquired, when she'd taken his hand and put it between her legs. *Feeling good about this, Rosa?*

When the sex was over, they ended up on the floor. From her vantage point, she could see dust bunnies underneath the sofa, and the carpet made her skin itch. She forced herself to ignore it, to act like this was the best sex she'd ever had, like he was the lover of her dreams.

"So what's your name?" she asked.

That was when the guilt grabbed him. His face had gone pale as he'd pulled his sweaty body away from hers.

"What?" she'd asked.

"I'm married," he'd said. As if she didn't know. As if she hadn't seen the ring, or the framed photo of the man and a woman, in front of City Hall, holding a marriage license; the man in a suit and tie, the woman with a scrap of a veil perched on her head.

Rosa told him that his wife was a fool, that it was her fault for letting such a handsome man out alone. *He'll never believe a line that cheesy*, she'd thought, and she'd been astonished, and the tiniest bit disgusted, when it was clear that he had. *It's her fault*, Rosa told him, and twined herself around him, thinking the more times they did it, the more likely the man was to believe her eventual lie.

"I can't," the man had muttered.

"You already did," Rosa pointed out. She'd gotten to her feet, pretending she was Catwoman, some slinky, sexy, half-animal femme fatale. When she'd stretched her arms up over her head and felt the man's gaze on her, she knew that she had him.

"You got a bed in this place?" she asked. He'd nodded, and he'd taken her there.

It had all been so easy. A little dirty talk, a lot of moaning. Rosa even found herself occasionally enjoying the feeling of that clean, strong body working against hers (not everybody Rosa encountered was clean and strong). *Deeper*, she'd said. *Harder. More.* And that was pretty much all that it took.

After the third time, he'd fallen asleep, passing out so fast it was like he'd been bludgeoned. Rosa had slipped out of bed and crept barefoot through the apartment, pausing to extract his wallet from his pants. She learned that the man's name was Eli Danhauser, and, from the textbooks, she guessed he was studying to be a dentist. Folded in one of the books she found a scrap of a letter, one she guessed he hadn't sent. *I know this isn't what you wanted, but we can make it work. I'll do anything I can to make you happy.*

Rosa swallowed hard. She moved on to the kitchen, opening the refrigerator, helping herself to a few swigs of white wine and a banana. In the bathroom, she'd brushed her teeth with her index finger and reapplied her makeup. When she heard Eli stirring she'd hurried back to the bedroom, slipped under the sheets, and pretended to be asleep, so she could do that slow, languorous stretching-and-blinking-into-wakefulness thing that men seemed to like so much (and how, she wondered, did none of them ever notice when the woman who'd ostensibly been sleeping beside them all night woke up wearing lipstick and mascara? *They're all idiots*, her sister, Amanda, said in her head). "Good morning, handsome," she'd crooned.

"No," he said, and sat up straight, looking terrified and sick. "No, you have to go."

That was fine, Rosa figured. They'd done it three times, which was more than enough to convince him that he'd slipped one past the goalie. She'd taken a shower, using the wife's bodywash and shampoo. When she'd come out of the steamy bathroom, Eli was standing there, looking pale and twitchy. He had money in his hand.

Part of Rosa felt the insult like a slap. Another part thought, *Maybe it's going to be this easy. Maybe I won't have to lie to him at all.*

"I'm not a prostitute," she'd said.

"A gift, then," he'd said, and she'd taken the money, thinking, sadly, *Why not?* It wasn't until she was in the elevator that she'd realized that maybe she was a prostitute, after all.

Rosa had gone home. She'd called in sick at the restaurant, again. She'd ignored the two messages Benji had left for her. She took off her clothes, put on her bathrobe, and got into bed, where she tried not to think.

She told herself that the guy, Eli, had plenty of money. Six hundred dollars was nothing to a guy like that, a guy who was going to be a dentist and would probably end up living in a mansion in some fancy suburb, driving his kids to private school in some fancy car. But the words of the letter she'd found kept playing, twisting through her brain on an infinite loop: *I'll do anything I can to make you happy.* He'd tried to stop. He'd tried to be faithful. He was a good guy, and she'd seduced him into misbehavior; playing Eve to his Adam, holding out the apple, telling him it was fine if he took a bite.

Rosa made herself go back to the bar that night. He was there again, the way she'd known he would be, so she'd done her slinky, sexy, Catwoman thing again and let him take her home. The second time with Eli was even worse, because the previous evening's engagement seemed to have taken the edge off. Eli didn't just want to fuck her; he seemed intent on pleasing her. Rosa had been forced to fake two separate orgasms, lying on a stranger's bed with a stranger's face between her legs, before she could get him inside of her again. Rosa had moaned and sighed and thrashed around, all the while thinking what a sin it was to destroy someone else's marriage, to take a good man and tempt him into indulging his own darkest nature.

"What's your name?" he'd asked when it was over.

Oh, shit, thought Rosa. "Jane," she'd said. "Call me Jane." Time to change the subject, she thought, so she'd given him her very best blow job, burning with shame as she licked and sighed and swallowed, feeling like the very worst person in the world. When, on the third morning, he'd finally called it off, she'd felt nothing but relief, chased immediately by regret at what she knew she had to do to him next.

Two weeks later, she'd sat on a bench outside of his apartment and waited until he'd emerged. As soon as he saw her, his eyes had gone wide. He'd come racing across the street toward her, oblivious to the honking cars and the cursing cabdrivers, looking terrified and sick with guilt. Rosa had shuddered, thinking, *If he feels bad, I feel worse.*

Briefly, tersely, she told him what had happened, and what she needed. He'd looked faint when she'd said that she wanted an abortion and had agreed to give her money immediately. He'd gone running back to his apartment (more honks, more curses), leaving her standing there, weak-kneed and nauseated, sick with guilt. She thought, *I could leave, right now. I've already taken away his chance to be a faithful husband and honor his marriage vows. I could at least leave him his money.*

But she'd needed his money. So she'd waited. She'd walked with Eli to the bank. When he'd offered to go with her when she had the procedure and had insisted on giving her his name and his phone number, she'd thought she would die, right then and there, just burst into flames from the shame of it. A dozen times she'd come close to blurting out a confession: *I was pregnant before we hooked up, I just needed money, I'm using you, I'm a liar.* A dozen times, she made herself keep quiet.

He can afford it, she told herself fiercely. But Rosa knew that it wasn't the money that mattered, it was what she'd done, how she'd taken a good man and pulled him down into the dirt. She'd taken a faithful man and made him a cheater; she'd taken an honest man and made him a liar. For six hundred dollars, she had found a good man and corrupted him . . . and she would have to carry that knowledge with her, about what she'd done and what kind of person that made her, for the rest of her life.

On the beach, with the waves muttering to the sand, tumbling rocks and shells and bits of sea glass until their hard edges were rounded down and softened, Rosa stood in front of Eli and made her confession. She told him she'd come to New York because she wanted to be a singer. She told him she'd gotten pregnant, and that she wasn't sure who the father was, because she'd been sleeping with a few different men, all of whom were broke. So she'd set out to find a guy who could do what her boyfriend couldn't, and pay for an abortion.

"And that was me." Eli's voice was very dry.

"That was you. Only, once I had the money, when I was flying back home, I changed my mind." Rosa hung her head, looking down at her bare feet on the sand. "I've felt awful about it—about what I did to you—almost every day of my life," she said. "And then, when I realized that Gabe was living with you—that you were his girlfriend's father . . ."

Eli shook his head. "What are the chances, right?" He turned and looked at her.

"Here's what I don't understand," he said. "When you realized that Ruby was my daughter—when you recognized me—why didn't you call me? Or return any of my emails?" His voice was loud, splintered with anger. "Do you have any idea what the last year of my life has been like?"

"I was ashamed." Rosa hung her head. "I lied to you. I thought you'd be mad."

Eli gave a squawk of laughter. "I would have been too

busy being relieved that my daughter wasn't going to marry her half-brother to be angry."

"I'm sorry," Rosa said. "I know that doesn't mean much now, but I am. I've felt awful about what I did—about lying to you—for as long as Gabe's been alive. It was a terrible thing to do."

Eli barely acknowledged her apology. "I just want to make sure I've got this right. You were already pregnant when we were together. There is absolutely no chance that Gabe is my son." Eli's hair was wind-tossed, his cheeks stained red.

"That's how it happened," said Rosa. "If you were Gabe's father, he would have been about two months premature when he was born. And he weighed almost nine pounds."

"Oh, thank God," Eli said. "Oh, thank God." He wrapped his arms around Rosa's waist and spun her, delightedly, in the air, whooping with joy, blurting out fragments of sentences, half-finished thoughts. "You have no idea—the whole time he was living with us, I kept looking at him, and seeing you, and thinking—but I didn't know your name, either—and when I found out, you weren't answering my texts or my calls—and I couldn't tell Ruby, and Sarah would have killed me—"

He spun Rosa around again, then kissed her, resoundingly, on her cheek. "Thank you," he said, and hugged her hard. "*Thank you.*"

When he pulled away, Rosa was crying. "Do you forgive me?" she asked.

"Yes," said Eli. He took her hands. "Yes, Rosa, I forgive you," he said. "And look. You might have started things with me for your own reasons, but I was a willing participant." He gave a scoffing laugh. "An extremely willing participant. If there's bad behavior, it was on both of our parts. Maybe I deserved to go through a little hell for what I did."

She nodded, sniffling. Tears were still sliding down her cheeks. "I've told Gabe his whole life I don't know who his father is, when I do." She paused. "I raised him without a father, when he could have had one." She bent her head. "I don't know what kind of father Benji would have been, but he would have been better than nothing. And that's what I gave my son. Nothing. I was selfish," she said, very quietly. "The truth is, I wasn't good enough to make it as a singer, and I wanted something that would just be mine. I wanted Gabe all for myself."

"You did the best you could," Eli began, but Rosa was shaking her head.

"No. I knew it would be better for him if I at least tried. If I'd told his real father the truth; if I'd given him the chance to be part of Gabriel's life, instead of doing . . ." She gestured toward him, and said, in a muted voice, "Instead of doing what I did."

"Gabriel's a young man," Eli said. "It isn't too late for you to reach out to his real father. And I can tell you, I'm honored to be his father-in-law."

Rosa bent her head. "Thank you."

"I should go see how Ruby's doing," Eli said.

Rosa nodded, her eyes on the sand. "And I should go talk to my son."

SARAH

$\sim\sim\sim$

Most mornings in Brooklyn, Sarah was up by six o'clock, six thirty at the latest. She'd enjoy a half hour of solitude in the kitchen before she'd need to start chivvying the boys out of bed, serving breakfasts, and assembling lunches and checking that homework assignments made it into backpacks. On the Cape, fretting over Owen, and her mother's revelation, must have taken a toll. When she opened her eyes on Friday morning, it was almost eight o'clock. Eli's side of the bed was empty. His suitcase yawned open on the dresser; yesterday's dirty clothes had been kicked into a corner of the bedroom. In the bathroom, his toothbrush was resting on the side of the sink, and a strand of floss dangled over the side of the wastebasket like a thin albino snake, but Eli wasn't upstairs in the kitchen, or out by the pool, and when she checked her phone for texts, the only new ones she saw were from Owen. *I'm here. Can I see you? Call me.*

Sarah poured coffee into one of the pottery mugs her dad had made. After a career as a lawyer, Lee Weinberg surprised his wife and children by enrolling in an Introduction to Pottery class at the Castle Hill Arts Center, and discovering what he would loftily refer to as "unsuspected artistic depths." He'd become proficient enough to make plates and bowls and a dozen mugs, generously sized, with a pleasant heft and a purplish-blue glaze.

Sarah added cream to her cup, slid the screen door open, and walked, barefoot, onto the dew-glistening deck. A breeze lifted her hair, and the hem of her robe. She set her mug on the railing and leaned over, looking down at the beach. A jogger in hot-pink shorts plodded along the shoreline; a group of six walkers with eight dogs, large and small, came from the other direction. Sarah watched as the frolicking dog pack swarmed toward the jogger, jumping and prancing. The jogger, clearly used to their welcome, unzipped her fanny pack and made each dog sit for a treat. The waves came curling and foaming up onto the shore; out past the sandbar, a pair of clammers waded through the shallows, working their rakes through the sand. Sarah took in the familiar scent of salt and seaweed and wild roses. In spite of her confusion and her heartache, and her mother's confession, which Sarah had barely begun to think through, she felt a sense of comfort and rightness, the security that came from having her family nearby and in this place, the repository of so many happy memories, from knowing her boys were safe, still sleeping in the children's room on the ground floor. She imagined she could feel her father here, his comforting, steadfast presence. He'd been an early riser, too. Sometimes, they'd find one another in the kitchen just after sunrise, and her dad would coax her into a walk on the shore or a bike ride to Provincetown, just the two of them. *All will be well*, she told herself, just as her cup, which had been resting securely on the ledge, rolled off and down into the overgrown thicket of rose hips and what was probably poison ivy, bouncing off the deck and splashing coffee onto her feet on its way down.

"Shit!" Sarah crouched low, looking down to see if

she could reach the mug from the deck. She discovered that she couldn't, and, when she was getting back up, she bumped her head on the deck's railing. "Shit!" she hissed again. Was this what things had come to? Was the house itself, once her favorite place in the world, now out to get her?

She pressed her hand against the top of her head, probing for any swelling, shaking coffee off first her left foot, then her right. She turned back to the house, meaning to rinse off her feet and try to find something—barbecue tongs?—that would let her retrieve the mug, and she almost missed what was happening below her on the beach. Namely, her husband, with his arm wrapped around the shoulders of an unfamiliar dark-haired woman.

Sarah jerked backward. Then she leaned forward, as far as she could, standing on her tiptoes as she bent over the railing, trying to see more. She realized that she was making a noise, a pained, wordless cry; and that she was gripping the railing hard enough to give herself splinters. It was Eli, absolutely Eli. Those had been Eli's curls, coming out from the brim of his baseball cap; those were Eli's familiar legs, pale and a little bowed beneath his blue swim trunks; that was Eli's dark-blue Yankees T-shirt, the one that Sarah had washed and folded and put away a hundred times, and those were Eli's goddamn plantar fasciitis flip-flops, two tiny black dots at the base of the beach stairs.

Sarah stood, with her head aching and coffee dripping off her ankles and her toes, watching as her husband wrapped his arms around the dark-haired woman's waist and spun her around. When Eli bent his head to the other woman's, Sarah took two giant, blundering steps backward, reeling like she'd been punched, until she felt the screen door against her back.

She got herself down to the outdoor shower and used the handheld attachment to clean her feet. She pulled off her robe and her nightgown and stood, letting the water pound down against her, eyes closed, hands fisted, mind full of roaring static; no words, only rage.

Without a towel, she'd been forced to put her robe back on. It clung unpleasantly to her wet skin as she hurried back to the bedroom. She made the bed where she and Eli had slept, grabbed her swimsuit and clothes from the dresser—a pair of loose, bleach-stained shorts and a T-shirt that had once been her dad's that read I GOT SHUCKED AT THE WELLFLEET OYSTERFEST. She pulled the shirt and shorts on over her swimsuit, and went, barefoot, to the kitchen. Her mother was at the sink, rinsing breakfast dishes. Ari was at the table, talking to a dark-haired woman who introduced herself as Gabe's aunt Amanda. "I'm the fun aunt!" she said with a bright smile. Sarah made herself smile back. She was trying to look normal, even as her entire body was thrumming with fury. How could Eli do this to her? (Never mind that Sarah herself had done the same thing to him.) How could he do it here, flaunting his indiscretions right under her nose? (Never mind that her old boyfriend was currently blowing up her phone, beseeching her to meet him less than five miles away.)

Platters of pastries, muffins, and croissants were set out on the kitchen counter. Sarah could smell bacon and eggs and could see a bowl of fruit salad. Eli had made it. She could recognize the way he cut his kiwis.

She excused herself, started down the stairs, and almost tripped over Lord Farquaad. "Oh, no you don't," she growled in a voice so low and scary that the dog, who was usually indifferent to Sarah's commands, gave a small, frightened whimper and went waddling quickly away. She was furious. Furious and betrayed, and so angry that she felt ready to start hurling crockery at the walls. Except that wasn't fair to Ruby. Ruby didn't deserve drama or distractions, no matter what kind of an asshole her father had turned out to be.

From the floor below, she heard the screen door slide open, the outdoor shower turn on. It was probably her traitorous slimebag of a husband, come to rinse off the sand, and whatever else was clinging to him after his early-morning adventure. In her pocket, her phone started buzzing. Owen again. She read his text and returned the phone to her pocket without answering. She turned and called upstairs.

"Sarah! Good morning!" Ronnie said.

"Hey, Mom? If I go for a pond swim, are you okay keeping an eye on the boys? I think Eli went down to the beach."

"No problem," Ronnie called back. "It's a perfect morning for a swim. In fact, if you wait a minute, I could—"

"No," Sarah interrupted. She drew a deep breath. "I'm sorry, but if it's okay, I think I could use a little alone time."

"Of course," Ronnie said. Her voice was calm, but Sarah thought she could detect hurt.

"I'll be back in an hour. Two at the most." She hurried away before Eli could see her, closing the bedroom door just as above her she heard him slide the kitchen door open. She tapped out a quick text to Owen—*I'm on my way*—and grabbed her white linen cover-up from its hook in the closet. She slid her feet into new red sandals that matched her pedicure and let her hair fall down over her shoulders. She was a long way from eighteen, especially in the bright summer sunshine, but her heart lifted at the thought of Owen, waiting for her by the water; Owen, who loved her more than he'd ever loved anyone. Owen, who still thought she was beautiful.

ELI

~~~~~~~

After Rosa went inside, in search of Gabe, Eli trotted up to the kitchen, desperate to find his wife and deliver the most important and sincere apology of his life. He wanted to find Ruby, too. There was something tugging at the back of his mind—something Ruby had said? Something she'd asked him? He couldn't quite call it into focus, but he wanted to be certain that his daughter was okay.

He found Ronnie standing at the stove, and Amanda and Ari sitting at the table. Ronnie wore a bathrobe belted over pajama bottoms; Sam, looking a little bleary, was in swim trunks and a T-shirt, standing by the coffee machine, waiting for the pot to fill.

"Good morning. Has anyone seen Sarah?" Eli asked.

"You just missed her," Ronnie said. "She went for a swim in the pond."

Eli smiled at his mother-in-law, his brother-in-law, Rosa's sister, the boys as they went racing past on the deck. He felt ten years younger, twenty pounds lighter. He wanted to sing, to dance, to find his wife and hold her in his arms, pouring out all his shame and fear, telling her how much he loved her, how much he would always love her. He would promise he'd do better and make her believe him. He'd tell Sarah that he would never let her down again; that everything would be fine.

Eli was putting the half-and-half back into the refrigerator when he figured out what had been bothering him, like a piece of lettuce stuck between a second pre-molar and a first molar. It wasn't anything Ruby had said; it was how she'd looked, back in Brooklyn, when they'd been loading the car. She'd laid her wedding dress flat on top of the suitcases in the trunk. She'd been smiling, Eli remembered; she'd teased him about his tux still fitting, and that had been fine, but the expression in her eyes when she'd turned away was the exact same way she'd looked when she was six years old and he'd taken her to Disney World and she'd insisted on riding Space Mountain by herself. Right after the safety bar had come down over her chest, she'd had that same expression—*Get me out of here, Daddy. I don't want to be on this ride after all.*

"Oh, God," Eli said out loud. He looked around wildly. "Where's Ruby?"

More headshakes. "We got in pretty late last night," said Amanda, with a broad wink. "Maybe the two of them are sleeping in."

That was the moment that Gabe came up to the kitchen, moving at a brisk clip instead of his usual slow-motion amble.

"Um, guys?" he said. His sleepy eyes were wide-open, his typical half-smile replaced with a tight-lipped frown.

Ronnie and Amanda and Ari all stared at Gabe. Sam looked at him, then seemed to cringe and look away. Before Eli could make sense of that, Gabe rocked on his feet and cleared his throat.

"What?" Eli asked. "What is it?"

"Um. I—well." Gabe shifted his feet again, shoved his hands in his pockets, and said, "The wedding's off."

A murmur of concern went up from the Levy/Weinberg/Danhausers. "Oh, no!" Amanda cried.

"Holy shit," said Ari.

Thank God, thought Eli.

"What happened?" asked Ronnie.

"I don't know," Gabe said. "Ruby left me a note. She said she didn't feel ready." His gaze drifted from Ronnie's face to a point on the wall. "Honestly, I don't think either of us was ready. She was just the one who was brave enough to do something about it."

Eli felt his chest expanding and his shoulders drop, as if another great weight had slid off them. Of course she didn't want to get married, he thought. *How could I have missed it? And,* he wondered, *what else did I miss?* Ruby was probably with Sarah. He could imagine his wife comforting his daughter, telling Ruby she had nothing to worry about or feel sorry for; telling her that things always worked out for the best. She'd been such a good stepmother, the best of wives and women, and he'd been a fool to take her for granted. Which he planned on telling her, the minute he could get her alone. He'd lock the door, and light a few candles, and draw her a bubble bath for starters, and then—

"And Ruby's gone," Gabe concluded.

Eli stared at his daughter's former fiancé.

"What?" he said.

"Her phone's still plugged in, back in the guesthouse, and I can't find her anywhere."

"She's probably down on the beach," said Ronnie.

"No," Sam and Gabe said at the same instant. The two of them exchanged another puzzling glance, and Sam said, "I was just down there, and I didn't see her." He looked away, adding, "But I wasn't really looking."

Ronnie stared at her son. "You've been down to the beach already?"

Sam fidgeted and murmured something about wanting to see the sunrise.

"I didn't see her down there, either," said Eli.

"I checked, and her swimsuit and her hat and her cover-up are all still in the bedroom," Gabe said. "And she never even unpacked her sunscreen." He didn't have to explain that Ruby never went out in the sun without protecting her fair skin. "And wouldn't she take her phone?"

"No reception down there," Eli said. His face felt frozen, all his joy and relief replaced by worry.

"Maybe she went to get muffins. Or into P-town for breakfast," said Ronnie. "Are all the cars still here?"

"I'll check." Sam trotted down the stairs.

"I'll go with you," said Gabe, and hurried after him.

Eli pulled out his phone and dialed his daughter's number, before remembering that Gabe had said she'd left her phone in the guesthouse. He tried Sarah, hoping she'd finished her swim, but the call went straight to voicemail. A moment later, Sam called upstairs. "The minivan's gone, but the rest of the cars are here."

"Sarah took the minivan," said Ronnie, forehead wrinkling as she frowned.

"Okay," Eli said. "Where would Ruby go? What should we do?"

"She could have taken a bike," Ronnie said, almost to herself. "Eli, why don't you take the boys down to the beach. See if the paddleboard or any of the kayaks are gone. I'll stay here to answer the phone. Someone should head into P-town . . ."

"I can do that," Sam volunteered.

"And hit the ocean beaches, too. Head of the Meadow and Longnook. Maybe she went for a swim," said Ronnie. "And I'll text Sarah and tell her to check Gull Pond and Slough Pond."

"How would she have gotten to a pond without a car?" asked Eli.

"It's not that far on a bike," Ronnie said. "Or maybe she's got friends out here?"

"I don't think her friends are coming until tomorrow." Eli tried to sound confident, even though he didn't know for sure. The wedding plans had swirled around him while he'd been oblivious.

"Sarah used to have a boyfriend whose family had a house out that way," Ronnie said. "Which is how I know it's bikeable. It's even walkable, if you're really committed."

Eli frowned. Had his wife ever mentioned a Cape Cod boyfriend? Had that been one more thing he'd missed? *I'll talk to her as soon as I can*, he thought. For now, the important thing was finding Ruby, and making sure that she was all right.

SARAH

Owen was waiting for her at the edge of the pond, right where he said he'd be. Sarah looked at him and felt time rewinding. His smile, when he looked at her, was just the same as it had been, all those years ago.

"Hey, beautiful," he said, wrapping his arms around her, pulling her close. Sarah spared a thought for anyone who might have recognized her, then decided that she didn't care. Had Eli held back for even a minute? Let them look; let them see.

"Want to swim?"

"Yes," he said, and took her hand. "But there's something else I want to do first." He took her by the hand, picked up his towel, and led her deeper into the woods, to the clearing where they'd been together for the first time.

She thought it would be bliss, the same ecstatic reunion they'd had back in New York City. Only this time, for some reason, it wasn't. Maybe it was because Sarah was still furious about what she'd seen down on the beach, her mind heavy with things she wanted to say to Eli, trembling not with lust but rage. Maybe it was because of what Ronnie had told her, how her mother had said that her affair hadn't been about the other man, but about how he'd made her feel, and how she'd decided she didn't like who she was when she was with him. Sarah detested the idea of her mother betraying her father . . . and yet, here she was, betraying the father of her own sons, becoming someone she didn't like.

Whatever the reason, she couldn't get out of her own head. And Owen seemed oblivious to the way her body was there but her mind was somewhere else.

She let him kiss her, and tried to kiss him back. She ran her hands against his shoulders, feeling the broadness of his back, the smoothness of his skin, the muscles working underneath. She touched his hair, caressed his cheek, tasted salt on his neck, tried to enjoy the sensation of his body, strong and agile, against hers, but she couldn't turn off her brain. Not even as she raised her arms to let Owen remove her cover-up; not even as he bent his stubble-raspy cheeks to her breasts, not even when he slid himself inside her. All of it felt strange, and forced, and even a little cheesy. Owen's strangled gasps of "Oh, God" sounded silly and dramatic; the way he squeezed his eyes shut as he thrust made her wonder if he didn't want to look at her. When he swung one of her legs up over his shoulder, Sarah felt a twinge of pain, and was reminded that Eli knew not to pull too hard on that hamstring, because she'd injured it years before during the single time she'd run the New York City Marathon. When she moaned, he mistook the noise for pleasure—another thing that Eli would never do.

Wrong, wrong, wrong, she thought. Maybe it was Ruby's misbegotten wedding; maybe it was Ronnie's confession; maybe it was how it had felt to see Eli embracing that strange woman, but it was starting to feel increasingly likely that the main thing really troubling her at the moment was that Owen was not her husband. It was also starting to feel more and more probable that fucking Owen was just a way of getting back at the man she really cared about, the man who'd disappointed her so badly. She was using Owen—Owen, who still loved her! It wasn't fair, Sarah thought miserably, feeling guilt settle against her like a smudgy cloud. This wasn't right. She'd have to tell him. They'd have to stop.

When it was over, Owen gathered her against him. Sarah shut her eyes, resting her cheek against his chest. Owen tangled his fingers in her hair.

"Do you think it's always going to be like this with us?" Owen asked. Sarah wondered what he'd felt; what, exactly, he'd experienced as her brain had hovered outside of her body and watched two middle-aged people get it on. "Is it always going to be this good?"

Sarah didn't reply, even though she knew the answer: after a few months, every infatuation fades. The passion ramps down, the fairy dust evaporates, the pheromones calm, and, instead of two people who float on clouds of ecstasy, who think of one another endlessly when they're apart and can't stop touching when they're together, you end up two people who have to decide, every day, whether or not you still want to be a couple; whether to stay or go. She'd seen it happen with her friends; she'd felt it herself, with her college boyfriend, Tommy, and then with Eli. But not with Owen, who'd turned himself into a ghost before it could. *Did you miss me?* Sarah wanted to ask. *Did you think of me, the way I thought of you? When did it stop, and who did you meet who stopped it?* There had to have been someone for him, the same way for her there'd been Tommy, then Eli.

Owen sounded dreamy and lovestruck, still in the clouds. "It's never been anyone but you for me."

Sarah spoke slowly at first. "Last night, my mother told me she had an affair. A long time ago, before my brother and I were born."

Owen made a startled noise.

"And she's selling her house."

Owen sat up, bringing her with him, reaching around to brush pine needles out of his hair, "I'm so sorry, I know how that feels, to lose your place here."

Sarah inhaled, then blurted out the final confession. "And Eli—my husband—Eli is cheating on me."

Owen looked down at her, frowning. "Really?"

"He's been weird and secretive for months, and I saw him on the beach this morning. With another woman."

"Brazen," said Owen, who'd come all the way from New York City and had made love to her right out in the open, five miles from the bed where she'd slept with her husband.

"Shameless," Sarah replied. When Owen leaned forward to kiss her, she shut her eyes, wishing that she could enjoy it and, if she couldn't feel pleasure, that she could feel nothing, just oblivion, no thoughts or sensations at all. Overhead, a mourning dove called—*too-WHIT, too-WHOO.* Another bird chattered back, almost angrily, and some small four-legged creature scampered by, rustling the grass.

"It's so beautiful here," said Sarah. She tried to appreciate it, the warmth of the sun, the sound of the water—but she just felt exhausted, drained and sad and empty, so preoccupied that when Owen said something she didn't hear what it was. She turned toward him, squinting in the sunlight. "What?"

"It's for sale," Owen repeated.

Sarah blinked at him. "What's for sale?"

"This." Owen gestured. "The land. My family's old place." He gestured toward the woods. "There's a house back there, and the people who owned it sold the property to developers. They were going to build, but I guess they got cold feet, or maybe their plans weren't approved. They put the property on the market again."

"Are you . . ." Sarah looked at him curiously. "Are you going to buy it?"

"Me? Hah." Owen's voice was bitter. "After the divorce, I've barely got two nickels to rub together."

Sarah jolted upright. "Divorce?"

Owen had the grace to look ashamed. "It was three years ago."

"You didn't mention it."

"Well, I am single." He had the nerve to sound affronted. "I didn't lie about that."

"Leaving out a marriage is a pretty significant omission. Kids?"

When Owen didn't answer, Sarah stared at him for a long moment. Finally, she reached for her cover-up and scanned the ground for her sandals. "So was this your plan? Find me, seduce me, and talk me into buying back the old place for you?"

Owen looked shocked. Maybe he was shocked. "Sarah, no. Absolutely not. I never planned on finding you, I swear. That was just luck, or fate, or karma."

Maybe you never planned it, she thought, yanking her swimsuit up over her legs. *But once it happened, you were pretty quick to take advantage of it.*

"Besides, if you decide to get a place here, it wouldn't be for me. It would be for us."

She shook her head. "This isn't my place, Owen. It never was. I'm not a Pond Person."

"You could be one, by marriage." He reached for her hands. His eyes, still such a lovely bright blue, were shining, brilliant with hope. "We could be together here.

Our kids could spend their summers here." He looked at her solemnly. "I have never loved anyone the way I loved you."

"I believe you." Sarah sounded remote. She certainly felt that way, like, in a few short breaths, she'd moved far, far away from Owen, even though he was still right beside her. "I don't think anyone ever loves anyone else the way they do when it's their first love. Maybe it's more about falling in love with love than with another person."

"No!" Owen looked, and sounded, genuinely anguished. With his palms, he rubbed at his hair. "Sarah, you're the most incredible woman I've ever known. I loved you then, and I love you now."

Sarah bent down and brushed the crushed bits of leaves and grass from the backs of her legs, so that Owen wouldn't be able to see her face. Maybe he was telling the truth—or at least, the truth as he understood it. Maybe he did love her . . . but it seemed more likely that what he loved was who he'd been back then, young and beautiful, full of unspoiled promise, before life had dinged or dented him. Sarah could remember him that way; could reflect that version of Owen back at him. Maybe that was what he loved, that previous, perfect, eighteen-year-old self . . . or maybe what Owen really loved was this place, and his family's former status. Maybe he'd been longing not for her but for his lost throne, from which he would reign as King of the Pond People.

Whatever his reasoning, Sarah had told him the truth. This, here, was not where Sarah Levy-Weinberg Danhauser's belonged, and it never would be. Her place was with her stepdaughter and her sons, her mother and her brother. Her place was with Eli, if they could fix what was broken between them. Not with Owen. Not anymore.

"Owen, I need to get back home."

Owen looked wretched. Probably as wretched as she'd looked, when she'd been eighteen and a freshman in college, when, after she'd spent five days telling everyone about her lacrosse-playing boyfriend at Duke, Owen had dumped her and never told her why. Sarah remembered the agony of it, how she'd tried to figure out what she'd done wrong, how she had tortured herself with thoughts of the prettier, skinnier girls he was meeting in Durham, girls who'd be cooler, and less clingy. Crying alone in her bed while her roommates went to parties, never knowing what she'd done wrong.

"Sarah, please."

She shook her head. It felt like she'd been sleeping and had woken up; like she'd been ensorcelled, under some enchantment, and the spell had broken. She remembered a long-ago line from a Shakespeare class: *Methought I was enamoured of an ass.*

"I have to go," she said again. "I'm sorry, but I need to get back home."

ANNETTE

~~~~~

Annette woke to the sounds of Ruby sliding the curtains open on their metal rods. Bright sunshine poured into the room, along with the sound of kids in the parking lot. "Daddy, will you teach me to ride the waves?" Annette heard a boy ask. Through the window, she saw a toddler, in a pink-and-white-striped bathing suit, sitting in a backpack on her father's shoulders, as an older sibling glided in circles on a push-bike.

"Coffee?" she asked. Ruby gave her a bleak smile.

"Sure. And then we'd better go back and face the music."

"Should you call them?" Annette asked.

Ruby looked shamefaced. "I don't have my phone."

Annette felt a trill of alarm. "You didn't tell anyone you were leaving?"

Ruby shook her head. "I left Gabe a note. Then I just took off." She sounded almost proud as she said, "It's the most irresponsible thing I've done in my entire life." Smoothing her curls, she considered, then added, "Maybe it's the only irresponsible thing I've done in my life."

"Don't worry," Annette said. "I've done enough irresponsible things for both of us."

Ruby restored her neat bun. She sat on the edge of the bed and looked up at her mother. "This is terrible to say, but I feel like I dodged a bullet. It's not Gabe," she added quickly. "He's not a bad guy. And he loved me. Loves me," she quickly corrected. "I guess I'm just not ready." Ruby smiled bleakly. "I guess it's better to figure it out now, before anything irrevocable happens."

"I couldn't agree more," said Annette. She tried to keep her tone light, but she felt, in the room, the ghost of something dark and woeful, the specter of Ruby's nonexistence. "I love you," she said, because it was true. "And I'm not sorry, if that's what you're wondering. I didn't want to have children, and I was crap at being a mother." She paused. "But I do love you. And I know your dad loves you, and Sarah does, too. And I want to be here for you now. As best I can."

"Maybe I wouldn't have been sorry." Ruby's voice was low and musing. "Maybe I would have been happy, married to Gabe."

Annette took her daughter's hand. "What do you want? Not your stepmother or your father or your grandmother or Gabe. Or me, for that matter. Just you. Close your eyes and ask yourself: What do I want?"

Ruby shut her eyes and sat quietly for a moment. Then she gave Annette a smile of surpassing sweetness. "I want coffee and a malasada. And then, I think, I want to go home."

SAM

~~~~~~~~

Sam drove Gabe and his mother to Provincetown, parking in the same lot where he'd left the car the night before. He paid a different evening attendant ten dollars—a third of what the price had been, he noted with amusement.

"Maybe we should start at the center of town, and then I'll head east and you two"—he nodded at Gabe and Rosa—"can head west?" He wanted to walk with Gabe—there were still a number of things that needed saying and, now that they were in public, there was less of a chance that they'd end up, as they had that morning, making out for fifteen minutes instead of talking—but of the three of them, only he and Gabe could be guaranteed to recognize Ruby, unlike Rosa, who still hadn't met her son's former intended in person.

Sam nodded. Gabe did, too, and then, when his mother's back was turned, he reached out and squeezed Sam's hand. "Weirdest second date ever," Gabe murmured in a voice pitched for Sam's ears alone. Sam's heart took a great, joyful leap. He tried, sternly, to tell himself that he was being ridiculous, that this entire situation was impossible, and that, of all the men in the world, he was not, could not, be falling in love with his niece's jilted suitor. Except, he realized, as he set off along Commercial Street, maybe he already had.

ROSA

~~~~~

Rosa and Gabe had just made it past the Lobster Pot, and were maneuvering through the morning crowd of bright-eyed families pushing strollers and hungover single men gulping coffee, when Rosa said, "Gabriel, I need to tell you something."

Gabe looked at his mother curiously. Rosa almost never used his full name. "What's up? Are you okay?"

"Yes. No. I mean, I'm fine—I'm not sick. It's just—" She paused and rubbed her forehead with her fingertips. "There's something I have to say to you."

"Come on," said Gabe. "We can look for Ruby on the beach while we talk." He led her along a narrow path that twisted through the knee-high grass to the sand.

"How'd you know about this?" she asked.

Gabe bent his head, turning so she couldn't see his face. "Uh, I did a little exploring last night."

"You went out?"

"Ruby left me a note," Gabe said. "And, after I got it, I didn't want to just sit around waiting for her."

Rosa looked at her son carefully, searching his face for an indication of how he was handling things. "Are you okay?"

He sighed, then nodded. "Yeah. Weirdly okay. Relieved, actually. I think both of us were rushing. And then neither of us was brave enough to say so. At least, I wasn't. I'm glad that she was."

"If it's not what you wanted . . ." Rosa said hesitantly. She didn't want to admit it, but she, too, was relieved. *A daughter's a daughter all her life, but a son's a son 'til he takes a wife*, was what her own mother had told her. She'd already lost Gabriel to the East Coast, to New York City, and part of her was glad that at least she wouldn't be losing him to another woman quite yet.

"I'm fine," Gabe said. "At least, I will be." He had the strangest expression on his face, something that looked like sorrow mixed with what seemed to be hope. "And maybe I won't be single for too long."

Rosa wanted to ask about that, but she couldn't let herself be distracted.

"So what do you want to tell me?" he asked.

Rosa had promised herself that she wouldn't cry. At her son's teasing tone, she bit her lower lip, hard, letting the pain distract her, so she'd be able to get through what she needed to say without tears.

"I always told you that I never knew who your father was, right?" When Gabe nodded, Rosa said, "That wasn't true. I know who it was. But I never told him I was pregnant. I never gave him a chance to be a father."

Gabe looked at her for a moment without speaking. "Who was he?" he finally asked.

"His name was—is, I guess—Benji. He was a musician. Someone I knew in New York City. I wanted to tell you that, and also . . ." *Just say it*, Rosa told herself. "I hadn't planned on having a baby. I wanted to have an abortion, but I didn't have the money, and Benji didn't, either, and so I decided that I'd find a guy . . ."

Gabe put his hand on her arm. "Mami," he said gently. "You don't need to tell me this."

"I do, though." The sea air felt like it was stinging

her lungs. She could smell coffee, suntan lotion, sweet pastries. She could feel the grit of the sand beneath her feet and hear a snatch of music as a car drove past with its windows down. It seemed impossible that the world was moving on all around them, people going about their normal days, leading normal lives, while she had to deliver this kind of news. "The man I found to give me money—the man who thought he'd gotten me pregnant—he was Ruby's father."

For a moment, Gabe just stared. "What?" he finally squawked. "You slept with Ruby's dad?"

"But he isn't your father," Rosa hastened to add.

"That's—well." Gabe opened his mouth, then closed it, then shook his head and settled for "Holy shit." He looked at his mother. "So, wait. When Ruby's dad saw you, on that FaceTime, did he think . . ." Gabe stopped talking and covered his face with his hands. His shoulders were shaking, and, for a terrible moment, Rosa thought he was crying. Then, when he raised his head, she saw that he was laughing, so hard that there were tears on his cheeks. "Ruby's dad thought he was my father, too," he snorted, shaking his head. "Mami. *Escándalo!*"

"I know."

"It's crazy!"

"Crazy," Rosa confirmed. "And I'm sorry. Ruby's father is a good man, and I took advantage of him. And . . ." She swallowed hard. "It wasn't right."

"Oh, Mami." Gabe took her hands, and smiled at her—his old smile, full of that surpassing sweetness. It took her breath away. "It's not that bad."

"Yes! Yes, it is!"

"People make mistakes."

"People, sure. Not mothers!"

"Aren't mothers people?"

Without thinking, Rosa shook her head in negation. "Do you forgive me?" she whispered.

Gabe opened his arms, and she stepped into his embrace, pressing her cheek to his chest as she started to cry. "Don't cry. It's going to be fine. It's okay. I forgive you. It's okay."

RONNIE

~~~~~~~

When she heard a car coming up the driveway, Ronnie made herself hurry down to meet it. That nagging stitch in her side was back—more nagging, now that she knew what it portended. *Can't think about it now,* she told herself. "Oh, thank God," she said as Annette and then Ruby emerged from the car. She hugged Ruby hard. Then she hugged Annette. Then, for good measure, she hugged them both again.

"You had us so worried!" she said.

"I'm sorry," Ruby said, shamefaced. "It was inconsiderate. I—I left Gabe a note, and then I think I just freaked out."

"It's okay," said Ronnie, and kissed her cheek. "I understand. We've all been through a lot, you know. The pandemic, and the quarantines. All of that was traumatic, right? Everyone's life got turned upside down. I've listened to podcasts about it. You're allowed to freak out."

"You listen to podcasts?"

Ronnie drew herself upright. "Your *safta* is extremely hip and of the moment. And the point is, I understand if you're not feeling quite yourself."

"I'm not even sure I know who 'myself' is," Ruby said, sounding mournful. She had her hair up in a bun, with curls falling around her cheeks. There was a bit of powdered sugar on her cheek, and she looked, to Ronnie, very young. Ronnie and Annette exchanged a smile, and

Ronnie said, "You've got your whole life to figure it out. As mistakes go, this isn't a terrible one."

"Where's Gabe?" Ruby asked.

"In P-town, with his mom and Sam. Looking for you. Your dad's down on the beach, and your mom went to Gull Pond, I think. I should probably call off the dogs." Ronnie paused. "And your bridesmaids, right? And your friends?"

"And the florist. And the caterer. And Gabe's grandparents." Ruby pulled her hair out of its bun, then used both hands to gather it up again. "I feel awful about this. I should never have let it get this far."

"Hey, at least it was going to be a small wedding, right?" Ronnie said. "Don't worry," she said, and gave Ruby her biggest, warmest, everything's-going-to-be-fine smile, even as she felt her side aching and tears threatening. "You brought us all together here. You gave me a gift."

Ruby raised her eyes as Eli came across the deck, with the boys behind him. "Dad!" she called. Eli quickened his pace to a near-run, hurrying down the stairs and across the driveway to sweep her into his arms.

"Ruby!"

"Hi, Dad," Ruby said sheepishly. Ronnie watched, amused, as Eli did exactly what she'd done, hugging Ruby, then Annette, then both of them at once.

"Where were you?" he asked his daughter.

"I went for a walk, and I ran into Annette, and we drove for a while, and then we went to her hotel."

"I didn't realize that she didn't have her phone, or that you were all out looking for her," Annette interjected. Eli barely spared his ex-wife a glance. He held Ruby by the shoulders, then raised his hands to cup her face.

"But you're okay," he said.

"Fine." Ruby looked pale, and sounded chastened, but, Ronnie thought, also fundamentally okay. She wished she felt okay and wondered which bombshell she'd deliver first when she could sit down with her children.

"I'm sorry," Eli said, and hugged his daughter hard. "I should've noticed that you were, ah, on the fence."

Ruby made a face. "That's one way to put it."

"I should have been paying more attention."

When Ruby looked at him curiously, he shoved his hands in his pockets. "There's a story," he said. "I'll tell you later." He looked around. "Where's Sarah?"

"Still swimming, I guess," said Ronnie. "I just texted her. Meanwhile, I've been thinking about how we should let the guests know."

"Ah," said Eli. "The guests."

"Why don't you give me the list, and I'll start making calls," Annette said. "Please. Put me to work."

Ronnie didn't miss the grateful look that daughter gave mother. She noticed how Eli and Annette went off together, talking quietly, probably about Ruby, how she was doing, how they could help. *All will be well*, she thought. *And as soon as I tell Sarah and Sam what I need to tell them, I'll be able to breathe again.*

She walked back to the kitchen slowly, rehearsing the speech she'd give, pausing twice to lean on the railing, pressing her hand against her side. She was bending over the dishwasher, unloading the mugs, when a wave of dizziness swept through her, the dull pain in her midsection flaring into agony. The windows and the water all went gray around the edges. *No*, she thought. *Oh, no. Not yet. Please not yet.* Ronnie grabbed for the counter, then the dishwasher door, and then the floor came rushing up to meet her. She heard the sound of her body falling, her head thudding against the hardwood, and then the darkness spilled over everything, the black erasing every bit of bright.

SARAH

Owen insisted on walking her to the car, even though Sarah said, "I'll be fine." When she arrived at the minivan, she stood on her tiptoes to kiss his cheek. She could see the brilliant blue of his eyes, but also the wrinkles around them; she could see the broadness of his shoulders, but also their weary droop. He was a man, not a prince or a magical escape hatch, the living embodiment of a Plan B. He was just a man, with good parts and bad, like all men (and all women).

"Goodbye, Owen," she said gravely. "I hope it all works out. Take care."

He bowed his head and nodded without making a reply.

Sarah climbed into her minivan and clicked her seat belt into place. She hoped he found a way to purchase his family's former land; that he could bring his children there for the summer, watch them swim across the pond, and grow up and fall in love.

She plugged her phone into the charger and had gone about fifty yards down the rutted dirt path when it started to buzz with incoming texts, one after another after another, until the buzzing was interrupted by an incoming call.

"Sarah?" Eli's voice rang out through the car's speakers. "Where are you?"

"I went for a swim." A shamed flush spread from the

crown of her head down over her throat and her chest. "I'm on my way home. Is everything all right?"

"Well," Eli began. "Ruby and Gabe have called off the wedding."

"What?" Sarah blurted. Then, "Oh, thank God."

"Ruby was missing for a while, but she just came back, with Annette."

"Annette?" Sarah blinked, and felt surprise, and a stab of rejection that she forced herself to ignore. Eli lowered his voice.

"Annette said that Ruby left Gabe a note, and then she kind of freaked out. She took off without her phone. She was walking down the road when Annette found her. She spent the night at Annette's hotel."

Sarah shook her head, stunned at the thought of Ruby doing something so impetuous and irresponsible. "And it didn't occur to Annette to text us?"

"She didn't know that Ruby didn't have her phone. She thought we knew where she was. Or at least that we had a way to get in touch with her."

Sarah rolled her eyes. "But Ruby's okay, though? You're sure?"

"She seems to be. She and Annette are here now. They brought doughnuts."

"That was thoughtful."

"Sarah," Eli said. Sarah waited. A pulse of unease worked its way up her spine. Did he know what she'd been doing? Had he seen something? Had he spotted some text message, overheard some call? Quickly, her fear was replaced by anger: after the way he'd treated her, the way he'd ignored her; after what she'd seen that morning, on the beach, how dare Eli accuse her of anything?

"Come home," said Eli. "Please. I need to talk to you."

She swallowed hard and remembered what her mother had said to her, the night before. *Marriages can survive a little resentment. Marriages can survive a lot of things.*

She braced herself, getting ready for whatever would come next, and told her husband that she was on her way. She drove up Corn Hill, down the curve of the road and turned left into the driveway. Before she'd put the car in Park, Miles and Dexter were racing across the deck, with Lord Farquaad barking and wiggle-bottoming after them, and Eli was running behind the dog.

"What?" asked Sarah, jumping out of the car. "What is it?"

"It's your mother," Eli said, his voice low and his expression troubled as the boys came pelting across the driveway.

"Mommy!" shouted Miles.

"Safta fell down!" Dexter said.

Sarah ran up to the kitchen, with Eli right behind her, telling her he'd already called 911 and that an ambulance was on its way. "Keep the boys outside," she told him, and ran up to the kitchen, where her mother lay on the floor, with Rosa kneeling beside her, holding Ronnie's hand, with two fingers on her wrist, monitoring her pulse.

"Mom!" Sarah cried, skidding across the floor.

"Let's not move her," Rosa said quietly. She sent Sarah for a glass of water and pillow to put under Ronnie's head. When Sarah touched her mother's shoulder, Ronnie groaned and opened her eyes.

"What happened?" she whispered.

"You fainted," Sarah said.

Ronnie closed her eyes. "I was going to tell you," she said.

"What?" Sarah asked. "Tell me what?"

Ronnie tried to sit up and groaned again, a horrible, pained sound.

"Don't move," Rosa said. "Just relax. Everything's fine. We're going to take good care of you." Then the paramedics were there, thumping up the stairs with their equipment. Sarah watched as they lifted her mother's body onto the stretcher and fastened the straps, carrying it down the stairs and into the ambulance. Sarah followed after them. In the driveway, she squeezed her mother's hand and repeated, "I love you," over and over, holding on tight, until the ambulance doors were closed.

"What happened? Did you see?" she asked Rosa. "Is she going to be all right?"

Rosa's face was somber. "You should go to the hospital. They'll know what's going on."

Eli put his hand on Sarah's shoulder. "Go get your purse and your phone charger. I can drive." He got into the car. Sarah took the seat beside him. She called her brother and told him what had happened as they followed the ambulance along Route 6 to Hyannis, and the Cape's only hospital.

"Maybe it's just stress," Eli said.

"She is getting older," said Sarah, and sat motionless and frozen, willing the car to go faster, staring at her hands, bunched in fists in her lap.

An hour after Ronnie was admitted, Dr. Dominguez ushered Eli and Sarah and Sam, who'd just arrived, into a conference room. The doctor wore a tennis dress and a matching visor over her dark-brown hair and had a dab of sunscreen on her nose.

"Why don't we sit," she said to Sam and Sarah and Eli, who had his arm around Sarah's shoulders.

"What's wrong?" Sarah asked.

"Your mom hasn't spoken to you?" asked the doctor.

The twins shook their head. "She said she had something to talk to us about," Sam said.

"But there was supposed to be a wedding tomorrow," said Sarah. "She wanted to wait."

The doctor nodded and opened a folder. "Let me get you up to speed: your mother signed a medical power of attorney stating that you both have the right to make decisions for her, in the event that she becomes incapacitated. There's more here, spelling out her wishes, but—"

"Please," Sarah said. Her voice was raw. "Please, just tell us what's wrong."

The doctor closed the folder and set her hands on top of it. "Three weeks ago, when your mother came in for her checkup, she was complaining of fatigue and stomach pain. When I did an exam, I felt a mass in her abdomen."

Sam gasped. Sarah started to cry. Eli handed her tissues he'd found somewhere and put his hand on the back of her neck.

"I sent her right to the hospital for an ultrasound and some bloodwork. Her blood tests showed very elevated levels of calcium, which is one of the markers for cancer. That was what the ultrasound and the biopsy of her pancreas confirmed."

"Oh," Sarah whispered. "Oh, Mom."

"We had surgery scheduled for next week, to remove as much of the tumor as we could. After that, our plan was to begin chemotherapy and radiation right away."

"So what happens now?" asked Eli.

"They're prepping her for that surgery. We'll get a sense of what we're dealing with. But, I should tell you . . ." She sighed and removed her visor. "Everything we've seen so far suggests that this is quite advanced."

"Could it be benign?" Sarah asked, in a small voice. "Could the tests be wrong?"

"Anything is possible."

"But not likely." Sam's voice was flat.

"No," the doctor said, and shook her head. "Not likely." She made eye contact with each of them, and said, "Your mom's a wonderful lady. I'm so very, very sorry."

ELI

~~~~~~~

I n an alcove near a window, on the hospital's second floor, there were chairs and a coffee table. Sam and Sarah sat down, staring at each other bleakly as Eli went to get them water and call home to tell Ruby what had happened.

"I can't believe this," said Sam as Eli set his cup down on the table.

"My God. Poor Mom. I hope she hasn't been in any pain . . ." Sarah buried her face in her hands.

Eli touched his wife's shoulder. He rubbed her back. He saw the bits of crushed leaves in her hair, a grass stain on the back of her skirt. He pictured her sitting out by her favorite pond, fretting about Ruby, worried about him. He had failed her. He'd failed her for months, for more than a year, for too long. He was not going to fail her now. Whatever she needed, she would have; whatever he could do for her, for her mother, for her family, he would.

SAM

~~~~~~

Two hours after the exploratory surgery was over, Sam was sitting beside his mother's bed when Ronnie opened her eyes.

". . . time is it?" she asked. Her words were slurred.

Sam told her, and held a cup of water for her, raising the top of the bed, angling the straw so she could sip. "We talked to your doctor," he said. "She told us what's going on. How are you feeling?"

Ronnie shrugged. In a raspy voice, she whispered, "Didn't want to ruin Ruby's big day."

"It's okay," Sam said. He held his mother's right hand, rubbing it between both of his hands. "Everything's okay."

A few minutes later, Ronnie whispered, "What's going on with you?" She touched his sleeve, looked into his eyes. "I know it's something."

"Oh." Sam thought, and said, "It can wait until you're feeling better."

Ronnie managed a laugh. "Not . . . sure I will."

Sam did his best to keep his voice steady. "They're going to try to get you stable enough so that you can come home. That's the plan." *We can make her comfortable*, Dr. Dominguez had told him and his sister, when the surgery was over and they knew just how dire things were. *We can coordinate with the palliative care team. We will make sure she's not in any pain. And there's a hospice nearby, if you're interested?*

At the word "hospice," Sam and Sarah looked at each other, communicating in that old twin telepathy. As always, Sarah spoke for them both. "No. If that's where we are in this, if she's dying, she'll want to be home. And we can stay with her . . ." Her voice cracked and Sam was the one to finish her sentence.

"We can stay with her for as long as it takes."

In her hospital room, Ronnie took another sip of water, and looked up at her son. "I'm sorry," Ronnie whispered to Sam. "Sorry about all this."

"No," said Sam. "Mom, please. You have nothing to be sorry about."

I do, though, Ronnie thought, and cursed her sister and those DNA kits, and wondered how to begin.

"Just rest," Sam said, and patted her shoulder. Ronnie tried to keep talking, but the breath wasn't there, and her tongue wouldn't move, and then a nurse came into the room and did something with her IV. She felt the blackness rise up again, an irresistible wave, and was powerless as it swept her away.

SARAH

~~~~~~

It was after midnight when Sarah made it home, and the lights in the guesthouse were still on. Sarah climbed the stairs, knocked softly on the door, and waited until Ruby, clad in a white T-shirt and pajama bottoms patterned with Snoopy, opened the door. She hugged Sarah hard, then pulled away to look at her.

"What's going on? Is Safta okay?" Ruby asked.

Sarah felt her eyes fill with tears. Not trusting herself to speak, she just shook her head. Ruby's eyes got wide. "Oh, no," she whispered. Sarah pulled her close and reminded herself that she was a stepmother, a mother; the de facto matriarch of the clan, which meant she did not have the luxury of falling apart.

"She has pancreatic cancer," she said in a voice that only wobbled a little. "It's . . . advanced. She's very ill. I guess—it seems like she's known she was sick for a little while, and she didn't want to tell anyone until the wedding was over."

"Oh." Ruby's shoulders shook with sobs. "It's all my fault."

"No, honey," Sarah said, and held her tight. "No, no, no," she said, but Ruby was inconsolable.

"I'm sorry!" she cried. "I'm sorry for all the trouble I put everyone through."

Sarah made a crooning noise, rubbing the spot just below Ruby's ponytail, right at the nape of her neck.

"You have no reason to feel responsible. You didn't make this happen."

"But she kept it a secret," Ruby said. "If it hadn't been for the wedding, she would have told you guys what was going on."

Sarah shook her head. "I don't think that would have changed anything. She knew her diagnosis, and she had a treatment plan. Her doctor said . . ." She swallowed hard against the lump in her throat. "Her doctor said this is a very aggressive, very fast-moving cancer. Even if Safta told us three weeks ago, when she got her diagnosis, it wouldn't have changed anything."

She held Ruby, patting her stepdaughter's back as Ruby sobbed, "And now there's not even a wedding!"

"It's okay," Sarah repeated. "I promise." She held Ruby by the shoulders. "Tomorrow we are going to eat a delicious catered dinner, underneath those pretty lights, with beautiful flowers on the table, and we'll go home with some fabulous door prizes." She thought for a moment. "And new dresses. New dresses that your dad can't get mad at us for buying. As far as I'm concerned, it's a win-win."

Ruby made a weepy, hiccuping noise, and looked at Sarah with red-rimmed eyes, her pale lashes darkened with tears.

"Want tea?" Sarah asked.

Ruby nodded. Sarah went to the galley kitchen, pleased that the kettle was already full, and that the normally recalcitrant burner on the half-sized stove turned on with her first twist of its dial. Ruby had pulled the shades down but left the sliding doors open. The fabric stirred and rippled with the wind; their bottom rails clinked gently against the screens. A quick glance revealed no sign of the erstwhile groom or his family, no suitcases or garment bags, not even a stray coffee cup or sock. Sarah didn't want to ask, but Ruby volunteered.

"My—Annette talked to the manager at the hotel where she's staying. They had a last-minute cancellation, so Gabe's mom and aunt are staying there. Gabe's sleeping with the rest of the boys." She smiled, a little sadly. "Maybe it's crazy, but it actually feels good to have him here."

Sarah heard what Ruby had stopped herself from saying. "It's good that Gabe's your friend. And you can call Annette your mom, honey."

Ruby made a face. "After one day of actual maternal behavior? I think she needs to earn it." She met Sarah's eyes and said, "You've been more of a mother to me than she ever was."

Sarah felt her throat get tight. "Well, I'm glad she was there for you when you needed her," she said. She carried a mug of jasmine tea over to the couch, where Ruby was curled, bundled up in a soft, fringed blue throw.

"Do you think I'm being selfish?" Ruby asked. Sarah heard what Ruby wasn't asking, the words Ruby couldn't, wouldn't say out loud: *Do you think I'm like my mother?*

"I think," Sarah began, reaching for all the wisdom that she'd amassed in her almost forty years. "Well, I know, for sure, that it's a lot better to walk away from a wedding than a marriage. It's better to leave a fiancé at the altar than to leave a husband and children."

Ruby nodded.

"I think it's better to go into a marriage with as few doubts or regrets as you can. And if you aren't ready, if you want to be an artist, or a stage manager or a director, or if you want to go live in Paris—whatever you want your life to be, that's fine."

"Fine for now," Ruby muttered. Sarah knew what she

meant. Young women who wanted children—or who thought that someday they might—those women lived with the sound of a clock eternally ticking in their ears. At twenty-two, it felt like you had all the time you could want. The world looked different when you were thirty-two, and thirty-five, and forty. But, for now, she'd told the truth. Ruby was fine.

"You have time," Sarah told her. "And you have a lot of people who love you." She didn't add that there weren't any perfect solutions, that you always ended up regretting something. Pick a husband and children, maybe you never reach the summits of your profession. Pick your career, and maybe you end up alone, with a shelf lined with awards and a bank account full of cash and a bed that feels empty when you lay your head down at night. Maybe you couldn't get *the* life you wanted, but you could have *a* life you wanted. Artists had the best shot at having it all, but even an artist who eventually set her ambitions aside in favor of staying home with her children might end up, as Ronnie had, with kids who resented her. And even the luckiest woman artist with the most supportive spouse didn't have it, in Sarah's opinion, as easy as the average man with a wife.

She thought about her studio apartment, with its single bed and its piano, of that version of her life. Maybe, if she'd kept at it, she could have been a star. Maybe, if she hadn't felt like she'd never had her mother's full attention, she would not have been so intent on giving her boys every scrap of her own. Maybe if she'd realized what her mother had sacrificed, maybe if she'd understood that her mother, too, had a road not taken, a version of herself that she hadn't been, she would have seen the world differently.

Maybe, maybe, maybe, Sarah thought. And meanwhile, here was Ruby, staring at her with tear-filled eyes like Sarah was the font of all the wisdom in the world. Soon enough, life would teach Ruby those difficult lessons. Soon enough, she'd have to make hard choices. Sarah didn't need to offer instruction when, right now, what Ruby needed was comfort.

"I don't think walking away from something is ever easy," she said, and touched Ruby's hair. "Not even when it's the right thing to do." She thought of her mother's confession and wondered how it had felt for her mother to leave her New York City man, even knowing that he was wrong for her; that she was wrong with him. "I'm glad you're safe."

"I never thanked you for giving me your mom. Or Cape Cod." Ruby's voice was raspy, her cheeks blotchy from crying. "I felt so lucky when I got to stay here. Like I was a princess and this was my kingdom."

"I remember," said Sarah. "I felt that way when I was a girl. I'm glad my mom had someone to share this with. You were one of the best gifts I could ever give her."

Ruby raised her chin, her voice getting stronger, more resolute. "If I ever have kids, I'll bring them here, every summer."

Sarah felt her heart crack open, and her vision blur with sudden tears. *This was all I ever wanted*, she heard her mother say. Maybe it wasn't too late, and Dexter and Miles and Connor could all have the kind of summer that Ruby had cherished; the summers she and her twin had once spent, with the bay and the ponds and the ocean. She'd talk to Sam; they'd talk to her mother, they'd call Paul Norman. Maybe there was still enough time.

"You did what?" Sarah asked her husband later that night. Sam was still at the hospital; Ruby had finally gone to bed.

"A long time ago, when Annette and I were still married, I slept with Gabe's mother," Eli repeated. He was dressed for bed in a white undershirt and plaid pajama bottoms, smelling of toothpaste, his hair damp from the shower and feet bare and flip-flop free, for once.

Sarah stared at her husband in horror. "You . . . what?"

"She was pregnant already, as it turns out. She needed money for an abortion, and she went out to find a guy who looked like he had some. And that guy was me."

Sarah shook her head. "Wait. Back up. You slept with your daughter's fiancé's mother . . ."

"And when I saw Gabe, I thought that she'd changed her mind about having an abortion. When Gabe told me where he was from, and when he'd been born, I thought that Gabe was my son." Eli made a noise of bitter amusement. "He looks just like her. Or, at least, just the way she did twenty-two years ago."

"I don't know what to say." Sarah clasped her hands in her lap, and stared at her husband. "Why didn't you tell me?"

Eli shook his head. "I should have. I was just so ashamed. I thought that if you knew I'd been unfaithful to Annette, you'd think that I could do the same thing to you."

She looked at him, thinking that the evidence of her own infidelity was probably still visible on her body, if Eli had cared to look. "Why didn't you just ask Gabe's mom to tell you the truth?"

"Couldn't reach her," Eli said. "It seems that she recognized me when she saw me on that FaceTime and was worried I'd be angry when I realized what she'd done."

Sarah thought back to her husband's behavior—all the conversations he'd ignored, all the dinners and movies and board games he'd sat through, preoccupied, his mind somewhere else. Now, at least, she knew where his mind had been, and what he'd been preoccupied with.

Eli reached for her hands. "When you and Sam were at the hospital, I had some time to think. I didn't do a very good job of listening to Annette when we were together. I haven't been listening to Ruby." He made a face. "If I had been, maybe I would have figured out she didn't want this wedding, and I could have helped her find a better exit strategy." He looked into her eyes. "And the worst thing is that I haven't been listening to you."

Sarah didn't speak. Eli looked right into her eyes.

"I can't ask you to forgive me, or to trust me. I'll have to earn your forgiveness and your trust. But I'm going to do everything I can, now and for the rest of my life, to show that I deserve to be your husband."

Sarah closed her eyes, not trusting her voice. Not knowing if she'd ever tell Eli what she'd done, if she'd ever ask him to forgive her, or if what had happened with Owen would be her secret to keep, her burden to bear, alone. Someday, maybe, she'd be the one making a confession; the one in need of forgiveness, and grace.

My mother is dying, Sarah thought. She was going to be an orphan soon, a woman without parents in the world. Which meant that she was the parent now; the one who had to set the example and do the right thing, even when it was the hard thing, and bear some of her burdens and hurts alone.

When Eli stood up, Sarah stood with him. She leaned against him, pressing her cheek to his chest as he wrapped his arms around her, holding her close, as if he'd never let go.

"I wish she'd told us." At one in the morning, with everyone else in the house asleep, Sam and his sister sat together on the pool deck, side by side with their feet in the water.

"She was going to," Sarah said glumly. "Remember? She said she had something to tell us, but she wanted to wait until after the wedding." Sarah shook her head. "Maybe that's why she was in such a rush to put the house on the market. Maybe she wanted to sell it before she . . ." Sarah swallowed hard, unable to go further.

Sam sipped the coffee he'd poured into one of their father's mugs. "Poor Mom." He circled his feet in the water. "Did you and Eli get a chance to talk?"

"We did," said Sarah.

"And are things okay?" Sam asked, after it was clear she didn't intend to say more. "Are you okay?"

"I am," Sarah said. She was smiling a little, a crooked, rueful smile. "It's a crazy story. But yes, I think that we will be. Eventually."

Surprisingly, Sam didn't press her for details. "I'm glad," he said. "Eli's a good guy. And I think you'll need him now, with Mom . . ."

"With Mom dying," said Sarah, who, of the two of them, had always been braver, the one to say the hard things out loud. Her voice softened as she looked at her twin. "I just wish you had someone, too."

Sam shrugged . . . but Sarah knew her brother's face almost as well as she knew her own. She narrowed her eyes, peering out at him in the dim light from the house.

"Wait a minute. Did you go out last night?"

Sam nodded, his lips curling upward.

"Did you meet someone?"

Sam shrugged.

"Yes or no!"

Sam mumbled something that sounded like *I don't want to talk about it.* Sarah leaned over and grabbed her brother by the shoulders.

"You met someone, didn't you? Oh my God! Sam!"

He shook his head and waved his hand. "It's complicated," he said. "Like, extremely complicated." His voice was grave, but his face was flushed, his eyes were bright, and he looked young, and vital, and handsome. Even in her sorrow, Sarah felt happy for him.

"Tell me!" Sarah gave him a little shake. "Tell me everything!"

"I can't. Not yet."

"But you're happy?" Sarah asked.

Sam smiled even more widely. "You know how you once told me that it felt like I had something missing? That there was some part of myself that I hadn't figured out?"

Sarah's eyes widened. "Did you figure it out? Did you find your missing piece?"

Sam nodded, beaming. "I think that I did."

RUBY

~~~

Y ou did what?" Ruby asked, and glared at Gabe on the morning of what was to have been their wedding day. They were out on the deck where the caterers were playing ABBA's greatest hits and setting the table for the non-wedding feast that night.

Gabe held his hands, palms out, in front of him, like a boxer preparing to deflect a blow. "Look, just remember that, technically, you had broken up with me."

"Technically!" Ruby repeated. She shook her head. "Couldn't you have waited a little while before you hooked up with someone else? Like a week? Or a day? Or a few hours?"

"I'm sorry!" said Gabe, who was apologizing and laughing all at once. "Believe me, I wasn't planning on meeting anyone."

"Well. They do say you meet your special someone when you stop looking," said Ruby, who was laughing a little bit, too. "So who's the lucky . . . person?" she asked.

Gabe's eyebrows twitched. He cleared his throat. "Um. Well. It's kind of a funny story . . ." He licked his lips, then shook his head. "Maybe for another time." He looked at the guesthouse, then at Ruby. "If it's not too weird having me here, I can just crash with Miles and Dexter again tonight."

"Or you could stay in the guesthouse." Ruby sounded

a little shy. "There's more room. And I think, tonight, I'm going to go back to P-town, and stay with my mom."

"Really?" asked Gabe, who knew how complicated things had been between Ruby and Annette.

Ruby nodded, smiling a little. "Really."

"And that's a good thing?"

"You know she isn't perfect. And I don't know, maybe this is a onetime deal. An anomaly. But last night, for the first time in my entire life, she was actually right there when I needed her."

Gabe smiled shyly. "I'm happy for you." He held out his arms. "Friends?"

"Always," said Ruby, and hugged him tight.

EPILOGUE

IF WE SHADOWS

~~~~~~

ONE YEAR LATER

They stood on the edge of the water below the house, their faces turned toward the sun and the sea.

Sam and Gabe and Eli all wore dark suits. Sarah's dress was black; Ruby's was navy-blue. Connor and Miles and Dexter were dressed in neatly pressed khakis and button-down shirts. Each boy carried a bouquet of wildflowers, cosmos and zinnias in shades of red and pink and cream. Sarah held a box made of black plastic with a sticker that read VERONICA LEVY on its top. Her mother, it turned out, had arranged for the disposal of her physical remains, at a place called (Sarah still cringed when she thought about it) Budget Cremations of New England. This, it emerged, was the same place that had handled their father's cremation, one of a great many facts that, for better or worse, her mother hadn't chosen to share.

Sarah surveyed the assembled mourners. "Is everyone ready?" she asked.

"Could someone check the wind?" Ruby asked. "Not to be morbid, but we don't want a *Big Lebowski* situation."

Gabe licked his thumb and held it in the air. "I think we're good."

Carefully, Sarah removed the top from the box and looked down at her mother's ashes: grainy and gray, with glittering flecks here and there. Heavier than she thought that ashes would be; lighter than the weight of a person's life should have been. "You don't think I should have gotten an urn?" she whispered to Sam, just as her mother's sister, their aunt Suzanne, asked, loudly, from her spot three landings above the beach, "They couldn't get an urn?"

"We didn't need one," Sam said. He turned to give Aunt Suzanne a big wave, and a bigger smile, and said to his sister, "Mom didn't want to sit on someone's mantel. She wanted to be with Dad. And this was their favorite place in the world."

Sarah remembered the conversation she'd had with Ronnie the night before the wedding-that-wasn't, how her mom had told Sarah that the Cape had been her favorite place, not her father's. And yet, they'd scattered his ashes in the water, at his request. *Marriage is compromise*, Sarah thought, and smiled a little, hoping her dad hadn't doomed himself to an eternity of seasickness or endured a lifetime of subordinating his wishes to his wife's. That wasn't the way Sarah remembered it . . . but if the last months of her mother's life had taught her anything, it was that memory was subjective. Veronica remembered summers with her children, with occasional breaks to write or grade papers; Sarah remembered a mother constantly working, with occasional breaks to be with her children. "I'm probably wrong," she finally admitted, during one of her last talks with her mother, but her mother had said, "No matter what really happened, it's how you felt that mattered. I'm sorry if I ever made you feel anything else but loved. Because I wanted to be a mother. I loved you and your brother very much."

Sarah held the box out to her brother and his partner, then her husband, then her stepdaughter, then the boys. One by one, they used the silver scoop to remove a portion of the ashes and sprinkle them into the water. When Sam started to cry, Gabe put his hand on Sam's back. When Eli saw Ruby sniffling, he reached into his pocket and handed her what turned out to be an honest-to-God handkerchief. When everyone had taken a scoop, Sarah waded into the surf and turned the box upside down, letting the wind take the last of her mother and blow her out to sea.

"Goodbye, Mom," Sarah said softly as the ashes skirted over the tops of the waves. The wind turned them into a mist, thinning and spreading them out until they were invisible. "I love you."

Up at the house, there were muffins and danish, bagels and lox and cream cheese, pitchers of fresh juice and champagne for mimosas. Lord Farquaad cruised the room on his stumpy legs, nosing for scraps. The boys were playing Monopoly in the living room. Aunt Suzanne and Uncle Matt sat at the dining-room table with overflowing plates in front of them, announcing, loudly, to anyone who came near, what a shame it was that the kids were selling the place, and, really, were they sure it was what Veronica would have wanted?

Eli's brother, Ari, and Gabe's aunt Amanda had

retreated to a corner, where they stood, almost touching, deep in conversation. Sarah lifted her eyebrows at her brother. Sam pressed his lips together and shook his head. Twin-speak for Sam saying, *That isn't going to end well*, and Sarah replying, *Yes, but there's nothing we can do to stop it*. As part of his attempts to be a better person, Eli had announced he was going to try to give his brother some grace—or at least, when possible, the benefit of the doubt. "If all I do is expect him to screw up, when he does, it's just a self-fulfilling prophecy," he'd explained. Sarah wasn't sure that Ari was capable of being anything but the troubled and trouble-making rapscallion she'd always known, but she loved her husband for trying.

Fifteen minutes into the reception, Suzanne got to her feet and cornered her niece and nephew in the kitchen.

"Did you two ever do those DNA kits I sent you?"

Sarah looked at her brother. Sam shook his head. "I know I meant to, but I think it got packed in the move, and it hasn't been unpacked yet." Sam and Connor were permanent East Coast residents now. Six months ago, they'd left California and moved to Brooklyn, so Connor could go to the same school as his cousins, and the families could have Shabbat dinners together each week, and so that Sam could see Gabe every night, instead of every month, which was what they'd done for the first six months of their courtship. "Young love," Eli had said indulgently when Sarah gave him the news. "Isn't it grand?"

"At least one of them's young," Sarah muttered . . . but Eli knew how happy she was that her brother had found someone; that he'd finally found himself.

"Sarah?" Aunt Suzanne blared. "What about you?"

Sarah shrugged. "I was going to, but then my mom told me she'd heard a podcast about how there's privacy issues, and that the government can force companies to turn over your data if they think you committed a crime. It sounded too risky."

"Hear, hear," said Uncle Matt. "I told Suze it was a bad idea."

"Oh, you said no such thing," said Aunt Suzanne, and slapped playfully at her husband's shoulder.

Uncle Matt wandered over to the bookcase. He pulled one of Veronica's books off the shelf and flipped through the pages. "You ever wonder why your mom stopped writing?"

Sam and Sarah exchanged a look. "I got the impression that she liked writing, but she didn't enjoy publishing very much," Sarah said.

"Fame," said Matt, and nodded like he'd spent his life dodging the paparazzi instead of unclogging toilets. "It's not for everyone."

"Who knows?" Sarah asked lightly. "Maybe she never stopped writing at all. Maybe there's a treasure trove of unpublished novels around here."

"Oh, you haven't gone through her things?" Suzanne's eyes gleamed with sudden interest.

"Not yet," Sarah said.

"We've been putting it off," Sam said. "We were going to do a big clean-out before we put the place on the market."

"But then," said Sarah, "we decided to hang on to the house."

Suzanne's and Matt's heads swung around in unison. Together, they asked, "Oh?"

Sarah nodded. "Mom always wanted us to come here

and spend time together. She wanted the cousins to get to know each other, and have the kinds of summers that we did, and she wanted to spend a lot of time with her grandkids." Brother and sister exchanged another look. "We weren't great about it when she was alive," Sarah said. "We want to do better now."

"Well, that's lovely," said Suzanne, hands clasped at her ample bosom. "And, of course, we're so *close!*"

"Happy to visit," said Uncle Matt, through a mouthful of cheese danish. "Just a phone call away!"

Sarah smiled politely, grabbed Sam's sleeve, and towed her brother into a far corner of the living room. "Good God," she whispered.

"When are we going to tell them about the books?" Sam whispered back. "We can't keep it a secret forever."

"Oh, let them be surprised," said Sarah. Her mother's death had been mercifully fast, and at home, as she'd wanted. They'd set up a bed in the living room, in front of the windows, making sure Ronnie could see every sunset. During one of her last lucid days she'd told Sarah that she'd left books behind, in a closet, and Sarah had found the boxes, an even dozen of them, each in its own plastic box, in the closet on the guesthouse's second floor. Ronnie had left a letter on top, with a man's name and address. When Sarah had asked who Gregory Bates was, her mother had said, "Old friend," before falling asleep— or pretending to fall asleep. Sarah was almost completely convinced that he was her mother's old lover, the man she'd been with while she'd been with Sarah's father and had eventually decided to leave behind. But so far, Gregory hadn't suggested that he'd known their mother as anything but author and a colleague. He told Sarah he was surprised to learn that Ronnie had named him her literary executor—"we hadn't spoken in years"—but that he was honored. And, now that he'd retired, he had plenty of time to read the books. Six weeks after Sarah had sent him the boxes, Gregory had called to say that he'd read the first three manuscripts, that he had found them sharply observed and smart and compelling—"just the way I remember your mother's work"—and that, with Sarah's permission, he would show them to editors in the new year. He felt confident, he said, that Veronica Levy was going to be a published author again. "It's too bad she won't be around to enjoy it," Gregory said, "but I guess she had her reasons." Sarah was sure he would have welcomed an explanation, had Sarah chosen to give him one; to explain why Ronnie had stepped away from her writing life and how, maybe, he'd played a part in that. So far, though, she hadn't said a word.

When Eli had asked what the stories were about, Sarah told him about the first book she'd read. "There're two families in Cape Cod; three generations apiece. One family's old-money WASPs, in the process of losing their money. The other family's Jewish, so they're the new arrivals. There's a dispute over a property line, and kind of a Romeo and Juliet thing when the youngest son of the WASP family falls in love with the daughter of the Jewish family." She'd found more than one echo of her own story with Owen Lassiter, and there was a character, a woman who walked away from her husband and her family, who Sarah was pretty sure was inspired by Annette. She hadn't decided how it felt to have her life mined for fiction, and had been swinging between feeling deeply flattered and slightly exploited. She could hear her mother in her head: *That's what writers do.* Maybe it explained why her mom hadn't liked who she'd been while she was a published author. It certainly explained why Veronica hadn't wanted these books read until she was gone. Sarah could be angry, but now there was no one to be angry at.

As for Owen Lassiter, he'd texted Sarah for a while, telling her he wanted to explain, pleading for a second chance. Sarah had tried ignoring him. Finally, she'd written back, *It was good to see you again, but I think we should leave the past in the past.* Sometimes, she worried about Owen getting angry, maybe showing up at her house or, worse, Eli's office and telling her husband what had happened, but she was pretty sure he wouldn't. He'd lied to her and broken her heart when they were teenagers. She hoped he'd be honorable enough to respect her wishes now.

"Are you concerned about this?" Gabe murmured, sidling over to Sam and nodding at Ari, who'd just brought Amanda another mimosa.

"We are," Sam replied, "but what can we do?"

"We can tell her no," Gabe offered. "We can tell her there's a moratorium on people from my family dating people from yours."

Eli opened his mouth, then pressed his lips together. "I'm trying to give my brother the benefit of the doubt."

Sarah smiled at her husband, and Gabe gave Sam's shoulder a squeeze. Sam had been worried—terrified, really—that his sister and his step-niece would judge him for hooking up with Ruby's former fiancé, no matter how many times Gabe had told him that Ruby had been the one to do the dumping. "Tell her one woman's trash is another man's treasure," Gabe urged him. Sam had buried his face in his hands.

"You have to admit that it's strange," he'd grumbled.

"Life is strange," said Gabe. In December, Rosa had

flown out to Brooklyn with Gabe, to help him move into the apartment he'd rented, and to introduce him to Benji, who had long since put away his bass and now went by Benjamin Scott. He sold commercial real estate, and was married with two children. He'd been, unsurprisingly, angry to learn about Rosa's duplicity, and their first meeting, at a diner in New Jersey, had started off feeling excruciatingly awkward, but Ben had warmed to Gabe. He'd even helped him find a job, calling a friend of a friend who owned a skateboard shop in Jackson Heights and who'd hired Gabe to organize its special events and run its social media accounts.

Connor was delighted to be in school with his cousins, and thrilled with Sam's new companion, who'd assumed a role in his life somewhere between cool uncle and big brother. Sam was happy—especially when he imagined Julie looking down at him with understanding.

Sarah didn't feel it when a microscopic fleck of her mother's ashes fell from the hem of her dress into a crack between the floorboards in the kitchen . . . but the house did. She opened herself and welcomed her former mistress.

It's all right now, said the house. *See? Everything worked out the way it was supposed to work out.*

Oh, look! said what used to be Veronica. She could see Sarah, deep in conversation with Eli, who was listening attentively, and Sam holding hands with Gabe. She could see her grandchildren and her step-grandchildren, Dexter and Miles and Connor, begging to be allowed to go to the pool, Ruby gesticulating with both hands as she told Paul Norman all about her newest project, which was outdoors and interactive, Shakespeare's *A Midsummer Night's Dream* staged in a shuttered suburban mall as a choose-your-own adventure for middle-school-age kids. She could even see her sister and her sister's husband, stuffing their faces at the kitchen table. *No, we're not selling,* she heard Sarah say, and she was glad.

Veronica heard, and felt, the vibrations of her grandsons' feet on the deck. She smelled, and felt, the scents of linguine with clam sauce, her son-in-law's specialty, which he'd made for dinner the night before. She could feel the presence of all the people she'd loved; all the people who'd loved her.

And you'll be able to see everything, the house assured her. *This is your place. Your home. And you're a part of it now, forever. All you have to do is sit back and watch.*

ACKNOWLEDGMENTS

The Summer Place was written during the latter part of our shared COVID year. I started it in the fall, wrote through the dark, cold winter, and was completing a first draft in the spring of 2021, when the vaccine rollout began. It felt—briefly—as if a return to something like normal was on the horizon, and all of us were waking from some strange, enchanted interlude, during which our lives had been reordered. Stuck at home, together, we saw the people with whom we were closest— our children, our spouses, our parents—out of context and in a new light.

I wanted to write about that time, about a family whose members had come through the pandemic year, as opposed to a book set during the heart of it. A fun, light-hearted book. A wedding weekend! I thought. Family drama! A man making sense of his sexuality, a husband, confronted by an old mistake, and a wife, tempted by an old love! I wanted the story to have a feeling somewhere between a Noël Coward farce and *A Midsummer Night's Dream*, where the pairings are driven by otherworldly interference. I also knew I wanted to write about the ways that quarantine exposed the fault lines in relationships and the buried foundations of money and privilege and sacrifice that hold up our lives, whether or not we acknowledge that they're there.

Then, in March 2021, my mom, Fran, was diagnosed with pancreatic cancer. Nine weeks later, she was dead. My mom was the first person who brought me to Cape Cod, on family vacations, when I was a girl. When I became a mother myself, I brought my daughters to the Cape, where they spent big chunks of the last eighteen summers with their Granny Franny. So I knew that I also wanted to write about loss, and mothers and daughters and how the torch gets passed from one mother to the next. My mother's spirit infuses every page, and I hope that when you read it, you can feel her humor and intelligence and her big, embracing heart.

I will always be grateful to Joanna Pulcini for being one of the first people who believed I had stories to tell.

I'm grateful to my agent, Celeste Fine, and to John Maas at Park/Fine, who edited this book with kindness and incisive skill and made every page, person, and plot point better. I am also grateful for the hard work of Emily Sweet, Andrea Mai, Susana Alvarez, Anna Petkovich, and Theresa Park.

At Atria, my editor, Lindsay Sagnette, loved these characters, the setting, and the story from the very first draft. Her encouragement and support and her enthusiastic love for the Levy/Weinberg/Danhauser family meant the world to me. Thanks to her assistants, Fiora Elbers-Tibbitts and Jade Hui.

I'm lucky to work with a brilliant, supportive publisher like Libby McGuire, and with Jonathan Karp, who has always been a great champion of my work.